RENEGADE PATH

A Lost Kings MC World Novel

AUTUMN JONES LAKE

COPYRIGHT

Renegade Path

A Lost Kings MC World Novel
by USA Today bestselling author Autumn Jones Lake
Copyright 2018, 2021 Autumn Jones Lake
Portions of *Renegade Path* were previously published as
Cards of Love: Knight of Swords
Model: Forest H
Photographer: Wander Aguiar
Cover Designer: Shanoff Designs
Proofread by: Julie Barney
Digital ISBN: 978-1-943950-67-6
Paperback ISBN: 978-1-943950-68-3
Hardcover ISBN: 978-1-943950-69-0

USA Today bestselling author Autumn Jones Lake delivers an unforgettable story of heart-wrenching first love.

ROMAN
From the minute I met Juliet, I wanted to shield her from the world's ugliness. We'd both already suffered more heartache than anyone should experience in a lifetime. I didn't have anything of value to offer—just my jaded heart, broken soul, and undying love. But for her, I'd sacrifice my pride, my hostility, and my heart. Anything to see her smile. Consequences meant nothing. I would've given up anything, even my life, to keep her safe.

JULIET
Both our lives were soaked in tragedy from day one. That's why we were drawn to each other the moment we met. I ignored the people who warned me he was dead inside. The truth was, he was as broken as I was. Together, we'd heal our hearts and stitch together our souls.

At seventeen, we fell in love for the first—and last—time.

ACKNOWLEDGMENTS

2021 hasn't been much easier than 2020. I planned to re-write and add a "few" things to *Cards of Love: Knight of Swords* and republish it with a new title and new cover back in, oh, March. Then Rooster and Shelby got into more adventures than I bargained for and Grinder took a little longer than I expected to find his lady. After the release of *Crown of Ghosts*, I said, "let me take a week and make those changes so I can finally show the world the beautiful new cover for Roman and Juliet's story."

Four months of labor, fifty-two thousand brand new words, or 234 extra pages, later here we are. *Renegade Path* has been reborn, rewritten, and massively expanded. It feels wrong to even mention it in the same breath as *Knight of Swords*. They are two completely different things as far as I am concerned. But still, I know someone will complain. Because, *you know.*

I loved the first iteration of Roman and Juliet's story. And I know it held a special place in a lot of my readers' hearts. But I wanted to go deeper and really explore more in their story. While you don't need to have read any of the Lost Kings MC books to enjoy this book, I think if you have, this book will make the Lost Kings MC world a lot richer for you. I think my lovely LOKI ninjas will adore the additions and relish uncovering those elusive Easter eggs I so enjoy dropping or possibly discover unintentional breadcrumbs I left behind.

If this is your first time dipping your toes into the Lost Kings MC world, welcome! I hope you fall in love with my characters and become part of the family.

A very special thank you to Julie for helping me catch those last bugs in the story. By the end, I'm so blurry-eyed, all the words look fine to me, but she always catches the smallest thing! Thank you so much!

Thank you to Jezzie for always taking a final look and wrapping me up in your words of encouragement.

Thank you to my lovely early readers for being so enthusiastic when I dropped this on their e-readers at the last possible minute. The fear that this is the time you'll finally tell me to fuck off always hovers, and yet, you always chase it away. I appreciate that *so* much.

Extra love and thanks to Mr. Lake for reading through Renegade Path even though his work schedule has been crazy lately. Don't tell Wrath, but I think Roman might be Mr. Lake's new favorite hero I've written and that was the final boost I needed.

Much love and gratitude.
Autumn

DEDICATION

Sometimes the most beautiful souls are the most broken.

CHAPTER ONE

Roman

I FELL IN LOVE FOR THE FIRST TIME WHEN I WAS SEVENTEEN.

One simple mistake altered the course of my future, of my very existence.

Until that day, feelings had always seemed irrelevant and illogical. My world was too dark and chaotic for something as obscure as love to develop.

It was my first day at another new high school. That made— three? four? —this year alone.

The locker I'd been assigned wouldn't open no matter how many times I spun the combination or slammed my filthy, worn boot into the rusty metal front.

"Do you mind?" A soft voice came from beside me.

I glanced down. Five-feet-nothing of waist-length red-gold hair, soft blue eyes, and freckles stared up at me. A smile played over her full pink lips that I already had an urge to kiss.

"I can't get it open."

Amusement flickered over her stern expression. "Maybe that's because it's *my* locker."

"No, it's not." Even though I already had a bad feeling in my gut that she was right, I handed over the yellow slip of paper I'd been given this morning.

"Hmm." She tapped her finger against that plump bottom lip that I wanted to suck into my mouth and run my tongue against. "It says seventy-six, but that can't be right."

She stepped forward, not at all intimidated by my size—I had to be at least a foot taller than her. Her warm shoulder brushed against my chest, and her long hair tickled my arm. She smelled like flowers after a rainstorm. I'm not ashamed to admit I stood there and inhaled her.

The lock clicked, and she opened the door. "See? It's *my* locker. *My* combination works on it. Yours doesn't."

"Well, shoot."

She grinned at me. "What's your name?"

"Roman."

Laughter spilled out of her. "I'm Juliet. I'll tell you what, Roman, I'm willing to share my locker with you. *If* you promise not to leave any gross boy things in it."

I scratched the back of my neck. "Give me an example of a 'gross boy thing.'"

"Uh, dirty socks."

"No problem."

"Jockstraps."

A grin threatened to break free at the corners of my mouth. "Don't have one."

"Anything smelly."

"Okay."

Pink raced over her cheeks, and I wondered what else she was going to say, but instead, she shook her head. "Welcome to locker seventy-six, roomie."

She held out her hand. I took it, meaning to give a quick shake. Instead, an electric current of attraction sparked between us. I stood there staring into her eyes, trying to decide if they were turquoise or teal, and stroked her soft skin.

"Thank you, Juliet." I loved the way her name felt rolling off my tongue.

She didn't jerk her hand away, and she held my gaze.

I made up my mind right then and there.

One day, I'm going to marry this girl.

CHAPTER TWO

Roman

PROTECT.

That's all I wanted to do once I laid eyes on Juliet. She consumed my thoughts as I drifted through my morning classes. Her laughter played over and over in my head. Her smile. Her kind eyes.

And then there she was. Waiting for me by the lockers, under the glare of cheap fluorescent lights. She was so damn tiny. Defenseless and innocent. An unfamiliar urge thrummed through my veins—to scoop her up and carry her away.

People seemed to avoid her, which both bothered and pleased me. I wanted her to myself, but I also wanted to kill anyone who hurt her feelings.

"How is your first day progressing?" The corners of her mouth twitched, but I didn't feel like she was mocking me. More like we were both in on the same joke.

"Lame. Just as boring as the last three schools."

Her eyes widened. "Why so many? Do your parents move around a lot?"

My eyes darted away. I didn't like talking about my situation. It was one of those things that made people uncomfortable and eager to get away from the conversation. But I sensed I could trust Juliet.

"I live at the group home over on Pine," I explained in a lowered voice. "Foster care. Before that, I stayed with a few families. None of 'em stuck."

My story was more complicated than that. Ten years, twelve different families, and three separate group homes to be exact. But I feared sharing too much, getting too real, might scare her away.

Sadness clouded her eyes. "I live with my aunt and uncle. Not the same thing, but I understand what it feels like…not to…"

I waited for her to finish, anticipating what she'd say.

"Feel wanted," she finished.

She'd never have to worry about that again. I wanted her like nothing I'd ever wanted in my life.

But I had absolutely nothing to offer her.

No family. No money. Hell, I didn't even have access to a vehicle to take her out on a date. I had the clothes on my back and a few other things stuffed in a drawer at the home. My luggage was a Hefty bag. I'd had a job lined up at the last place I lived, but that was gone now.

"Sucks, right?" I said to fill the silence between us.

Her lips curved up in a soft smile. "It's not so bad. One day I'll have my own family, and I'll know all the right things to give them."

The longing in her voice hit me on a primal level. I didn't understand what having a family meant. It had always seemed too unattainable. But the way Juliet talked about it made me want to figure it out. *With her.*

I'd never had the luxury of thinking that far ahead in my life.

I was too busy surviving from one day to the next. But Juliet made me want to think ahead. She made me hope for things I'd been afraid to admit to myself I even wanted.

Before I opened my mouth and offered to make some babies with her, someone slammed into me from behind. My shoulder hit the corner of the open locker door and I narrowly missed knocking Juliet over.

"Watch it, new guy," the brawny football player I'd showed up in gym class earlier said. He high-fived his equally jackass friends.

It wasn't pride that forced me to go after him. I didn't care that Juliet saw me get shoved like a little kid.

No, it was blind *rage*. That fucker had pushed me right into her. She could've been hurt, and he did it without thinking.

I'd been pushed around enough at that point in my life. By foster parents, teachers, other kids. I'd learned early that the world was cruel.

I also learned not to take shit from anyone.

If you couldn't stand up for yourself, no one would do it for you. And if I couldn't defend myself, how could I protect anyone else?

"Roman—" Juliet said, but I was already sailing through the air, tackling Doug to his knees and punching him in the side.

The violence in my eyes and fists made his two buddies back away instead of helping their unfortunate friend.

Two teachers and a security guard pulled me off the kid, but I still kept fighting.

Until I saw Juliet shaking her head. Tears in her eyes.

"Don't," she mouthed at me.

It was a bucket of ice water over my hot-tempered head.

CHAPTER THREE

Juliet

"Roman, don't."

I wasn't afraid *he'd* get hurt.

No, obviously, Roman was the kind of guy who could take care of himself. I was more worried he'd kill Doug Winstead and end up in jail. Doug deserved the ass-kicking. He'd been picking on younger, weaker kids for as long as I could remember.

My bigger fear was that Roman would get expelled from school before I got to know him better.

Selfish? Maybe. But I'd never met anyone who affected me the way he did. Despite the fact that we'd met while he was kicking in my locker, he was the most beautiful boy I'd ever seen.

Boy probably wasn't accurate. He had the seriousness of a man who'd already seen it all. Survived it all. Rich, brown hair fell over his forehead, complimenting his green eyes. The brief smile he flashed made me weak in the knees. He didn't seem to notice that half the girls in the school were gawking at him, practically running into walls because they were staring so hard.

But he never took his eyes off me.

Destiny.

Before Roman, I believed my sad story was already written.

Love at first sight.

My cousin Debbie had always reminisced about how she fell in love with her husband the minute she met him in ninth grade. I loved her, but her story made zero sense to me. Only when I looked into Roman's olive-green eyes did I finally understand.

Maybe I affected him too. He stopped resisting and allowed the security guard to drag him down the hall. I chased after him, but Mrs. Johnson, my AP English teacher, stopped me.

"Don't, honey. You don't need to be involved with trash like that. He's not going anywhere good in life."

My temper flared. "Doug started it. He's always starting trouble. Hurting kids who can't fight back. This time he picked on the wrong person and got what he deserved."

She recoiled. I hardly ever spoke up or talked back to teachers. I earned high marks, but I kept to myself.

My outburst seemed to change her mind. "Go ahead down to the principal's office and let Mr. W. know what happened." She glanced over my shoulder. "I'll give you a pass."

Relief that at least one adult in my life seemed to have some decency flooded through me. I accepted the pass and hurried downstairs.

Mr. W. was no-nonsense. We called him Mr. W. because no one could pronounce or spell his last name. I'd never been in his office before.

I stepped into the main office and his secretary glanced up. "Juliet? What are you doing down here?"

"I have a pass." I swallowed hard, finding my courage. "I need to speak to Mr. W. about the fight. I saw what happened."

She stared at me for a minute. "All right. Wait here."

I turned and found Roman sitting on the bench outside the principal's office. Staring at me.

"What are you doing, Juliet?" he asked in a low voice when I approached.

"Someone needs to tell the truth about what happened."

He stared at me as if no one had ever offered to stand up for him before. "Don't get in trouble over me. I'm not worth it."

My fingers nudged his chin, trying to angle his head back so I could see his eyes. Roman was stubborn though. "You're wrong."

Behind us, the door opened and the secretary spoke to Mr. W.

"Juliet, come on inside."

I felt the weight of Roman's stare with every step I took toward the open door.

CHAPTER FOUR

Roman

JULIET STUNNED ME. NOT ONLY WAS SHE BEAUTIFUL ON THE outside, she was pure beauty on the inside.

I glanced down at my bruised knuckles, already covered in a life's worth of scars.

No one had ever stood up for me before. Not my parents before they died, not my grandmother when the state took me away from her, not my teachers who saw the bruises on me from my first set of foster parents, not my "good" foster parents that I prayed would adopt me, not the social workers or the lawyers appointed to me by the system. No one.

Juliet barely knew me, yet she'd done more for me in one day than anyone else in my entire life.

The door opened, and Juliet stepped out, a whole lot more confident than when she went inside.

The principal spoke quietly to his secretary for a second then motioned me over.

"Miss Hayworth explained that you were defending yourself and that the other student almost hurt her as well." His eyes scanned my face to see if I was surprised. If Juliet lied.

"Yes, sir."

"No more trouble from you, Roman. It's only your first day."

"I'll do my best."

That didn't seem to reassure him, but he dismissed me anyway.

Juliet waited in the hallway for me. Smiled when she saw me.

"Why'd you do that?" I asked, falling into step beside her. "Where's your next class?"

"AP English."

I pulled out my schedule. "That's where I'm headed too."

She raised an eyebrow as if it surprised her that I had been placed in an advanced class.

"What's wrong? I don't look like someone who'd take advanced anything, do I?"

She shrugged. "That's not what I was going to say, but since you said it, yes."

Feeling fired up after the fight and narrowly escaping trouble, I gave her a cocky wink. "I'm full of surprises, sweetheart."

Her lips curled into a playful smile. "I'm sure you are."

Trading jokes back and forth on our way to class soothed me somehow. I couldn't explain it, but I didn't even want to punch one of Doug's smug buddies when we passed him in the hallway. That's the effect Juliet had on me.

The class was about to discuss *Death of a Salesman*. I'd already read it at my last school which seemed to make the cute little English teacher happy.

A kid everyone, even the teacher, called Stubby raised his hand first. I recognized him as one of Doug's sycophantic friends.

"It's about the fakeness of the American dream. Like that Biff dude should've been more successful, but he's not because it's all a lie." He sat back looking like a proud puppy who'd just taken his first piss outside.

I'd taken the seat directly behind Juliet—of course—and was pleasantly surprised when she raised her hand.

"Biff's an unemployed loser who peaked in high school. He thought his looks would open doors to opportunities he didn't deserve. He wasn't willing to put in the work."

I was hanging on every word out of her mouth and couldn't help jumping in. "But by the end, I think it's clear the American dream *isn't* dead. You just have to work for it."

"Very good, Roman, but next time raise your hand." The teacher scowled at me.

Typical.

Juliet turned slightly and gave me a smile.

After class, she packed up her things slowly. I held out my hand for her bag and she tilted her head at me. "Where you headed next?"

"Gym."

Shit, I wouldn't mind watching her running around in the tiny gym shorts I'd seen other girls wearing in my class.

"I'll walk you."

"Don't you have a class?"

"Technology. It's right by the gym, isn't it?"

"It is."

"Let's go."

She handed me her backpack and I slung it over my shoulder, marveling that she managed to lug it around all day. "You smuggling a body in this thing? It must weigh as much as you," I teased.

"Usually I don't like stopping at my locker during the day." She blushed and looked away. "Never had a good reason to before," she said in a softer voice.

It says a lot about how gone I was over this girl that it took me a minute to realize she was talking about me.

This feeling between us was mutual. I wasn't imagining this attraction. She wasn't a polite girl taking pity on the new kid.

I almost leaned over and kissed her when I handed over her backpack in front of the girls' locker room. At the last second, I stopped. When our lips touched for the first time, it wasn't going to be in a dimly lit, sweat-scented hallway in front of sixty of our fellow classmates.

No, I wanted it to be special. And private.

CHAPTER FIVE

Juliet

My stomach fluttered as Roman and I stared at each other.

"I'll pick you up when the bell rings," he said.

"Okay."

He grabbed the notebook out of my hand and quickly scribbled down some notes.

"We have the rest of our classes together."

"Oh, good."

Someone shoved me. Roman all but snarled at the offender.

"Ooo, Juliet, who's your scary friend?" my friend Vienna asked.

"Vienna, this is Roman. This is his first day."

Vienna raked her gaze over him and I had a violent urge to strangle her.

"I heard all about how you taught Douchebag Dougie some manners this afternoon," Vienna said, still staring at him with too much interest. "Well done."

Roman didn't puff out his chest or even smile like most guys would. "Seems like someone should've done it a long time ago."

"Got that right," Vienna said. "That asshole lifted my dress in second grade and showed everyone my underwear. Got called 'polka dots' forever because of him."

Leave it to Vienna to mention her underpants within five seconds of meeting a guy.

"We're going to be late." I dug my fingers into Vienna's arm and tugged her toward the door.

"See you in an hour," Roman reminded me.

"Wow," Vienna said in a dreamy voice that I didn't care for. "You lucky bitch. How did you meet him?"

"Trying to break into my locker."

She scrunched up her nose, trying to decide if I was kidding or not, I think.

"He seems to like you." She evil-grinned at me. "A birdie told me you went to the principal's office to defend him."

"Dougie started it. Why should he always get away with—"

"Don't get me wrong. I'm thrilled. Doug can't get enough ass-kickings as far as I'm concerned."

We stripped out of our clothes and into the insultingly small gym uniforms the school insisted we wear. Thankfully, I was so height-challenged the shorts and polo looked almost normal on me. On Vienna's tall, slender frame, the white shirt and shorts looked positively obscene.

"Come on, let's get this over with."

It was volleyball day, the one sport I was actually good at. I tossed the ball in the air to serve and almost missed when I spotted Roman watching me from the hallway.

I smashed the ball over the net, happy he caught me doing something I'm good at.

When I looked again, he'd vanished.

Something whooshed through the air and thudded against the side of my head. "Ow!"

The volleyball *thunk, thunk, thunked* against the gymnasium floor and lazily rolled away. "Look alive, Juliet!" the gym teacher yelled.

My face flamed hot. At least Roman hadn't seen that.

After class, Vienna elbowed me. "Were you fantasizing about your knight in shining hottie?"

"That doesn't even make sense."

Not offended, she grinned and flounced into the locker room ahead of me.

True to his word, Roman was waiting in the hallway for me after class.

Again, he took my backpack, but this time he winced when he slung it over his shoulder.

"Are you okay?"

"I'm fine."

Apparently we'd reached a stage in our relationship where I felt comfortable rolling up his sleeve to inspect his arm.

Black and blue stained most of his upper arm and shoulder. "We need to get you some ice for this."

"I'm fine." He glanced down at his bruised skin. "I've had worse."

"Doug's such an asshole," I seethed. "Principal W. better have had a chat with him too."

He grinned at me. "You're pretty cute all fierce."

He thought I was cute? My heart tapped out an erratic rhythm that sounded a lot like one of my favorite love songs.

Again, he took the seat behind me in class, glaring at Steve Lennon who usually occupied that seat. With Roman at my back, I felt safe and protected.

Normally I loved history, but today, I couldn't stop thinking about the boy behind me.

After the final bell, he followed me outside. "Do you take the bus?" he asked.

"Not usually." No, I'd had enough of being picked on and called names on the bus years ago and decided I'd rather walk than put up with my obnoxious classmates.

"Do you drive?" I winced after I asked. He was in foster care; I doubt he owned a vehicle.

"No car." His jaw tightened and I wondered if I offended him.

"I'm sorry. That was thoughtless of me."

"It's no big deal, Juliet." But he seemed to relax again.

My already shaky nerves rattled as we got closer to my street.

"I'm actually not that far from you," Roman said. "A couple streets over."

"Oh."

The fear that had crawled up my spine disappeared when we approached the driveway and I saw my uncle's truck was missing. I wasn't in the mood to have him be rude to chase Roman off. And I had no doubt, that's exactly what would happen.

My gaze searched the neighborhood, searching for any nosy neighbors who might report back to my aunt and uncle that I'd had a boy over.

The coast seemed clear.

"Come in so I can put ice on that," I said.

He only hesitated for a second. "Thanks."

Inside I tried not to cringe as he stooped to avoid smacking his head on the low ceiling. "My aunt and uncle are short like me."

"I'm fine."

"You can set my bag there. Thank you for carrying it."

"No problem."

Each answer came out shorter and more clipped than the last and I worried I was keeping him from doing something more important.

"Here." I reached into the freezer and grabbed an ice pack, then wrapped it in a kitchen towel.

I froze when I turned and found his green eyes focused on me, waiting as if he expected me to treat his injury.

Carefully, I lifted his sleeve and rested the pack against the bruised area. He hissed in a pained breath but otherwise gave no indication it hurt.

He was so warm and solid against me. Smelled so good. I closed my eyes, soaking in the moment.

"Are you okay, Juliet?" His raspy voice broke the spell.

The concern in his voice caught me off guard. "Tired." I forced a smile. "I got whacked in the head with a volleyball in gym."

That same fierce protectiveness I'd witnessed earlier resurfaced. "Who did it?"

"It was my fault, I wasn't paying attention." I dropped my gaze to his shoulder. "I got distracted by someone peeking in the door."

He chuckled softly. "Busted."

His warm hand covered my chilled one. "I think I'm all better. Thank you."

Too bad I wasn't ready to let him go.

CHAPTER SIX

Roman

THE FIRST TIME I TRIED TO KISS JULIET, I MADE HER CRY.

I slipped the ice pack out of her hand and tossed it on the kitchen counter. No one in my life had ever shown me as much concern as this girl I barely even knew. Kindness in response to my pain felt so foreign.

Maybe I didn't have any experience with love, but something big I'd never felt before settled in my chest.

Her hands were chilly and I took them in mine, pulling her closer.

"Thank you."

She stared up at me with those big eyes; I still hadn't decided if they were teal or turquoise. Whatever the color, it was now my favorite shade of blue.

"You're welcome."

I might not have had years of experience to draw from, but I knew the moment demanded something.

My hands cupped her cheeks, angling her head so I could lean down and finally taste her lips.

The briefest warm, shivery sensation brushed against my lips before she jerked away.

"Roman," she whispered.

Obviously, I'd read the situation completely wrong.

"Shit. I'm sorry."

Tears shone in her eyes and dread crawled through my chest. Everything in me wanted to protect her, not upset her.

"It's not you. I'm sorry." The anguish in her voice killed me.

I rubbed my thumb over her cheek. "No, I'm sorry. I'm—"

Outside, a car door slammed and her eyes widened with fear. "You have to go. I'm not supposed to have boys in the house."

"Shit. Yeah. Okay."

I scooped up my bag and she pushed me onto the back porch, locking the door behind us. She shoved me onto a bench and threw herself into the chair across from me. Before one "what the fuck" left my mouth, someone clomped up the porch steps.

"Juliet? What you doin' out here, girl?" a gruff voice asked.

I turned and took in the short, stocky man who must be Juliet's uncle.

I may not have been the smartest kid in any class, but I'd met enough people to develop a bit of intuition about them. And Juliet's uncle gave me the fuckin' creeps.

"Who's your friend?" he asked with the least welcoming smile possible.

I stood and held out my hand, hoping manners might erase whatever notions he was forming about me.

"Roman Hawkins, sir."

"Roman's new in school," Juliet said, scrambling to stand beside me. "We share a few classes."

The older man grunted and shook my hand. "Jared Samson." He gave Juliet a pointed look. "Your aunt will be home soon, Jules. You need to help her with dinner. Say goodbye to your guest."

I wanted to punch him in the throat for the disrespectful

way he spoke to his niece, but I didn't think it would help the situation.

"Yes, sir. I was just leaving. Good to meet you," I said, trying to force something that sounded polite into my voice. I wasn't about to do anything that might keep me away from Juliet.

Under her uncle's watchful eye, I faced Juliet. "See you tomorrow."

Her cheeks were bright pink and she kept her hands clasped in front of her. "Yup."

It was awkward as hell with her uncle standing in my way, but I managed to get past him without knocking one of us off the steps.

I glanced back at Juliet once before jogging down the street and turning the corner.

CHAPTER SEVEN

Roman

ONE OF THE COUNSELORS MET ME AT THE FRONT DOOR WHEN I walked into the group home.

I still wasn't used to the place. The constant noise. The way it smelled. Institutional like all the others but still unique. Discount Lysol instead of the real thing maybe.

"How did your first day go?" he asked. "Stay out of trouble?"

"More or less."

He tilted his head, not liking my non-answer. I hadn't figured out this dude yet, so I wasn't sure if honesty would keep me out of trouble or get me sent to a new facility.

From the moment I landed in the foster care system, it felt like I'd been handed a lottery ticket to a game I'd never win.

"It's always hard for the kids from here," he said, almost sounding sympathetic. "But we didn't get any calls from the school, so that's encouraging."

Thanks to Juliet. If she hadn't vouched for me, I bet I'd be stuffing my Hefty bag and waiting on the front porch right about now.

"Go on up and do your homework. Dinner prep starts at five-thirty."

"Thanks."

And that was the extent of my counseling for the day. Suited me fine. After years of dealing with sympathetic and unsympathetic counselors, therapists, social workers, teachers, and other appointed do-gooders, I was all talked out. Any feelings had long ago been stuffed down deep in my rotted soul in order to survive.

I'd worked my way to "level two" in the house, which meant I didn't need the constant supervision of the house monitors, and I intended to keep it that way. Leaving the door open every time I had to take a piss got tedious. And it was really hard to jerk off in the shower when you had someone asking what was taking so long every five seconds.

"Hey, Pip," I greeted my roommate and tossed my frayed backpack on the bed.

Foster homes were required to give every child over the age of three their own room. In the few foster homes I'd been dropped off at, that usually meant an attic or basement room. Dark, cold—or hot—and far away from the rest of the family.

Didn't really help you feel welcomed.

In group homes, I'd lived by myself, had a roommate, or been crammed with up to three other kids in a space the size of a broom closet.

As long as no one touched me or tried to crawl into bed with me, I'd ceased caring who I shared space with a long time ago.

Phillip Plant was a pipsqueak of a kid. I dubbed him Pip for short and he seemed pleased by the nickname. He'd only been in the system long enough to develop a healthy fear of everyone and everything. Little shit almost stabbed me with a pair of sewing scissors the first night, when the last-shift counselor showed me to my room without informing Pip he had a new bunkmate.

Fun times.

Small for his age, he made an easy target for the older,

rougher kids in the house. Something I'd put an end to my second night here.

"How'd it go?" he asked. "You're back late."

My first two weeks here were spent taking exams, going to therapy and adjusting to the new house and its many rules. All valuable time spent in the eyes of the state. Not like I was already behind or anything.

And teachers wondered why I struggled to live up to my "academic potential."

"Not bad." Was I going to sit and gush about Juliet to my roommate? Hell fucking no. I didn't talk about personal shit with anyone.

"Evie said she saw you with a girl."

I blew out an irritated breath. A few girls were housed on the third floor here. Evie Potts was their ringleader and she'd made it clear she wanted to bag the new guy. Girl couldn't take a not-fucking-happening hint for shit.

"Evie needs to mind her own business."

Pip shrugged. "Hottest girl in the house wants to blow you. Cry me a river."

Dating, or even setting foot on the girls' floor, was forbidden. Grounds for immediate removal to a much more secure facility. Even if I had been interested in what Evie was offering, I wasn't going near her. I'd had enough of being yanked around. I planned to do whatever I could to make this the last stop on the foster care train. At least until graduation. If I ever fucking graduated. Some days I wasn't so sure sticking it out was worth the effort.

I threw myself on my bed and dug out my history book. At some point, I'd need to gain access to the sole house computer to turn my assignment in, but I'd ask one of the counselors on the next shift. They seemed less stressed. I steadily read through the assigned chapters and scribbled down some notes. There was a lot to catch up on and I briefly considered asking Juliet to "tutor" me.

Normally, I could hyper-focus on my schoolwork for short chunks of time—the result of rarely having a quiet place to study—but this afternoon, I found my mind wandering to Juliet often.

What was she doing?

Was she wondering the same about me?

Did her aunt and uncle treat her well?

I moved from history to my English assignment and groaned when I considered the instructions.

"Roman?" Pip's quiet voice invaded my musings and I found him standing next to me holding out a bunch of worksheets.

"What's up?" I asked, setting aside my notebook.

"Can you...?"

Understanding his reluctance to ask anyone for help, I took mercy on him. "Math homework?"

"Yeah. We got like three methods for solving this and I still don't get it."

I jerked my chin toward his desk. "I'll help, but I ain't doing it for ya."

I pulled over another chair and sat next to him. For the next half hour we steadily worked through the problems until he felt confident he could work the rest out on his own.

"Thank you, Roman. You explain it way better than Mr. Chin does."

Uncomfortable with the compliment, I shrugged. "Hopefully, I'm right. Hey, I found something for you."

I dug out the pink mechanical pencil I'd swiped from the secretary's desk when I'd been in the principal's office. Lady had like a hundred of 'em, so I didn't think she'd mind donating one to Pip. Kid had an affinity for all things pink—something that got him picked on exactly as much as you'd expect—and I figured a pencil was small enough to hide.

His whole face lit up. "Oh, cool. The lead's pink too!" He ran over to the desk and pulled a small sketch pad from the bottom drawer to try it out. I chuckled and went back to my homework.

"Aw, ain't you two sweet," someone said outside our room.

I jerked my head up and glared at the shaggy-haired brute of a kid darkening our doorway. "Get lost, Squire."

Sam Squire was the first kid to learn that the days of picking on Pip were over. Apparently, he already needed a refresher.

"Get down to the kitchen, Squire!" someone else shouted. Sounded like a counselor. Squire slumped away and Pip relaxed.

Five minutes. Just five minutes of peace and quiet was all I wanted.

CHAPTER EIGHT

Juliet

AFTER ROMAN LEFT AND MY UNCLE WENT INSIDE, I REMAINED ON the porch pretending to do my homework.

Really I was just waiting for my aunt to get home.

I learned as a little girl not to be alone in the house with my uncle if I could help it.

The awkward feeling from Roman's almost-kiss lingered. I wanted to kiss him. Wanted him to kiss me. But the sick feeling rolling in my stomach stopped me cold. I didn't want our first kiss to be in a house that held so many bad memories.

Thankfully, Aunt Susan arrived not much later, pulling me out of my obsessive thoughts.

She and I got along okay. I didn't necessarily trust her to keep me safe, but she'd kept a roof over my head and food in my belly after my mother died, so I owed her some loyalty.

"Your niece has a boyfriend," Uncle Jared said as soon as he saw his wife.

I rolled my eyes and went to the refrigerator to take out ingredients for tonight's dinner.

"Who is he?" Aunt Susan asked.

"A new kid. His locker's next to mine." I didn't volunteer that we were actually sharing my locker. It was my secret and I didn't want them butting in or trying to "fix" it with the school. "We have a few classes together."

"He looks like a troublemaker," Uncle Jared said.

I wanted to say, "No one asked you," but I bit my tongue. It wouldn't matter anyway.

Together, Aunt Susan and I fixed a quick dinner of roast chicken and vegetables with mashed potatoes. I thought about how I wished I were in a different situation where I could've asked Roman to stay for dinner. That I had normal parents who'd be interested in meeting my friends from school and allow them to hang out at my house.

But that wasn't my life.

It was never my life.

My life was being raised by a single mother who worked her ass off to give me what she could—which wasn't much with her high school education and waitressing job. But I loved her and felt loved by her and that was enough.

One night, my mother went out with her sister, Sharon, to celebrate her birthday, and never came home. A drunk driver hit them head-on. In an instant, my Aunt Susan lost both of her younger sisters and got stuck raising me. She and her husband never had children of their own, so I felt like the world's worst consolation prize.

Aunt Sharon's daughter, Debbie, was old enough to fend for herself when our moms died. Cousin Debbie met her own tragic end a few years later. Something we never talked about in this house. Once in a while, her husband still checked in on me. I called him Uncle Dex and used to beg him to let me live with him when I was younger. I stopped asking a few years ago when I realized trying to guilt him into keeping me might drive him away.

"Why so quiet, sweetie?" Aunt Susan asked, passing me the bowl of mashed potatoes. "Thinking about the boy?"

As if I'd ever talk about a boy at the dinner table. "I have a lot of homework. That's all."

"No boy's gonna be interested in you if you make him feel stupid all the time," Uncle Jared pointed out.

I bit my tongue again. So many retorts raced into my mind.

I'm not interested in a boy who's intimidated by my good grades.

Boys don't factor into how I approach my schoolwork.

And my personal favorite—*Fuck right off, Uncle Jared. Secure men don't fear smart women.*

Roman doesn't. Not that we had a lot of time to talk, but I sensed his interest in what I had to say during English class. He didn't mock me or call me *nerd girl*.

No, I could picture Roman encouraging me. I wondered if he wanted to go to college and what he wanted to study. He was in the foster care system, so was college even a possibility for him?

I don't know why the thought distressed me so much. My academic future didn't look all that bright.

Ever since I'd visited my cousin Debbie in the hospital after she gave birth, I'd wanted to be a NICU nurse. But no matter how good my grades were, my aunt and uncle had made it clear they didn't have money to send me to college, nor would they be taking out any student loans on my behalf. I'd have to pray for one hell of an all-inclusive scholarship if I wanted out of this dump.

After dinner, I helped my aunt clean the kitchen and then quietly went upstairs to my room, locking the door behind me.

CHAPTER NINE

Roman

WHILE "LEVEL TWO" GAVE ME SOME FREEDOM IN THE HOUSE, I had to be on the van with all the other kids at seven a.m. sharp so I could be unloaded in front of the high school with the rest of the herd. I was allowed to walk home after school, but I couldn't walk *to* school in the morning.

None of that made sense to me. I mean, wasn't I more likely to get in trouble lingering *after* school?

Since I had no desire to lose my privileges, I kept my opinions to myself and had my ass in the van on time.

Besides, maybe I'd get to see Juliet before school. She struck me as the type who might show up early.

Cheap, powdery perfume choked my nostrils and I glared at the offender standing over me. "Let me have the window seat," Evie said, pressing her breasts into my arm.

"Get your own seat," I growled, irritated she was putting me in a position where I might end up in trouble.

I stared straight ahead, ignoring her until Greg, one of the counselors who rode with us, saw her and jumped up. "Find a seat, Evie. Now!"

She huffed and bitched the whole way, finally throwing herself into a seat in the back. I nodded my thanks at Greg and resumed looking out the window.

Pip ended up next to me, chattering away about an art project he had planned. High school students got dropped off first, so I ruffled his hair before squeezing past him and bounding down the steps.

Being dropped off early wasn't so bad. At least there weren't a lot of people around to see me exit the navy blue van with *Pine Bluff Group Home* written along the side in big, bold, white letters.

Evie and her friend Janet lingered behind me, and I ignored them. Most of the other kids went on ahead, but I was busy searching for a certain redhead.

"You're supposed to go inside to the cafeteria," Evie informed me.

I continued ignoring her as I entered the building.

Thankfully, my lack of responses seemed to bore her and she gave up. I wandered to my locker so at least I'd have an excuse if I got caught not reporting to the cafeteria right away.

There she was.

Sitting on the floor in front of our locker with her knees pulled up to her chest, reading.

"Morning," I said.

She startled then smiled when she looked up and saw me. "Hey, I was hoping I'd see you."

My heart stopped.

Just fucking *stopped.* "Were you waiting for me?"

She blushed and ducked her head. "Sort of."

I held out my hand and helped her up off the floor. "Well, I was looking for you, so we're even."

She still couldn't seem to meet my eyes. "I'm really sorry about yesterday," she whispered.

Yesterday was pretty fantastic, all things considered. Meeting her was the best day I'd had so far this entire year. Maybe in my whole life.

Finding her courage, she straightened up and met my eyes. "At my house...when you..."

Shit. So far gone over her, I forgot that she'd blocked my clumsy attempt to kiss her. Maybe she was waiting here to tell me to find my own locker and get lost.

"I shouldn't have done that. I'm sorry." It felt wrong to apologize, because I wasn't sorry for wanting to kiss her, but I *was* sorry I'd made her uncomfortable. I didn't want whatever this was to end before it even started.

"Oh." She looked down again. "Right."

Shit, we're getting our wires crossed all over the place.

I decided to lay it out. "Juliet." I grabbed her hand, tugging her closer, forcing her to look at me. "I'm sorry if I made things awkward. I won't try to kiss you again if you don't want me to." Her friendship meant more to me than a quick make-out session.

She blinked. "It's not you. It wasn't you, I mean. It was...not there."

It took me a minute. Shit, her uncle came home about five seconds later. How dense was I?

"You didn't want to get caught?"

Finally, a half-smile formed on her gorgeous lips. "Sort of. Yeah."

I stepped closer, backing her up against the lockers. Her breathing sped up, drawing my attention to the hint of cleavage bared by the V of her T-shirt. Her pale skin was flushed and dotted with little freckles. I had the sudden urge to dip my tongue into the hollow at the base of her neck and run it over her collarbones, tasting every inch of exposed, creamy skin.

Not here.

It was almost impossible to pull away. But if I got caught making out with a girl at school, they'd notify the home, and best-case scenario, I'd be stripped of all privileges. Worst case— I'd be moved to a different home and seeing Juliet again would be almost impossible.

Already happened to me once before with a girl at another school. I was curious and she was willing. We got caught making out. Later that night, I was given fifteen minutes to pack my Hefty bag and shipped off someplace new.

I wasn't ready to disappear from Juliet's life yet, so I backed away and ran my hand through my hair instead of kissing her senseless the way I wanted.

"I'm supposed to be down in the cafeteria until first bell." It was embarrassing to admit that to her, but I really wanted to stay out of trouble. Even when I was out of the house, it still felt like I was in prison.

"Oh, okay." She stared up at me. "Am I allowed too?"

"Yeah, I don't see why not." Lots of kids other than the ones from the group home seemed to hang out there in the morning.

I grabbed her bag again, but before I slung it over my shoulder, she stopped me. "How's your arm today?"

"I'm fine."

She gestured toward the locker. "Did you need to grab anything?"

I grinned at her. "I found what I was looking for." The tone of my voice left no doubt I was talking about her.

Her cheeks flushed pink. "I'm glad."

No one looked up when we walked into the cafeteria together. I slid into a seat at a table in the back near the windows and Juliet sat across from me.

I had an insane urge to pull her into my lap. I was convinced having her warm body weight pressing into me and wrapping my arms around her would keep every bad thing in my life at bay.

To keep myself focused and out of trouble, I asked about our English assignment—writing a personal narrative—and she shyly handed over a couple of stapled-together pages.

"What about yours?" she asked.

I hesitated. With all the chaos at the home, I hadn't delved too deep with my essay. It was too damn depressing to relive all my defining moments.

Finally her pleading eyes convinced me to hand it over. Mine was scribbled in my blocky handwriting because I still hadn't gotten access to the computer at the house.

The defining moment in my life was the death of my mother. Before that my mother and I lived in an apartment not far from my two aunts. We didn't have a lot, but life was good. I never doubted that I was safe and loved.

Fearing what was coming next, I swallowed hard and continued.

Everything changed one night when my mother went out with her younger sister to celebrate her birthday. Neither of them made it home.

My aunt woke me in the morning. I'll never forget the blank look on her face when she said my mother had gone to heaven and wouldn't be coming back for me.

Safety, comfort, security all disappeared in an instant. I packed a few favorite toys and clothes to stay with Aunt Susan and her husband until they could "figure out something else."

Except for cousin Debbie, they were the only family I had left, so I wasn't sure what there was to "figure out." Where did they want me to go? Where did orphaned girls end up when no one wanted them?

It was a short ride to my new home and I remember looking at the familiar house in an unfamiliar way as we pulled into the driveway.

This was a new start to my life. In a way, the old Juliet died with her mother. New Juliet had to learn to accept a fresh start. I promised myself I'd behave so my aunt and uncle wouldn't have a reason to send me away...

"Juliet," I breathed out when I finished, stunned by her words.

"It's bad, right? Too maudlin?"

"I'm not sure what that means, but no. It's very powerful. Raw."

"I think she was looking for a *positive* life-changing event." She glanced down and flicked the pages in her notebook. "But I don't have one of those. I haven't decided how to finish the assignment yet."

"That's because your story isn't written. You still have a long road ahead of you."

"I hope so."

She tapped my pages on the table. "This is good. You're really talented," she said. I'm pretty sure it was the first time anyone said I was good at anything other than getting into trouble.

The compliment sucked in a way because my piece was completely superficial and lacked any real emotion. I wrote about how learning martial arts changed my life. The dull, predictable type of essay the teacher probably had in mind. I hadn't sliced open a vein and bled all over the pages the way Juliet had.

"Is it true?" she asked.

"Mostly. One of my foster homes, the dad taught martial arts, so I learned from him."

"Was it a good home?"

She seemed so genuinely concerned, I actually wanted to talk about it, something I hadn't done in a long time.

"Yeah, they were nice people. Probably the best home I've been in."

"What happened?"

"They had a baby." I shrugged as if the memory didn't sting. "My time was up."

"Do you still keep in touch—"

I shook my head, cutting her off. "No, that's discouraged."

"That's so sad."

Her mouth turned down. She seemed so damn distressed by my story. Maybe I should've kept it to myself. I'd never thought of my situation as happy or sad.

It was all I knew.

CHAPTER TEN

Roman

THE REST OF THE DAY WASN'T AS EXCITING AS MY MORNING. I DID manage to stay out of trouble. Doug and his friends avoided me.

Actually, everyone except Juliet acted like I had a contagious disease. Maybe word had spread that I was one of the kids from the group home. I didn't dwell on it because I didn't care.

Before our last class of the day, I found Juliet waiting for me, just as pretty as she'd been first thing this morning.

"We have to stop meeting this way," she teased, stepping aside so I could chuck my books in the locker before we headed to art class.

I liked art. Maybe not as much as Pip enjoyed it, but I could draw a decent portrait if I had a worthy subject.

Juliet would be worth drawing.

Hell, my notebook already contained half a dozen doodles of her long hair, secret smile, and perfect profile.

It was a small, advanced art class taught by a somewhat eccentric middle-aged guy—Mr. Broom. I'd joined the class right before they started a section on photography. A subject that interested me, but I'd never had the luxury of exploring. Hell, I wasn't even allowed to have a flip phone. While all my peers were busy snapping selfies and fucking around on social media, I was busy with therapy sessions, learning house rules, protecting myself, and chores.

There was an extra fee for this part of the class and I'd have to ask one of the counselors or my caseworker to approve it. I usually avoided asking for anything, but I didn't want to drop out of the class.

We sat two to four kids to a table and naturally I sat right next to Juliet. So close our legs touched from thigh to knee. A thrill ran through me at the contact, and she peeked up at me as if she sensed it too.

After the opening lecture, Mr. Broom strolled through the room, passing out magazines that demonstrated different styles of photography.

Mr. Broom stopped by my table and leaned down. My whole body tensed, afraid I was already in trouble.

"Your fee has been taken care of, so you don't need to worry about it, Mr. Hawkins," he said quietly before straightening up and walking away.

It was a relief, but it also bothered me. Who paid it? The school? Mr. Broom? He didn't even know me. My social worker? She barely seemed to know where I was half the time.

It was a mystery I couldn't solve, but I was grateful that for once in my life something wouldn't be a big deal. Grateful he went out of his way not to embarrass me, allowing me to avoid the shame of being the poor orphan begging for scraps.

We took the magazines home, and I was supposed to decide what subjects moved me. People, nature, animals, objects?

After class, I wanted to talk to Mr. Broom, but he was surrounded by students, so I followed Juliet into the hallway instead.

"What did he say to you?" she asked.

"Nothing."

Her face fell as if she expected to share things with me and I'd disappointed her. "I'll tell you on the way home," I added.

The way home. On the way to *her* home. I didn't have one.

"Oh, I can't wait until we get an actual camera. And we're going to develop the film ourselves. That will be so much fun!" Juliet skipped ahead of me, hair flying behind her. I jogged to catch up to her, grabbing her hand to slow her down.

Her enthusiasm was infectious and I found myself smiling.

That smile didn't fade until we got closer to her house and I spotted some guy crouched in front of an all matte-black Harley-Davidson motorcycle in her driveway. I pulled her back, stopping her in her tracks. "Who is that?"

"Who? Where?" She glanced around and when her gaze landed on the leather-clad biker, she broke into a grin. "Uncle Dex!" She jerked out of my hold and ran toward the stranger.

I sprinted after her, still unsure whether the guy was a danger. At the sound of her voice, he stood and turned. A grin broke out over his face. He held out his arms and she launched herself at him.

Who the fuck was this dude?

She laughed and chattered a mile a minute as he spun her in a quick circle, then set her on her feet. His gaze landed on me and he placed a protective arm around her. "Who's your friend, Julez?"

She grabbed his hand and tugged him in my direction. "Dex, this is my friend, Roman. He's new in school and we share a locker and a bunch of classes," she said in a rush.

Dex was no fool. He took one look at me and knew I wanted to be a hell of a lot more than Juliet's *friend.* I'd gotten similar looks from girls' fathers in the past. This guy might not be her dad, but he had overprotective instincts like one. Not in a creepy-asshole way like the uncle I met yesterday. No, this guy's demeanor was completely different. Stern, but curious. Something I respected.

I nodded and held out my hand. "Roman Hawkins, sir. Moved to the area recently and Juliet's been kind enough to show me around school."

He shook my hand and released Juliet. "Nice to meet you, Roman." His shrewd gaze lingered, observing everything no doubt. I stood up straight under his scrutiny because anything else wouldn't earn his respect.

"Are you staying for dinner?" Juliet asked with a pleading note in her voice I hadn't heard her use before.

"Can't, Julez. You know that. I did want to give you an early birthday present though."

"Really?" She squeezed her hands together and squealed a bunch of happy noises. Damn, she was fucking cute all excited. She grabbed each of our hands and dragged us toward the back porch. While we settled into chairs, she ran inside.

"So where you from, Roman?"

"All over." I wasn't trying to be evasive. That was the truth.

"Where do you live?" he asked in a more specific, don't-bullshit-me tone.

I swallowed hard and met his stare head-on. "At the Pine Bluff Group Home, sir."

His eyes narrowed and he nodded. "How'd you end up there?"

I knew what he was asking. Was I a delinquent who got tossed into the system by the criminal courts—someone who might hurt his niece—or was I an orphan?

Instead of giving him my whole sad history, I answered the question he really wanted to know. "Been bouncing around the foster care system since I was seven years old. Never found the right family to adopt me, sir."

That seemed to relieve some of his tension about me and he settled back in his chair just as Juliet burst out of the house carrying a tray with a pitcher of iced tea and several glasses. I jumped up to help her, taking the tray and setting it on the low table in front of her uncle.

"Thank you," Juliet said breathlessly. "I was worried I would drop it for a minute."

I caught Dex watching me again as I sat back in my chair and looked away. My grandmother had been strict when I lived with her. She firmly believed that being polite never went out of style. That meant holding doors open, carrying heavy things, and generally helping ladies instead of standing by and watching. It was probably childish, but I liked to think if Grandma was somewhere watching over me, she'd be proud I hadn't let the system beat her lessons out of me.

Juliet sat facing her uncle and gave him her full attention while he handed over a package tightly wrapped with dazzling silver paper. I'll admit I was a little jealous. First, I didn't realize Juliet had a birthday coming up. Second, even if I did know about her birthday, I didn't have a penny to buy her anything.

She gasped and squealed when she pulled out the dark green leather jacket.

"Oh my God, it's beautiful. So perfect!" She jumped up and slipped it on, zipping it up to her chin. "Am I ready to ride with you now?" she asked her uncle.

He stood and fixed the collar for her. "Gotta get you a helmet and Aunt Suzy's permission first."

Juliet rolled her eyes. "Never gonna happen."

"If not, I promise I'll take you out for your eighteenth birthday, okay?"

"I'm holding you to it."

He laughed. "Expect nothing less from you, Julez."

She sat down and peppered him with questions about his travels, and I gathered she hadn't seen him in a long time.

"What do you do that keeps you on the road so much?" I blurted out, genuinely curious. Having never been outside of New York State—except for a miserable six weeks at a "youth wilderness camp" in Massachusetts—I was dying to travel and it sounded like Dex did a lot of it.

"Different things," he answered with practiced evasiveness.

"He does a lot of charity runs with his motorcycle club too, right Uncle Dex?"

His lips twisted into a half-smile. "That's right."

My gaze traveled over his black leather vest again, this time taking in some of the patches decorating the front.

Loyal Brother. Lost Kings MC. On the left side. *Brother's Keeper. Respect Few, Fear None.* On the right.

Huh. That last one I could definitely relate to.

"You ride, Roman?" Dex asked.

"No, sir. Don't have a license." Motorcycles had always interested me. But since the probability of ever being able to afford one seemed about the same as sprouting wings and learning to fly, I didn't give them much thought on a daily basis. I liked the look of Harleys over crotch-rockets and that was about the extent of my knowledge on the subject.

Since Juliet seemed safe with this guy, I decided I should take off and let them visit.

I stood and picked up my bag. "I should head out. Nice to meet you, sir."

"You need a ride?" he asked.

"Nah, I'm only a few streets over. Thank you, though."

Juliet stood, her mouth turning down with unhappiness. "You don't have to go—"

"No, it's fine." I reached out and grabbed her hand, giving it a quick squeeze. "I really do need to get home before someone comes looking for me. I'll see you tomorrow."

"Early?" She batted her lashes and smiled.

Damn did I want to kiss her, but not in front of Dex, who was watching us like a damn cobra about to strike.

"Early," I promised.

CHAPTER ELEVEN

Juliet

I watched Roman go with a mixture of sadness and guilt. It hadn't occurred to me that he might need to be back at the home by a particular time. I didn't want to be responsible for getting him in trouble.

"So, he your boyfriend?" Dex asked as soon as Roman was out of sight.

The stern note in his voice made me proceed with caution. "Just a friend."

"Seems to like you a whole lot more than *just a friend*."

"You think so?" I gushed. Caution be damned.

Dex groaned and sat back. "You're making me feel old, Julez. Weren't you eleven last week?"

"Uh, no. Try five years ago." I thought for a minute about how to express myself. "I like Roman a lot. He's really kind and thoughtful."

Dex nodded to my backpack on the floor in front of me. "Noticed that," he said. I liked the approval in his voice. It was good timing that he saw Roman walking me home. I wanted Dex to like Roman as much as I did.

Even though my cousin Debbie was a lot older than me,

she'd been like the big sister I never had. I'd tagged along with her and Dex frequently when I was little. His approval meant something to me.

"Just be careful. Boys his age can't be trusted." Dex laughed. "I was one. I remember."

I rolled my eyes. "He's really not like that." I leaned in and lowered my voice. "He tried to kiss me yesterday, but when I said I wasn't ready, he backed off. He told me today he won't try again unless I want him to."

Dex shifted, his gaze darting around the porch. "Why you gotta tell me stuff like this?"

I suppose I could've talked about it with Vienna, but I didn't feel comfortable sharing this with her for some reason. She'd tell me I was silly for turning Roman down or make a joke about how he needs a "real woman." Both would fire up my temper.

"What should I do?"

"Revisit when you're twenty-one?" Dex suggested.

"I'm serious."

He blew out a breath and stared straight ahead as if he was searching for someone out of sight to provide the right words. "What do *you* want?"

"I want to get to know him more. I like being around him. Talking to him. He really listens. And he's smart. And he doesn't mind that *I'm* smart." I stopped myself before I crazy-babbled any more silly high school girl stuff.

"Then get to know him more. There's nothing wrong with that."

"But how do I tell him I *want* him to kiss me?" I whispered, then quickly added, "When I do."

I couldn't confide the real reason why being so close to a boy scared me the way it did. Not to Dex. Not to anyone ever. But I fell asleep last night wondering what it would feel like to have a boy I liked kiss me. To *want* to be close to him more than my next breath.

Dex groaned and looked away. "When the time's right, you'll both know." He shook his head. "Can't you talk to Suzy about any of this?"

"Heck no. She'd probably scream at me about getting knocked up in high school like her sister did."

He winced at the mention of Debbie's mom, my aunt Sharon. "She scream at you often?"

I shrugged it off like it was no big deal.

He reached over and patted my leg. "I'm sorry, peanut. I wish...well, what I wish doesn't matter. You don't have long until you're out on your own."

And doesn't that terrify me almost as much as being trapped here forever.

My fear must have shown on my face, because Dex looked even more troubled. "You still want to be a nurse?"

"Don't know how I'll pay for it, but yes."

"It will work itself out, Juliet. Somehow."

I doubted that. "I miss them. Mom and Debbie. She was like the big sister I never had. I could've told her this."

Sadness clouded his eyes and I wished I'd kept my mouth shut. "She loved you," he rasped. "Her little peanut."

In the driveway, a truck door slammed and someone shouted, "Why is this piece of shit in my driveway!"

Dex clenched his jaw. "I planned to be out of here before he came home."

"He works second shift now," I whispered.

"When's Suzy get home? She still working nights?"

"No, she should be here soon."

He sat back as if he had no plans to leave, even with Uncle Jared muttering and cursing his way around the house.

One heavy boot thudded against the porch steps and I shuddered. Dex glanced at me and frowned.

"That your bike in my driveway?" Jared asked.

"Who else's would it be, old man?" Dex stood and shook my uncle's hand, even though Jared seemed pretty cranky. Dex always ignored my uncle's moodiness but never backed down because of it. Something I admired and respected. If I was Dex's size, I could probably get away with it too.

"What're you doing here, Dex?"

"Wanted to stop by and give Juliet an early birthday present," he said, as if he was trying to remind my uncle that I had a birthday coming up.

Good luck with that.

Uncle Jared and Aunt Susan hadn't acknowledged my birthday in years.

Jared grunted at the explanation.

"I'm going to wait around so I can say hi to Susan," Dex said, leaving no room for discussion.

My uncle slammed the door open and stomped into the house without answering.

Shaking his head, Dex dropped into the chair next to me. "He seems angrier than ever."

I shrugged. Uncle Jared had always been unpleasant. That was nothing new.

CHAPTER TWELVE

Roman

THE NEXT MORNING WHEN I GOT OFF THE VAN IN FRONT OF THE school, there was a Harley parked at the curb.

I recognized the owner right away and wasn't one bit surprised.

"Hi, Dex," I said, approaching him first. Guess it was time to prepare for the "Stay away from Juliet" speech. Too bad I had no intention of staying away from her.

"Morning, Roman." He reached out and shook my hand.

Maybe he wasn't here to tell me to back off.

I crossed my arms over my chest and waited. "You looking for Juliet?" I asked when he didn't start the conversation.

"Nope. Looking for you."

"Well, you found me." I glanced at the school. "I need to be inside."

He cocked his head. "It's ass-crack early in the morning."

"Yeah, well, I don't exactly get a lot of freedom."

He nodded. "You like Juliet?"

"Yeah, I like her a lot," I said, deciding to forgo cockiness in favor of honesty.

"You got a job?"

Okay, didn't expect that question.

"Haven't been here long enough to look for one."

"I might be able to hook you up with something."

No one did favors for free. "And why would you do that?"

He blew out a breath and glanced away before answering. "Because if you're gonna be hanging around Juliet, I don't want her dating a bum."

"You don't have a problem with me dating her?"

He shook his head. "I ain't her fuckin' dad. I'm not even really her uncle. But I care about her. Known her since she was little. Figure you're teenagers. Gonna do whatever the fuck you wanna do anyway. Least I should do is make sure you can take her out and shit."

I wasn't quite sure I believed that explanation.

"Although, if you ever hurt her, I will fucking kill you." The casual way he tossed out the threat made me believe he meant every word.

"I'd never hurt her."

"Sometimes we can't help hurting the ones we love the most," he said in a low voice I barely made out over the noise in the parking lot.

"Don't get ahead of yourself, Dex. Juliet and I just met."

"Doesn't matter. Sometimes you just know when you meet the right person."

An uncomfortable sensation rolled through my chest. Juliet was the one for me. Knew it the second I met her. Our souls connected. My rational brain knew that was absurd, but the rest of me didn't care.

Dex saw it too and didn't think I was crazy?

He handed over a card with a name and address.

"What's Crystal Ball?" The address was way the fuck down in the city of Empire. Not sure how he expected me to find my way there.

"Club owned by my MC. Come down and see me. I'll find you some work."

"Uh…" I hesitated and considered handing the card back. "Whatever the job is, it has to be legal and I have to get it approved by my caseworker. Plus, I have no way to get there."

He stared at me for a second. "You always such a rule-follower, Roman?"

"No, but I'm not really in a position to do anything about it, unless I want to get moved to another home, which I'd rather avoid." I glanced at the low brick building behind us. "I like it here."

He nodded as if he approved of my answer. "You're awfully level-headed for your age."

"Sometimes."

"Give me some time to come up with another lead. In the meantime, do me a favor."

Finally, the reason he came to see me. I lifted my chin and waited for him to continue.

"Look out for Juliet. Her uncle's nastier than ever. Make sure everything's okay there. If it's not, let me know and I'll handle him."

"I noticed he's a prick. You think he'd hurt her?"

"Don't know. Not sure she'd tell me if he did."

"But you think she'll tell *me*?"

"If she trusts you."

He picked his helmet up off the seat of his bike and strapped it on.

"Wait," I said. "When's her birthday?" It had been bugging me all night that I didn't know.

Dex smirked and gave me the date which was three weeks from today. That made her younger than me by about eight months.

"My cell's on the back of that card," he said. "Call me if she needs anything."

As if he just thought of it, he reached into the pocket of his leather vest and pulled out a silver flip phone. "It's nothing fancy, but if you need to get a hold of me, or if she needs to reach you, use it."

Phones, or any electronics besides small MP3 players, were strictly forbidden. Plenty of kids at the home had contraband phones. I'd considered it myself once or twice, except who the fuck was I gonna call? I had no brothers or sisters I wanted to keep in touch with. No parents. The risk of getting in trouble seemed pointless. But now I had Juliet, and Dex was right. If she needed me, I wanted her to be able to call. I didn't enjoy taking charity from anyone, but it would be stupid to turn it down.

"Thanks. Appreciate it."

He shook my hand again before taking off. I made sure the phone was turned off and slipped it in my bag before going inside.

"Morning, stranger," Juliet greeted me at our locker. A teasing smile played over her lips. She was wearing the jacket Dex gave her yesterday and a pair of brown leather boots.

"Dex give you a ride?" I asked.

She blinked. "How'd you know?"

I nodded at her jacket. "The outfit. And the fact that he was outside waiting to talk to me."

"He what?"

"It's cool. He said he might be able to help me find a job."

"Why? So you're too busy to spend time with me?"

I snorted and emptied my backpack into our locker, pulling out the books and notebook I'd need for first period. "I think he just doesn't want you dating a bum."

I was staring right at her when I said it, so I didn't miss the way her jaw dropped and her eyes widened. Or the way her cheeks turned an even deeper shade of pink. "Are we dating?" she whispered.

The air in my lungs vanished and my stomach bottomed out. Did I move too fast?

I closed the locker door with a quiet metallic click and braced my hand against the cool metal, considering all the possible answers.

"Roman?" she prodded.

Finally I met her troubled blue eyes and let it all out. "I don't have anything to offer you, Juliet. Not a penny to my name to give you the things you deserve. My time's regulated more than an inmate. Can't spend hours online with you or even call you without someone listening in on our conversation. Got no car or way to take you out—"

"Stop."

"Don't have a family to introduce you to," I continued.

"Roman, I don't care."

"You deserve more."

"So do you."

Do I?

I hated dwelling on it but living in the system for so long left me bitter, jaded, and full of anger. I hadn't done anything wrong to be placed in foster care, but I'd been treated like a criminal since I was seven years old. Eventually you started to believe you deserved your shitty life and weren't worthy of a better one.

Our eyes locked and to my utter shock, she placed her hand on my chest, over my heart. Blood thundered through my veins. My heart was literally in the palm of her hand. Could she feel it throbbing and ready to jump out of my chest?

Looking up at me through her lashes, she raised up on her tiptoes and gently pressed her lips against mine.

Sweet, beautiful mercy she was so soft and shy. It took everything I had not to grab her and devour her completely. She trembled as she opened her mouth, running her tongue over my bottom lip. She tasted like cinnamon and crisp spring air.

I snapped. The attraction that had been building between us

for days flared like a lit match. I captured her lips with mine and swept my tongue inside her mouth. Tasting and teasing her. She moaned, the soft vibration firing me up even more.

"Roman." Either she whispered my name or thought it. We were so entwined I wasn't sure where I ended and she began.

My cock jerked against my zipper so hard, it shook me from head to toe. I framed her face with my hands, holding her still for more kisses. She fell into me, pushing her perfect tits tight against my chest. Fuck, I burned with the need to sneak my hand under her shirt and run my thumb over her nipple.

She smelled so damn good. I wanted her scent embedded in my clothes and skin so everyone knew I was hers.

"Yeah, dawg. Get some!" a kid shouted.

As quickly as it blazed, our kiss fizzled. I pulled back enough to lean my forehead against hers and whispered, "I want to do that again, Juliet. Soon. And often. But not here."

She closed her eyes tightly, her lips curving up with happiness, relief, or satisfaction, I wasn't sure.

That short, searing kiss was a cataclysmic shift in our relationship. We were no longer locker buddies or new friends getting to know each other.

We were soul mates.

Deep, deep down, my heart twisted with anguish. Nothing good had ever come from caring for someone before. I wasn't sure I even knew how. And even if I learned how to love someone...

I always lost them anyway.

CHAPTER THIRTEEN

Juliet

Who knew one little kiss could devastate and electrify you at the same time?

For the rest of the day, I floated through school on a cloud.

Nerves consumed me after our last class. I jittered all the way to our locker, my thoughts bouncing around like a bunny in the forest. Roman said he wanted to kiss me again. And often. Did he mean right now? At school? Where else could we go to have some privacy?

"Hey," he greeted me.

"Hey." For the first time since we met, I felt shy and unsure around him. I ended up staring at his feet.

"Juliet? Is everything okay?" The concern laced into his question drew my attention to his face. The confusion and uncertainty swirling inside me seemed to be reflected in his eyes.

"I'm fine."

"Ready to head home?"

Not really. I wanted to go somewhere I could be alone with him, but I wasn't sure how to float the idea.

"Can we walk through the park?" The path through the park

would take us half a mile out of our way, giving us time together.

"Planning to do some bird-watching?" he teased.

"Not really." A nervous smile twitched over my lips.

"Sure. Let's go."

The grounds behind the school backed right into the park and we took the well-worn trail up over the first small hill separating the two places. Lots of kids headed this way after the final bell. Usually to hide and sneak cigarettes. Or ambush other kids. I never went home this way because it didn't seem safe. But with Roman I felt completely protected.

As we entered the deep grove of trees surrounding the park, Roman slipped his warm, rough fingers around mine.

A dizzying rush of heat spread through me. The contact was so simple but felt so right.

"How was your day?" he asked quietly as we kept walking.

"Not as good as my morning."

He stopped, turned, and stared at me. "Juliet." So much longing colored his voice, I leaned closer and pressed my hand against his chest.

His eyes closed briefly, then he seemed to make a decision. He gently nudged me off the path, into a cluster of trees. Bright, afternoon sunlight beamed through the canopy of leaves, turning the hidden spot into a magical chamber. Our bags hit the ground with thuds muted by layers of leaves and pine needles.

I looped my arms around his neck and his hands threaded into my hair. Our lips met and fire raced over my skin.

A groan ripped out of him and he lifted me, moving us until I was trapped between a tree at my back and his hard chest against mine.

"Roman." Without thinking, I teased my hands under the hem of his T-shirt.

"I love the way you touch me and say my name," he whispered against my lips.

"Roman," I said again. My fingers tugged at his shirt. I had no idea what I was doing, I just moved on instinct, want, and need. To be closer to him. Skin on skin.

He stripped off his shirt and my breath caught. He was beautiful. Muscular, strong, but scarred. "What happened?" I asked, tracing my fingers over faded white and red lines.

"Nothing I want to talk about." He glanced down as if seeing the scars for the first time in ages. "One day I want to cover them up with some ink."

I easily pictured a tapestry of vivid, bold colors splashed over his skin. "What kind of tattoos do you want?"

"Haven't decided yet. I'm sure I'll find inspiration when the time is right." He bent down to kiss me again and I tipped my head back, offering myself.

He kissed and nipped at my neck all the way to a spot behind my ear that made me dizzy with desire. His thumbs brushed against my sides, under my jacket and shirt. The urge to have his hands on my bare skin made me reckless. Pinned between him and the tree, I struggled for leverage to take my jacket off, then tugged my shirt up over my head.

Roman stared at me with awe in his wide, green eyes.

I hesitated and crossed my arms over my chest. Did he think I was moving too fast? How far did I want this to go?

Then his lips were on mine again and I stopped questioning the moment.

Slowly, almost reverently, he skimmed his palms up my sides, over my back, and finally stopped to gently tug my arms away from my chest.

He stared.

Heat crawled over my skin.

I didn't own any fancy underwear like Vienna or the other girls in my gym class. But by the hungry look in Roman's eyes, I don't think he minded the plain, white cotton bra one bit. He reverently cupped my breasts, his thumbs brushing over my bra where my nipples pushed against the fabric. A zap of electricity shot straight to my center. My head fell back, lazily rolling to the side.

I'd never felt this way before. Wild and desperate. Yet, safe in Roman's arms.

"Juliet?" he whispered.

I opened my eyes and watched as he dipped his head low, kissing the swell of my breast peeking over the top of my too-small bra. Any lingering embarrassment over my basic undergarments evaporated. His tongue gently teased over my nipple straining against the cotton.

"Roman." My hands dug into his hair. I wanted so much more. He answered my desperate grip by moving to my other breast, gently biting at my nipple.

"Oh my God." Tingles of pleasure flooded my body from that simple nip.

With great reluctance, he slowly dragged himself away from my breasts and stood straighter, peering down at me.

He opened his mouth to say something and since I sensed it was something I didn't want to hear, I hooked my hand behind his neck and pulled him toward me for another kiss.

I wasn't ready for our magical moment to end.

Roman

Gone. My brain had switched to feral mode. The need to claim Juliet right this second beat through my blood. I lifted her, marveling at how light but solid she felt in my arms. This wasn't a dream. She was real. Her thighs hugged my hips, her ankles hooked behind me, drawing me closer.

She kissed me with the same determined passion. I rolled

my hips, and my painfully hard cock nudged the warmth straight between her legs.

Heaven.

I was convinced it was behind that denim.

The wind rustled through the leaves and a few splatters of water from the earlier storm rained down. A cooler breeze swirled around us, whispering that we couldn't continue down this path.

"We have to stop," I rasped.

She tightened her legs around my waist and I groaned. I was two seconds from shredding her jeans and discovering all her hidden spots.

I cupped her cheeks and kissed her lips one last time before pulling back for good.

"We can't," I whispered. "Not now."

For one thing, even though our current spot was secluded, we were still in a public park where anyone could stumble on us. I didn't want to take that chance.

There was also the fact that I didn't have a condom. I'd encountered enough pregnant girls in foster care to know I didn't want to be the kind of asshole who knocked up his high school girlfriend. Especially since I had no way to provide for Juliet.

Yeah, I was thinking that far ahead.

At a couple of the group homes I'd been in, the counselors would hand out condoms on the sly. Others preached abstinence only. You can guess which ones had the higher rates of teen pregnancies. I had been at mine long enough to think of at least two counselors who might help me out.

Fuck, I was harder than a damn rock.

"I'm sorry," she whispered.

"Why are you sorry?" *Please tell me she doesn't regret this already.*

Pink bloomed over her skin, creeping up her neck. She lowered her feet to the ground. My gaze dropped to her chest. The innocent, white cotton bra she filled out so nicely didn't look as wholesome now that I'd left two wet circles over her nipples. My mouth watered, eager to discover the taste of her skin.

She leaned over to grab her T-shirt, snapping me out of my trance. "I don't know what came over me." She ducked her head and slipped into the shirt. "I don't usually...I've never done this before."

She peeked up at me, searching for a reaction, and I tried not to beat my chest like a proud gorilla.

"I don't usually either." Maybe some guys wouldn't admit that, but I didn't care. Foolish pride served no purpose. I wanted total honesty with Juliet.

Her mouth twisted in a *yeah right* smile. I leaned down and kissed her, then whispered in her ear, "I think I've been waiting for *you*."

I wasn't deliberately trying to come up with lines to get in her jeans. Around her, my mouth seemed to open and whatever was in my head or heart poured out.

Her disbelieving smile softened, but something painful flashed in her eyes. A memory maybe. Whatever it was had nothing to do with me. I wouldn't push her now, but I wanted to know what bothered her so I could fix it.

She glanced at her chest, cupped her tits and adjusted herself. The sexy shimmy and jiggle didn't do a damn thing to calm the erection she'd given me.

To keep myself from grabbing her again, I scooped her jacket and my shirt off the ground.

When we were finally dressed, I led her out of the trees and back onto the path toward her house.

"I'm sorry. Do you get in trouble if you're late?" she asked.

I captured her hand and tugged her closer while we walked.

"Yeah, I can get in trouble," I admitted. "It's like being in prison. Except, they give us just enough freedom to know we're not really free."

"Roman."

The sadness in her voice stopped me. I turned and faced her, distressed to see tears shining in her eyes.

"It's okay, Juliet," I tried to reassure her. "It's only temporary. I just need to make it through this phase in my life to get to the next one."

"You're so brave. And clever."

I wasn't worthy of being called either of those things, but her mouth tipped from sad to happy, so I didn't argue.

"What happens if you get in trouble?" The note of fear in her voice proved she was the clever one in this relationship.

I blew out a breath. "Anything from getting demoted to level one, which means round-the-clock supervision, to being removed and sent to a stricter home."

"You've already moved around a lot, right?"

"Yup. They prefer to ambush you at night when you're not expecting it." I tried to keep my tone light and teasing, but my stomach churned with so many memories of being dragged out of bed and given fifteen minutes to shove my shit in a garbage bag. I didn't share those depressing flashbacks. She seemed to have enough of her own sadness, no need to pile on my years of misery. I wanted to shield her from the bad in the world. Not alert her to even more depressing situations.

"That's awful."

I shrugged like I didn't care, which after years of trying to convince myself, sometimes I actually believed. "It sucks, but whatever."

Her eyes searched my face as if my cool demeanor didn't fool her. But she didn't press me any further.

"Do you have a roommate?"

I chuckled. "Yeah, he's in middle school, though. I call him Pip. He's a crazy-talented artist, but super shy." Actually, poor

Pip was probably wondering where I was, scared he'd have to fend off the bigger bullies in the house all by himself.

Those fuckers should've known by now not to fuck with Pip, but I worried anyway.

I tried to never get attached to anyone. Not that I was attached to Pip, but I felt responsible for him, and that bothered me. Eventually, I'd let him down.

I was definitely getting attached to Juliet.

Today, there was no one waiting in her driveway. I walked her to the back door and gave her a quick kiss before jogging away.

For a brief moment, in the midst of the chaos that was my life, I'd found peace.

CHAPTER FOURTEEN

Juliet

DAYS AND WEEKS MELTED INTO ONE ANOTHER. ROMAN AND I were inseparable. We never had as much time together as we wanted but the moments we shared were intense.

Half the time we ended up making out in the park, other times we stole a few moments in the photography lab. Mr. Broom seemed oblivious, which worked in our favor.

Roman somehow had his gym class switched to mine. The days the boys and girls were grouped together were my favorite.

Even if it was something idiotic like teaching us ballroom dancing. We lived in a poor, rural area. The likelihood of anyone in this class ever using ballroom dancing skills was pretty slim.

It might have been a silly, frivolous thing to teach us, but I secretly loved the lessons. Especially the way Roman made it clear to every boy in our class that I was off-limits. And the *step away* stare he shot at every girl who approached him to be their dance partner.

Yeah, his new-guy-with-the-violent-temper reputation commanded the interest of every single girl in our school. They seemed to be caught up in some fantasy of "fixing" the bad boy.

Only I knew the truth. Roman wasn't bad. He *was* angry—

but he had plenty of valid reasons for that rage. He didn't need *fixing*, he needed someone to see his goodness.

I was happy to be that someone.

"Lift your head, Juliet," the teacher shouted. "Feel where he leads."

"I feel where you lead all the time," I mumbled.

Roman rumbled with laughter. I loved making him laugh and seemed to be the only person capable of teasing a genuine smile onto his oh-so-serious face. Occasionally, some wacky thing that came out of Vienna's mouth would make him chuckle, and I loved those moments too.

We truly understood each other. He laughed at my jokes, no matter how random they seemed. Roman was the first person who truly got my quirky sense of humor and appreciated it instead of thinking I was a weirdo.

"Sometimes I'm not sure who leads who." Roman winked and spun me around.

That was ridiculous. I was so under his spell, it wasn't funny. He pulled me in and I pressed myself against his chest for a brief moment—even though we were supposed to remain at arm's length.

Besides giving me an opportunity to publicly touch my boyfriend for a solid forty-five minutes without fear of getting in trouble, the dance lessons were great because we didn't have to change into our dorky, inappropriately sized gym uniforms. Today, I'd worn a short, floaty chiffon dress Vienna had given me for Christmas. It was frilly, with layers that fanned out each time Roman spun me around, making me feel like a modern fairy-tale princess.

Class finished and Roman gave me a quick peck on the lips before I dashed off to the locker room with Vienna. I didn't need to change, but I did need to collect my backpack for our next class.

"Girl, the way that boy looks at you," Vienna sighed. "Gives me goosebumps."

"He's kinda *ew*. Like doesn't he live in a detention center or something?" One of my cattier classmates—Diane—said without looking at me.

"You didn't seem to think he was *ew* when you asked him to take you to prom," I said sweetly. As if the whole school hadn't been talking about the way Roman flatly turned her down.

Vienna laughed and slammed her locker shut. "Don't be such a bitter bitch, Diane, it'll give you wrinkles."

More nastiness came out of Diane, but I'd stopped caring about what my shallow classmates thought of me a long time ago.

I grabbed my stuff and hugged Vienna before taking off to meet up with Roman.

Except he wasn't in the hallway waiting for me like he normally was.

A sick feeling settled in my stomach.

Doug and his friends had been increasing the verbal attacks on Roman whenever they could get away with it. So far, Roman ignored the insults, but I didn't doubt if one of them laid a hand on him, they might not get it back.

Finally, he emerged from the gym, smiling when he saw me. A whoosh of relief passed my lips and I took his outstretched hand. "Were you waiting long?"

"Is everything okay?" I blurted instead of answering his question.

"Mr. Dawson wanted to talk to me about trying out for baseball."

"Isn't it too late in the season?"

He shrugged. "They're down a player. I know zip about baseball, except that it looks boring as fuck."

"I hope you didn't say that to him." I snort-giggled and covered my mouth.

"Nah, I just said I didn't have time and I don't think I could get permission from Pine Bluff." He peered down at me. "Would you rather be dating a baseball player?"

I almost laughed again. As if any other boy in this school could compare to Roman. Yet, I sensed a hint of seriousness in his voice and wanted to reassure him. "Only if it's *you*."

"If I'm doing anything after school, it's finding a job."

"I hear that," I mumbled.

He raised an eyebrow. "What did you have in mind?"

"Maybe the ice cream shop connected to the drive-in theater for the summer? That could be fun." Fun *and* keep me out of the house until late.

"Fun huh?" He slipped his arm around my shoulders and I soaked up his warmth.

The soft patter of Vienna's heels over the tile was the only warning I had before she plowed into us from behind. "Ugh, Diane is such an uber bitch. You were smart to run."

Laughing, I shrugged her arm off my shoulder.

Roman frowned. "She say something to you?"

"No," I answered quickly. I didn't want Vienna to repeat Diane's comments about Roman.

"Maybe we can drown her on our class trip." Vienna skipped ahead, raising her arms in the air. "Another tragedy at Fletcher Park, news at eleven." Her eyes widened and she stopped dead in front of us. "Or we could push her over the cliff." She mimed pushing someone and watching them fall. "*Weeeeee, splat!*"

"You're terrible," I scoffed, stepping around her and linking hands with Roman again.

"What class trip?" he asked.

"Oh, you'll be thrilled, lover boy," Vienna sang, hurrying to catch up to us. "You'll get to ogle your girl in a bikini all afternoon."

Roman raised an eyebrow. "Oh, really?"

Laughing nervously, I pushed Vienna. "I'm *so* not wearing a two-piece in front of these cretins."

"Not even for me?" Roman teased.

"Maybe. If you ask me nicely."

"Later!" Vienna waggled her fingers at us and took off running down the hall.

Roman and I strolled into art class a few minutes before the bell and sat in our usual spots. Chloe and Jameson, another couple in our grade, sat across from us, eagerly discussing their prom plans. I shifted uncomfortably. I hadn't brought up prom because I figured there was no way Roman could afford to go and I didn't want to make him feel bad.

Under the table, he found my hand and twined our fingers together. He leaned over and whispered in my ear, "Do you have a date for prom?"

"What? No." How could he ask me that?

Then I looked into his laughing green eyes and knew he was only teasing. He winked but didn't have a chance to add anything to our conversation. Mr. Broom started class.

Naturally, Roman and I had worked on our photography projects together. He'd taken an embarrassingly large number of photos of me for his assignment.

He also had a talent for capturing breathtaking landscapes and pretty much anything else he turned his lens on.

After the introductory lecture, Roman leaned over. "How do you feel about sticking around after class?"

A tingle of excitement zipped through me. "Sounds good. Are you allowed to?" I whispered back, making sure to keep my voice low. Enough rumors about Roman had been spread around the school without me adding to them.

"I have special permission for this project," he assured me.

That Roman sought out permission from the counselors—when I knew how much he hated asking anyone for anything—just to spend time with me meant a lot.

Mr. Broom seemed oblivious to why maybe two teenagers shouldn't be left alone in a darkroom together without supervision, but yet, he did.

Not just us either.

Other kids used the space to get high. Roman and I had no interest in drugs.

We were too high on each other.

CHAPTER FIFTEEN

Roman

MY PHOTOGRAPHY PROJECT REALLY DID NEED TO BE FINISHED, BUT it was impossible to concentrate around Juliet. Not in the sexy dress I'd been admiring since the moment I saw her this morning. It appeared to be see-through but wasn't. Trust me, I'd been staring holes through it all day long.

We focused on finishing her photos first, before moving to mine. That way if we ran out of time, she wouldn't be late turning in her assignment. Of course I didn't phrase it that way. Then she'd insist on me going first and I just wasn't that kind of guy.

She always came first.

While we waited for the photos to develop, she perched on the counter, swinging her legs and lightly tapping the cabinets below with her heels.

The project was to make something that scares you look beautiful. Working on the assignment together gave us a chance to learn more about each other. I'd discovered Juliet was terrified of bees. So we spent a couple afternoons in the park photographing honeybees as they buzzed from flower to flower.

"This one's too fuzzy," she said, pointing to a half-processed picture hanging in front of her.

"It's too soon to tell."

"I think I understand why the world moved to digital photography," she grumbled.

"You're cute."

She scrunched up her nose at me, only proving my point.

I stepped in between her legs, resting my hands at a spot right above her knees, pushing her dress up to run my hands over her soft skin. Those amazing little legs of hers wrapped around me, pulling me closer.

A shiver of pleasure raced down my spine as she slid her arms over my shoulders, threading her fingers through my hair and raking her nails over my scalp. I'd come to crave her touch. It felt so good to be touched and wanted. Even a look from her had the power to light a fire inside me I never knew existed.

Our lips met. Juliet wasn't shy about kissing me anymore. We kissed for hours some afternoons. Never going further than stroking our hands over each other. I was dying to do more. On those days, my body thrummed with the need to be inside her for hours after we'd said goodbye. No amount of shower jerk-off sessions cured the ache.

I wanted to be surrounded by her warmth, swallowed whole by her desire. With Juliet I could shut off my brain for a few merciful minutes and be *happy*. I never pressured her to go further. Just like with kissing, I wanted to wait until she was ready. Until she came to me.

I'd take it from there.

That afternoon, I found it harder to restrain myself than usual. I blamed the damn dress. All day long I fantasized about sliding my hands up her legs, under the filmy material. I'd sat through all my classes but couldn't remember a word of the teachers' lectures.

She licked her tongue against mine. My hands slid higher. I

swear I almost came in my pants when my thumbs grazed her inner thighs and she ever so slightly spread her legs apart.

Inviting me to do more?

The tip of my thumb brushed against her hot center. No, that was her satin underwear. Her *damp* satin underwear.

That was a good sign, right?

Keeping one hand clamped around her thigh, I continued to brush my thumb along her seam, pressing harder with each pass. Exploring. Discovering. Her breath hitched and she moaned as I slowed at the top. I pressed harder over that spot and she squirmed.

Christ, I needed another hand to touch her in all the ways I wanted. Her hard nipples poked against my chest and I so badly wanted to tease my fingers over the tips. But then I'd have to take my hand out from under her dress and release her thigh and I didn't want to let go.

I ground my finger into her harder, moving my thumb in slow circles. Her breathing sped up, sharp panting puffs of air against my cheek.

She tore her mouth from mine. "Roman," she whispered, harsh and urgent.

Our foreheads touched. "Does that feel good? Do you like me touching you there?"

"Y…yes," she stuttered and squeezed her eyes shut.

I was definitely on the cusp of something major. "Tell me what you need, Juliet."

"I…I don't know." Another low moan tore out of her throat and her hips jerked, pressing her warm, wet, satin-covered center into my hand.

"Oh!" she gasped.

I caught her louder moans with my kisses. My hand squeezed her ass, dragging her to the very edge of the counter. I pressed my hardness against her and she went off completely. Crying out too loud for me to silence with a few kisses. I clamped one hand over her mouth. The last thing we needed was someone busting in on us and ruining what was probably the high point of my life. She bucked and jerked her body against mine. Clothes in the way or not, the friction felt amazing.

Oh, shit.

Familiar white lightning shot down *my* spine. I squeezed my eyes shut, hoping to rein it in, but it was too late. We both came, panting, sweating, and whispering each other's names.

"Roman?" She cupped my face with her hands and dragged me down for a long, lingering kiss.

So intoxicated with the moment, at first I didn't realize what the sound coming from the door meant.

"Hello?" Mr. Broom shouted, then knocked again.

Our teacher's voice snapped me into action. I flipped Juliet's dress down, smoothing it over her legs before reaching over and unlocking the door. "Hey, Mr. Broom," I greeted, trying to sound casual while ignoring the sticky mess in my shorts.

"Oh! It's you two. I wasn't sure who was in here. How's it going?" he asked without a hint of I-caught-you-in-the-act coloring his voice.

Behind me, I heard the soft rustle of Juliet's dress and click of her sandals as she slid off the counter to the floor. "I'm not so sure, Mr. Broom. I don't think mine came out very well."

She sounded perfectly normal and calm. Was I the only one with a heart about to explode from my chest?

"Let's have a look," Mr. Broom said, leaning over the counter.

Juliet peeked over his shoulder and gave me a soft, reassuring smile.

"I'll, uh, be right back." I escaped the room, leaving the door slightly ajar and ran to the bathroom to clean up.

Juliet

My heart wouldn't stop racing even after Roman left the room. Mr. Broom went over my photos with me, but I barely heard a word. I nodded and smiled, even took some notes while he explained things to me, but the instructions were nothing more than petals floating away in the breeze.

"Did Roman get to his photos yet?" Mr. Broom asked.

"No, we were going to work on them next."

"Very well." He touched the edge of one of Roman's photos from last week's assignment. "He's very talented."

"He is," I agreed.

Mr. Broom's gaze strayed to the open door, and he almost seemed troubled. My stomach clenched in fear. Did he know what Roman and I were doing before he came in here? Could he smell it? Was I blushing?

"Your friendship seems to be a good influence on him, Juliet."

"You think so?"

"Yes. The kids I've seen from Pine Bluff..." his voice trailed off for a moment. "They don't receive a lot of encouragement. Half the time, they drop out or end up in jail."

I wasn't sure what to say besides, "That's awful."

"It really is. It's unfair. They're not given the same chance most of the kids here are." He blew out an annoyed breath. "Even some of my co-workers don't want kids in the system here." He shook his head. "Anyway, I shouldn't be discussing this with you. Forget I said anything."

"Okay, Mr. Broom."

He glanced at the clock. "You two should probably wrap up for the day. I'm sure Mr. Hawkins has to—"

"I have to be back by four," Roman interrupted, coming inside.

"Ah, very good. You probably have time to develop one more set. I'll let you get to it," Mr. Broom nodded at both of us before backing out of the room.

Shaking his head, Roman gave me a half-smile. "You okay?" he asked in a low voice.

I nodded slowly. The fear and tension from Mr. Broom almost walking in on us overshadowed all the amazing feelings Roman had given me earlier.

"Are *you*?" I asked. He seemed like he was in pain right before Mr. Broom's interruption.

I swear Roman blushed. His gaze strayed to the side. "I, uh, haven't had an *accident* like that since…well, never."

Accident? I wasn't sure what he meant. Well, I had some idea. My own cheeks turned hot and I looked away. "Sorry."

"Don't apologize." He picked up my hand and pressed it against his chest. "Feel that? My heart's still racing." He swooped in closer for a kiss. "It was amazing. Thank you."

My heart responded with its own quickstep. Feeling bold, daring, sexy even, I raised up on my tiptoes and whispered in his ear, "I think my panties are ruined."

He groaned in response. "What are you trying to do to me, woman?"

Woman. I liked the way that sounded coming from his lips. I certainly felt womanly around him. But I also knew we had work to do, and I wanted him to get home on time so that I could see him again tomorrow.

Selfish, but I couldn't bear him getting into trouble because of me.

"Come on, we need to finish your photos." Another streak of boldness forced me to add, "If you do a good job, I'll let you see how damp you made my panties."

"Jesus, you're killing me," he grumbled but got to work.

Roman

The photos turned out pretty damn good and I'm not usually

one to compliment my own work. We hurried to clean up and put everything away before leaving school.

Juliet danced ahead of me as we walked toward the park. "I wish I could take you out to celebrate." The wistful catch in her tone pierced my chest.

Every day it got harder and harder to say goodbye to her after school. The weekends were torture because I couldn't see her at all. Sometimes I'd sneak in a phone call or two. Most of the time I spent writing letters that I'd hand her Monday morning.

"Oh, look at all the daisies!" She took off running toward an open field in the park.

Damn she was cute. Excited over a bunch of raggedy-looking white and yellow flowers. I helped her pluck daisies until she had a decent-sized bunch.

As she stood there smiling at the flowers a large yellow and blue butterfly fluttered between us and landed on her hand.

"Oh my God," she whispered. "Look!"

"I see him." As carefully as possible, I slipped her cell phone out of her backpack to grab a picture. "Don't move."

The pretty creature sat still long enough for me to take two pictures. One close-up of him on her hand and one of her staring down at him.

Then the breeze picked up again and he floated away.

"Wow. That's never happened to me before. I used to pick daisies with my mom when I was little." Her face fell. "They're my favorite. My mom wore them in her hair on her wedding day. I always wanted to—"

"What?"

She blushed and looked away. "Nothing."

"What?"

The pink on her cheeks spread to the tips of her ears and down her neck. I think I knew what she was going to say. I even guessed why she was hesitant to tell me. But I wanted to hear the words from her mouth.

"If I ever get married," she twirled a few locks of hair around, "I want to wear them too."

I stepped closer and bent down, touching my nose to her. "What do you mean *if*?"

"I don't know. *If*."

"Juliet, the day I met you, I knew I was gonna marry you."

Her mouth fell open. "What?"

My fingers grazed her chin, tipping her head back. I swallowed hard. "I need some time to get my life sorted. Graduate. Find a job so I can take care of you the way you deserve. But yeah, then we're getting married."

She placed her hand on her hip and tilted her head. "That sounds more like a statement than a question."

My lips quirked at the challenge in her voice. "I'm not ready to ask you, yet."

She went up on tiptoes and slipped an arm around my neck, threading her fingers into my hair. "You don't need to take care of me. We'll take care of each other."

I didn't have a chance to respond. She leaned in and kissed me. Slow and soft.

That sweet kiss saved me, because I had no words.

"Where are we going to live?" she whispered when she backed away.

"Near wherever you're going to college, I guess."

"You're not going to college?"

I snorted. "Not likely."

"Your grades are even better than mine. You should. If you could go anywhere and do anything, what would you want to do?"

"Something outdoors maybe. Or a pilot."

"You don't like being caged in."

"Nope. Hate it. Hate not having any damn control over my life."

She wrapped her arms around me and pressed her cheek to my chest, squeezing me tight. "We will one day, Roman. I promise."

Christ, I couldn't breathe. I liked the sound of *we*. I'd never been part of a *we* before. I slipped my arms around her and hugged her back. "I like cars. Fixing them and stuff."

She gave me a curious look.

"One of the foster families I lived with when I was younger. They fostered a bunch of kids and owned a garage. Used to race cars on the weekends. Something always needed fixing at their house. I used to hang out in the garage and help out after school."

"That must have been fun."

Fun wasn't quite the right word. "They expected their foster kids to work. For free. To earn our keep. I guess what the state paid them wasn't enough."

"Oh. I'm sorry."

"It's all right. The husband was cool. He taught me how to do the easier stuff. Oil changes. Tire rotations. That kept me busy. But I'd also help him on the bigger jobs so I could learn."

"That was smart."

"I guess." I glanced down at my hands, turning them over. "I like solving problems. Fixing stuff that's broken."

"You're good at it." She squeezed my arm. "You fixed me."

"You're not broken."

Her gaze skipped away from mine, sparking a desire to seek and destroy anyone who hurt her.

"Everyone's a little broken, don't you think?" she said softly. "But when I'm around you, I feel whole."

Relief crashed over me with the force of a ten-foot wave. In a few words, she summed up all the feelings I couldn't name whenever we were together. "I feel the same way."

She took my hand and we started walking. More than any other day I didn't want to say goodbye to her.

As if she'd heard my thought she pointed at an old, Victorian house on the edge of the park. It was pink, yellow, and white. Gaudy as hell, but somehow still pretty. "I wish we lived there. You and me."

"Oh yeah?"

She nodded and bounced on her toes as she walked, dragging me along faster. "The park would be our backyard and it would be close to school, so when it snowed we wouldn't have to ride the bus."

"You mean right now?"

"Right now," she confirmed. Her cheeks turned that pretty shade of pink again. "I'd like to fall asleep next to you every night and wake up with you every morning."

I stopped, dropping our bags on the ground with a thud. I yanked her against me. "I think of you every night when I go to bed, wishing you were next to me."

She smiled up at me. "I do the same."

My hands slid down to her waist. It didn't matter that we were in a public park in the middle of the afternoon. I wanted to strip her down and finish what we started in the photo lab.

"Roman?" she whispered. "We need to get going."

Damn, she was right. I grazed her cheek with my knuckles and gave her one last kiss. "You've given me a lot of memories to replay when I fall asleep tonight." I'd also probably have to get up a few times and rub one out, but I couldn't say that to her. My hands ached to cup her breasts again. To touch her without anything in between us. "Juliet, was that okay before? Are you okay?"

"God, yes." She lowered her voice. "That was amazing. I've never felt anything like it."

I brought my lips to her ear. "Don't you ever touch yourself?"

She gasped and shook her head slightly. "Never."

Great, so I was the pervert in this relationship.

I kissed her cheek and along her jaw. "I'd make you feel like that every night, Juliet." My gaze dropped to the V of her dress. Just low enough to give a glimpse of the creamy swell of her breasts and the valley between. "I'd kiss you everywhere."

She shivered and closed her eyes.

"Are you cold?"

"No, I'm hot all over."

I inhaled a long, deep breath, savoring her scent mixed with the sweet spring air. "So am I."

Finally, I found the strength to move my feet. In front of her house, I kissed her cheek one last time before jogging down the street.

Not toward home. No, that day I felt like I was running *away* from home.

CHAPTER SIXTEEN

Juliet

I watched Roman sprint down the street, praying he made it home in time. It was almost impossible to swallow over the lump in my throat. I hated it when he left.

My uncle's truck rolled into the driveway and a knot of fear pulled my stomach tight.

"You messing around with that boy again?" he called out.

Mortification heated my cheeks. The whole neighborhood didn't need to know the details of my life.

"We're not messing around. He's my friend."

His eyes roamed over my dress, making me wish I hadn't left my cardigan in my locker.

"I heard he lives in that group home. I want you to stay away from him. And don't you dare be lettin' him in my house. He's probably got criminal tendencies."

The knot in my belly twisted. Why was he checking up on Roman? How? When? "I don't let any of my friends in the house."

"Good. Keep it that way."

I wanted to run back to school. Or run after Roman. Or run *away* with Roman.

Unwilling to be alone in the house with my uncle, I puttered around outside until my aunt pulled up. "What are you doing, Juliet?"

I gestured toward the flowerbeds I'd been absently weeding. "Thought I'd get a head start."

She eyed my dress and grimy hands. "You should've changed first."

"Oh." I glanced down and a thin laugh escaped me. "I guess so."

"This is why I don't like to waste money on nice clothes for you, Juliet."

I was aware. I'd worn thrift store finds and hand-me-downs forever. Until Dex started slipping me money and gift cards to go clothes shopping and Vienna had let me "borrow" her hand-me-downs. Never mind we weren't anywhere near the same size.

"Well, go wash up and change so you can help me with dinner."

"Sure." I scooped up my bag and wandered inside. My uncle was stretched out on the couch with a bottle of Jim Beam at his side. That was never a good sign. I wondered if he'd lost another job.

If that was the case, I really might run away. I'd had enough of living through their arguments and weeks of his drunken rages when he was out of work. Lots of bad things happened during those times.

I was almost seventeen. Maybe Roman and I could get an apartment like we talked about. We'd need to find jobs. I could work a few hours in the afternoons and still keep up on my schoolwork. Weekends I could work all day and night.

It wasn't fair for me to expect Roman to do that, though. Except he didn't seem to love the group home too much. Maybe I'd ask him tomorrow.

I held onto thoughts of tomorrow all through the night. It helped drown out the fighting of my aunt and uncle. One day, this misery would be a distant memory.

One day.

CHAPTER SEVENTEEN

Juliet

"HURRY UP!" VIENNA CALLED.

"I'm coming. Sheesh!" I hiked my backpack over my shoulder and moved faster through the school's rear parking lot.

Roman had to help out with chores at the house in order to be allowed to go on tomorrow's class field trip. Vienna decided we should go shopping.

I tossed my backpack behind my seat and folded myself into her car.

"We need to find you something hot to wear," she declared. "We're going to be lounging by the pool all afternoon." She twisted the key in the ignition and the throaty engine of her sports car roared to life.

I clicked my seat belt into place.

The wheels chirped as she took off. "Now, I know you and Roman are all lovey-dovey, but it won't hurt for him to see that other guys think you're hot too."

"I don't care about other guys." I hit the button and my window slid down. The wind ruffled through my hair and I closed my eyes.

"I know you don't, Juliet." Her voice held the final threads of her patience. "But he should appreciate how lucky he is and see how desirable you are."

I rolled my eyes. "Roman appreciates me."

"Ooo, do tell."

"I don't need to play games with him. He lets me know how he feels all the time."

She huffed. "Fine. Then at least help *me* pick out a suit."

Finally, I smiled. "No problem." I had a few dollars in my purse. Probably not enough to buy a fancy bathing suit, though. Not unless I could convince Vienna to stop at the discount mart.

She parked right by one of the side entrances to the Stonewall Mall on the lower level and marched us inside to a store full of bathing suits. Since it wasn't officially summer, nothing was on sale yet.

"Eighty dollars for three pieces of tissue paper?" I hissed in her ear as I carefully returned a bright orange bikini to its rack.

She rattled off the name of a designer I'd never heard of before and pushed me toward the next rack. "This!" She yanked a hanger with a jewel-green two-piece. "Not too revealing. And that emerald shade will look so pretty on you." She fluffed my hair.

"It's beautiful." My eyes bugged at the price tag. "Maybe later in the summer when it's on sale, though."

"It's your size. At least go try it on."

Reluctantly, I followed her to the dressing room. A few minutes later, I wished I hadn't bothered. The suit actually flattered my figure, making my legs look longer and my hips perfectly curved.

"Holy boobs." Vienna adjusted the straps of my top and glanced at her own chest. "I wish I filled out the top as well as you do."

I scanned the white and blue suit she was wearing. "That looks perfect on you."

"Hmm." She stared in the mirror, posing every which way, adjusting the material and straps with each pose.

"Vienna, you're not going to be sitting still in one pose all day long. Buy something you're comfortable wearing."

"You know they'll be taking yearbook pictures tomorrow." She lifted her chin at an awkward slant and pouted at the mirror. "I want to make sure I look good from every possible angle."

"Wouldn't it just be easier to join the yearbook committee and choose the pictures yourself?"

Her mouth widened into a happy "O." "You're a genius!"

"I have my moments." I picked up my clothes. "Can I change now?"

"Sure." She ducked out of my dressing room and into hers. "I have a few more to try on. Do you mind?"

"Nope. I'm going to run next door and get a lemonade. Do you want one?"

"Too much sugar."

I rolled my eyes and zipped my jeans. Grabbing the suit, I placed it neatly on the hanger. Outside the dressing room, I gave it one last longing look, before hooking it over the bar for the salesgirl to put away.

Instead of returning to the store with my drink, I waited for Vienna outside the entrance. I turned, watching other shoppers hurrying by. Moms with little kids. A couple arguing in front of the hair salon.

"Ready?" Vienna chirped.

I glanced down the long, wide corridor of the mall. None of the other stores would have a bikini in my budget. My plain navy swimsuit from last year would probably still fit. Or maybe I wouldn't even bother swimming. It might be too chilly anyway. There were plenty of other things to do at Fletcher

Park. I'd rather go hiking with Roman than swim in a chlorinated pool of my classmate's pee, anyway.

"Let's get out of here." I forced a smile so I didn't ruin her fun. "Are you happy with what you got?"

She hugged the bag to her chest. "Oh, yes. I'm very pleased. Come home with me for dinner? My mom's making mac and cheese."

"Okay."

By "making" mac and cheese, Vienna meant her mom had left it in the crock pot before going out. Which was fine, since I always felt uncomfortable under her mother's intense stare and rapid-fire questions. Vienna scooped heaping portions out for both of us. She picked at hers while I stuffed my face with cheesy, gooey goodness.

"So, you didn't ask which one I ended up with," she said.

I finished and set my fork down. "I assumed the white and blue one. Did you try on others?"

"A whole bunch."

"Okay, so which one did you get?"

She tossed her fork on the counter and grabbed my hand, yanking me off the stool.

"Easy," I laughed as I followed her up the stairs.

I'd always been jealous of Vienna's room. The whole downstairs of my aunt and uncle's house could fit in her bedroom. Someone had put a lot of thought into picking out fine, white, feminine furniture for Vienna when she was little. A matching dresser, desk, vanity table, nightstand and bed frame. She even had a pink upholstered reading chair in the corner with a fluffy pink rug and pink lamp.

Knowing Vienna would want to put on a show, I took a seat in the chair. She pranced over to the bed and turned the bag upside down. A tumble of colorful suits landed in a pile along with something in another separate bag.

She held up each suit, asking for my opinion.

"I like that peach one." I frowned as I shifted my gaze between the two choices. "But the white and blue is still my favorite. It has an older, sophisticated vibe."

That's all I needed to say. She squealed and tossed it on her pillows. "That's the one, then. I have these cute blue shorts and a white peasant blouse with embroidery all over the sleeves that I'll wear with it."

"That'll be pretty."

"Here." She thrust the extra bag into my hands.

"What's this?" The smooth plastic bag crinkled against my fingers.

"Open it."

Heat seared my cheeks as I opened the bag. At the bottom was the green suit I'd tried on earlier. "Vienna," I sighed. "I can't accept this. It's too expensive."

She waved her hands in the air. "I bought it for *me*. Just in case the others didn't work out."

I leveled a "don't b.s. me" stare at her. "You bought a suit four sizes too big for yourself? Just in case." I raised my eyebrows to punctuate my disbelief. "Convenient."

"I know, right?" she gasped and pulled an exaggerated shocked face.

The corners of my mouth twitched. "Vienna, I can't. I have a bathing suit. I'll be fine."

"It's non-refundable." She shrugged. "Besides, it looks *so* good on you. I can't be the hottest girl there. It's not fair to the rest of our class."

I snort-laughed.

"You have to help divert some of the attention," she pleaded. "Otherwise, I'll get a giant, inflated ego."

I laughed even harder. "Too late."

"Come on. If you won't do it for me, do it for Roman. He deserves a hot woman on his arm."

"V, aren't your parents going to be upset? This wasn't cheap."

"They don't pay attention to what I spend." Her mouth turned down. "Please. I had fun with you today. No one ever goes shopping with me anymore."

That finally did it. Even though some awkwardness lingered, I caved. "Remember that weird, see-through, long blouse I found at the Salvation Army last year? I think I'm going to use that as a cover-up. It'll match."

"Ooo, that was such a pretty print." She squeezed her eyes shut as if she was trying to picture the ensemble. "I like it."

"I still need to pack a bag for tomorrow." I tucked the suit away and stood.

"I've got loads of sunscreen." She led me into the hallway, to the family linen closet, digging through her parents' neatly folded towels until she found what she wanted. "SPF 50. You burn like toast," she said as she handed it over.

Laughing, I accepted the tube. "True."

Next, she pushed two plush towels into my arms. "Just in case I forget mine," she said to ease the sting of embarrassment. We both knew she wouldn't forget and that I didn't have beach towels at home. Not nice ones that I'd want to use in front of my classmates anyway. "Thank you."

"You know the towels the school's gonna give us won't cover up an arm, let alone anything else."

"Probably."

Downstairs, she stuffed everything into a shopping bag for me. "Let's get you home before your aunt has a conniption."

"Hey." I stopped her with a hand on her arm. "Thank you, V."

Her determined expression softened and she reached out, hugging me tight. "We're going to have so much fun tomorrow."

For once, I believed her. All the normal anxiety I'd usually have over a field trip had been replaced with excited anticipation.

CHAPTER EIGHTEEN

Roman

Sitting next to Juliet was the only thing that made the long bus ride to Fletcher Park tolerable. Our classmates were wild. Yelling, singing, jumping up and down on their seats like monkeys. Hard to imagine these fools would be seniors in a few months.

Juliet's giant tote bag took up a large chunk of space next to the window, forcing us closer together. She'd worn tiny denim shorts. It was a lot of bare skin for my overheated brain to handle all at once. Having her so close, sitting so we were touching from hip to knee, I just wanted to skim my fingers over the inside of her leg. Every time I did, she giggled and leaned into me.

I stopped to stroke an especially ticklish spot behind her knee and bent down, getting a face-full of her honey-scented hair blown in my face. "I want to kiss you right here," I whispered in her ear.

Her giggles cut off with a gasp. "Roman!"

"What?" I traced a little higher. "Here too."

Squire popped up over the seat in front of us like a deranged jack-in-the-box. "What are you two up to?"

"None of your business," I growled.

His gaze dropped to Juliet and I wanted to throw one of her beach towels over her legs. Squire didn't deserve to breathe the same air as Juliet and he sure as shit shouldn't have the honor of staring at an inch of her bare skin.

"Sit down and face forward!" the bus driver yelled.

One of the teachers lurched down the aisle to scold Squire.

I smirked, happy to see him getting in trouble for once.

"Everything okay here?" the teacher asked. He raised an eyebrow and stared at where my hand was clamped around Juliet's thigh.

She curled her fingers around mine. "We're fine. Squire was bothering us. Thank you for having him take his seat."

The teacher grunted and turned around.

Something tugged on the seat behind us. "You're going to flip when you see Juliet's bikini, Roman," Vienna said. "She looks *so* hot in it."

"She looks hot in everything," I answered without turning around.

"Aww." Vienna's hand reached over and mussed the top of Juliet's head.

"Quit it!" Juliet laughed and smacked her friend away.

A second later, Vienna tugged on my arm. "Can we switch places for a minute?"

I wanted to say *no* and keep Juliet all to myself. But I also didn't want to be an asshole to Juliet's friend. "Sure."

When the bus driver seemed occupied with the road ahead, Vienna and I quickly swapped places. For some reason, she'd been sitting with Stubby and now I was stuck sitting next to him.

"Hey." He nodded at me. After word spread about the coach trying to recruit me for the baseball team, Doug Winstead—and all his other jock buddies—had grudgingly begun to accept me.

Not that I cared. But at least I wasn't getting into fights in the hallways.

I perched on the edge of the seat, feeling like an intruder.

"If they give us the option, take the tour of the falls," Stubby said. "You'll be able to sneak off the trail with your girl for a few minutes alone."

He said it in a matter-of-fact way, not a creepy wink-wink-nudge-nudge way. "Thanks."

"The pool's gross anyway. They talk about closing it every year." He snorted. "But it gives the girls a chance to show off. You'll see what I mean."

I wasn't interested in checking out any other girls, but I nodded anyway.

Vienna stayed with Juliet until the bus pulled into the oversized parking lot. As soon as it stopped, kids jumped out of their seats, eagerly pushing each other to be the first one off the bus. Stubby and I hung back.

"No point gettin' crushed by these doofs," he grumbled, crossing his arms over his chest.

"Got that right," I muttered.

Juliet leaned over her seat and smiled down at me. "Hey, you."

"Hey, yourself."

Vienna popped up. "Sorry I hogged your girl."

Stubby nudged me with his elbow. "It's okay. Gave us some bro time."

I hadn't realized we were bros but didn't want to seem like a dick, so I nodded and shrugged.

When the herd finally thinned, I jumped out of my seat. My swim trunks were under my jeans. All I'd brought with me was a towel one of the teachers had handed me before boarding the bus. My backpack and everything else, I'd left in our locker back at the school.

I hefted Juliet's tote over my shoulder. "This *is* a day trip, right?" I joked.

Her forehead crinkled. "What?"

"What's in here?"

"Oh!" she laughed. "Sunscreen, towels, change of clothes, extra shoes, bottles of water, and some sandwiches."

Vienna had packed a similar-sized bag. As I glanced around, I realized most of the kids had brought stuff with them. *Oops.*

"Don't worry." Juliet linked her hand with mine. "I've got you covered, Roman," she said so quietly, I almost didn't hear her.

Shame prickled at me. Juliet didn't seem to have a whole lot more than I did. I appreciated her thinking of me, but I hated taking advantage of her.

"Thanks," I mumbled.

"Thank *you* for carrying all my stuff." She nodded to her bag.

At least I could do something useful for her. "Anytime."

Our classmates ran screaming toward the chain-link fence surrounding the pool. Teachers shouted orders to line up.

Vienna shook her head. "They're like animals freed from the zoo."

"Exactly," Juliet agreed.

Stubby howled something unintelligible and darted across the parking lot, leaping on top of his baseball buddies.

Vienna played with her phone and handed it to me. "Get a pic of us, please?" She wrapped her arm around Juliet's neck and smiled wide.

I snapped a few nice shots and returned her phone.

"Now you two." She shoved Juliet toward me. "Over here, so I can get the mountains behind you."

I hugged Juliet to my side for a few pictures. Then lifted her in the air. Her laughter rang out over the parking lot.

"Perfect!" Vienna yelped. She shoved her phone in her pocket. "Let's go!"

Juliet and I lagged behind with another couple, Chloe and Jameson.

"We're going to go on the waterfall tour and ditch the group, if you want to join us," Chloe offered.

Juliet glanced up at me with hope dancing in her eyes.

"Whatever you want," I answered.

Once inside, boys and girls split up to visit the separate locker rooms. Someone handed me a key for a locker. I shoved my jeans inside and followed the long, winding hallway back outside. After the darkened locker room, the brightness stabbed my eyes. I blinked and frowned until my eyes adjusted.

Sunlight glittered off the pool's wavy blue surface. Kids were already cannonballing into the water and splashing each other.

I squinted and searched the area for Juliet or Vienna.

Vienna emerged from the girls' locker room first. In big sunglasses, high sandals, and her barely-there white two-piece she looked like she belonged on a runway, not a high school field trip.

As if someone had tossed raw meat on the sizzling concrete, a wild pack of horny teenage boys stopped what they were doing and zeroed in on her.

Juliet popped out of the exit next. Unlike her friend, she kept her head down and shoulders hunched. My gaze traveled over the weird, loose dress-thing she was wearing. It was a dark, green abstract print with a ruffle at the bottom. The sheer material hinted at the bathing suit underneath.

Some sort of territorial need to stake my claim washed over me, and I stalked to her side, brushing my hand against her arm.

"Oh! There you are." She grinned up at me.

"Let's set up camp somewhere now," Vienna ordered. "Before all the good spots are taken." She grabbed Juliet's hand and dragged her toward the far edge of the concrete pool deck.

"We saved you a spot, Vienna!" Stubby called out.

She nodded and waved but kept powering toward three lounge chairs clustered under an umbrella and a small table.

"Here!" She plopped her bag on the first chair and nodded to Juliet to take the one in the middle with the most shade. "You'll fry like bacon if you sit directly in the sun," she said to Juliet.

"I've got my SPF 50, remember?" Juliet wiggled a large green tube at her friend.

I spread my towel out on the chair and watched the girls arrange their stuff. They'd brought an awful lot for a day trip. "Do you need help?" I asked.

"No." Juliet handed me a larger beach towel and a bottle of ice-cold water.

"Thanks. What else are you hiding in that bag?"

Her lips twisted with amusement. "Not much."

I uncapped the water and took a swig, keeping my eyes on Juliet.

She lifted her dress, slowly pulling it up over her head.

I choked and sputtered on the swallow of water.

Vienna smirked at me and helped Juliet untangle herself from the sleeves of the dress. Still coughing, my eyes bugged.

What...the...

My gaze slipped from the deep green top that molded perfectly to Juliet's chest all the way to the slick green fabric hugging her hips. My heart stomped a frantic beat. My fingers tingled as all my blood reversed course and headed south of my waistband.

Almost shyly, Juliet shimmied her shoulders. "What do you think?"

You're stunning. Someone hand me a blanket to toss over my girl. I want to lick your stomach. Lots of answers popped into my mind. None seemed appropriate. I continued stuttering and drooling on myself in front of everyone.

"He's speechless." Vienna patted Juliet's shoulder. "Perfect."

Juliet blinked and reached for her towel. *Aw, shit.* My doofus act had punched a hole in her confidence.

"No." I grabbed the towel, stopping her from covering herself. "You look spectacular. I, uh, love that color on you."

Color, good one.

Her hesitant smile transformed into a full, glowing one.

Phew. I managed to compliment her without mentioning my hard dick, how fantastic her tits looked, or asking her to turn around. My brain still functioned. What a relief.

I held out my hand to her. "Want to test the pool?"

She wrinkled her nose. "If we're going to swim, let's do it now, before it's just a sea of pee."

"Eww," Vienna groaned.

"When you put it that way…" I glanced at the pool again. The scent of chlorine hung heavy enough in the air to burn my nostrils. Bet the staff had tossed in extra when they found out a wild pack of hormonal teenagers was about to invade.

"Come on!" Vienna ran past us and launched herself into the pool, neatly slicing through the water, narrowly missing a group of kids slapping each other with long, foam noodles.

"Do you know how to swim?" Juliet asked.

I watched, fascinated and dumbstruck as she pulled an elastic off her wrist and bound her hair into a high, bouncy knot on the top of her head. Was it weird how much I loved watching her just do *stuff*?

"I can keep my head above water." *What a metaphor for my entire life.* "Had a few lessons when I was a kid."

We walked over the scratchy, burning concrete to the shallow steps leading into the pool.

"Same." She laughed and dipped her toe in. "It's warmer than I expected."

I splashed down the steps and turned, holding my arms out for her. She jumped off the top step and I caught her, spinning us in a slow circle.

"Take it easy!" one of the teachers shouted. I couldn't tell if it was directed at us or someone else. We were hardly the only couple with their hands all over each other.

I set Juliet on her feet. The water lapped at her stomach, right about the spot where I wanted to dip my tongue in her navel. She fluttered her hands through the water and stared at the ripples.

"You okay?" I asked.

She cast a furtive glance around, then leaned up on her toes to whisper in my ear. "I've never worn a two-piece before. I'm afraid my top will come off if I move too fast or something."

"Trust me, I won't let that happen."

I crouched until the water was up to my chin and slid my arms through the water. "Let's do a lazy lap to the end and back."

"All right."

We pushed off the edge and navigated our way through clusters of our classmates. We narrowly missed having someone belly flop right on top of us. Finally, we reached the other side. Both of us clung to the cement lip of the pool, slowly moving our legs back and forth.

"This would be fun without everyone else here," she said.

"Uh-huh." I wanted to kiss her in the worst way. Under the water, I grabbed her waist with my free hand and pulled her closer.

"Hands above deck, Mr. Hawkins!" someone shouted. The principal? I wasn't sure and didn't bother to look. Juliet drifted out of my grasp and I raised my arms in the air like I was being held at gunpoint.

"Whoopsie!" Juliet whispered. She slapped her hand over her mouth to contain her laughter.

She pushed off the wall, slowly paddling toward the shallow end. I followed behind her.

In the middle of the pool, Vienna hooked her arm around Juliet's shoulders and whispered in her ear.

"Listen up!" one of the teachers shouted. It took a few more tries for the noise to die down so she could be heard. "We'll be starting group tours down to Ladder Falls in about an hour. It's an easy hike but you'll need sneakers or hiking boots."

She droned on and on with more information and a list of rules. Most people seemed to tune out after the initial announcement.

"Let's grab lunch," Vienna said. She turned and splash-ran through the water to the steps.

I stayed as close to Juliet as humanly possible. Our skin sliding and bodies bumping against each other under the water. Juliet slipped on the first step out of the pool. I was close enough to grab and steady her, keeping my hands on her hips all the way out of the water. For safety purposes, of course.

One of our classmates, a kid named Toby, pushed between us, getting in my face. "Look at you, panting after her like a dog."

"Get out of my way," I warned.

He chest-bumped me, looking like a wild turkey trying to establish himself in the pecking order. I stared him down and raised an eyebrow. "You sure you wanna go there, bro?"

He flinched. Hesitated. Glanced over his shoulder, looking for backup. His buddies looked away, pretending to see nothing.

"Hope she puts out," he muttered, stepping away.

My fist curled at my side. But he wasn't worth the trouble I'd get into if I threw a punch.

"Hey, Roman." A girl I recognized brushed her arm up against my wet chest.

I couldn't remember her name. "Hey."

Toby blocked me again. "All the chicks wanna bang you, dumbfuck. And you're wasting your time on the stuck-up nerd girl?"

"Who asked you, dick?" I pushed him out of my way and kept walking.

Juliet handed me my towel when I reached our chairs. "What was that all about?"

"Who knows." I shrugged and roughed the terrycloth over my damp skin.

"*Romannnn*," Vienna sang. "Who knew you were so ripped?" She nodded at my stomach.

"Looks like you skipped a few leg days, though, bro," Stubby added.

"Jesus Christ." I finished drying off and slipped my T-shirt over my head. "You're a bunch of fuckin' creeps."

Juliet stretched out on her chair and pulled her bag into her lap. A few seconds later she passed a thick, foil square to me.

"I like your legs," she whispered.

My lips twitched. "Yours are better."

"It's chicken salad." She nodded at the sandwich in my hands.

I peeled open the cool foil, revealing a dark, nutty-looking, whole-grain bread stuffed with lettuce, tomatoes, and overflowing with chicken salad. My stomach rumbled.

"I made it last night," she said. "The chicken salad, I mean."

"Looks great." I realized I was starving and made quick work of it, almost eating the foil in my rush.

Juliet handed me half of her sandwich. "I can't eat the whole thing."

"You sure?"

She gestured for me to eat up.

Vienna passed bags of M&Ms, Twizzlers, and loads of other candy out and pretty soon, a good portion of our class was clustered around our chairs. I reached over and wrapped my hand around the leg of Juliet's lounger and dragged it closer to mine.

"Hey, you." She bent her knee and shifted closer, dragging her toe along my calf.

"Careful, we'll get yelled at again," I warned, my gaze fixated on her red-painted toenails.

"Worth it."

After lunch, guys from the baseball team started picking up girls and tossing them in the pool. Doug approached our group and I stood up in front of Juliet's chair, blocking his path. Like hell was he putting his hands on Juliet. "Keep moving."

He smirked and swaggered past us.

Out of the corner of my eye, I caught Stubby guarding Vienna and chuckled.

"Want to go on the hike?" Juliet asked.

"Definitely." I bent over and grabbed my scruffy sneakers.

Juliet wiggled into her shorts and I almost lost my damn mind. I helped her pack most of her stuff and we left the bag on her chair. Just in case, I grabbed one of the towels and slung it around my neck.

"Are you coming?" Juliet asked Vienna.

Vienna lazily tipped her sunglasses up and squinted at us. "Nah, I'm sleepy. Going to take a nap in the sun. Maybe later."

I curled my hand around Juliet's and we made our way toward the gate where one of the teachers was taking a head count.

"Stay together!" the teacher shouted to our group.

There were maybe twenty of us and we formed a loose line. Juliet and I deliberately drifted toward the back of the herd, where we ran into Chloe and Jameson.

Jameson lifted his chin and nodded with a knowing smirk stretched across his face.

Juliet squeezed my hand as we started our trek across the grassy field. I studied the signs and landmarks we passed, trying to orient myself. Eventually, we reached a flat expanse of rock. A short post-and-rail fence marked the edge of the cliff.

"Damn, not much to keep someone from going over," I muttered.

"Search and rescue gets called up here a couple times a year," Jameson confirmed. "Someone gets drunk and misjudges the distance to the edge."

Juliet shivered.

I wrapped my arm around her shoulders. "I won't let anything happen to you."

"It's not always drunks," Chloe said. "Remember that old man who got lost on the trail? They didn't find his body until the following year."

"I guess the takeaway is, stay away from the edge of the cliff?" I whispered to Juliet.

The tension melted from her expression. "I guess so."

"Everyone stay to the right!" the teacher shouted.

Like good little lambs, we held onto the wooden railing and trooped down a narrow set of stone steps. I leaned over to get a glimpse of what was below us and just saw rocks and trees.

The stone steps led to another flat surface where the teacher stopped to explain some geological history of the area. Then we continued down a set of narrower wooden stairs. Our group stopped on a wide ledge. A waterfall shot out from the rocks above and to our left. Another narrow wooden railing ran along a narrow path carved into the mountain. More stairs lay in front of us.

Jameson nudged my shoulder and jerked his head. The ledge ran behind where we were standing to another waterfall. Another set of wooden steps appeared to be past the water.

"Okay, let's continue." The teacher waved her hands in the air.

Jameson grabbed Chloe's hand. They ducked and ran in the opposite direction of our class.

Juliet grinned up at me. "Let's go."

The staircase we'd just come down provided cover. We skirted around it and caught up with Jameson and Chloe.

"There's a cave behind that waterfall." Chloe pointed ahead.

I was game for whatever, as long as we didn't get caught.

Juliet

My heart hammered as we jogged after Jameson and Chloe. I'd never ditched a group activity before. A cool mist splashed my cheeks and forehead as we approached the waterfall. Jameson expertly ducked behind the water, moving over the slippery rocks like he'd done it dozens of times. Maybe he had.

I hesitated.

My gaze locked on the falling water rushing to a rocky pool hundreds of feet below. Maybe not that far. I wasn't a good judge of heights. I just knew I didn't want to slip and go for a ride. I glanced behind us but our class was already out of sight.

"Are you okay?" Roman asked.

"I don't want to fall."

"I won't let you." He grabbed onto a rock and flattened himself against the wall. Firmly gripping my hand, he followed the same steps Jameson had taken and pulled us behind the curtain of water.

The rocks opened into a large, wet cave. Water dripped from above. Light filtered in from the outside. Enough to see a few feet in front of us. Then, it was only inky darkness cut by the rough silhouettes of rocks.

Chloe shrieked from somewhere deeper inside the cave. Her laughter echoed and bounced around us.

"I guess they're okay," I said.

"Let's pray they don't scare any bats out of hiding," he grumbled.

"Bats! Are you kidding?" I ducked and glanced up at the ceiling.

Roman chuckled and wrapped his arms around me. "Sorry. I was just kidding." He leaned down and kissed my cheek. "I won't let anything get you."

The protective way he cocooned me against his body made me believe every promise.

I tipped my head and caught his lips. He inhaled a sharp breath, then groaned. His body pressed against mine until my back bumped against the uneven wall.

"Roman," I gasped, and blinked up at him.

"Keep kissing me." He brushed his lips against my forehead, my cheek, the tip of my nose, and finally my lips. He slipped a finger under the strap of my bikini top, sliding it back and forth. "You look so sexy today."

"Really?" I ran my hands down my sides. "I'm not all tall and skinny like Vienna—"

He drew back so sharply my words dried in my throat.

"Juliet, I haven't been able to keep my eyes off you all day. And I couldn't even remember what color Vienna is wearing if you offered me a million dollars."

"Yeah?"

"Yeah." He stared down and squeezed my hips, his thumbs rubbing against my stomach. "I'm obsessed with your belly button. It's so damn adorable."

"What?" I burst into laughter.

"Uh-huh." He knelt in front of me and kissed my stomach, stopping to trace his tongue around my navel.

Laughter died on my lips. The ticklish sensation exploded into a streak of tingling warmth shooting to my center.

"Roman." My voice shook.

He lifted his gaze to meet mine and ran his fingers from my knee to the hem of my shorts. "Want to kiss you here." He pressed his lips to my inner thigh.

My whole body trembled.

He slid his hand between my legs, gently cupping me. I inched my feet apart to give him room.

"I want to kiss you here, too."

I didn't know what to say. My bottom lip quivered. I felt hot and tight where his hand touched me. Why were there shorts and bikini bottoms blocking him?

He turned toward the curtain of water protecting the entrance to the cave. Daylight filtered through. Anyone could pop inside, just the way we had.

He slid his hand to the button of my shorts, toying with it for a second before standing again.

A distinctive moaning and slapping sound echoed from the back of the cave.

Roman scowled.

We both turned and stared into the darkness. I caught the faint glow of a flashlight but nothing else, thank goodness.

"We can hear you!" Roman shouted.

Jameson added some grunting noises to the rhythmic thumping.

Roman rolled his eyes and returned his attention to me.

"That's quite a soundtrack." I smiled up at him and wrapped my arms around his neck, drawing him closer. "Forget about them."

He slid his hands to my hips, then my legs, urging me up. Using the rock behind me for leverage, I hooked my legs around his waist, crossing my ankles to tether myself.

"That's better," he whispered against my lips.

He leaned into me, his hardness pressing into my center in exactly the right spot. I moaned into his mouth and tightened my arms around his neck. His body froze and he eased back.

"Nooo." I tightened my legs around him.

He ran his hand over one of my legs and it took me a second to realize he wanted to set me down. Shaking so hard I thought I'd fall, I touched my toes to the ground.

Roman kissed me deeper, his tongue diving past my lips. I opened for him, stroking my tongue against his. He groaned and slid his palm over my stomach, quickly working the button of my shorts loose and sliding his hand underneath.

My body froze.

His movements stopped.

He broke our kiss. "I...I won't go under your suit."

"Okay," I whispered. My heart pounded harder than the water falling outside.

He pressed two fingers against me and slid them lower.

"Oh!" I gasped and slapped my hand over my mouth.

"Here?" Roman pressed harder and gently rubbed his fingers back and forth.

Sparks fired behind my eyelids. Dizziness swirled around me.

"Or like this?" He dragged his lips from my cheek to my neck, while down below he changed direction, rubbing his fingers in a slow circle.

"Oh my God!"

"Mmm." He smiled against my skin. "Like that."

"Roman?" I whispered, desperate for something I didn't know how to name. This was different from the day in the photography lab. More intentional, less accidental.

He kept tracing circles against me, gradually increasing the speed and pressure. My body squirmed and rocked in time with his movements. Everything in my world narrowed to where he touched me. We stayed like that for the sweetest eternity.

"Ah." My body jerked.

The fire he'd lit inside me exploded.

"That's it," he encouraged.

All of a sudden, his touch was too much and I pressed my palms to his chest.

"Stop?" he asked.

"Yes...I can't. Too much."

He withdrew his hand and quickly buttoned my shorts. "Was that...okay?"

I slowly opened my eyes. My lips curled into a goofy smile. "Oh, yeah."

Feeling brave or maybe drunk on whatever feel-good chemicals he'd released in my body, I tugged on his shorts. I tried to shove my hand between the elastic of his waistband and his hard stomach. "I want to make *you* feel good too."

He sucked in a breath as my fingers grazed his rigid flesh.

I tried to lower myself to the ground like he had earlier.

"No." He grabbed my elbow. "Absolutely not."

I blinked. "What?"

"Not here. Anyone could find us and...I don't want that for you."

I raised an eyebrow. "And your hand down my pants was better?"

He frowned. "Than you on your knees? Yeah. Much better. No one would be able to tell what I was doing."

Protecting me. Always. I reached up and kissed him.

"Give me a minute." He squeezed his eyes shut.

I withdrew my hand and leaned against the wall, watching him take several deep breaths.

"Let's go explore the park," he finally suggested.

The noises from the back of the cave had died down. Embarrassed they might have overheard us, I was eager to leave.

"We can go to the overlook."

"Guys!" Roman yelled. "We're heading to the overlook."

"Okay," Chloe answered. "We'll catch up later."

Roman grabbed my hand and dragged me toward waterfall. We studied the cascading water and the rocks to the right—opposite of where we'd come into the cave. This path looked easier. Roman went first, carefully testing the rocks. When he touched dry ground, he held out his hand.

"Watch yourself. It's slippery in the middle," he warned.

I gripped him hard with one hand and braced my other against the wall. Maybe my steps were *too* cautious.

On the second rock, I slipped.

Terror burned through my limbs. An image of plunging to

the jagged rocks below flashed through my mind. I yelped and flailed my arms in the air.

Roman grabbed my elbows and yanked me into the safety of his arms. "You're okay. I got you," he breathed out. "I got you," he repeated several more times.

He hugged me tight to his body and rested his back against the side of the mountain.

Below us, shrill threads of screams and laughter pierced the air. We carefully walked to the edge of the trail and peered over the railing. Looking like a line of marching ants, our classmates traveled the trail below us.

We quickly pulled back.

"I hope no one saw us," I said.

He shrugged. "What are they going to do about it?"

I nodded toward the wooden staircase about a hundred feet in front of us. "Let's get up on flat ground. I'm not cut out for extreme hiking."

"I wouldn't call it *extreme*, but yeah, let's get off this cliff."

"Whatever."

Even though I wanted to break into a sprint, we kept close to the wall. I breathed a sigh of relief when we reached the stairs. I sprinted to the first landing and groaned. There had to be a hundred more steps to reach the top.

My legs were on fire by the time we made it.

"Why didn't it seem like that many stairs on the way down?" I huffed.

"We were moving at a snail's pace with twenty other kids?" Roman grinned at me. "Which way are we going?"

I pointed to a large, grassy path under a canopy of trees. "That way."

Since it was a weekday, the park wasn't crowded. We passed a few people walking their dogs. No one looked at us twice or asked if we were lost.

It took longer than I remembered to make it to the parking

lot with the low stone wall overlooking Empire County and beyond. But when we finally did, Roman stopped and stared.

"Wow."

"It's pretty, right? You can see all the way to Vermont." I pointed in what I hoped was the right direction.

We found a spot with the least number of trees obstructing our view and sat on the wall, staring out at the Empire City skyline, farmlands, lush green fields, and trees. "I've always wanted to come up here to watch the sunrise."

"I bet that would be pretty." Roman shifted closer and wrapped his arm around my waist. I leaned into him, resting my head on his shoulder.

After a few minutes, he curled his free hand around mine and rubbed his thumb over my knuckles. "Was that okay? What we...what I did back there?"

I lifted my head and met his concerned stare. "More than okay." I touched my forehead to his cheek, my nose grazing the slight stubble along his jaw. "I wanted to do *more* with you. To make you feel good too."

He skimmed his fingers over my cheek. "I feel good. I really liked...doing that...watching you. I just wish we'd been alone."

"Me too," I sighed.

"Hawkins! Hayworth!" an angry male voice shouted our names.

We whipped around. A furious Mr. Broom marched over the parking lot toward us. We both scrambled to get off the wall. I felt half-naked and silly in nothing but my bikini top and denim shorts.

"Thank God." Mr. Broom panted and wiped his forehead with the back of his hand. "I've been looking all over for you two. The buses are getting ready to leave."

"Oh, sorry. We got cut off from the group on the trail and I wanted to show Roman the view from the overlook," I said in an apologetic rush.

Mr. Broom's gaze flicked to the view behind us and he blew out a breath. "Well, okay. At least that's all you were doing. Can't blame you. It's a beautiful view. You're probably the only two students who'd appreciate it," he grumbled, turning and motioning for us to follow him. "Two students were caught *in flagrante delicto* and it's been a mess. So when I realized you two were missing…"

Roman and I frowned at each other.

"What the…?" he mouthed to me.

"Sex?" I whispered back and shrugged.

His shoulders shook with laughter.

Like properly chastised puppies, we followed Mr. Broom all the way back to the buses.

"Oh! I left my bag and everything by the pool!" I lunged toward the gate.

"Vienna has your things," Mr. Broom assured me.

Sheesh. How long was everyone looking for us? My cheeks burned hot as we approached the buses. Kids hung out of the windows to heckle us and make obscene noises.

Mr. Broom stopped in front of our bus. "Due to the circumstances, boys and girls are being separated. Girls on the left, boys on the right." He stepped aside so we could climb the steps.

"Great," I muttered.

Roman kept his hand on my back. I glanced over my shoulder and caught the defiant lift of his chin and rigid posture. It helped me lift my head and not worry about the whispers and stares as we shuffled down the aisle.

Vienna bounced in her seat and waved to me. When we got closer, she pointed at the bench across from her where Stubby was holding a seat for Roman.

"Thanks." I slid in next to her, noting my tote bag stuffed on the floor under her legs. "Thank you so much for grabbing my stuff."

"I got you, girl." She flashed a wicked smile. "Where did you two disappear to?"

"We explored this cool cave and then walked down to the overlook."

"Uh-huh." The skeptical lilt to her voice wasn't lost on me.

I leaned in closer to her. "Who got caught having sex?"

She burst into giggles. "Diane and Brody."

"Oh," I said, relieved it wasn't Chloe and Jameson.

Roman stretched across the aisle and brushed his knuckles over my leg. "You okay?" he asked in a low voice.

My heart melted at the sweet way he always looked after me. "Better than okay."

It was too noisy to talk much. I spent the rest of the trip back to school staring out the window, listening to the chatter around me. More than ever, I didn't want to go home. I wished I was back in the cave with Roman. Just the two of us. Alone and together.

CHAPTER NINETEEN

Roman

THE BUZZ FROM MY DAY WITH JULIET LASTED UNTIL I RETURNED to the home.

I pushed open the bedroom door and found Pip curled in a ball on the floor.

"What's wrong, Pip?"

It wasn't unusual to find him huddled in the corner of our room or even wedged into our tiny closet after school. On those days I knew he'd either had a rough day or I was about to whoop someone's ass in this house for picking on him.

He glanced up at me with red tear-streaked cheeks. "Where were you?"

"We had that field trip today. The buses got back late. Why? What happened?"

"Nothing." His gaze darted to the open door. "Evie. Stay away from her, Roman."

I crouched down next to him. "What do you mean?"

He wiped his cheeks and stared at me with glassy eyes. "I overheard her talking to Janet. They want to get you in trouble, so you get sent away. Squire's in on it too. But Evie, man. She's pissed you have a girlfriend."

Shit. I thought Evie had finally gotten bored with me and latched onto Squire. Figured they'd both leave me alone if they were busy with each other. I should've known two unhappy souls couldn't comfort one another. It was more fun for them to spread the misery.

I swallowed hard. I hated lying to people I cared about. "I'm not going anywhere, Pip." I had no business making that promise. I had no control over my life or what happened to me.

"But you are. Once you graduate, you'll have to move out. Then I'll be here all alone."

It wasn't like I hadn't considered that before. As much as I worried about where *I'd* end up, I also feared what would happen to Pip once I moved on.

"We gotta bulk you up a little, kid," I teased, reaching out to squeeze his bicep.

He shrugged away from me. "I don't wanna bulk up. I just wanna be left alone."

"I know." Damn, I felt inadequate. What would Juliet say? Somehow, she always made the shitty stuff in my life seem fleeting.

He turned his hopeful, puppy eyes on me. "Maybe I can come with you? Like, you could adopt me."

"Shit, kid. If I thought they'd say yes, I'd do it in a heartbeat."

At least that seemed to comfort him. I held out my hand and helped him up off the floor.

"How's Juliet?" he asked.

I'd finally relented and shared a little about her with Pip. Nothing important. I liked Pip and would do what I could to protect him, but I didn't trust him not to betray my secrets if things got rough. He just wasn't made of strong enough stuff to lie for me, and it probably wasn't fair to expect him to, either.

"She's good. We had a lot of fun today. Fletcher Park is pretty. You'd like the view." I didn't share any of the R-rated details. Everything about those stolen moments with Juliet belonged to me alone.

"You think..." he gazed at the small bedroom window, "you're gonna marry her after you get out of here?"

"Once I have a job and can afford to, yeah, I want to marry her," I admitted.

His eager puppy dog eyes returned. "Maybe the two of you could adopt me? A married couple would have a better chance."

Damn he was smart. The gentle pleading in his tone almost undid me. By the time Juliet and I were settled, he'd be aging out of foster care himself. "That would be pretty cool, wouldn't it?" I carefully sidestepped the question and clapped his shoulder. "Come on, finish your homework. You have to set the table tonight."

He groaned but got to work.

My body and mind clashed with the desire to seek out Squire and punch him in his smug face for plotting with Evie. I'm not proud of it, but I wanted to shake some damn sense into Evie as well. I was sure she arrived with baggage and damage of her own that led her into making stupid decisions. And while that was sad in its own way, my sympathy ended where her problems started to interfere with my life.

Pip and I went downstairs early. I wanted to talk to counselor Mike about my options for finding an after-school job. And Pip had talked Judy, the counselor we'd dubbed "house mom," into buying cloth napkins he wanted to fold into swans. To bring some culture to our dinner table, he'd said. Judy was too amused to say no, and I'm pretty sure she'd used her own money to purchase the napkins.

Pip and his napkin-swans saved my ass.

"Help!" a voice I recognized as Janet's screamed from the top of the stairs.

The girl screamed for help once or twice a week, so no one exactly jumped to attention.

Mike groaned and nodded at Judy as she power-walked by to see what the emergency was.

Thuds and bangs bounced over the ceiling above our heads. A few minutes later Judy rushed down. "Where's Roman?"

I leaned over and waved at her. "Right here."

"What's going on?" Mike asked. "We're in the middle of something."

"How long has he been down here?"

Mike shrugged and glanced at the clock. "I dunno. Twenty or thirty minutes."

Her mouth flattened and she marched away without explaining.

Panic tightened my chest. "What's going on?"

"Don't know," Mike answered.

I swallowed hard. I wasn't a tattletale. Snitching on other kids always seemed wrong. But this was self-preservation. "Listen, when I got home, Pip was upset."

"He's always upset about something," Mike said.

"Yeah, I know, but this was different. He said Evie and Janet were talking about getting me in trouble."

Mike rolled his eyes. "That girl is always up to no good." His jaw settled into a grim line. "I clocked you in when you got home from the field trip, Roman. You've been with me for the last half hour. You're good, kid. Besides, I know you wouldn't mess with either of those girls."

"I wouldn't." I hesitated. "I have a girl at school I'm into. Evie's jealous."

His face transformed into a broad grin. "Yeah? Good for you. Just don't get her into trouble."

I assumed that was code for "don't get her pregnant," especially when he slipped a handful of condoms out of his desk drawer and passed them to me.

"Uh, thanks." I shoved them in my pocket and looked away.

I coughed to cover up the awkwardness. "So, what are my chances of being allowed to get an after-school job?"

"So you can work with your girlfriend?"

"No. She doesn't have a job."

He nodded. "I can talk to Ms. Simpson and see what she says."

My overloaded caseworker wasn't easy to get in touch with, but she'd probably answer Mike's calls quicker than she'd ever answer mine.

"Your grades are good," he added. "You haven't caused any trouble at the house. She might approve a couple hours a week somewhere."

A couple hours a week wasn't going to earn me nearly enough money to do what I wanted, but I had to start somewhere.

Screams ricocheted through the house, followed by shrill curses. Mike jumped to investigate. "Stay here," he ordered.

Left alone in his office and having no interest in involving myself with whatever drama was unfolding in the rest of the house, I eyed the phone on the desk. I'd love to give Juliet a call. Had her number memorized from the day she wrote it on my arm. My secret phone was stashed upstairs in my backpack.

The yelling and swearing grew louder and I craned my neck to peer out into the hallway.

Judy wrestled a crying and struggling Evie down the hall with Mike following behind them.

"Roman did it!" Evie screeched.

I jumped out of my chair and ran to the doorway. "What the fuck is she talking about?" I shouted at Mike.

He shook his head. "Nothing. We got it handled, Roman." He nodded to his office. "Stay put for a few minutes, okay?"

My heart thundered as he closed the door.

Evie was trying to set me up for who the hell knew what.

Fear rolled through my stomach as I staggered back to my

chair. Obviously, I hadn't done anything wrong. Mike knew that.

But no matter how hard I tried to convince myself everything would be okay, deep down a voice whispered reminders of all the times I'd been let down and betrayed before.

CHAPTER TWENTY

Juliet

MY CELL PHONE RANG AND I LEANED OVER TO SCOOP IT UP OFF my nightstand. No one but Roman, Vienna, and sometimes Uncle Dex ever called.

I didn't recognize the number, but I answered anyway. Uncle Dex frequently used different unknown numbers.

"Hello?"

"Juliet? It's me."

"Roman." A happy sigh followed his name. We'd spent the whole day together and I still couldn't get enough of his voice. "What's up?"

"I'm not sure." Tension radiated over the line, wiping the dreamy smile off my face.

"Are you okay?"

"I'm not sure. When I got home, Pip was babbling about Evie trying to set me up and now there's some commotion. My name was thrown around. I'm worried."

He didn't talk a lot about the home when we were together, but he'd mentioned Pip often enough. And Evie had confronted me once or twice at school—although I'd never told Roman—so I knew who she was and what she was after.

"Roman, what are you going to do?"

"Nothing I *can* do right now. If something happens…If I get sent away again. I want you to know—"

"Don't. You're not going anywhere. Please," I added. A tear rolled down my cheek. I couldn't stand the helplessness or the injustice of his situation. "Let's look for a place together now," I blurted.

Silence.

"Juliet, I'd love that more than anything, but—"

"Maybe Uncle Dex can loan us some money."

"I can't take money from your family, Juliet. A job offer is one thing, but—"

He had his pride. Having everything else out of his control, I understood it. To a certain extent.

In the background there was knocking. "I gotta go, Juliet."

The call ended.

I didn't dare try calling him back and risk getting him in trouble.

All night I worried and wondered what was happening.

Roman

I'd seen a lot of legitimate issues get swept away or ignored during my time in the system. So the attention Evie got for her false allegations shocked me into silence at first.

Then I came out fighting.

"I wasn't even here when she claims whatever happened, happened!" I roared. "Did you talk to Janet? I guarantee she's involved too!"

No one cared.

I still had to be questioned.

Interviewed.

Examined.

Questioned again.

What pissed me off the most was that somehow Janet and Squire skated out of the whole mess. I had no doubt they helped concoct this idiotic plan and encouraged Evie to go through with it. While Evie had been a source of annoyance since I moved into the house, I'd never suspected she was this downright devious.

"For the last time, I got home late from our school field trip," I explained to my caseworker. Ms. Simpson did *not* seem pleased she'd been dragged out of her house after business hours. I couldn't blame her, honestly. But I didn't want her to somehow blame *me* and block me from getting a job or something.

"Why so late?" she asked, tapping her pencil against her yellow notepad.

"It was an all-day field trip. You approved it," I reminded her.

"So someone can confirm you were on this school trip?"

Guilt, because I'd snuck off with Juliet, crowded my conscience. Mr. Broom had caught us far away from where we were supposed to be. But because he trusted us, he'd let it slide. And now I might be dragging him into vouching for me.

Thankfully, the moral compass I'd developed over the years spun in its own direction. I swallowed hard but kept my voice and gaze steady. "Only my entire class, the principal, and the six teachers there to supervise all of us."

Supervise was a bit of a stretch since I'd spent a good portion of the afternoon making out with Juliet.

"All right, I'll call the school tomorrow."

How embarrassing.

"Ms. Simpson," Mike finally piped up. "Roman's been a good resident. Haven't had a single disciplinary problem with him since he got here. Evie has had multiple infractions. I've caught her lying on several occasions. And I personally spoke to Roman when he came home today, so I can confirm the time."

About time. I wondered when Mike planned to pipe up on my behalf. Ms. Simpson's face unwrinkled a bit.

"Very well." She slid her pencil into her briefcase and pulled out a stack of paperwork. "I still need to write up a report and have you both sign statements."

Great. Not like I had homework or wanted to eat dinner or anything.

"While I have you here, Ms. Simpson." Mike pasted on a phony but polite smile. "Roman expressed some interest in finding a part-time job after school. I think it would be a benefit to him." He lowered his voice as if I might be too tender to hear the next part. "It would be good for him to get some job experience since he'll be aging out of care next year."

She blew out a long breath and stared at me until I wanted to squirm in my seat.

"Your grades are good, Roman," she finally said. "I was planning to discuss this with you at a later time, but if you continue to do well in school, I might be able to get you into a program that will help you transition out of foster care. Tuition for a state school or trade school would be covered and you'd have a stipend for living expenses as long as you're enrolled until you turn twenty-one."

"Really?" I sat up, more interested in the conversation. I'd never heard of this program before.

"Not many of my clients qualify for it and funding gets slashed every year," she sighed, "but it's an option I planned to explore for you."

She glanced at Mike again. "As long as his grades don't suffer, I'll sign off on a job. It needs to be appropriate, though."

"Of course. Thank you, Linda."

Huh. I'd never heard anyone call her by her first name before.

It was still a long night after that. But at least I had a shred of hope to cling to. And for once in my life someone who wielded some power believed in me.

By the end of the night, Evie was the one who was sent away. Her banishment didn't give me much comfort.

What if next time I wasn't so lucky?

CHAPTER TWENTY-ONE

Juliet

ROMAN DIDN'T SHOW UP TO SCHOOL THE NEXT MORNING. I lingered in the cafeteria. Then waited by our locker before the first bell, but he never showed.

There was no sign of Evie either. We weren't exactly friends, so it wasn't abnormal not to run into her. Still, after Roman's strange phone call an uneasy sensation settled in my stomach and wouldn't leave.

Finally, around noon he strolled into the lunchroom and headed straight for me. I jumped out of my chair, knocking it over and drawing everyone's attention as it clattered to the floor.

I didn't care about making a spectacle of myself. Roman caught me as I threw my arms around him. "Are you okay?"

"Better now, butterfly," he murmured against my hair.

Kids whistled and commented on our display. To avoid attracting any more attention, he released me and we sat at the table.

"Hey, Romeo." Vienna wiggled her fingers our way. "So nice of you to roll into school today."

I hadn't told her about Roman's phone call last night. It wasn't my place to discuss his troubles with anyone.

He shrugged off her teasing. "Long night. Did I miss anything good?"

Vienna rattled off a bunch of gossip about the morning. While he listened, he inched his fingers across the table and took my hand.

"Did you eat?" I asked after Vienna finished her monologue.

"Nah, I'm fine."

I pushed my apple slices with sunflower butter across the table and he accepted the offering without comment.

"Okay, lovebirds," Vienna announced. "I have to run to the office." She leaned over the back of my chair and planted a loud smooch on my cheek. "See you in a few."

Roman switched chairs, claiming her empty seat.

"Are you okay?" I asked.

His expression remained somber. Stoic. Unreadable. "Nothing I can talk about. I did get some good news out of the situation."

I raised an eyebrow, encouraging him to continue.

"My caseworker's going to let me get a part-time job and she said I might qualify for a program to go to college where they'll pay me a small stipend to cover living expenses."

"Roman, that's great!" I threw my arms around his neck. Then it hit me—we couldn't run away and live together any time soon. "Are you allowed to have a roommate?"

"I didn't ask, but probably. I doubt the stipend is enough to live on my own." He cast a sly look my way. "You know of someone?"

I gave him my own heat-filled stare. "I do. She's tidy and knows how to cook."

"Works for me." He leaned back and patted his stomach. "I'm neat and like to eat."

"Sounds like a perfect match."

He returned my happy smile and kissed my cheek.

Despite the good news, for the rest of the day his movements remained robotic and his gaze distant. He didn't speak up in class at all. Not that he was a know-it-all who always raised his hand, but he usually participated at least a little bit.

I wished he could tell me what happened.

On the way home after school, I tried to think of a tactful way to ask.

"You're quiet today," Roman said.

"So are you."

"I'm tired."

I hesitated, my steps slowing until he stopped. "What's wrong?"

"Nothing. You had me worried last night."

He sighed and shifted his gaze to the side. "I'm sorry. I was near a phone and just wanted to hear your voice."

I waited.

Finally, he relented. "I'm not *allowed* to talk about it."

"Oh." Well, that was better than not *wanting* to tell me.

He jammed his hands in his pockets and stared at the ground. "I got accused of doing something I didn't do. Thank fuck we got back late from the field trip yesterday."

"Was it that bad?"

"Could've been."

Frustrated, I felt so helpless to do anything for him.

We kept walking toward my house in silence. On the corner my neighbor, Mrs. Shields, waved at me.

"Juliet!" she called. "Sweetheart, can you come here a second?"

"Do you mind?" I asked Roman. In a lower voice I explained, "Her husband died last year and she's all alone. I try to stop by and help her out when I can."

"Sure." He gestured for me to go ahead.

We strolled up the short driveway together. Mrs. Shields smiled as soon as she saw Roman.

"Who's your friend, Juliet?"

I hesitated. Would she tell my uncle if I introduced Roman as my boyfriend? When was the last time they even spoke to each other? Who cared if he found out? I liked Mrs. Shields too much to lie.

"Mrs. Shields, this is my boyfriend Roman."

"Boyfriend," she repeated. Her raised eyebrow and slightly curved lips hinted at her approval. "Aren't you a good-looking young man. So tall!" she gushed.

One glance at Roman showed he was blushing.

Did he really not realize how attractive he was or was it just because someone old enough to be his grandmother was pointing it out?

"Nice to meet you, Mrs. Shields." He extended his hand and she shook it briefly, beaming the whole time.

I gestured to the open trunk of her car. "Do you need help carrying your groceries inside?"

"Would you mind? They packed them too heavy at the store again."

"Sure," I answered, reaching for the closest brown paper bag.

Roman waved me off. "I got 'em. Help her inside."

Mrs. Shields did indeed need help navigating her way to the front door. She dropped her keys several times and seemed extremely frustrated.

"This is why I stay home most of the time," she muttered, squinting at the lock.

"I can do it, Mrs. Shields." I eased the keys from her hands and opened the door.

"Thank you."

"Maybe you shouldn't go to the store alone," I suggested gently. "Where's your daughter?"

She rolled her eyes and shuffled into the kitchen. "Who knows? Following some band around the country last I knew."

"Where do you want 'em?" Roman asked, as he followed us into the kitchen.

"On the counter, please."

He set everything down and the two of us unpacked the bags, following Mrs. Shields' instructions for where to put all the supplies.

"Oh! This is really why I called you over, Juliet." She took a brick-sized package neatly wrapped in foil out of the fridge. "I made banana bread."

My mouth watered as soon as she placed the bread in my hands. She was a phenomenal baker.

I eyed Roman. "It's a good thing I like you so much. Normally I wouldn't share."

Both of them laughed.

"That's for you to take home, dear. The two of you can help me finish mine."

"No, I can't do that," Roman said.

"Are you allergic, dear?" she asked, setting the plates on the counter and slipping a knife out of the drawer.

"Uh, no. I just…"

When she looked away, I shook my head at him. Mrs. Shields shared her affection for people by feeding them. It would hurt her feelings if he turned down her offer.

While she brewed a pot of coffee, I set the table. Roman kept eying the front door like he planned to make a run for it any second.

"This is amazing," he said a few minutes later after we were all seated with coffee and cake.

"Told ya," I mumbled around a forkful of moist banana goodness.

She had lots of questions for me about school and I answered in detail, even though none of it seemed very exciting.

Finally she turned her bright-eyed expression on Roman. But not to pry into his school day.

"Do you know anything about cars, dear?"

"A little."

"Would you mind checking my windshield wiper fluid?"

Roman seemed so relieved to have something to do, he practically jumped up from the table. "Sure."

We followed him outside. Mrs. Shields stood back and watched as he popped the hood.

"I hate doing that," she explained. "Ray always did all the car maintenance." She let out a short, sad laugh. "I was always afraid I'd lose a finger if the hood snapped shut. Silly, but Ray didn't want me to worry, so he took care of everything..."

I slipped an arm around her shoulders. "I'm so sorry, Mrs. Shields."

"We had so many good years together." She forced a smile that didn't quite reach her eyes. "Not everyone is so lucky. I just...miss him."

I hugged her a little tighter, unsure of what else I could say to ease her pain.

Roman pulled out a gallon jug of green wiper fluid from the trunk. "Good choice, Mrs. Shields. This stuff helps keep the bug guts off the windshield."

She wrinkled her nose. "It's what Ray always used in the spring and summer."

He finished with the car and even got in and turned the key to check the wipers before declaring her good to go.

"Thank you so much." She turned to me. "Let me grab your bread. I'm sure you two need to get home."

Roman smiled at me when she went inside.

"Thank you for doing that."

He shoved his hands in his pockets and glanced away. "I don't mind. She's a nice woman. Seems to like you a lot."

"I've known her since I moved in with my aunt and uncle. She and her husband were always nice to me."

Mrs. Shields returned with my bread in one hand and a couple of folded-over dollar bills in her other.

"If I'd known you were coming, I'd be sending you home with bread too, Roman."

The corners of his mouth twitched.

She held out the money to him and he put his hands in the air. "No, ma'am. I can't take your money."

"Nonsense. You saved me a lot of trouble."

He shook his head again. She gave up and handed the money to me. "Seriously, make sure he takes this. It would've cost me twice that if I'd taken it into the shop."

"Yes, Mrs. Shields. Thank you."

She gave me a kiss on the cheek and waved to Roman before going inside.

At the bottom of her driveway, he shook his head again. "I can't take her money, Juliet. It's not right."

"She's a proud woman, Roman. I think it would hurt her feelings if she felt like she took advantage of you."

He groaned and relented, allowing me to slip the money in his pocket. "I didn't do much."

His wary gaze darted down the street and I realized he was probably antsy to get back to the house.

"Do you need to be home earlier than usual?"

"No one said so. But after last night, I don't want to do anything to call attention to myself."

My throat tightened and maybe it looked like I was about to cry because he squeezed my shoulder. "It's okay, Juliet. Everything's going to be okay," he promised.

"I don't want anything bad to happen to you."

He sighed and took my hands. "The only thing I was upset about last night was that I might not be able to see you again. I didn't want to disappear on you. Especially after we had such a nice day together."

Disappear. That's what would happen, wasn't it? One day, he'd just be gone. Maybe I'd gather bits and pieces of gossip from the other kids.

As if he heard my thoughts, he brushed his knuckles over my cheek. "I'll always find my way to you, Juliet. I promise. The rest doesn't matter."

"*You* matter to me."

His jaw flexed and he swallowed hard before nodding once. "I haven't mattered to anyone in a long time."

"Well, you matter to me," I repeated.

I'd say it a hundred more times until he believed me.

CHAPTER TWENTY-TWO

Roman

I HATED LIKE HELL TAKING MONEY FROM ANYONE. BUT THE money from Mrs. Shields provided me with a way to buy Juliet a birthday present.

Sometimes on the weekends, the home took us to the mall and turned us loose. Dangerous probably. Only level twos were allowed on these special trips. The counselors were supposed to stick with us, but more often, they'd hand us a couple dollars and tell us to meet them in the food court in an hour or two.

Pip always stuck with me. This trip was no different. His curious eyes were full of questions when I ventured into the small world crafts store.

"What do you want in *here?*" he sputtered.

"I'm not sure yet."

As soon as the words left my mouth, I saw it. A wide green leather bracelet with daisies embossed into the leather.

I had just enough money to cover the cost.

Until they added the tax.

"Dammit," I muttered, desperately scraping the lint out of my pockets, praying for a hidden, mangled dollar bill.

"Here." Pip thrust his lunch money into my hands. "Last time I ate at the food court I had the shits for a week."

The salesclerk groaned.

"You sure?"

"Yeah, take it," Pip insisted. "Is it for the girl?"

"Her birthday's coming up."

"Take it," he said again.

I accepted the money and finished paying for the bracelet.

"Thanks, Pip." We walked into the mall, and I glanced left and right. "Anywhere you want to go?"

"Nope."

We had just enough money left over to buy two sodas. There wasn't much time before we had to meet up with the rest of the group, so we sat and waited.

"Thanks for doing that," I said.

"You really like this girl?"

I couldn't hide my excitement when I thought of Juliet. *Liked* wasn't nearly strong enough to describe what I felt for her. "Oh yeah."

"Is she hot?"

"She's beautiful."

"When can I meet her?"

"I don't know."

He wiggled in his seat, as if he couldn't contain his enthusiasm. "I'll be in high school next year. If you're still together, I can eat lunch with you guys."

I snorted and leaned over to ruffle his hair. "You got it, Pip."

CHAPTER TWENTY-THREE

Juliet

I WOKE UP THE MORNING OF MY SEVENTEENTH BIRTHDAY WITH A crushing weight on my chest. More than anything I wanted to yank the covers over my head and go back to sleep until the next day.

I never liked birthdays. It just seemed like celebrating that you're one day closer to death.

My own birth had caused my father to disappear. When I started school, I was always *that girl*. The one who got excluded from the other kids' birthday celebrations. My mother and aunt had died when they'd gone out to celebrate a birthday. My cousin died after *giving* birth. Birthdays were bad news in my family. Every year, it seemed like yet another reminder that no one loved me. My aunt and uncle barely acknowledged my existence, let alone my birthday.

Buzz!

I flung my hand out and grabbed my cell phone off the nightstand.

Uncle Dex: Happy Birthday, Julez!

That forced a hint of a smile onto my face.

Even though he was in and out of my life, Dex usually

remembered my birthday.

My phone vibrated again.

Roman: Happy birthday, butterfly! Can't wait to see you today.

How did he know it was my birthday?

Intrigued and smiling, I flung the covers away and raced to get dressed. Even though the weather was warm, I pulled on the green leather jacket Dex had given me as my early birthday present weeks ago and trotted down the stairs.

No one was waiting for me in the kitchen. I grabbed the brown bag lunch I'd packed the night before and shoved it in my backpack before hurrying out the door.

I tried to get to school as early as possible to give me as many extra possible seconds with Roman as I could squeeze into a day.

That morning he was waiting for me on the front steps.

"Hey, birthday girl," he said in that low, gravelly voice I felt down to my toes. He swept me into an embrace and pressed his lips to mine.

The school, the noises around us, even the fact that it was my birthday all faded away. Nothing else mattered.

My mind flashed back to the cave at Fletcher Park. When would we have another chance to be alone like that again?

Breathless, we parted. We stared at each other for a few simmering seconds. Was he thinking about the cave too? Did he want to do more next time?

He smiled and lifted a small, square box between us. "Happy birthday."

"Roman! You didn't! How'd you know?"

One corner of his mouth curled in a sly smile. "I have my methods."

The pretty blue paper had daisies and butterflies dotted all over it and I hated to rip it open. "This is so pretty!"

"Please open it. I want you to see what's inside before school starts."

"Okay." This was already the best day. I carefully eased my nail under the tape and peeled the paper apart without ripping it. I'd cut out a piece and tape it into my diary tonight.

Inside was a square purple box and I gently pried off the lid. "Oh!" My breath caught. "It's beautiful!"

Daisies! He remembered how much I love daisies.

The dark hunter green matched the leather of my jacket—my favorite color. I ran my finger over the embossed leather, tracing the carved lines of each petal. "It's beautiful. I love it so much. Thank you."

He brushed his knuckles over my cheek. "Nothing's as beautiful as you and you're welcome."

Tears pricked my eyes. I couldn't believe how sweet and thoughtful he was.

"Juliet, is it okay? You look like you're going to cry." He sounded so distressed, I forced a smile onto my face.

"If I am, they're happy tears. Thank you for thinking of me."

"I'm always thinking of you." His voice held nothing but sincerity. "Every day. All day. All night too."

To stop myself from blubbering all over him, I held out the bracelet. "Put it on for me, please?"

A delightful shiver raced down my spine as he wrapped his fingers around my wrist and pulled me closer. He swept his thumb over my pulse point. Desire quickened my blood. "Roman."

"Sorry. You're just so soft." His voice lowered to a raspy rumble. "I love touching you."

My heart raced so fast, I couldn't answer. He wrapped the bracelet around my wrist and snapped it secure.

"I'm never taking it off," I swore.

"Well, you might want to when you shower." He closed his eyes. "Damn," he whispered. "Now I'm picturing you in the shower in nothing but the bracelet."

I burst into giggles and smacked his chest. Instead of the playful smile I expected, he captured my hand and held it over his heart. "I'm not kidding, butterfly."

So much heat pulsed between us.

"Roman? Can I tell you something?"

"Always. Anything." His concerned eyes bored into me.

"I can't stop thinking about kissing you in that cave." I lowered my lashes. "And other things."

He slid his hands from my hips to my waist. "What other things?"

Heat flared across my face. Was he going to make me say it?

But when I peeked up at him, mischief glinted in his eyes. "I can't stop picturing you in that green bikini. Been going to sleep and dreaming about you in it every night."

Pleasure warmed me from the tips of my ears to the tips of my toes. "I'll wear it for you again."

He groaned and closed his eyes.

I reached up on tiptoes and softly kissed his lips. "One day soon."

"I can't wait." He cupped my cheek and stroked his thumb over my bottom lip. "You know that's not *all* I want to do with you, though, right?"

"Of course, silly." I poked his stomach. "You want to eat banana bread at my neighbor's house in the afternoons, too."

He chuckled, his stomach rippling under my finger with the movement. I had the urge to slip my hand under the hem of his shirt.

The bell rang, startling us apart. "Shoot. We're going to be late." He picked up my bag and took my hand. "I doubt birthday girls get a pass."

"Nope."

Several times throughout the morning, he caught me staring at my bracelet, touching the intricately carved lines.

For the first time in my life, I didn't hate my birthday.

CHAPTER TWENTY-FOUR

Roman

THE HAPPINESS ON JULIET'S FACE BECAME AN ADDICTION. I LOVED making her smile more than anything in the world.

I needed a damn job

Not just to buy her trinkets. More than that. I was trying to plan ahead. For our future.

I wanted to slip a ring on her finger, find a place for us to live, and send her to school.

After that, I wasn't sure. Maybe I'd consider going to college myself. For the first time in my life, I wasn't just trying to survive from day to day.

Juliet gave me hope.

Every now and then she'd hint about having a family. I knew from the day we met she wanted pretty babies she could give all the things she'd never had.

How she held onto that dream mystified me. My life had taught me how unpredictable the world could be. Death claimed who it wanted when it wanted. I could have all the best intentions to be there for my children and still let them down. Leaving them at the mercy of the foster care system. It wasn't like either one of us had any reliable relatives I'd trust to raise my kid. I wasn't sure I trusted myself.

My phone buzzed, pulling me away from thoughts of the future. I glanced around the cafeteria before pulling out my phone.

It was the call I'd been both hoping for and dreading since the morning he showed up at school.

"I have a lead on a job for you," Dex said as soon as I answered.

Perfect timing.

Even though I'd gotten the okay to accept a job, I hadn't been able to find anyone willing to *offer* me one.

I cautioned myself not to get too excited.

Somehow, I knew Dex's help would come with strings attached.

But I needed some way to earn money so I could take care of Juliet and treat her the way she deserved. So I'd pretty much do whatever he asked of me.

I answered with a mix of appreciation and restraint. "How about some details?"

He chuckled as if that was the response he expected.

"Buddy of mine owns the Jericho Two, you know it?"

I only knew that it was the drive-in movie theater Juliet was hoping to get a job at over the summer. "I've heard of it."

"He needs help landscaping and cleaning it up for when they open in a couple weeks. So it's probably not a long-term job, but if you do well, he might be able to find you something through the season."

"Sounds good." Fuck knew I'd done plenty of manual labor over the years for foster parents who had "foster kid" confused with "slave labor." It'd be nice to earn some cash in exchange for breaking my back.

"It's a little bit of a walk off the bus line," Dex added. "Nothing you can't handle."

I doubted the home was going to hand over a bus pass and be cool about the job. Things were never that easy for me. But I didn't want to sound anything less than enthusiastic with Dex. My counselor was right, at some point I needed to start thinking about what the hell to do with myself once I aged out of foster care. I'd convince them to let me accept this arrangement.

One thing I knew for damn sure, stipend or not, I'd need money. For some reason, Dex seemed determined to help me. I'd be an idiot to piss him off by saying no.

"Thank you, Dex."

He gave me the information and I scribbled it down. Shit, a job would mean a lot less time for sneaking around with Juliet after school. Unless she was able to get hired too. Maybe if I was already working there and the owner liked me, I could give her some sort of edge. Or maybe once I proved myself, I'd ask Dex if he'd put in a good word for Juliet.

We said goodbye and I hung up feeling more hopeful about the future.

The "lead" turned out to be a sure thing. The owner of the place, another biker who went by the name of Ulfric, hired me on the spot.

"Dex's word is good enough for me," he'd said.

I wasn't sure how I felt about that. If I fucked up, it would make Dex look bad. Then I'd have to deal with not one, but *two* pissed-off bikers.

"Set your own hours. Just get this cleaned up by opening day," Ulfric said in his gruff no-bullshit way. Not that he was rude, he just never seemed to use more words than absolutely necessary.

We walked the property and he showed me the spots where

fallen trees needed to be cut and hauled away. Grass and leaves needed mowing and bagging. The fence surrounding the place needed to be repaired, potholes in the dirt road needed filling in. A lot of labor. But I formulated a plan for how to tackle each task. Every day after school, I hauled my ass out there and worked the solid four hours the home allowed.

The counselors were so impressed with my work ethic, they even arranged a schedule to pick me up at the end of my shifts. Of all my years in foster care, this was the first time my life didn't feel like a clusterfuck of chaos and frustration.

Ulfric worked me hard. But at least he had the right equipment for all the jobs he wanted done. If I needed something he didn't have, he bought it right away. He taught me how to use a bunch of different tools and how to fix shit when it broke. Anytime I was able to pick up a new skill, I was happy.

This new, tighter schedule didn't allow me much time with Juliet. We still met every morning. In the afternoons, I'd walk her home before jumping on the bus.

"I miss you," she said as we passed Mrs. Shields' house one afternoon.

"Miss you too, butterfly, but—"

"No, I'm not trying to make you feel bad. I'm really proud of you." The corners of her mouth curled up. "Maybe a little jealous."

"Ulfric's going to be hiring for the ice cream shop out front in a few weeks. I'll get you an application."

"That would be perfect. We can spend all summer working together."

"Juliet!" Mrs. Shields called. "Roman!"

I smiled and waved as Juliet and I headed up the driveway.

"How are you, Mrs. Shields?" I asked.

"Good!" She focused on Juliet. "I wanted to talk to you, dear. I'm going to go visit some friends for a couple weeks and wanted to know if you'd watch the house for me?"

"Oh." Juliet glanced at me. "Sure. I can do that."

"You can stay here. I'll make up the guest room for you and you can use my car."

"Oh no. I don't need…You don't have to do that."

"Please, dear? I'd feel much better if someone I trust is here watching the place. And your aunt and uncle aren't far if you need anything." An edge crept into her voice, surprising, since Mrs. Shields was generally such a pleasant woman. Maybe she knew how useless Juliet's guardians were.

"You have your license, right?" she insisted.

"Well, yes."

"So, there you go!" Mrs. Shields ushered us into the house and pressed a set of keys into Juliet's hands. "There is some food here, but I'll leave you grocery money on the counter."

"Mrs. Shields—-"

"No, no. No arguing." Mrs. Shields pressed a finger against her lips, making Juliet laugh.

"When are you leaving?"

"Tomorrow morning."

"Oh! Wow. Okay."

Mrs. Shields shrugged. "Might as well live a little and be spontaneous, right?"

Juliet laughed. "I guess so."

We left Mrs. Shields to finish packing for her trip. At the end of the driveway, Juliet stopped. A tentative smile trembled over her lips. "I'll have the place to myself. Think you'll find time to keep me company?"

My pulse charged. Dozens of images of all the things we could do alone together flooded my overheated brain. Privacy. No worries about teachers walking in on us or other people around.

Juliet must have mistaken my silence for a no.

"I'm sorry." She dropped her gaze to the pavement. "That was kind of forward. I didn't mean—"

"Juliet, of course I want to be alone with you." I flicked a glance toward the house. "I want it more than anything. You know that."

She raised her head, a relieved expression replacing her uncertain one.

The shitty reality of my impossible situation obliterated the moment. "My schedule is so tight. The job's given me a small taste of freedom. I'm scared to do anything that jeopardizes it."

A guilty blush spread over her cheeks. "That was selfish. I'm so sorry. I shouldn't have—"

"Don't apologize, butterfly." I wrapped my arms around her and brushed my lips over her forehead. "I'll figure out a way."

Juliet

Was it wrong that the first thing I thought about was that house-sitting would give us an opportunity to be alone together? I was dying to have him all to myself. Total privacy. Where no teachers would burst in on us. No angry uncles would show up. Nothing but the two of us.

That's the only excuse I had for my selfish question.

I knew Roman cared about me. He showed me every day. But sometimes I couldn't help wanting extra reassurance that he was as into our relationship as I was.

We continued the walk to my house at a snail's pace. He needed to catch the bus to get to his job. I was about to remind him when he stopped.

"There's a chance our curfew will be extended for prom," he said. "I was going to talk to you about it."

A thrill went through me. He was thinking of ways for us to be together.

Prom would be expensive. For both of us. I knew he'd been working hard and saving money. I hated to have him blow it on one night of frivolous high school stuff. Not when he was trying to save for his future.

"Let's skip prom," I suggested.

He stared at me, a slight frown crinkling his brow. "You don't want to skip prom. Vienna said you already have a dress and everything."

Sure, before I met Roman, prom seemed like the height of my high school existence. Now, when our time together was so precious and rare, the last thing I wanted to do was waste it on bad food, loud music, and the people I saw every day in school.

I tugged on his hand, drawing him closer. "Let's have our own, private prom. You and me."

He swallowed hard and searched my face. "Are you sure? I don't want you to be mad at me later because you missed it."

"I think I'll be more upset if I waste the night with our classmates, when I could be alone with *you*."

A confident smile curved his lips. "I can't disagree with that."

CHAPTER TWENTY-FIVE

Roman

PROM—AN EVENT I NEVER THOUGHT I'D ATTEND.

Well, technically, I *wasn't* attending prom.

Juliet and I had formulated our plan. I'd be dropped off with the other four kids from the house who were going, but then I'd slip away and meet Juliet at Mrs. Shields' where she was still house-sitting.

The plan cost me a prom ticket and a tuxedo rental. Worth every penny.

"Slumming it with us tonight, Roman?" Squire sneered as I sat in the first seat in the van.

"Roman's been *so* busy lately," Janet added. "I'm surprised he can leave the house for some fun."

Both of them still blamed me for Evie's banishment. As usual, I ignored their taunts.

"You finally gonna smash that hot chick with the big tits?" Squire asked. "She looked hot as fuck in that bikini on the field trip."

"Fuck off," I snarled. The urge to yank out his tongue and tie it around his neck burned hot. I blew out a breath and counted to ten. I had too much to lose if I got into a fight. I'd worked too hard, planned tonight down to the second. I couldn't afford to get into trouble.

"She's not *that* hot," Janet simpered. "She's kinda short and chunky."

I stared down at my hands—Juliet's curves fit in them perfectly. Every inch of her was flawless. That's why girls like Janet tried to tear her down all the time.

At the school, Mike stepped out of the van with us and patted me on the shoulder. "Have fun. You deserve it. You've been working hard." He squinted at me. "Just not too much fun."

I swallowed a lump of guilt. "Thanks."

"Midnight!" he yelled to the others. "You're late, you're grounded."

Everyone groaned but promised to be waiting out front at midnight. I said hello to a few other kids I knew who were hanging around outside. Once Mike drove off, I edged away from the crowd into the shadows. When I was sure no one noticed my disappearance, I sprinted for the park.

Enough moonlight filtered through the trees to illuminate the way. Prom sounds from the school followed me into the woods. A few kids had also snuck away for some "alone time." Soft moaning and other noises came and went as I jogged along the dirt path that would take me to Juliet.

As I came out on the other side, the glow from one of the upstairs windows of Mrs. Shields' house caught my attention.

Low, soft lights. Candles?

My cock stirred in my too-tight, rented tuxedo trousers. We hadn't talked about what exactly we planned to do with our night. I couldn't deny that I was dying to make love to Juliet. I'd even taken a few of the condoms the counselors kept shoving at me and stuffed them in my pocket. Just in case.

Except, losing our virginity to each other when I couldn't even spend the whole night with her seemed wrong.

I pulled out my phone and sent her a text.

Almost there.

The lights downstairs winked on and I picked up my pace. By the time I arrived, I'd have sweat rolling down my ass crack, but I was so eager to see her, I didn't care.

This house-sitting gig of hers made me nervous. I hated that she was alone and unprotected all night. Not that her aunt and uncle provided much protection, but at least she wasn't by herself.

As promised, she didn't answer the door until I rang the bell and called her name.

My mind blanked when she appeared in the doorway.

"Juliet." My gaze roamed over every inch of her slight frame. From shoulders to just above her knees, she was encased in dark red, shimmering lace. The material hugged her curves and glimpses of skin at her shoulders and legs teased me through the lace. It still covered more than most of the girls' dresses I'd spotted at prom before slipping away. Maybe that's why it was so much sexier. "You're beautiful," I finally added, realizing I was staring at her like a slack-jawed moron.

"And you're very handsome." She stepped back. "Come in."

She'd been house-sitting for over a week now, and I hadn't come inside once. I'd been convinced we'd lose control and rip each other's clothes off if given the chance. Now, I cursed myself for being an idiot.

Her breath hitched when I brushed up against her. She peeked up at me from under her long, darkened lashes. She'd obviously spent time on curling her hair and all the other primping girls did for big events. A pang of regret resonated inside my chest. Maybe she'd be sorry we didn't go to prom after all. It wasn't too late. I still had my ticket and I could buy her one at the door.

"Are you sure you don't want to go?" I asked.

She tilted her head. "To prom? Yes. Why?"

"You look so pretty. You must have spent a lot of time getting ready. Seems wrong to waste it on me."

"It's not a waste." She fluffed her hair. "I did this *for* you."

Damn, how'd I get so lucky?

She closed the door behind us and nudged me into the living room. "I hung out with Vienna and helped her do her makeup."

"You're beautiful every single day." My gaze roamed over her body from shoulders to toes again. "But you're breathtaking tonight."

"Thank you." She glided over the carpet and flicked on the ancient stereo. Something soft and sultry came over the speakers. On the rare occasion I had a chance to pick the music I listened to, I usually chose something louder, angrier, and darker. This was light, sexy, and infused with hope.

Fitting because that was how I always felt in Juliet's presence.

Juliet

"I think those ballroom dancing classes are about to come in handy," I said.

One corner of Roman's mouth turned up. "Is that right?"

I offered him my hand and he took it, yanking me closer. His hands slid down, clutching my hips.

"Mr. Hawkins, I believe that's improper form."

He chuckled and curled one arm around my waist. "Better?" He twirled me away and pulled me back in before I answered.

"Those jerks at school would've made fun of us for using our nerdy dancing skills."

He snorted. "None of their opinions matter."

For several more songs we continued dancing. Nothing more than the simple waltz we'd learned in gym.

"Can we dance like this at our wedding?" The words tripped off my tongue without a second thought.

Sure, he'd said he wanted to marry me weeks ago, but he hadn't mentioned it again. We were way too young to contemplate marriage, but I couldn't help it. When I thought of my future, I always pictured Roman in my life.

His happy grin chased away my doubts. "We can do anything you want at our wedding."

"Oh, in that case, I want to get married on top of a mountain at sunrise." I rattled off some other outrageous scenarios and Roman agreed to each and every one.

"Are you planning to spoil me and let me have my way with everything?" I teased.

"You deserve to be spoiled." The smile slid off his face, replaced with raw desire flickering in his eyes. "I'll take over when you need me to."

"That sounds ominous."

His predatory look only intensified. "I'll always take care of you, Juliet."

I *tsked* at him. "We promised we'd take care of each other."

"I meant something slightly different."

He pulled me tight to his body and the hardness pressing into me left no doubt of his intentions.

A flutter of awareness stirred in my belly. "Are you hungry? I made some appetizer-type foods and mixed up this punch recipe I found."

"Prom food?"

"I wanted you to have the full experience."

He threw his head back and laughed. My favorite sound in the world. Roman's happiness.

"All right then, give me the full experience."

I led him into the kitchen and fixed him a plate of finger food. Stuffed mushrooms, tiny macaroni and cheese rounds and spinach puffs.

"These are so good." He grabbed a few more stuffed

mushrooms and took a seat at the kitchen table. "Come sit with me. I can't believe you made all this."

I had made most of it from scratch. Only the spinach puffs had come frozen from a box.

"Be right there." I poured him a glass of fruity red punch from a sparkling bowl I'd found in the pantry. Not knowing if he'd be tested for alcohol, I hadn't spiked it.

I set my own plate on the table and handed him his glass. "It's virgin punch."

"Good. I'm already drunk on you." A slow, simmering smile curved his lips. "And you need to be on your game."

Too startled by the second part of his statement, I didn't have a chance to bask in the first. "I do, huh? What are you planning to do to me?"

His sexy expression melted into seriousness. "Whatever you want me to do."

A thrill shot down to my toes. I popped a mushroom in my mouth and thought carefully about my answer.

"What if I want everything?"

He sipped his punch, watching me over the rim of the glass.

"Then I'll give you everything."

CHAPTER TWENTY-SIX

Roman

THINGS WERE MOVING FASTER THAN I EXPECTED. BUT IT FELT right. I flicked a glance at the clock behind Juliet. We had exactly three hours before I needed to be back at the school.

"Roman." Her soft, husky voice stirred up a storm inside me. "Will you come upstairs with me?"

I practically knocked my chair over in my eagerness to say yes. After a breath, I held out my hand. "Show me the way."

Every step shook me to my core. We were about to change everything. I'm not sure why I was so sentimental. I just knew that after tonight, our futures would be forever bound together.

"This is my room," she said, pushing a door at the end of the hallway open. As I'd guessed earlier, several candles were lit, throwing soft, dancing light over the space.

"You left all these candles unattended?" I teased.

"I was distracted."

I pushed her hair off her shoulder and kissed her neck. "What distracted you?"

"You."

"Were you planning on bringing me up here?"

She shivered under my touch. "Is that wrong?"

Some people might think so. Might think we were too young. Or she was too young and I was wrong for her. But *fuck them.*

We were the same age. Had both endured a lifetime of heartaches and disappointments. We understood each other better than anyone else. We belonged together. My need for her was stronger than finally getting off inside a girl. I loved her like I'd never loved anyone in my life.

I would never love anyone the way I loved Juliet.

How could that be wrong?

Except for one tiny snag. The only thing that made me consider waiting.

"Are you sure?" I glanced away. "I can't stay, Juliet. If we do this…I want to stay with you all night. Leaving feels wrong."

She cast a look at me over her shoulder. "How long until you'll be able to do that?"

Too long. Way too damn long.

I didn't have to say it. She knew.

"I won't feel abandoned or used, if that's what you're worried about."

Hell, she could voice my concerns better than I could.

I skimmed my hand over her cheek. "I love you, Juliet."

She stared up at me with sincere, unblinking eyes. "I love you too, Roman. I want to be with you forever."

That one statement soothed my soul. Every awful thing I'd endured in my life was worth it to bring me to this moment. With this girl. "You're already the center of my world. You know that, right?"

"And you're mine." She turned, giving me her back, and lifted her long, heavy hair. "Will you help me with my dress?"

Hell yes.

My fingers trembled as I gripped the tiny, hidden zipper and tugged it down, revealing creamy skin and little freckles. I leaned down to kiss the back of her neck, inhaling her scent. Roses and vanilla frosting.

The dress dropped to the floor in a puddle at her feet and she carefully stepped out of it. Leaning over, she picked it up and I almost lost my damn mind.

Her breasts swelled up over the cups of her strapless bra. My gaze traveled lower, enthralled with my unobstructed, unhurried view of her stomach and hips. Her cute belly button that I couldn't wait to tease with my tongue. Lower, my gaze stopped on the small satin panties in the same shade of deep red as her dress. When I could breathe again, I continued drinking her in. Long, smooth, bare legs. Black heels. A fantasy come to life.

We'd spent a lot of afternoons making out. Quick, stolen moments, forever etched in my mind. But this was different. I didn't have to hurry. I wasn't afraid we'd get caught. Music continued to flow from the speakers downstairs and Juliet swayed to the melody.

But it was her gaze that pinned me in place.

She held out her hands. "Dance with me."

Her invitation snapped me out of my trance and I took her hands in mine. This dance had nothing to do with what we'd learned in gym class. I spun her around and kissed the sensitive spot on her neck. Her body perfectly molded to mine. I nipped at her earlobe and she leaned against me even more. I dropped my hands to her hips and we settled into a slow grind. The curve of her backside fit so perfectly against me. I was free to take my time exploring every exposed inch of her.

Spinning her around, I took her mouth, kissing her until the music faded away, replaced by our beating hearts. My overheated blood shot through my veins. The electricity sparking between us had my cock harder than ever. Stiff and throbbing. If I came in my pants again—like the day in the photo lab—I'd never forgive myself.

"Juliet," I whispered, squeezing the firm globes of her ass to slow her down.

"Roman," she answered. Her fingers reached for the cheap bow tie at my neck, pulling it loose. She went to work on my buttons, stripping off my jacket and shirt. I couldn't let her near my belt, or I'd definitely come in my pants.

"Lie on the bed for me." I nodded to the neatly made-up queen-sized bed against the wall. "Let me see you."

A pretty flush spread down her neck and chest as she hurried over and climbed onto the bed.

Oh, fuck. That didn't slow down my racing heart at all. Especially when she kicked off the heels and stretched out on her side. She propped her head up on her hand and watched me fumble with the unfamiliar buckle and trousers.

"Oh, Roman," she gasped, covering her mouth with one hand.

I glanced down, afraid I'd already shot my load and just hadn't realized it. But no, I was still harder than a motherfuckin' log.

"What's wrong?"

"I'm afraid that's going to hurt."

My mouth curled into a smug smile and I approached the bed with surer steps. "I'll go slow. I'd never hurt you."

"I know," she whispered.

She watched with wide eyes while I took the three condoms from my pocket and set them on the nightstand.

I placed a knee on the bed and stared down at her. "Are you sure?"

"Surer than I've ever been about anything." She rolled to her back and curled a finger, inviting me closer.

I settled myself between her legs, holding my weight above her. "Kiss me, butterfly." I lowered my head and feasted on her full lips. She rubbed her tongue against mine, panting into my mouth.

"I love kissing you," she whispered against my lips.

She slid her palms over my freshly shaved face and kissed me even harder. I desperately needed to be skin on skin with her. Slipping my arms under her, I rolled us so she was on top. She laughed as she settled over me.

"What are you doing?"

"I need to see you. All of you."

My fingers fumbled with the stubborn clasp of her bra. "May I?"

The smile vanished. "Yes, Roman," she answered.

I continued grappling with her bra hooks until she finally took mercy on me. "Need some help?"

"Go easy on me. It's my first one."

She raised an eyebrow.

I pressed my hands against her cheeks, needing her to understand how serious I was. "I've never done this with anyone else."

Her gaze skittered away. Or maybe the flickering candles made it seem that way. "I never wanted this with anyone else," she finally said.

I was too overwhelmed to puzzle that out. Then she reached behind her and unsnapped the hooks. With no straps to keep it in place, the bra fell between us and I was more than ready to catch the soft weight of her breasts in my hands.

"Roman," she whispered as my thumbs rubbed over her nipples. She was even prettier than I'd imagined. And I was so glad we hadn't gone further that day in the cave.

She spread her legs wider, grinding herself against me. With her head thrown back and her eyes shut, I wasn't even sure if she was aware of what she was doing.

"Juliet."

I wanted her with me every step of the way.

I flipped us again and her eyes popped open. "Eyes on me, Juliet."

She bit her lip and nodded. Watched while I kissed my way to her breasts. Slowly, I ran my tongue over the hard tips of her nipples, stopping to savor each one. Writhing underneath me, she looked like pure sin. Then I'd find her eyes, full of innocence and longing.

Her hands reached for me, stroking my cock. Even through my underwear, her touch burned. "Take me out," I whispered.

She wasted no time, shoving the elastic band down over my hips. My cock sprung free and she eagerly wrapped her hands around me, softly touching and exploring.

I sucked in a sharp breath. My own hand never felt that damn good.

"Is this okay?" she asked.

I closed my eyes and gritted my teeth. "Fuck yes."

"I wanted to do this that day in the cave." She flicked her thumb over a sensitive spot and my whole body jolted.

This was going to be over quick if she kept that up.

"Believe me, I wanted you to." I kissed her cheek. "But I'm really glad we weren't the ones who got caught *in flagrante delicto*." I said the unfamiliar phrase with a silly accent and she broke into soft laughter. I traced my finger over her collarbones. "I wanted to strip you down, explore every inch of you."

Her breath caught.

"But I just kept thinking if Jameson or someone else caught a glimpse of you, I'd probably shove them over the cliff." I cupped my hands over her breasts to show her I wasn't kidding.

She brushed her fingers over my cheek. "It's just you and me, now."

I slid my hand down her belly.

Her entire body froze. Plump thighs clamped around my wrist. "Juliet? Is this okay?"

She seemed to shake off whatever pulled her out of the moment. "Touch me," she whispered.

Slower this time, I rubbed my fingers down her center. Her panties were soaked. This time, I knew it was all Juliet, not from a dip in the pool. The satin material was so much thinner than her bathing suit had been, leaving little to my wild imagination.

I was dying to shove the thin strip of fabric aside and sink my fingers deep inside her, but I took it slow. With each pass, I added more pressure, which she seemed to enjoy, but I wanted her overwhelmed with need.

I took two fingers and settled them over the spot that seemed to drive her nuts before and rubbed in slow circles.

"Oh, Roman. Right there. That's so good."

I kept up the rubbing, moving in slightly faster circles until she was moaning and begging for more.

"What do you need?" I asked.

"I don't know. More?"

I watched her face closely, taking note of each reaction. If we only did *this* all night long, I'd be perfectly happy.

"God, you're so good," she whispered. "So gentle." The awe in her face made me pause. Had she expected me to claw at her like a wild animal? I mean, the instinct was there. I couldn't help it. But I was in control of myself. My desire to please her, make this satisfying *for* her, overrode my baser instincts. Most of them, anyway.

She reached for me and I grabbed her hands, gently pinning them over her head.

"Oh!" She arched her back, brushing her bare breasts against my chest. "I like that." She pushed herself against my hand, seeking more.

I stretched out next to her, keeping her arms over her head and my hand between her legs.

A soft, frustrated whimper worked out of her. I leaned over and kissed her cheek, then her lips. We were lost in another soul-entwining kiss when I slipped my fingers under her panties. I brushed my knuckles against soft, damp curls and rubbed against her seam. She was so hot, so wet, so much more than I ever imagined.

She shook herself out of our kiss. "Please. I want you." She dropped her gaze to my cock. "All of you."

Why she was so eager to rush, I wasn't sure. I slipped a finger inside her impossibly tight center, slowly working in and out, then added another. "I don't want to hurt you."

"You won't." She bit her lip and squeezed her eyes shut. "I know you won't."

Someday when I wasn't five seconds from coming all over myself and I had more patience, I wanted to draw out this part. Leave her trembling and writhing beneath me for hours. Touch and taste every part of her. Command every moment. Tonight wasn't that night. I only possessed the patience of a seventeen-year-old boy who'd waited his entire life to be with the right girl.

Still, I took my time sliding off her panties and kissing my way down her body. I stopped and took a moment to dip my tongue in her navel. She sucked in a breath as I kissed lower.

Her scent utterly intoxicated me, and I couldn't help tasting her.

"Roman, please!"

I sat up and chuckled, stroking my hand over my painfully hard cock. I reached over and grabbed one of the condoms, tearing into it like a man possessed.

Other than my mindless need to be inside of her and to make her happy, I had no idea what I was doing. She watched with bright, eager eyes while I rolled on the condom.

Her breathing sped up as I covered her with my body. She spread her legs wider to accommodate me. "Make me yours, Roman. Please."

"You're already mine, butterfly." I crushed my mouth to hers.

Shaking with the need to be inside her, I slid the head of my cock along her slit. Our lips connected again and I rocked against her, seeking entrance. She let out a strangled cry as I pushed inside, her smaller body squirming underneath me. The impulse to pound into her seized my body, but I willed myself to take my time.

Slow and gentle. We had our whole lives for fast and hard.

"Still good?" I asked.

"I think so." She wiggled her hips again and a burst of pleasure seized my entire body.

"Easy," I breathed out. "Am I hurting you?"

She seemed to think over the question and my heart stopped while I waited for the answer. "No. It feels...different. Full, but not in a bad way."

I grunted and pushed into her with a little more force. "I want it to feel *amazing* for you."

She stroked her hands down my sides and dug her nails into my ass. "You can go faster. I can feel how much you're holding back."

"I don't want to hurt you."

"You won't."

She was so tight but dripping with arousal. I clutched one breast and scraped my teeth over her nipple. Her moaning spurred me on and I drove into her faster. Harder. Bit down on her other nipple.

"Roman, I'm..." she strained, tense and so close. I reached between us and rubbed her secret spot until her eyes rolled back in her head and her little body jerked underneath me.

Having the whole house to ourselves was a blessing. Juliet came hard and *loud*. So many different noises I'd never heard from her before.

I wanted to hold back my own release as long as possible but lost the fight as soon as her muscles clamped down around me.

We lay there panting, slick with sweat, staring into each other's eyes.

Juliet

We fell asleep for a few minutes. Well, I did. Roman darted into the bathroom to clean up before slipping under the covers with me. He pulled my naked body against his. The warmth from his still-sweaty skin seeped into me.

I sighed as his hand restlessly traced patterns over my hip and belly, down to my thighs and up between my breasts. He still seemed eager to roam and explore. And honestly, so was I.

"Will you think I'm weird if I show you something?" I whispered.

His hand stopped moving. "Never."

I reached out and yanked open the nightstand drawer. My cheeks heated as I pulled the vibrant book out of its hiding spot.

Roman sat up. "What's that?"

"It's silly. When I told Vienna I wasn't going to prom, she gave me this."

Despite how intimate we'd just been, I had a hard time meeting his eyes as I handed over the colorful *101 Sensual Positions* guide.

His whole face lit up. "Remind me to thank her."

"Don't you dare."

He chuckled and flipped over onto his belly, encouraging me to do the same so we could look through the book together.

"What do you want to try next?" he asked.

I hesitated. I truly didn't know. When I'd first looked through the book, all of it seemed too overwhelming. Exciting but overwhelming. I wanted to wait to study it until Roman and I were together.

"Come on." He slipped his hand around mine, intertwining our fingers. "Which one makes you tingle when you look at it?"

"Hmmm." I flicked through the pages. "We already kind of did this."

"Not quite." He pointed to the way the woman's feet were

braced against the man's chest. "We'll give that variation another try later. Right now let's figure out what excites you."

"You excite me." I leaned over and kissed him. When I pulled back, he was smiling and still waiting for an answer.

"There was this…" I flipped the pages, finally landing on one called *The Basket.*

He read the short description out loud and sat up. "Sounds sexy. Let's do it."

"Now?"

He reached over and grabbed another condom, tearing into it before answering me. "Right now."

My insides ignited at his eagerness. To please me.

He put his back against the wall and stretched out one leg. "Come on." He pulled me on top of him, arranging me in his lap the way the picture showed.

"Yeah, this is hot. I like this." He held my breasts in his hands, kissing and licking, while I figured out how to ease down his length. He lowered one hand to my hip, guiding me.

"Oh!" I gasped and raised up.

"Easy," he encouraged. "You control how much you can take."

I liked that. Actively participating. The way other girls gossiped in school, it always seemed like sex was something boys did *to* you, not *with* you.

I balanced my hands on his shoulders and tried again. The strange, almost painful fullness eased into something hotter and more pleasurable. "Ohhh."

"There you go." His voice had turned into a choppy rasp. "You're so beautiful. You feel so good. Don't stop. Please."

I raised and lowered myself a few more times before falling into a faster, satisfying rhythm. That same heat from before swept over me, pulling me under and turning me inside out. "Oh my God," I gasped and kept on riding him.

When the overwhelming tingles faded and I opened my eyes, Roman gripped my hips and took control of my movements, wringing another orgasm out of me before finding his own release.

I fell forward, resting my forehead against his shoulder.

He stroked his hands up and down my back. "Ninety-nine positions to go, butterfly," he whispered against my hair.

CHAPTER TWENTY-SEVEN

Roman

WE DIDN'T MAKE IT THROUGH THE WHOLE BOOK, BUT WE DID eventually use the third condom.

Then the part I'd been dreading all night came. Juliet's alarm went off.

"I set it in case we fell asleep," she explained. "I don't want you to be late getting back."

I groaned and untangled myself from her. "I don't want to leave."

"I don't want you to either, but I can't have you get in trouble. Not when things are going so well."

She was right. I still hated it.

"Stay like that. I want to burn this image in my head," I said as I stood and yanked on my underwear and pants.

She pulled the sheet back, giving me an unobstructed view of her naked body.

"I didn't get to do a fraction of the things I wanted to do to you," I groaned.

"We'll have more chances," she promised.

I dropped to my knees beside the bed and took her hands in mine. "We will, Juliet. You're my present. My future. When we're together I'm something, and I'm nothing when we're apart."

She stroked my cheek with the back of her hand. "Roman, you're everything."

Her alarm chirped again. I kissed her once more, then finished getting dressed.

To my disappointment, she also got dressed. "I'll walk you downstairs."

"I'd tell you to stay up here and tuck you in, but I want to make sure you lock the door behind me."

"I will."

I followed her downstairs and checked the windows and back door before we said goodbye. "If I kiss you again, I won't stop."

She nodded as if she had the same dilemma. "Go. I don't want you to be late." She reached up and pecked my cheek. "I love you."

"Love you too, butterfly."

Then I raced into the night, leaving my heart behind.

Thoughts of Juliet and everything we'd done consumed me as I ran through the park. I arrived a few minutes before midnight and sat on the brick wall in front of the school to wait for the van.

"Where were you?" Squire shouted. "Didn't see you all night."

"I was around," I muttered.

"You sneak off with your girlfriend?" Janet's nasal voice irritated me, but I shrugged off the question.

I was saved from any more probing by the van pulling up to the curb. Judy opened the door and we clambered in.

"How was it?" she asked.

"Fun," I answered quickly. Maybe too quick because she squinted at me for a second.

"Yeah, *Raman Noodles* had so much fun, no one saw him all night long," Squire tattled.

I slapped his hand off my shoulder and took my seat. "Didn't see you either. Where'd you and Janet sneak off to?"

My hunch was correct and he finally shut his big mouth.

Judy shook her head. "I hope you guys behaved. You know if you didn't that means the kids next year won't be able to go."

"Why's that our problem?" Squire scoffed.

Juliet's scent clung to my skin and to my jacket. I stared out the window into the night, wondering if she was okay. Hating that I had to leave her after such a big step in our relationship. Furious that I wouldn't see her until Monday morning.

My body might have been on the van on the way to the group home. But my heart and mind were still in the bed with Juliet.

CHAPTER TWENTY-EIGHT

Roman

ONE OF THE REASONS I'D WANTED TO WAIT WAS THAT I KNEW THE second Juliet and I had sex, I wouldn't want to stop. After our "prom night," we took any and every opportunity to sneak away for privacy and a quickie.

She was still house-sitting for Mrs. Shields, so most days we raced there and tore each other's clothes off as soon as we stepped in the front door.

I spent a portion of my next paycheck on a jumbo-sized box of condoms that I stashed in Juliet's room.

"I don't think I've ever been happier," I said as I bent her over a mountain of pillows stacked on the couch for a position the book promised would allow for "deeper penetration."

"No kidding." She laughed into her hands then moaned as I pushed into her.

I lightly smacked her ass. "Not just because of this."

She glanced at me over her shoulder. "I know."

We ended up on the floor after that. Slow and gentle. Her on top. Side by side. You name it, we tried it.

When I couldn't put off leaving for work any longer, we got

dressed. "Let me make you a sandwich to take to work," she said.

"I'll be fine." Juliet already did enough for me. I hated mooching food off her all the time.

"We take care of *each other*," she reminded me as if she knew what I'd been thinking.

She packed up more than just a sandwich for me while I watched. Like always, she added cut up fruit and vegetables. A few cookies. Somehow, she just knew food was scarce at the home and was always trying to feed me.

"Wouldn't it be nice if we lived here together?" she said over her shoulder.

As if I hadn't thought the same thing a million times.

I wrapped my arms around her waist, hugging her to me. "I'd love nothing more. Soon, butterfly. I promise."

She rubbed her hands over my arms. "I know."

"I probably won't be able to afford a place as nice as this—"

"But at least we'll be together," she finished for me.

"Right."

Since she still had Mrs. Shields' car to use, she drove me to work so I didn't have to take the bus and risk being late.

I kissed her goodbye and watched her drive off before heading inside.

Ulfric had a line of paint cans waiting for me. "Touch up the building. Ain't supposed to rain for a few days."

And that was the extent of the instructions I received for the day.

That suited me fine.

I worked better alone and uninterrupted. Ulfric had let it slip one day that he had hidden cameras stashed all over the place. He waited until after he'd confirmed that I didn't fuck off while I was working to share that tidbit.

Didn't matter. Camera or not, I wasn't a slacker.

In the middle of my shift, I was twelve feet in the air dabbing white paint over bare patches of concrete when I heard the crunch of gravel below. I glanced down and groaned.

"Dex, what are you doing here?" I greeted my surprise visitor.

He smirked at the paintbrush in my hand as I climbed down the ladder. "Very good, kid." He raised one finger in the air. "First rule of the streets, never let anyone get the jump on you."

"Uh, okay." I glanced around. We were way in the suburbs. "This isn't exactly the streets, Dex."

He rolled his lips like he was trying to bite back his laughter. "Need you to help me run an errand tonight."

Was he joking? My gaze skimmed the area. "I'm kinda in the middle of my actual job."

He grunted at the sarcasm. "Already spoke to Ulfric. He knows you're leaving with me for a couple hours."

"A couple of *hours*?"

"I'll have you back by curfew, Cinderella." He cocked his head toward the parking lot. "Come on."

I unzipped my coveralls and stopped in Ulfric's office to confirm he was okay with me leaving before walking outside with Dex.

"You're not gonna make me ride bitch, are you?" I asked.

He snorted. "No, smart-ass."

Instead of the bike, he led me to a fancy black sports car. "Somehow I expected you to drive a truck."

"I usually do. Get in."

"Aren't you part of an MC? Why can't any of your buddies help you with this errand?" I asked once we were on the road.

"They're busy."

"And I was your next best option?"

"I'll pay you double what you make the whole night painting cinderblocks."

I took that as my cue to quit bitching. "Okay."

After a few miles, he glanced over. "Tonight's adventure stays between us. Juliet doesn't need to be involved."

I wasn't sure how I felt about that. Juliet and I weren't in the habit of keeping secrets. But in the end, I figured the less she knew about whatever Dex was into, the safer she probably was.

We pulled up in front of a large brick apartment building and Dex cut the engine. "Stay in the hallway and bang on the door if anyone's coming. Then haul your ass down here and start the car." He handed over the keys.

"You're not worried I'll steal it and leave you behind?"

He leveled a hard stare my way. "You're not that stupid, Roman."

No, I wasn't.

"Are we doing something illegal?" I asked. Apparently, I *was* stupid enough to keep asking questions.

"Nope."

That wasn't reassuring.

He punched a code into a keypad by the front doors and we went inside. He looked around for a second before jogging up the wide staircase in front of us. On the second floor, he scanned each apartment door before stopping in front of 4F.

"Stay right *here*." He pointed to the wall next to the door like I was an unruly puppy in need of training. "Keep your mouth shut."

"All right." I hated everything about this situation, but I was also intrigued. What exactly was he willing to pay me so much money to do?

Satisfied I'd stay like a good boy, he banged on the door.

From inside, someone shouted, "What?"

Dex mumbled something incoherent.

The door opened. "What do you want?"

Dex shoved his way inside.

"What the fuck!? Who are—"

Thump! The unmistakable sound of a fist smashing into someone's face.

The door slammed shut, but the sounds of the beating on the other side continued.

What did Dex drag me into?

Crash! Thwack! More thumping. I scanned the hallway. All the doors remained shut. None of the neighbors were concerned about the situation in 4F.

Another smash. A loud grunt.

Shit, what if the guy had gotten the upper hand and *Dex* was the one getting his ass kicked? The dude was obviously nuts, but Juliet loved him. I didn't want him to get hurt.

I nudged the door open and peeked inside.

"You like beatin' up on girls, motherfucker?" Dex sneered.

Boom! He slugged the guy in the stomach. With his foot.

"She fell!" the guy on the floor hollered.

Thwack!

"Fell my ass." Dex pummeled the guy in the face. "This ain't the first time you put your hands on that girl. But it *will* be your last."

And the beating continued.

The guy had *not* gotten the upper hand. I don't think he'd even touched Dex.

More punches. A few kicks.

The guy either died or passed out. I couldn't tell and didn't care to investigate.

Dex looked up and focused on me. I fought the urge to piss my damn pants under his intense stare.

"Christ you're a sneaky bastard. Didn't I tell you to stay outside?" His tone wasn't that sharp. He didn't seem all that concerned that I'd just witnessed him beating a man half to death. No, the scariest thing about him was how calm and controlled he acted.

"I heard a crash." I shrugged. "Thought you might need help."

He cocked his head. "So you ran in here?"

"Well, yeah."

He chuckled, but I got the sense he approved. The guy at his feet groaned and Dex spit on him.

"Let's go." He slipped off his black leather gloves and stuffed them in his vest pocket. Eager to get the hell away from the scene, I followed.

On the sidewalk, he held out his hand for the keys.

"You make a habit of breaking into strangers' homes and beating the hell out of 'em?" I asked once we were in the car.

"Who said he's a stranger?"

"Okay, you make a habit of busting—"

"Don't ask more questions than you want answers to, kid." He waited a second to see if I'd open my mouth again. "That piece of shit broke a girl's wrist and shoved her down the stairs so hard she sprained her ankle. She can't work for weeks now. And she's got a kid to support."

Who? His sister? A friend? "You must care about her a lot."

He glanced over but didn't say anything at first. We navigated out of the neighborhood and back onto the highway before he spoke again. "Someone who works for me."

"Calling the police wasn't an option?"

"Why?" His tone sharpened. "So they can harass her for being a stripper, humiliate her, and then do nothing about it anyway? My way's more effective."

"Stripper?"

"Crystal Ball." He smirked. "What'd you think it was?"

I shrugged. "Fortune-teller's parlor?"

The asshole laughed for a solid minute. "Maybe we'll host your eighteenth birthday party there. I'll make sure the girls show you a good time."

Disgust rolled through me. Watching strange girls dance around naked would feel like cheating on Juliet. "No thanks. Not interested."

He glanced over and quirked an eyebrow. Was this another test? Whatever. I crossed my arms over my chest and stared straight ahead.

"I see why Juliet likes you," he said quietly.

No wonder he wanted me to tag along. It solved two issues for him. Payback for the girl who'd been hurt, *and* the beating provided me with a powerful visual of what would happen to me if *I* ever hurt Juliet.

"What if that guy injures your employee worse next time? Because of what you did tonight?"

Dex growled and flicked the blinker on, taking a turn way too fast. "Then next time, I'll kill him."

The deathly calm tone of his voice left no doubt he meant it.

"You're a brave kid," he said after a few more miles. "Honorable too."

"How so?"

"Well," he drawled, "you could've taken the car keys and driven off. Sold it for parts."

"I couldn't do that to Juliet. You're her family."

He roared with laughter. "But if I was a stranger?"

"I wouldn't have gotten in your car in the first place. *Stranger danger.*"

He smirked. "How's work going?"

"All right."

"Ulfric treat you fairly?"

It seemed like an odd question. Weren't he and Ulfric friends? Why wouldn't he treat me fairly?

"He runs a different motorcycle club, but the clubs are friendly to each other," Dex said as if he'd read my mind.

That didn't exactly clear things up. "What does that mean?"

"You really don't know anything about MCs? Figured you woulda run into at least one or two MC brats in the system. A kid with a father in a club."

"I tend to stick to myself as much as possible."

"Hmm." My answer seemed to disappoint him.

"Hard to trust people you barely know," I added. Not that I owed him any explanation.

"Yeah, I get that." He drummed his fingers against the steering wheel. "I can't speak for every MC, but mine's a brotherhood. I'd die for any one of them and they'd do the same for me."

I couldn't think of anyone—except Juliet—I felt that strongly about. I'd protect Pip, but I don't know if I'd be willing to *die* for him.

"So why're you hiding tonight's adventures from your brothers, then?"

"I'm not hiding shit." He laughed again. "My president's more than okay with what just went down. He would've done it himself, but he had other business to attend to."

"Busy beating up the neighborhood drug dealer?"

"Not tonight."

There wasn't a lot more to say. He'd given me plenty to think about.

As promised, before I got out of the car, he handed over a wad of cash.

In a few short hours, the direction of my life had been steered onto an entirely new path.

CHAPTER TWENTY-NINE

Juliet

SCHOOL WAS FINALLY OUT FOR THE SUMMER.

Mrs. Shields had returned from her trip, which meant I needed another way to keep myself out of the house for as many hours a day as possible.

As Roman predicted, my "interview" at Jericho Two consisted of a brief meeting with Uncle Dex's friend where he asked me a few questions before handing over a pile of papers to fill out. His way of saying I was hired.

"Ice cream shop closes right after the second movie starts," Ulfric explained. "You'll be responsible for wiping everything down and cleaning out the machine with the flavor of the day. I'll handle the registers in the morning."

That suited me fine, I didn't want to be responsible for counting the money.

He glanced at the open doorway. "I understand you're Roman's girl. I can trust you two to behave, right?"

My cheeks heated. He wasn't asking in a creepy way, more in the way a father who actually cared about his daughter might warn.

"Yes, sir."

"I'm kidding, sweetheart," he said in his deep, rumbly voice. "Just don't do anything to get your uncle pissed at me."

I'm pretty sure Dex suspected how close Roman and I were. We didn't discuss it, but he'd gone out of his way to help Roman find this job. According to Roman, Dex also threw other side jobs at him. Although when I asked him for details he refused to elaborate.

Either way, I appreciated this opportunity, and I had no intentions of squandering it.

After my very first shift, Roman and I climbed into Mrs. Shields' car together.

"She's still letting you borrow her car?" he asked.

"Just to go to work. She said she doesn't drive at night and she didn't want me taking the bus." I still felt guilty about using her car and wasn't sure how Uncle Jared would tolerate this newfound independence of mine.

"She's a really nice woman." Roman cranked down the window on his side and stared into the night.

"She is. I want to do something to thank her, but I haven't decided what yet."

"I'll help you figure out something." He glanced around the car. "We could take it to get it detailed."

"It's not that dirty."

"Maybe some of those hanging flower baskets she likes for the front porch."

"Oh, that's a great idea! I can run over and water them in the mornings for her."

"Perfect." He leaned over and kissed my cheek. "I'll help you pick them out this weekend."

It would've made more sense to drop Roman off first, but he wouldn't allow it. I parked the car in Mrs. Shields' driveway and he walked me home, refusing to leave until I was safely inside. Then, he'd walk home by himself.

"What if someone mugs you?"

He snorted. "Good luck to them."

He had a point. I felt sorry for anyone who thought they could take Roman on. All the manual work around the movie theater had added a lot of muscle to his already large frame.

Still, I worried. I ran up to my room and watched him walk down the street until I couldn't see him anymore.

As soon as he was able to, he always sent me a text.

Home safe.

"Are you still hanging around with that boy after I told you not to?" Uncle Jared's voice reminded me that in my eagerness to watch Roman walking home, I'd forgotten to close and lock my bedroom door.

I turned and faced my uncle. "Yes. He's good to me." I wouldn't bother explaining that I loved Roman. Or that we were soul mates. Or that after high school we planned to get married. He didn't deserve to know those things.

He stepped into my room and fear knotted my stomach. He hadn't been in here in a very long time.

"Where's Aunt Susan?" I asked, backing up against the window.

The corners of his mouth twitched. "Asleep." He jerked his head toward the window. "You fucking him?"

"That's none of your business."

"Like fuck it's not. I've been taking care of you for years. You owe me some damn respect, girl."

I braced my hand against my nightstand, my fingers brushing against a pair of scissors I'd left there earlier. I curled my hand around them and brought them to my side.

Uncle Jared didn't miss the movement. He smirked. "What are you gonna do with those?"

I straightened my spine and stared back. "Do you really want to find out?"

That seemed to give him second thoughts.

I'm not a scared little girl you can bully and trick anymore.

Slowly, he backed out the door. As soon as he was gone, I raced over, closed, and locked it. Still not feeling it was enough, I tucked my desk chair under the door handle.

I needed out of this house. Where could I go? I couldn't confide in Roman. Not about this. I had no doubt he'd go after my uncle if he knew the truth about how he treated me. And I wouldn't be responsible for Roman getting in trouble.

Mrs. Shields might let me move in with her. But if Aunt Susan made an issue of it, Mrs. Shields might have to go to court and I didn't know if I could ask her to make that kind of commitment.

My eighteenth birthday had never seemed so far away.

CHAPTER THIRTY

Roman

THE SUMMER WAS OURS. JULIET AND I WORKED AS MANY SHIFTS together at the movie theater as possible. Ulfric put me in charge of collecting money at the gate. He said I was scary looking enough that no one would try to sneak in any extra people on my watch. I think it was supposed to be a compliment.

After a few weeks, Juliet was promoted to night manager of the ice cream shop. She had a knack for handling multiple orders with speed, grace, and a sweet smile for every customer.

Once the first movie started and the carloads of people entering slowed, someone else took over at the gate for me. My job was to walk the grounds. Make sure nothing nefarious was happening in one of the drive-in's many dark corners. When that was finished, I was supposed to help clean up in the ice cream shop.

My favorite part of the night.

Juliet and I raced to get the work done so we could sneak over to the darkest corner of the lot where her car was parked. We'd slip inside and frantically tear off our uniforms, sighing and groaning as we came together.

We fogged those windows up every night. Even left handprints on the back windows. Maybe a footprint on the ceiling of the car.

When we were spent, we'd crawl out of the steamy interior, spread a blanket over the grass, and watch the end of whatever movie was playing second that week. Some nights, Juliet fell asleep in my arms, and I hated when it was time to wake her.

It was almost the perfect fantasy life. Except for the end of the night when we had to go to separate homes.

One night, near the end of the summer, we talked about how we'd change up our shifts once school started back up. After Labor Day, the theater would only be open on the weekends. The ice cream shop was still open every afternoon, so Juliet's job was safe. I'd have to look for something else though.

"Chris is leaving to go back to college. Maybe you can take his shifts," she suggested.

"Maybe." I hated that guy. He'd tried asking Juliet out right in front of me on his first day. Never did it again once I'd made it clear who she belonged to.

She rolled her eyes, knowing where my thoughts had gone. "Get over it, Roman. That was weeks ago. He has a girlfriend now."

"Get over it? Get over it?" I reached over and pulled her into my lap. I tickled my hands over her ribs and kissed her neck. "A man doesn't get over another man hittin' on his woman. He gets *even*."

"You've terrorized him enough."

I reached down and squeezed her butt through the tiny denim cutoff shorts she was wearing. She placed a finger over my lips. "You're the only man I want." Her eyes narrowed. "And don't think I didn't notice Jessica flirting with you the other night."

I buried my face against her neck. "You've got nothing to worry about. But I do enjoy your jealousy."

She lightly smacked my shoulder while I shook with laughter.

We teased and joked around with each other all the way home. I hated saying goodnight, but I did it.

Eyes on the prize, I kept reminding myself. I had a good nest egg saved up. More than enough for first and last month's rent on an apartment near the college Juliet was thinking of attending. My eighteenth birthday was a few months away, but I wouldn't graduate until next June. I was hoping that as long as I stayed in school, I could move into my own place and still be eligible for the scholarship Ms. Simpson had told me about.

She hadn't checked in with me in weeks. That wasn't unusual. I hadn't noticed because I'd been too wrapped up in work and Juliet. But I should probably call her soon.

A counselor I didn't recognize met me at the front door.

"You're late."

I bit back the *Who the fuck are you* I wanted to say and glanced at the clock. It was exactly five minutes after midnight. As long as I made it home within fifteen minutes of midnight, Mike and Judy never had a problem.

"Sorry, my shift ran a little late."

"Don't let it happen again," he barked.

I sized him up. Short but bulky. Probably in his twenties. Could already tell he had a complex and would use what power he held over me to make him feel like a bigger man.

Just what I needed.

"Yes, sir," I said. I mentally patted myself on the back for keeping the sarcasm out of my voice. "I'm Roman by the way."

"I know who you are," he sneered.

Okay. "And you are...?"

"Jason. The new weekend counselor."

Great. So I'd be seeing more of this asshole.

He jerked his head toward the stairs. "Get to bed. You need to be up early tomorrow. It's chore day."

"I have to work at noon."

"Not my problem."

Fuck him. I wasn't missing a shift. My schedule had already been approved by the counselors and my caseworker. But I bit my tongue. No sense getting this jackass riled up now. I'd deal with it tomorrow.

"Look, it's golden boy," Squire taunted at the top of the stairs.

"Isn't it past your bedtime, Squire?" I shot back.

"Was waiting up to see if the new guy reamed you out."

I glanced behind me, sure I'd find Jason hot on my tail. He wasn't. "What a dick. Where'd he come from?"

For a minute Squire dropped the attitude and we were allies. Two inmates vs. the warden. "Don't know. But he's a prick for sure. Came down hard on everyone at dinner. Sent us upstairs at nine. On a weekend."

"What bullshit," I growled. "Who'd he replace?"

"Ozzie failed a drug test. So I guess whoever is higher up on the food chain is taking a harder look at this house now. That's why Officer Time Clock was sent here."

"Fuck." Not what I needed just when I had managed to carve out such a sweet setup for myself. I wanted to stay off this guy's radar.

To thank him for the information, I handed over one of the two packs of Twizzlers I'd brought home for Pip and said good night.

"You awake, Pip?" I whispered as I stepped into our room.

He flicked on his flashlight, the light nearly blinding me. I shut the door behind me quickly.

"Heard it was an exciting night."

A few sad sniffles were his only response.

"You okay, Pip?"

"Yeah," he answered.

"Brought you something." I walked closer to his bed and waved the candy at him.

He snatched it out of my hand, immediately tearing into the wrapper.

"Don't you want to wait until tomorrow?"

"No. Officer Hard-Ass will probably confiscate it."

"True."

All night long I tossed and turned, worrying over what trouble this new change would bring to my life.

CHAPTER THIRTY-ONE

Juliet

I couldn't miss the tension in Roman's shoulders when he finally showed up for work the next day.

"What happened?"

"Don't ask," he grumbled, walking past me. Roman had never brushed me off. Something was wrong.

"Hey." I grabbed his arm and tried to turn him to face me, but he might as well have been made of stone.

His shoulders dropped and he took a deep breath before turning around. "Sorry, butterfly." He reached out and tucked a piece of hair behind my ear. "Bad night. Bad morning. There's a new weekend counselor who has made it his mission to make our lives miserable."

"Oh no." Damn. Things had been going so well for him. This was the last thing he needed. "Just the weekends, though, right?"

"So far."

"You all right, son?" Ulfric's big voice boomed over the parking lot. He came up next to Roman and clapped him on the back.

"I'm sorry about getting here late, sir. The house—"

"I got your message. No worries." He nodded toward the lawn. "Grass ain't goin' anywhere."

"Thanks, I appreciate it."

"I feel for you, kid. Living under someone's thumb ain't right. Been avoiding it my whole life."

Ulfric frequently broke into long rambles about the "outlaw life" and "riding the wind." His were more colorful versions of the stories Uncle Dex gave when anyone asked him why he didn't work a regular nine-to-five.

When I'd asked Roman why Ulfric ran a business if he hated rules so much, he'd explained that most likely Ulfric used the drive-in theater and ice cream shop to launder money since they were cash-based businesses. All those "jobs" Uncle Dex had Roman help him with began to take a different shape in my mind after that conversation.

The throaty engine of a car pulling into the gravel parking lot signaled that I had a customer. I waved to Roman and Ulfric before taking off.

A few hours and what felt like a thousand sticky ice cream cones later, Roman snuck up behind me. His strong arms wrapped around my middle and anchored me to his chest. He buried his face against my neck. "Sorry I was a prick earlier," he murmured against my ear.

"It's okay."

He turned me around. "No it's not. You're the only good thing in my life."

"I'm always here for you, Roman. I wish I could do...something."

"Just knowing you love me gets me through, Juliet."

Tears pricked my eyelids. For someone so hard on the outside, he said the sweetest things.

"Do you mind leaving a few minutes early tonight?" he asked. "This clown busted me for being five minutes late last night. I don't wanna put up with his bullshit again."

"Of course." Damn, if we hadn't stopped to fool around last night, he would've been home on time.

Without meaning to, I'd gotten him into trouble.

He didn't send me the usual *home safe* text that night and I lay awake worrying until morning.

CHAPTER THIRTY-TWO

Roman

THE FIRST WEEK OF SCHOOL WAS FINALLY HERE AND THE HOME was utter chaos.

I marveled at the fact that I'd be starting the new school year at the same school that I'd ended the last one with. It had to be a first for me. Maybe I'd make it all the way through to graduation.

Maybe wasn't an option. There was no way I'd leave Juliet.

Pip couldn't contain his excitement. He couldn't wait to finally start high school. He'd found a navy blue polo and a pair of tan pants that looked like a Catholic school uniform. I shook my head and handed him his new backpack.

Jackass Jason—as all the kids in the house now called him— had picked up more shifts in the house. He drove us to school on the first day.

Pip was unusually quiet on the way to school. Maybe the reality of attending a school where more assholes like Sam Squire probably roamed the halls was finally sinking in.

I leaned over and spoke against his ear. Low enough that only he would hear what I had to say. "I got your back, kid. You're gonna be fine."

Finally, he smiled and seemed to relax.

Juliet waited for me at our usual table in the back of the cafeteria. I kissed her senseless before setting her down and introducing her to Pip.

He blinked up at her, completely in awe.

"I'm so happy to finally meet you, Phillip," she gushed. She reached out, pulling him into a sisterly hug which Pip surprisingly accepted.

"All right, that's enough of that," I said, breaking them up.

She snorted at me and returned to her seat. I took the chair next to her. Under the cover of the table, I put my hand on her leg, running it beneath the loose dress she was wearing until I gripped her thigh. Her body automatically responded to my touch. Her legs inched apart and I dared to brush my knuckles against her core.

Her entire body quivered and she took in a shuddering breath. "Roman," she warned in a low voice. "Don't."

"What are you doing?" Pip asked, ducking under the table.

"Get out of there." I reached over and tapped him on the back.

Juliet covered her mouth and laughed.

"I need you. Soon," I whispered in her ear.

Her lashes fluttered.

The magnetic pull to her never lessened. I'd spent the entire summer mapping the contours of her body, knowing her in the most intimate ways possible. Still, my desire for her never went away. It was always there, crackling under my skin when she was near.

Focus.

It was time to settle down and wrap my mind around schoolwork again. For the hundredth time this week, Juliet and I compared our schedules. I wouldn't see much of her in the morning, but we managed to have the same lunch period and shared all of our afternoon classes.

She reached over and plucked Pip's schedule out of his hands. "Do you want me to show you where your classes are?" she asked.

Did Pip want the prettiest girl in the school to show him around? Of course he did. He slowly bobbed his head up and down.

The bell rang. I kissed her cheek and wished Pip luck before heading to my first class.

THE FIRST WEEK back to school was a short one. Despite a bit of leftover restlessness from the summer break, classes had gone well.

I couldn't wait for Friday to be over. I was looking forward to working over the weekend. Both to spend time with Juliet and to make money.

Apparently work would have to wait. After my last class of the afternoon, I received a note from the office that I needed to go straight home.

A bad feeling settled in the pit of my stomach. This had never happened before.

"I have to go home first. But I'll see you at work later," I promised Juliet on the walk to her house.

"Okay."

I didn't dare give her more than a peck on the cheek in front of her uncle's house. Just in case the bastard was lurking nearby.

If I'd known the hell I was about to walk into, I would've taken Juliet's hand and run far, far away instead of going home.

Many cars lined the driveway. Not unusual. We frequently had visitors. Especially when kids were removed or placed here.

Jackass Jason was in the living room with my caseworker and two men I didn't recognize.

"Roman, come here."

My stomach bottomed out.

They were here for *me*.

Memories of all the other times I'd been packed up and shipped off flooded my brain.

I hadn't even done anything wrong.

"What's going on?"

Jason stood up, crossing his arms over his chest. I don't know what I did to piss this guy off, but he seemed to be enjoying himself way too much. "We executed a routine search of your room and found contraband."

"Routine search? I've lived here for months and never been searched before."

"You were overdue."

I took a step closer to Jason. "What contraband?"

He pointed to the coffee table and for the first time I noticed the items laid out in neat plastic bags with notes written in black marker on the outside. My brain struggled to catch up and make sense of what I was seeing. An iPad. Two different cell phones. Marijuana, rolling papers, and a pipe.

"None of that's mine."

"It was found in your room. Under *your* bed. So who else would it belong to?"

"Bullshit. I'm being set up." I turned to Ms. Simpson, seeking her assistance. She had to know this wasn't true. "Do something. You know I'm not a thief."

"Roman—"

"Why would I bust my ass working so many hours if I was gonna steal shit?" The injustice of it boiled my blood.

By this point in my life I already knew what was coming. Don't know why I bothered fighting it.

I was about to lose everything.

The freedom I'd worked so hard to carve out for myself.

Any chance of going to college.

The love I'd found.

Everything familiar was going to be ripped away once again.

"The electronics are bad enough. But you've also brought illegal narcotics into the house," one of the men I didn't know said.

"No I didn't." My hands went to my hair, grabbing a fistful. "Test me. I'll take any test you want. You won't find any drugs in my system." I pointed at the stuff on the table. "Fingerprint that shit. You won't find my prints on any of it."

Jason shifted and looked away. Guess none of that occurred to him.

For the first time, I thought maybe I was getting somewhere and this nightmare would go away. The two strangers looked at each other and then Ms. Simpson. She eyed Jason before addressing me.

"The items will be processed. For now, we need to remove you."

"No!"

Run! Get out!

The two strangers tackled me before I reached the front door, slamming me into the wall. "Relax, son. Relax."

"You fucking relax. I'm being set up."

They zip tied my hands behind my back. I glanced up the staircase and found Pip, Squire, Janet, and the rest of the kids watching the spectacle.

Squire pouted and wiped a fake tear off his cheek. Janet wiggled her fingers at me and mouthed, "Bye-bye."

They did this.

Tears ran down Pip's cheeks and he shook his head.

Who would protect him from the bigger kids if I wasn't here?

"Don't do this." Realizing Pip would be all alone reduced me to begging. "Ms. Simpson, please. You know I'm innocent." With my face mashed up against the wall, my words came out muffled.

"We'll sort it out, Roman," she said with a little more authority.

But it was too little too late.

They could sort it out later, but the damage would be done. My life would be upended. Even if I was vindicated, the chances of me being returned to Pine Bluff were slim.

The two officers marched me out the front door and into a van. "Where are we going?"

"A more secure facility."

Kiddie prison.

"I just started the school year."

"They have a school there."

Great, I was headed to a facility where I wouldn't be allowed to leave the grounds. Not even to go to school.

Juliet.

I had no way to contact her. Even if my backpack somehow made it to the place I was going, they'd search it and find my phone. She was going to be so worried.

My job would be gone too. I had no hope anyone involved would have the decency to call and let Ulfric know why I wouldn't be coming in this weekend.

I yanked at the restraints on my wrists. Tears of rage welled up, burning my eyes, but I gritted my teeth until they dried up.

I wouldn't give them the satisfaction of my tears.

They wouldn't break me.

CHAPTER THIRTY-THREE

Juliet

BY SUNDAY I WAS OUT OF MY MIND WITH WORRY. SOMETHING BAD must have happened to Roman.

As soon as I realized Roman wouldn't be showing up for work Friday night, I told Ulfric about the ominous message he had received at school.

He shook his head. "Fucking bastards," he'd muttered.

I called Uncle Dex to see if he could do anything.

"I'll see what I can find out, Julez. But I'm not family. I'll have a hard time getting anyone to talk to me."

After work Sunday night, I went to see Mrs. Shields. While watering the flowers Roman and I bought her earlier in the summer, I broke down crying.

Behind me the screen door clicked open and thumped shut.

"Honey, what's wrong?" Mrs. Shields pulled me into the warm circle of her arms and stroked her hand over my hair.

I spilled all my fears and worry to her.

"Oh, Juliet." She sounded so distressed, I felt bad for telling her. "Poor Roman. What can I do?"

For a moment we were both quiet. What could she do? What could I do? I'd never felt more powerless.

"Do you think I could apply to be his foster parent?" she finally asked.

I wiped the tears off my cheeks and stared at her. "You'd do that?"

"Of course. He's a good boy. He deserves some stability." She hesitated. "I might be too old to be approved as a foster parent, though. I don't know."

"I don't think so." My heart already felt lighter. They'd be crazy to turn her down. Mrs. Shields had a lovely home and lots of time to give. She'd be a perfect foster parent for Roman. This might actually work. It had to.

"I'll call my lawyer tomorrow morning and see if he can help me figure out where to start," she promised.

"Thank you. Thank you so much, Mrs. Shields."

MONDAY MORNING, I waited out front for the Pine Bluff van to arrive. Praying Roman would be on it. Maybe the home found his phone and he was grounded for the weekend, but he'd show up for school. Everything would be okay.

Everything was *not* okay.

The van pulled up to the curb. I didn't recognize the driver and I was afraid to approach. I doubted he'd answer any of my questions anyway. Instead, I waited for Pip.

He trudged down the van steps last.

"Pip!" I called out.

"Aw, you waiting for your fuck boy?" Sam taunted.

"Sorry, he's not coming today," Janet added. "So sorry."

I hated these two. Roman never talked about them much, but it didn't take a genius to know there was friction among the three of them. Sam Squire had bully written all over his aggressive posture. If I knew Roman, he stood up for the kids Sam probably enjoyed picking on.

"Where is he?" I asked, pushing into Sam's space.

"Back off, bitch." He lowered his filthy face until it was inches from mine. "He's *gone*."

My stomach churned. Gone where?

"What did you do?"

"Who, me?" Sam pretended to be offended. "Nothing, darlin'." He slung his arm around Janet's shoulders and the two of them strolled inside together, smug as two slugs.

A cry of pure fury burst out of me.

"They took him Friday night," Pip said in a quiet voice.

I glanced down at him and wanted to cry. Misery was written all over his pale face. In the dark circles under his eyes and the tension lines around his mouth. Losing Roman had hit him hard.

"Who took him? What happened?"

He gestured toward a bench away from the other kids and we moved over to it for privacy.

"Sam's been gunning for him for a while. First, Evie and he tried to set Roman up. Janet's been pissed since Evie got sent away. She stole some stuff from school and the two of them planted the stuff and some drugs under Roman's bed. Our room had a 'surprise' search and that was it."

"Where'd they send him?"

"I don't know." His bony shoulders lifted in a sad shrug. "They don't tell us stuff like that."

My heart broke at the note of acceptance in Pip's defeated voice. I understood, though. He'd probably gained and lost many friends while in foster care. My brain refused to accept the harsh reality of the situation. The connection Roman and I shared was special. Our futures were already woven together.

I wouldn't abandon him at the first bump in our road we encountered.

CHAPTER THIRTY-FOUR

Roman

THERE WAS NOTHING REGAL ABOUT THE CASTLE CORRECTIONAL Center. The gladiator-like environment had a different set of rules than the Pine Bluff home.

This was more like a prison. To prepare us for where most of us would end up once we were released from the state's "care."

In fact, we weren't far from the county jail. When kids acted up—pretty much every day—and the counselors didn't want to deal with it, they dialed 911 and let the cops cart us away.

It was a place designed to turn broken children into monsters.

I was isolated from the rest of the inmates—I mean kids—for the first week. That was fun. First, I'm kidnapped from "home." Everything normal in my life stripped away. Then, I'm shoved in a room by myself for my "safety."

Every nerve in my body was on edge. What was Juliet doing? Thinking? She must be so worried about me. Would she go to the house? Ask what happened? God, I hoped not. I couldn't stand the thought of someone telling her I was a thief.

She'd know it was lies. We were so deeply connected, she'd have to know I'd never do anything that would pull me away from her.

After five days, I finally wrangled a pen, envelope, stamp, and piece of paper from one of the counselors.

CHAPTER THIRTY-FIVE

Dear Juliet,

I can't imagine what you're thinking right now. But know this—I was set up. Probably by Janet and Squire. I never would've purposely done anything that would've taken me away from you.

You can write me here, just know someone will read your letters before I see them.

Please look out for Pip if you can.

Love,

Roman

I SOBBED with relief when I opened the mailbox and spotted Roman's familiar, blocky handwriting.

The envelope shredded under my eager fingers and I carefully tucked the pieces back together so I didn't lose the return address.

He was okay.

I ran up to my room and quickly wrote my own letter. If I hurried, I could run to the post office and mail it before they closed for the day.

CHAPTER THIRTY-SIX

Dear Roman,

I'm so happy to finally hear from you! Pip explained what happened. I'm so sorry and angry.

Don't be embarrassed, but I spoke to Mrs. Shields. I don't want to give you false hope, because I'm not sure how things will turn out, but she talked to her lawyer. They are working on getting her approved as a foster parent, so you can live with her. Wouldn't that be amazing? You could come back to school. And we'd see each other every day.

I'll be here waiting for you.

All my love,

Juliet

SADLY, Juliet's letter gave me no hope. Sure, I got choked up thinking of Mrs. Shields going through the trouble on my behalf. Did I think it would work out? Nope. Nothing in my life had ever gone in my favor. Why should my luck change?

"Letter from your girl?" my new roommate asked from the top bunk across from mine. So far, we had the room to ourselves, but there were two more spaces left. I dreaded who they might place with us. Griff was around my age and seemed to have the same fuck-off-and-let-me-do-my-time-in-peace attitude I'd developed. He wasn't an orphan, but from the brief things he'd said about his parents, he might as well have been. He'd already been at the Castle for a few months. As soon as I got tossed in his room, he took on a big brother role. It annoyed me almost as much as I appreciated the protection. His concern gave me some breathing room to get used to my surroundings.

"Yeah," I answered.

"Nice." He held up his own small stack of mail. "It's nice to know someone gives a shit, right?"

He tore into an envelope and tugged out a piece of notebook paper with a 4x6 photo tucked inside. Girlish writing in various shades of purple and pink filled the page.

"You got your own girl writing you letters?" I asked.

His face broke into a grin and he chuckled. "Nah. My best friend's baby sister." He reached down, placing his hand next to his knee. "Known her since she was little." He shook the neatly written page. "She writes me letters like this when I'm home, too."

"They live far away?"

He laughed even harder. "No. I live right around the block from them. She just likes writing letters. Has a thing for colorful pens." He waved the page at me again.

"Cute. Reminds me of my last roommate." A wave of sadness washed over me. Who was Pip's roommate now? Was he safe? At least Juliet got to talk to him at school. Who knew I'd miss the little bugger so much?

Shouts and scuffling echoed in the hallway outside of our room. I groaned and stared at the ceiling. Every damn day with this shit. Except here, the counselors didn't try to break up the pathetic battles for dominance. Hell, half the time they instigated the fights and placed bets.

My roommate also happened to be one of the best fighters currently housed at the Castle.

"Christ," Griff grumbled. He jumped off his bunk and shoved our door closed. "I only got a few weeks left. Don't need to be dragged into any bullshit."

"I hear that," I mumbled. I had an appointment with my caseworker this afternoon. Unless she was coming to tell me I was leaving this hellhole, I didn't want to see her. But it's not like I had a choice. I sure as shit didn't want to get written up for fighting right before our meeting.

"You got homework?" Griff asked.

I shot a glare at him. "No, Dad, I don't."

Education here was an exercise in futility. No one learned anything useful. Kids acted out, disrupting the class constantly. The "teachers" themselves barely paid attention. I opted to enroll in the GED program. From the practice tests they gave me, it didn't seem too difficult.

That was my new plan. Get my GED, turn eighteen, and get the fuck out of here.

The state couldn't hold me hostage after my birthday. Legally, I'd be an adult. They'd have to release me, right? A few phone calls to the attorney who once represented me hadn't yielded any meaningful answers.

One of the wardens popped into our room. "Griff, you wanna fight tonight?"

Griff raised his head and scowled. "Fuck no, Ollie. I'm outta here in two weeks."

Ollie scanned Griff in a long, slow way. As if he was trying to mentally calculate how much money he could make off of Griff's fighting skills before he got released. "As long as you win, I got your back," the guard promised.

Meaning he wouldn't write Griff up or call the cops and add time to his sentence.

How generous of you, asshole.

An uncomfortable silence stretched between them. I flattened myself against my bunk, breathing as quietly as possible, praying Ollie wouldn't notice my presence.

Over the last few weeks, I'd watched the counselors pressure and arrange several fights between the kids. If you said no, they'd set you up to get in trouble. If you answered yes, you had to either get the shit beaten out of you or pummel someone bloody.

Even with the rage brewing inside me, both seemed like shitty options.

When Griff didn't change his answer, Ollie turned his greedy eyes my way.

Fuck.

Ollie took a few steps toward my bunk. "How about you, pretty boy?"

"No thanks."

"Can't fight?" He crept closer to my bunk until he was staring in my eyes.

"Nope," I answered without flinching.

"Big guy like you." His calculating gaze studied me. "I don't believe that."

"You trying to date him or get him in the ring?" Griff muscled his way between us. "I'm in. Who you got for me to fuck up?"

I shook my head. "Griff, don't—"

He shrugged me off. "It's cool, Roman."

Ollie took Griff aside and in a hushed voice I couldn't overhear, gave him some instructions. A few seconds later, he left.

I sat up and swung my legs over the edge of the bunk. "You're so close to getting out, Griff," I reminded him. "Don't risk it. You got people who depend on you."

His jaw ticked and I wished I'd chosen better words to voice my concerns.

"I'll have to get in the ring at some point," I added, hating the note of defeat in my voice.

The hard expression on his face melted into the easier, casual grin he usually wore. "I'm gonna have to teach you a few things before I go." He squinted at me. "You really can't fight? Figured a guy your size would get challenged a lot, living in a group home."

"I can defend myself." Fuck knew I'd encountered enough bullies over the years. "And protect the younger kids in the house. But I don't willingly fling myself into a fight if I can help it."

"Gotcha." He clucked his tongue and tapped the side of his head. "Smart." He pointed to our small bar-covered window. "Out there, it's always better to diffuse a fight with words, if you can." His smile slipped. "I've never really had that opportunity."

I opened my mouth to mutter *sorry*, or something equally lame, but he cut me off.

"Real world rules don't apply in here. Always be ready to use your fists," he finished.

"Fantastic," I grumbled.

"It can get wild inside. But for the most part, you don't have to worry about weapons being pulled during an official fight. At least the guards keep things one-on-one. You won't get jumped by multiple people."

"*Greaaat.*" I drew out the word with slow sarcasm that Griff ignored. "I feel so safe and warm now. Thanks."

"No rounds. Fights go until someone taps out or they're physically unable to continue. Once they hit the floor, you gotta back off or the guards *will* hammer you." He reached out and tapped my jaw. "Tuck your chin to your chest if you're being taken down. Don't wanna crack that handsome noggin on the ground."

I blew out an annoyed breath. "I'd rather avoid getting taken down at all."

"Eh." he shrugged. "Sometimes, fighting from the ground gives you an advantage."

"I'll take your word for it."

He stretched his arms straight out in front of his chest. "Never try to save yourself from a fall with your arms out. Good way to break a bone. When striking—use elbows or palm strikes if possible, so you're not breaking bones in your hands or fingers." He held up his right hand to show off his slightly crooked ring finger. "We don't exactly enjoy platinum medical care in here."

No matter how much I tried to avoid it, fighting would become my means of survival.

CHAPTER THIRTY-SEVEN

Roman

MAJOR CHANGES IN OUR LIVING SITUATION HAPPENED WITHIN A few days.

Griff and I were hanging out in our room when our door swung wide open, banging into the wall with a thud.

"Got a new roomie for you two," Ollie said, shoving a tall, beefy kid holding a stack of blue sweats against his chest into our room. "Play nice." Ollie cackled and slammed the door shut.

"Fuck no!" Griff grinned, jumping off his bunk. "What are you doing here, Eraser?"

They embraced and thumped each other's backs like long-lost twins. Thank fuck. Maybe this would give Griff the opportunity to big brother all over someone else for a change.

"What's with the orange jammies?" Griff slapped his friend's chest.

"Just got out of solitary."

I lifted my head at the voice and looked at the kid closer. "Easton?"

He turned and stared at me. Yup, it had to be him. I jumped off my bunk.

"Roman. Holy shit. The fuck you been eating, Miracle-Gro?"

He ambled over and tossed his clothes on the bottom bunk, then crushed me in a big bear hug.

"I could say the same about you." I patted his back and pulled away to look him over again. "How you been?"

"Well," he ran his hands down the front of his orange scrub top, "not great, obviously. But I'm alive and still fuckin' shit up, so that's something, right?"

"Yeah." I slapped his outstretched hand, clasped it and yanked him in for another quick hug. "That's everything."

"So, I take it you two know each other," Griff said, joining us.

"We crossed paths at a foster home or two," I explained.

"Mrs. Camp's house for wayward kids," Easton agreed. "Heard she kicked the bucket awhile back."

"I heard her daughter's like a social worker or some shit now."

"Missy? That chick was always asking me to look at the moles on her vag."

I choked on a laugh. "All righty then. I could've lived a perfectly fine life never knowing that."

"She never pulled her pants down for you?"

I could barely get out an answer through my laughter. "No."

"Christ, that shit scarred me for life." He shivered with disgust. "Got bounced outta there because of her."

"That's fucked up."

Easton slapped Griff's shoulder, then mine. "I can't believe you two are roomies. Just when I thought this stint was gonna fuckin' break me."

"I only got a few weeks left," Griff said. "I hope."

Easton nodded. "What about you, Roman?"

"No idea. Got sent up from a group home on some bullshit."

"Sorry, bro."

Griff patted Easton's back. "You're in luck, Roman. Eraser's a beast in the cage. He'll help me train you."

"What's this *Eraser* shit?" I asked, ignoring the part about them training me.

The two of them shared a sly smirk.

"It's a ring name he picked up." Griff dropped to a low, dramatic crouch, sweeping his arms through the air like a dive-bar magician. "Our boy can make someone disappear with his fists," he added in a low, theatrical voice.

"Good to know." I chuckled and made a jerking off motion with my fist. "I was thinking it was 'cause you got caught rubbing one out."

Eraser burst out laughing. "Fuck no."

"Hey." Griff's expression turned serious. "How's Ella doing? Where's she at?"

Eraser side-eyed Griff. "I'm gonna ignore the fact that you brought my girl's name up after talk of rubbin' one out and assume your question is genuine."

Griff's mouth flattened to a thin line, but his cheeks twitched. "Bro, I swear I'm serious."

Whoever Ella was, the mention of her name sucked all the humor out of Eraser. "I don't know, Griff. I gotta get the fuck outta here so I can track her down."

"You best stop gettin' your ass thrown in solitary then."

"No shit."

"Give me whatever information you've got. I'll pass it along to Remy. See if he can find her."

"Thanks." The two of them shuffled over to the beat-up desk in the corner to talk quietly.

I hopped back in my bunk and pulled out one of Juliet's letters.

"You got a girl, Roman?" Eraser asked.

I held up the paper in my hand. "Yeah. Juliet."

"Roman and Juliet?" he snickered. "You serious?"

I rolled my eyes.

"Oh shit. I just got that." Griff giggled like a little fuckin' kid. "That's precious."

"I wouldn't announce it took you that long, Griff. Makes you sound like an illiterate fuck." Eraser gave his buddy a quick shove.

"Fuck both of you," I grumbled.

"She pretty?" Eraser asked.

"Who?"

"Your girl."

My mouth curved up. "Prettiest girl I've ever laid eyes on."

"Aww!" they shouted.

Eraser hopped up on my bunk, swinging his legs over the side.

"Don't get comfortable," I warned him. "I'm not trading." We'd shared a room for a couple months when we were kids, and I liked the guy well enough. This reunion was fun and all, but I wasn't going to let him push me around. Didn't give a fuck what his new nickname was.

"Ease up." He lifted his chin toward Griff's side of the room. "I'll take the bottom bunk on his side."

"Damn right," Griff muttered. "Your big ass ain't sleeping over my head."

"Dude, do you even fit on that mattress?" Eraser waved his hand at the bed. "Your mega clown feet probably hang over the edge."

"Keep it up and I'll shove one of my clown feet up your ass." Griff lifted one sneakered foot in the air.

They cracked up and continued trading insults.

"Hey, let's go down to the gym and teach Roman a few skills," Griff suggested.

Was he serious? Now? "I'm plenty skilled."

"In here, the fights are different from anything you've seen on the outside." Griff's grave tone got under my skin. "It's not the same as defending yourself when you know a teacher or counselor will break it up any minute."

"You've clearly never spent time in any group homes," I said.

"No, he's right, Roman," Eraser chimed in. "Guards place bets. They want a good show."

"I've noticed." I wasn't getting out of this. One way or another I'd probably get tossed in the ring at some point. If these two were that good, I'd be stupid not to let them train me.

I stashed Juliet's letter away and sat up. "All right. Let's go."

Griff glanced at the clock over the door. "We got time before dinner."

Eraser changed into his blue sweats. We looked like deranged triplets in our matching outfits and Velcro sneakers.

The gray corridor was dark and highlighted by a stripe of orange paint for us to line up on in the mornings. The guys took a left. I'd been down to the gym once or twice. Each time, a fight had broken out. I preferred to do some bodyweight exercises—push-ups, planks, pull-ups—in the comfort of my cell, without worrying about someone dropping a stack of weights on my back.

We passed a guard who remained expressionless. Griff and Eraser ignored him, so I did the same.

"Royal, pull your pants up," he barked when we were a few feet away. "You're not on the street. That gang look doesn't fly in here."

"Fucker." Griff yanked up his loose pants and fiddled with the drawstring. "Food is so shitty. I've dropped like ten pounds since I got here."

"Don't even," Eraser grumbled. "They legit fed me an apple and a bottle of water every day down in solitary. Nothin' else."

"Jesus Christ, how is this place still open?" Griff jumped up and tapped one of the signs hanging from the ceiling. "State shoulda shut it down by now."

"Maybe you can lead that crusade when you get out." Eraser

slapped his friend's shoulder. "No one gives a fuck about us delinquents."

"True that." Griff slapped another sign.

This time, the gym wasn't crowded. The few who were working out were already chiseled like stone statues. Hard, expressionless faces. Dead eyes following our every move. I recognized two from fights I'd witnessed in the cafeteria. They glared at us but no one uttered a word. Griff and Eraser glared right back, then headed straight for the dumbbells and a bench in the corner without exchanging words.

Griff didn't grab weights right away. He picked up a medicine ball and chucked it at me. "You know how to do mountain climbers?"

I caught the ball and held it against my side. "Yeah, I can do them."

"Try 'em with that. It'll ratchet up your balancing skills and work your core." He slapped his stomach.

"Uh, okay." I glanced at the ball and then the floor. Did he mean *right now*?

"Once you get in that ring, it's a few blows shy of kill or be killed," Griff said. His expression remained smooth and serious.

"The more scars you get, the better fighter you'll be," Eraser added.

"Let's try not to collect any scars." Griff scowled at his buddy. "But Eraser's got a point. The more opponents you spar with, the better you'll get over time."

"And there's no shortage of fuckers to fight in here." Eraser cast a malicious glare around the workout room.

They spent the next hour kicking my ass. My baby workouts were barely a warm-up for these two savages. Regular planks weren't good enough. They introduced me to side planks and star planks, then plank *push-ups* for fuck's sake.

"Enough with the fucking planks," I groaned. "I'm ready to throw up."

Eraser shoved a bottle of water at me.

I sucked down half of it before setting it on the floor. "I thought you wanted to teach me how to fight?"

"Nah. First we gotta build up your balance and core strength, little buddy." Griff gave me a pat on the head to go along with his patronizing tone.

I lifted my shirt. "My core strength is solid as a rock."

Griff launched his fist at my gut. It hit like a missile, pulsing through my body.

"The fuck?" I wheezed.

"That was a fraction of what he can do," Eraser said.

"Come on." Griff patted my shoulder. "Your girl will be all hot and bothered when you come back shredded."

I scowled at him. "My girl's never complained."

After that day, we spent every afternoon in the gym. They tortured—I mean *trained*—me with sadistic glee.

After a few sessions, I felt stronger mentally and physically. And by lights out, I was exhausted, which meant fewer sleepless nights staring at the ceiling worrying about my future.

CHAPTER THIRTY-EIGHT

Roman

THE PA SYSTEM CRACKLED TO LIFE. CONVERSATION IN THE cafeteria stopped while everyone waited for the announcement.

"Roman Hawkins to the front office."

My gaze shot to the door and I groaned.

A few people made obnoxious "you're in trouble" noises. But one quick glare from Eraser and they shut up fast.

"Think it's your caseworker?" Griff asked.

"It better be." I slammed my spork on the tray and stood.

"Good luck," Eraser called after me.

The guard at the door nodded as I dumped my tray. "Go ahead."

Behind me, the cafeteria returned to its usual level of noise.

I shuffled down the long, dim corridor, tucking my freezing fingers up under my sleeves. This place was so damn cold all the time.

I stopped in front of a set of locked double doors and waited to be buzzed into the office. Ms. Simpson stood when she saw me.

She flashed a bright smile. "How are you, Roman?"

Was she for real? *Kiddie prison's a blast, thanks.* "Fine."

"Let's talk."

I followed her into a smaller office without answering. There wasn't much to say. She was nothing more than another person, in a long line of people, who'd betrayed me in my lifetime.

She closed the door and gestured for me to take a seat in the crooked chair across from an empty, beat-up old wooden desk. She took a seat behind it. It didn't belong to anyone; no family photos, pen cups, or anything personal on the surface. The caseworkers just used this room to meet with us from time to time. It was as dismal as the rest of the place.

"It's official. No one's pressing charges for the stolen items." She smiled as if I should be grateful.

"Am I supposed to say thanks? You know damn well I didn't do it."

A slight frown wrinkled her brow and she ducked her head, shuffling through a folder full of forms in front of her. "I found another facility for you. We can work on the transfer papers now. It's in a different school district..."

"Of course it is." The best I could hope for now is that it would be somewhere near a bus line so I could see Juliet.

She sighed and shuffled through some papers, then opened her briefcase and pulled out another stack of forms. "Do you know a Mrs. Emma Shields?"

Finally, a spark of hope lit in my chest, but I answered with caution. "Yeah, why?"

"Her attorney has contacted the agency and inquired about fostering you. What's your connection to her?"

"She's my girlfriend's neighbor." I shrugged. "Juliet and I helped her out from time to time."

"Well, she's been very persistent."

The weight of the hope building inside me stole my breath.

"Really?" I choked out. Mrs. Shields was that worried about me? She cared that much?

"Yes. So, you can either wait here to see if her application is accepted and she passes the home evaluation. Or I can get you transferred to the new facility and if things work out, then you'd move in with her."

This was probably the first time I'd been given a choice over anything concerning my life. Stay in this hellhole or move into the unknown?

Both options sucked.

"How long will it take for her to get approved?"

"I've asked them to fast-track her application, but it could still be a few more weeks."

I was pathetically unprepared to make such a big decision, so I tried weighing the options. Here, was familiar. I knew what I was dealing with. Griff and Eraser had my back. A new facility could be worse. "Whatever. I'll stay here."

We both knew my answer didn't matter. No matter where I was placed, I was only killing time until I turned eighteen.

Unless I went to live with Mrs. Shields. Maybe I could salvage something of my former life if I had some stability.

For the first time in a long time, I had hope.

The long walk back to my room didn't seem like a march to death row for once.

I pushed open the door. Griff was instantly in my face.

"How'd it go? You getting out?"

"Not yet." I motioned for him to back up. "My girlfriend's neighbor is trying to apply to foster me. So Simpson's fast-tracking that application."

Griff held his hand up high and I clasped it, giving him a quick shoulder-bump. "All right."

Eraser gave me a quick thump on the back too. "That's good news."

"I'm trying not to get too excited about it," I confessed.

"I hear you." Eraser nodded. "My uncle's been trying to get

me placed with him for months, but they keep jerking him around."

From what I'd picked up about how the system operated, I assumed his uncle had a criminal record or major health condition. Otherwise, the state would be thrilled to drop a kid off with a relative. But I didn't want to pry. We shared a lot of information with each other, but some details were just off-limits.

"That sucks."

He shrugged.

I tried to shove it out of my head while I lined up with everyone else for the nighttime routine. Marched single-file to the dorm-style bathrooms. Only six of us allowed in at a time. Eyes forward. Use bathroom in front of everyone. Don't make eye contact. Three-minute shower. Watch my back. Brush teeth. Watch my back. Pretend none of this is happening. Shuffle into the changing area. Slip into my long-sleeved thermal night shirt that scratched my elbows every time I turned over, and another pair of sweatpants. Marched back to my room.

Fun times.

Kids yelled. Fights broke out. Guards talked shit.

I ignored it all, crawled into my bunk, closed my eyes, and waited for lights out.

Somewhere in his foster care journey Eraser had picked up some esoteric, manifesting, bullshit visualization techniques.

Since Griff and I had no idea what he was rambling about, Eraser had appointed himself our *visualization guide*, forcing us to name and visualize the things we wanted for our futures. So, after we were all tucked into our bunks and the guards had stopped by to make sure the lights were off, instead of falling asleep, Eraser expected me to ruminate about all the things I wanted but couldn't have.

"Come on, Roman," Eraser insisted. "I swear this works."

"And yet, you somehow haven't *manifested* your ass out of here," I commented.

"I'm taking the necessary steps to improve my situation."

Fuck if this guy didn't have an answer for everything.

Surprisingly, Griff went along with this woo-woo crap. "Keep your negative energy on that side of the room, Roman. We're all peace and light over here."

"Peace and light my ass. I saw that vicious jab you gave Egghead in the cafeteria when no one was looking."

"*That* was karmic justice," Griff said.

The two idiots across the room laughed and slapped palms.

"Okay, seriously," Eraser said. "Get clear on what you want in your life. You listening, Roman?"

"Zzzz," I fake snored.

Something that sounded like the soft rubber sole of a state-issued sneaker bounced off the metal frame of my bed.

"I'm serious," Eraser insisted.

"I'm visualizing you shutting the fuck up." I stretched my arm down, searching for something to throw back. That was the problem with the top bunk. Not much was within throwing distance.

"I'm visualizing my Seventies Chevelle," Griff said.

"What color?" Eraser prompted.

"Black. Red and purple pinstripes."

"Why red and purple?" I asked.

"Don't question," Eraser scolded.

I made a face at the ceiling. "Sheesh."

"What's your ride, Eraser?" Griff asked.

"Mustang for running at the track. F-250 for the winter," Eraser said. "Harley-Davidson Road King for the summer."

"A Harley?" Griff sputtered. "A sport bike will cut corners much better. Faster too."

I rolled over and propped my head on my hand. "I thought we weren't supposed to question?"

"Shh." Griff laughed.

"The Road King is a sweet ride," Eraser explained. "Better for two."

"I think my girlfriend's uncle has one of those," I said.

"You into bikes, Roman?" Eraser asked.

"Yeah, sure." I scoffed. "I dabble in motorcycles with all my trust fund money."

They snorted with laughter.

"He's in an MC and talks about riding all the time," I explained. "Sounds like fun, I guess."

"Whoa." The bed creaked under Eraser as he turned my way. "Around here? Which MC?"

"Uh, the Lost Kings? My old boss at the drive-in theater was in a different MC. The Wolf Knights."

"Jesus. Don't go around dropping biker's names. They get mad pissed about that," Griff said.

"He asked." I waved my hand at Eraser even though it was dark and they probably couldn't see me. "I'm not dropping names. Just stating facts."

"He means, outside of here," Eraser clarified. "Be careful talking about biker business. They're real secretive and shit."

I already knew that from working for Ulfric and tagging along on "jobs" with Dex. "How do *you* know so much about it?"

"My uncle used to run with a few clubs back in the day."

"That one fighter I told you about is a Lost King," Griff said. "He's like a fucking gladiator in the ring."

"I haven't met anyone else besides her uncle," I said, afraid to even mention Dex's name now.

"All right, so what's your vehicle, then, Roman?" Eraser asked.

"A magic fucking carpet to get me the hell out of here," I grumbled.

"He's afraid," Griff said with knowing smugness.

"I ain't afraid of shit."

"You gotta clear your resistance, Roman," Eraser said with an eager note that didn't annoy me as much as usual. "Whatever fear you have around achieving the life you want, remove it."

That struck a chord. Resistance came naturally to me. Everything in my life had always been out of my control. Any effort to change things seemed embarrassingly futile.

"All right," I sighed. "Go on."

"Work on getting a clear picture," Eraser said. "*Feel* what it would be like to have what you want."

The tiny seed of hope planted by Ms. Simpson's visit took root. I closed my eyes and allowed myself to picture Mrs. Shields' house. The warm, inviting kitchen. Her kind smile while she offered us banana bread. Juliet was there too, of course. Under the kitchen table, I slid my hand over Juliet's and we linked fingers.

My mind moved to the bedroom upstairs where Juliet and I had lost our virginity to each other.

Whoops.

Nope, shouldn't go there. Thinking about sex when I was supposed to be "manifesting" would probably make my dick fall off or something.

Flower baskets. The baskets we bought and hung for Mrs. Shields. Pretty flowers dangling over the sides, swinging in the gentle spring breeze. *Car.* Mrs. Shields' car. Adding wiper fluid. Changing the oil for her. *The lawn.* Mrs. Shields wouldn't have to hire people to do yardwork. I would earn my keep by mowing the lawn and weeding her flowerbeds while I lived there. I could go grocery shopping with her so she'd never have to worry about the clerks packing her bags too heavy again.

Outside our door, metal scraped against metal. The lock clicked. Light from the hallway grew brighter.

"Griff?" Ollie whispered. "You awake?"

None of us moved or breathed.

"Egghead's still running his mouth. You wanna fight him tonight?" Ollie asked.

Still no answer from any of us.

"What about you, Hawkins?" Footsteps approached my bed. I forced myself to remain blank-faced and my breathing slow and even. "Heard you been working out every day with these two clowns. Gettin' shredded for a reason, aren't you?"

The footsteps stopped. Hot breath warmed the side of my face and I tried not to recoil.

"Hmm," Ollie grunted. "Or you just wanna look pretty for your boyfriends? That it? The three of you up to some freaky shit in here when no one's lookin'?"

Slam. My whole bed rattled.

"The fuck?" I mumbled.

Ollie kicked the metal frame again.

"All right," Griff shouted. "I'll do it. Leave him alone."

"Griff, don't." I sat up and shook off the pretense of sleep.

Griff was so close to getting out, I didn't want to see this go bad and have him thrown in solitary or something.

"I'll go." Eraser sat up and pounded his fist against his palm.

"All three of you. Come on. We need an audience or it's no fun." Ollie jerked his head toward the door.

I jumped down off my bunk.

Griff moved in front of me, holding his arms out to the sides. "Roman's just there to watch."

I don't know why he bothered. Trying to bargain with Ollie was like signing a contract with a minion of the devil. It could be revoked at any time.

"Yeah, your boyfriend's safe tonight," Ollie said.

Not feeling reassured, I grabbed a hoodie and slipped it over my head. It didn't have drawstrings—just in case one of us tried to hang ourselves to escape this miserable place—so the hood flapped around my face, but at least it was warm.

Eraser shook his head but motioned for me to follow them.

Ollie stopped at another room and dragged two more kids out of bed. We all silently nodded to each other.

The five of us followed Ollie to the basement.

On the stairs, I caught Eraser's eye and I swear the two of us shared the same thought. Five against one. We could push Ollie down the stairs and make a run for it. Most likely the cameras were shut off to keep the other guards from finding out about the underground fights.

Where the fuck would we go, though?

This place was way the fuck out in the middle of nowhere. Five fugitives would stick out among the fields of grass and cows. It was getting colder. PJs and a hoodie wouldn't offer much protection.

Ollie unlocked a heavy metal door and pushed us through.

The room was a wide, concrete nightmare of flickering lights, dirty corners, and leaking overhead pipes. In the center, someone had painted a wide red circle. Several rusty splotches stained the inside of the circle.

My heart jumped in my throat. I didn't want to be here.

"Watch him," Griff said to Eraser in a low voice, his gaze shifting to me. "And stay out of it."

Eraser clenched his jaw but nodded.

"If things get out of control, find a corner and sit with your back to the wall. When the guards get here, lay down on your belly, hands on your head," Griff instructed. "Got it?"

If he thought I was going to sit and watch while these animals ganged up on him, he was out of his mind, but I nodded to reassure him. He needed to go into the fight with a clear head.

A guard I recognized from one of the other units walked in with three of his inmates. He and Ollie argued briefly, then shook hands. More guards and kids came down until the room was somewhat crowded. I even recognized off-duty guards in their street clothes among the people placing bets. So many people seemed to be taking part in this savagery that I started to wonder if *I* was the crazy one.

"All two-faced pieces of shit," Eraser whispered to me, as if he knew what was bubbling in my brain.

No one made any official announcements or anything like that. The guards huddled together. Someone walked around and collected money. Kids got called into the ring. The bloodshed began. No time to waste.

Griff had stripped down to his shorts by the time he got called into the ring. Most of the kids did. Easier to fight without worrying about being strangled by your sweatshirt.

He jumped in place to pump himself up and scanned the crowd. I lifted my hand quickly and he nodded.

Egghead really did have a head shaped like an egg. He was a mean bastard too. Always talking shit and lashing out at the other kids. At least I wouldn't feel bad when Griff kicked his ass.

"Go!" one of the guards shouted.

A hush fell over the room. Griff and Egghead circled each other slowly. Egghead was strong—I'd watched him throw a weight bench into the wall one afternoon and flip over a cafeteria table another time—but he was slow. Griff was strong *and* quick on his feet. In another life, he'd probably be training to be an MMA fighter or something.

Egghead rushed Griff, diving for his middle. Griff grabbed Egghead and shoved his face straight into his knee. Blood gushed from Egghead's nose and Griff shoved him away.

"Ooo!" The crowd erupted.

Lurching to his feet, Egghead came at Griff again. This time Griff threw two punches to the kid's face, turned, and threw an elbow to his jaw.

Egghead hit the ground and didn't get back up.

"Too short!" a guard yelled.

There was a commotion by the side of the ring. Ollie took Griff aside. At first Griff shook his head, then he nodded.

"What's going on?"

"Probably going to have him go another round."

I zeroed in on the side of the ring where someone had dragged an unconscious Egghead. "How? He's out."

"Someone else."

"Jesus." I rammed my fingers through my hair.

"Goodyear." Eraser elbowed me. "He's not as slow as Egghead but Griff can take him easy." He snorted. "Got that nickname because of the spare tire he's carrying around his middle."

"Genius," I muttered.

The second fight started right away.

Goodyear approached Griff with caution. He threw a fast fist, but Griff dodged it and rammed his shoulder into Goodyear's chest, pushing him back a few feet.

Goodyear wrapped his arms around Griff's body, lifted him in the air, and threw him to the ground in a bone-jarring slam.

"Fuck!" I yelled.

"It's okay," Eraser assured me.

They grappled on the floor for a few agonizing seconds. Goodyear landed several blows to Griff's face.

Finally, Griff gained the upper hand, trapping Goodyear beneath him on the floor. He jabbed several punches in Goodyear's face, grunting with each blow. Drops of blood and sweat popped in the air.

Goodyear stopped fighting back.

Griff jumped off him, slowly backing away. He grinned, his teeth stained bright red.

The guards called the fight and finally let Griff leave the circle. Someone dragged Goodyear out of the ring and dumped him next to Egghead.

Two other kids replaced them in the ring.

Griff wobbled a bit as he approached us.

"You all right?" I asked.

"Never better." He dabbed a dirty towel against his split lip. "Ollie said he'd share his winnings with me for the second fight."

Eraser slapped Griff's chest. "Good luck collecting that."

Weary and freaked the fuck out, I followed them back to our room.

That night, I manifested like a motherfucker, praying I'd get out of there before it was my turn to battle it out in the ring.

CHAPTER THIRTY-NINE

Juliet

Pip didn't seem to be doing well without Roman.

Every day he said less and less. Roman said he could be talkative, but I never saw that side of him.

"Is everything okay at the home?" I asked.

He shrugged.

"Can I see your notebook?"

In one of Roman's letters, he'd asked me to make sure Pip had a plain notebook to draw in every day.

He passed over the notebook in silence.

I flipped through pages of pretty scenes. Girls with big, expressive eyes and little clothing. The images gradually got more disturbing. They went from vibrant colors to black and red drawings of zombies and corpses.

"You should talk to Mr. Broom and see if you can get into his advanced art class. These are really good."

He shrugged. "Next semester. Maybe."

My phone rang. Praying it was Roman, I answered right away.

"Juliet Hayworth?"

"Yes?"

"Hayden Porter, attorney for Mrs. Shields."

"Oh! Hi!" I almost jumped out of my seat with excitement. Maybe he had good news about Roman.

"I'm so sorry to tell you this over the phone, but Mrs. Shields passed away this morning."

My stomach slid to my toes. "What? No. That can't be." This had to be a mistake. "I just saw her last night."

"You did?" His suspicious tone penetrated my fog of disbelief.

"Yes." Tears burned my eyes, but I kept my voice steady. "I try to stop by every night to help her water the plants and take care of things around the house."

"I see," he said slowly. In the background, it sounded as if he were taking notes. "That's good to hear, Miss Hayworth. She was very fond of you."

I swallowed hard but couldn't force out a single word.

"Juliet? Are you still there?"

"I'm here," I whispered.

"I understand this is a shock and a difficult time, but I'll need you to come by my office. She already made all her funeral arrangements after Raymond died, but you still need to—"

"Wait, what? Why do you need *me*?"

"It will be easier to explain in person. I can come to you, if that's easier."

"No. Give me the address. I'll be there after my last class."

The rest of my day was a painful blur. Mrs. Shields had been my most maternal influence. Until more recently our relationship had been mostly superficial greetings and chats over banana bread. She'd been good to me. And to Roman.

Oh God.

More bricks of reality slammed into my head. Roman wouldn't be moving in with Mrs. Shields now.

I ripped a piece of paper out of my notebook and jotted down a quick letter to Roman. He needed to know what was happening. I dropped the envelope in the mail on the way to Mr. Porter's office.

With Mrs. Shields gone, it didn't seem right to borrow her car anymore. It took two different city buses to find my way to his office.

Tears pricked my eyes. She was really gone.

Why hadn't I stayed later? She seemed fine last night, but I should have checked in on her this morning. What if I'd noticed she wasn't feeling well and I could've gotten her to the hospital or something?

"Come in, Juliet," Mr. Porter said.

I sank into the antique leather chair across from his desk and inhaled the musty scent of law books and yellowing paper.

"What happened?" I blurted out before he took his seat.

"It looks like she had a heart attack this morning."

A strangled cry escaped me. I'd been late to school and worried about Pip, so I hadn't stopped by her house. Hadn't even thought to check on her.

"CPS was conducting their home inspection. They were the ones to find her and call emergency services."

"Oh my God."

"Juliet, you're seventeen, correct?"

"Yes. Almost eighteen."

"Your aunt and uncle are your legal guardians?"

I frowned at the question. Why did he care? "Yes, why?"

He flipped open a folder on his desk and took out a stapled stack of papers. "Save for a few personal items, Mrs. Shields left everything she owned to you."

It took a few minutes for his words to sink in.

"She did what?"

"The house and its contents. Her car. Some investments. It's a small estate, but it should help you through college. In the event that she passed while you were underage, she appointed me as trustee until your twentieth birthday. I'll handle all the bills, taxes, and other matters for you."

"What about her daughter?"

He shook his head. "Kimmy was left some Christmas decorations and a jewelry box that contains items Mr. Shields gave his wife over the years. But everything else is yours." He gave me a sympathetic smile. "She said you were the only person who worried about her or checked up on her. She knew you had a rough life and she wanted to make things easier on you."

Tears freely streamed down my cheeks.

Because of Mrs. Shields, I'd be able to attend college without worrying about how to pay for it.

I could move out of my aunt and uncle's house.

"Can my aunt and uncle stop me from moving into the house?"

He frowned. "That's another reason why she appointed me as the trustee, she didn't want either of them having any control over this money." He consulted the papers in his hands again. "You'll be eighteen in less than a year. Legally, there isn't a lot they can do to compel you to remain in their home. As long as you stay out of trouble and keep going to school, the police won't get involved." He flipped to another page. "With your uncle's criminal record, I doubt he'll initiate any contact with law enforcement."

Criminal record? That was news to me, but not exactly surprising.

"What about Roman?"

"He's a different story. As a ward of the state, they *can* compel him to stay in foster care until he turns eighteen."

I chewed on my thumbnail. "Dammit."

"He's turning eighteen in another month, right? They'll have to let him out then. If not, I'll file a petition to get him released."

"Thank you."

He reviewed documents and deeds with me. None of it made a lot of sense. I trusted he would handle the legal papers.

Mr. Porter didn't want me taking the bus so late in the afternoon and offered to drive me home.

Home? I didn't even know where that was anymore. "Will you take me to Mrs. Shields' house?"

"Of course." He hesitated and tapped his thumb against the steering wheel. "Things may be a little messy from the paramedics and everyone else going through the home, but everything has been processed. You can stay there tonight if you want to."

Stay in the house where Mrs. Shields died? I hadn't considered that part. It didn't frighten me, though. If anything, it made me feel closer to her.

Mr. Porter walked me inside and helped me straighten up downstairs before shaking my hand and leaving.

I glanced at the clock. My aunt and uncle wouldn't be home yet.

I dialed the house phone and left a message explaining that I wouldn't be home tonight.

CHAPTER FORTY

Roman

OUR PEACEFUL CO-EXISTENCE WAS DISTURBED AGAIN BY THE addition of another roommate.

None of us knew the kid. And to say he didn't fit in with our group dynamic was the understatement of the year.

Everyone called him Wiggles. I assumed it was because he had long, wild black curls springing from his head that shook and jiggled when he moved.

He took the bed underneath mine. And *that's* how I discovered the origin of the name *Wiggles*—he liked to beat off every fucking night. Not all quiet and polite like the rest of us. Nope. He shook the whole damn bunk bed.

Bunking with Wiggles made me realize how good I'd had it all these years in the system.

"I assure you, it's much more horrifying to accidentally open your eyes and *see* him jacking off in the moonlight, than it is to hear it," Eraser complained while Wiggles was in the bathroom.

"I don't just *hear* it, though," I insisted. "He shakes the whole bed. I *feel* it."

"Yeah, that's worse." Griff pointed at me. "Roman's got it worse."

"Bullshit," Eraser argued.

"I think every other roommate has kicked his ass," Griff said.

"Yeah, I heard that too." As much as I couldn't stand Wiggles, I couldn't beat him up for the crime of being annoying. Besides his nocturnal activities, he was a meek kid. The kind of bullies who picked on him probably liked to kick puppies and punch babies too.

It was family visit day.

Griff and Wiggles headed down to the visitation area. Eraser's uncle wasn't allowed to visit for some reason. I had no family. We stayed in our room.

"Drugs'll be flowing tonight," Eraser said.

"Thought they searched everyone coming in here?"

"Stuff always gets by the guards."

Considering the fighting ring the guards ran, that didn't surprise me. "Shocker."

Tension was always high around family visitation days. A bunch of troubled kids already on edge before sitting down with their fucked-up families. Then afterwards, dealing with whatever trauma their family members inflicted during the visit. The Castle didn't have enough counselors on staff to deal with the fallout.

I kept my head down and stayed out of the way.

Eventually, it was time for lights out.

Wiggles was even more skeptical about the manifesting sessions than I had been in the beginning.

"You go first, Eraser," Griff's voice demanded in the darkness. "Where do you see yourself in seven years?"

"Seven, huh? Not five?" Eraser answered. "Let's see. I'm gonna help my uncle run the racetrack. Hustle, bring in new business. Ella and I will be married and shopping for the right piece of property to build our dream home." His voice lowered to an almost dreamy tone, the same way it did whenever he mentioned Ella.

"Dream home," Wiggles scoffed. The bed springs from his corner of the room squeaked. "You sound like a girl."

"I don't punch like a girl, though, do I?" Eraser threatened.

Wiggles grumbled but otherwise stayed quiet.

"Describe the dream home?" Griff asked.

"A log cabin. Lots of trees around us. Tall ones. No neighbors. A place that's hard to find with a big garage to work on cars."

"Nice. I'll be able to find it, right?" Griff teased.

"Fuck, yeah. You, Remy, Molly, and that's about it," Eraser chuckled.

"What are you wearing?" Griff prompted.

"Jesus, you serious with this shit?" Wiggles snapped.

"Shut up," Griff hissed. "If you want this visualization shit to work, you gotta be specific."

"Flannels," Eraser answered. "Nice, thick ones. Not those cheap, thin things they sell at the discount store. Not hand-me-downs out of a garbage bag. Like, L.L. Bean or some shit."

I couldn't help it. I burst out laughing.

"Careful, Roman, or you won't be gettin' directions to my secret log cabin in the woods," Eraser warned.

I laughed even harder. "Sorry. Go on."

"One nice handmade Italian suit. Because every man needs a tailored suit in his closet. Just in case. And one of those red plaid wool coats for chopping wood in the winter."

"Also L.L. Bean?" I snarked.

"Your turn, Stonewall," Eraser ignored my comment.

"I dunno," Griff drawled. "Eraser's gonna be such a dapper dresser, I can't compete with all that wool and flannel you'll be sportin'."

"Fuckin' A," Eraser agreed. "Women like a well-dressed man."

Griff cleared his throat. "All right. Seriously. I'm gonna earn enough money to come back and buy this place. Then I'm gonna fire every last one of these fuckers and burn it to the ground."

"It's mostly stone. Doesn't burn well," Wiggles said.

"Fuck off."

"Did I ever tell you guys about the time I fucked my girlfriend's mom?" Wiggles cackled.

"And on the next episode of *Things That Never Happened...*" Griff announced like a television voice-over in a bad detective show.

"First, we'd have to believe you've ever had a girlfriend," Eraser said.

A rhythmic smacking sound echoed through our small room. Metal squeaking served as background music.

The three of us went silent.

My bed shook.

"What the *fuuuck*?" I groaned.

"Wiggles, if you're whacking off again, I swear to fuck—" Griff threatened.

"I'm visualizing a clear picture of what I want," Wiggles moaned. "I'm *feeeeeeling* what it would be like to fuck your mom, Griff."

"*Daaamnnn*, someone's mouth is writin' checks his ass can't cash." I whistled. Wiggles must really hate our nightly visualization ritual to go *there*.

"Motherfucker." Griff's bare feet hit the floor with a thud.

"Don't, bro," Eraser hooked his arms around Griff's legs, holding him back.

"It's a compliment," Wiggles whined. "Your mom's hot. Couldn't stop staring at her titties during visitation today."

"I'm gonna slit your motherfuckin' throat!"

More struggling and rustling as Eraser tried to hold Griff back.

I jumped out of my bed, blocking Griff's way. "Bro, you're gonna get us all in trouble."

Faced with a snarling Griff and the possibility of eating his future meals through a straw, Wiggles wisely shut his mouth.

I reached into his bunk and smacked his face. "Apologize."

"I'm sorry your mom's so hot." Wiggles snickered into his pillow.

I grabbed his shirt and yanked him out of the bed. "Apologize, fucker."

Jerking off must've given Wiggles some kind of super-stupid power. Instead of an apology or another snarky comment, he reached past me and shoved Griff. "Why you so twisted about your hot mom?"

Fire exploded in Griff's eyes. He wouldn't have beat Wiggles over words but once he touched him, all bets were off. That was our unspoken rule.

I stepped aside. "Have at it, bro."

Eraser fell back on his bed laughing.

"Wait, what?" Wiggles screamed as Griff tackled him to the floor.

"We tried our best to save you, Wiggles." I jumped back up onto my bed and watched the scuffle below. "Shoulda kept your mouth shut and your hands down your pants."

Griff was pissed but controlled in his rage. Wiggles curled into a ball and covered his face.

After a few shots to the gut, Griff shoved Wiggles away and stared down at him. "Jesus Christ, you don't even fight back?"

Wiggles sniffled. "I can't."

"You should probably learn to shut your mouth then," Eraser said.

"I'm sorry," Wiggles whined with a lot more sincerity this time.

"Whatever," Griff growled. He toed Wiggles with his foot. "Get up, you little shithead. Time for bed."

"MAIL CALL!" Griff threw an envelope on my bed the next afternoon. "And, I have news. I'm finally getting the fuck out."

"Fuck yeah." I raised my hand in the air and Griff slapped it. Eraser joined our celebration, hugging Griff tight.

"Gonna miss you, bro," Eraser said.

"Yeah," I echoed. "Not gonna be the same."

"You'll both be out soon. You'll be all right, Roman. I got faith in you." Griff squeezed my shoulder. "Eraser has your back."

"For real." Eraser held out his fist and I tapped his knuckles.

"You two need to look out for each other," Griff reminded us. "Don't get separated. Try to stay out of the fights." He turned and squeezed Eraser's cheeks. "I'm gonna see what I can find out about Ella."

"Thanks, bro."

"We're all gonna get together and party once we're on the outside," Griff promised us.

Normally, I'd take that with a grain of salt. But I was confident the bonds we'd formed inside this hellhole would last.

Griff grabbed a notebook, his stack of letters, and a few other items.

"Wait, you're leaving *now*?" I asked.

He gave me an apologetic smile. "Yeah. I was told to pack my shit. My mom's on her way. I ain't questioning it."

"Don't blame you at all. Get out while you can."

Eraser and I walked Griff to the main office. I swallowed every embarrassing emotion trying to bubble to the surface. A guard met us and pushed Griff toward a small room to the right.

"Get back to your unit," he barked at us.

"See you on the other side." Griff waved at us.

Eraser and I walked the long way back toward our room in silence.

CHAPTER FORTY-ONE

Roman

AFTER GRIFF'S DEPARTURE, WE WERE HERDED TO THE CAFETERIA. It wasn't until after dinner that I was able to pick up Juliet's letter.

I slipped it out of the envelope and stared at the torn piece of notebook paper and hurried writing. Not the pretty stationery Juliet usually used or her neat script. After I read the few lines, I understood why.

DEAR ROMAN,

I wish I had better news to share. Mr. Potter called me at school today. Mrs. Shields passed away this morning. Mr. Potter said he needs to speak to me. I don't know why but I'm on my way to his office now.

I'll keep doing whatever I can to get you out.

I love you!

Juliet

· · ·

My sadness for Mrs. Shields twisted together with grief over my freedom. No amount of manifesting would bring Mrs. Shields back. And it wouldn't get me out of here any sooner, either.

"You all right, Roman?" Eraser stood and crossed to my side of the room.

"No." I folded the letter and shoved it under my pillow.

"Your girl break up with you?"

Huh, I guess things could've been worse.

"No, it's not that."

"You wanna talk about it?" He chuckled. "Before Wiggles returns and starts yanking his snake."

I couldn't even force a laugh. "Not really."

"Okay. I respect that."

Numbness settled in my chest.

When it was time, I shuffled to the showers with everyone else. Like a zombie I trudged through my night routine, then crawled into my bunk.

Eraser skipped the guided visualization. Griff's departure had hit him hard. Even Wiggles went to sleep without shaking the bed for once.

A few minutes or maybe an hour later, I was so out of it I didn't know, someone shook me awake.

"We need you tonight." Ollie's foul breath washed over my face.

"No." I rolled away.

Searing pain singed my scalp as he tore his hand through my hair and yanked me out of my bunk. I landed with a painful thump on the cold tile.

"What the fuck, Ollie?" Eraser's harsh whisper both comforted me and added to my humiliation.

"Shut your mouth and get up. You're coming too."

Eraser didn't need to be told twice. Careful to avoid Ollie, he slid out of his bed and knelt next to me. "Come on," he whispered.

"I'm ready." After Juliet's letter, I really didn't care what happened to me anymore. Or maybe that's what I told myself to survive an impossible situation.

I grabbed my sneakers and shoved them on. Ollie yanked us to our feet and pushed us out the door. Another guard, Danny, was waiting in the hallway with two other kids. They were new and I hadn't bothered to learn their names yet. We sized each other up carefully.

Danny's hand landed in the middle of my back and pushed. I stumbled, caught myself and began the long march down to the basement. The haze of sleep vanished. I was hyper-alert. Aware of everything around me. Even though it was futile, I kept searching for an avenue of escape or something to use as a weapon.

"Maintain your balance," Eraser reminded me in a low voice. "Stay on your feet as long as you can. Keep your hands up. Clench your teeth. Tighten your stomach and shift so any body shots land on your obliques instead of your kidneys."

Sweat rolled down my forehead. Eraser's last minute, desperate instructions sunk into my exhausted mind. This was happening.

Whether I wanted to or not, tonight it was my turn to get in the ring.

CHAPTER FORTY-TWO

Roman

THE FEAR LEFT AS SOON AS WE ENTERED THE BASEMENT. COLD detachment took its place. Acceptance. My whole life had been leading to this. No one was coming to my rescue. My only goal now was to make it out of here alive and with my body in one piece.

To do that, I'd have to win.

"You've got this, Roman." Eraser clasped my shoulder. "If that's the kid you're fighting," he pointed to a tall, stocky kid stalking the opposite side of the ring, "he's big, but no endurance. He hasn't completed a run yet."

I vaguely remembered the kid being harassed and called names for walking most of the five miles we had to run each morning. Fighting me was probably his punishment.

"Hawkins, get your ass over here," Ollie called. "My warriors against Danny's delinquents." Ollie laughed and held my arm in the air. Danny flashed his middle finger at us.

Great. So I was being used as a tool in their pissing match. At least I understood it better when it was just about placing bets and winning money. This was fucking ridiculous.

"I'll give you twenty-five percent of whatever I win tonight," Ollie promised.

I wouldn't hold my breath.

Focus. Griff said half the battle was mental. I had plenty of experience blocking out the world in order to survive. Except for the physical pain, this wasn't much different.

"Travis the street hustler versus Hawkins the foster kid!" Danny announced.

How creative.

The bloodthirsty bastards gathered around the ring roared with laughter. Travis came at me fast. For some reason, I expected we'd dance around the ring and size each other up before trading blows. He nailed me with a fist to my side and my jaw.

"Fuck." I shook off the punches and landed two of my own, to his face and chest.

"Block, Roman!" Eraser yelled.

I dodged a punch, sending Travis teetering forward. He recovered fast and raised his foot. I blocked the kick by snapping my hand around his shoe and yanking his leg high. Off-balance, he hopped on one foot. I pushed and he hit the floor hard. He lay there panting and staring up at the ceiling.

Was the fight over? Could I go back to bed now?

Or was I supposed to jump on top of the kid and punch him unconscious?

I turned, seeking a sign from Ollie.

The second of indecision cost me. Travis wrapped his arms around my legs and tackled me to the floor. Air whooshed out of my lungs but I managed to keep my head from hitting the concrete and rolled to the side, narrowly missing a kick to the ribs.

So that's how it was.

I jumped to my feet and circled my opponent. Blood dripped from a cut on his forehead and I strangled the guilt that rose over the damage I'd caused. Kill or be killed. No room for remorse.

Travis threw a punch. I ducked left and grabbed his arm, using his momentum to spin him around and put him in a chokehold. Travis struggled. Used his weight to drop us to our knees, but I didn't let up the pressure.

"Yes!" Ollie shouted.

The second I felt Travis go limp, I shoved him away. He rolled to the side, unconscious but still breathing.

Elation over the win and the relief of finishing my first fight drowned out the shame.

CHAPTER FORTY-THREE

Roman

"ONE MORE," ERASER SHOUTED IN MY FACE.

I completed the set of Spider-man crunches and jumped to my feet.

"Looking good."

I grunted in response.

We were both battle-worn. The nights Ollie was on shift, Eraser and I spent in the basement fighting for our lives. The fights became nastier. Bloodier.

The guards during the day shift started to get curious about where all the bruises were coming from. Not that they did anything about it.

And I wasn't a snitch.

As badly as I wanted to see the guards punished, I knew if I complained, the violence would only get worse.

Winning money for our captors came with its perks. Guards allowed us fuller plates at dinnertime. We were allowed to keep snacks in our room. Someone gave us a proper first-aid kit so we could patch each other up after the fights. Ollie brought us new sneakers, which was dumb, because Eraser always fought barefoot. For chores, we were assigned to laundry, which was the easiest job with the least amount of restriction.

My birthday was coming up. But I'd lost hope that I'd ever be let out of here. Why would they let their cash cow go? I was paranoid they'd tie me up in the basement and tell Ms. Simpson I'd run away or something. I stopped responding to Juliet's letters. I didn't know what to say to her anymore. She wrote to me about school and let me know how Pip was doing. All I had to share were stories of my nocturnal reign of terror in a pathetic underground fighting ring.

"My uncle finally got approved," Eraser said in a lowered voice. "I'm gonna go live with him when I get out of here."

I set down the medicine ball I'd just picked up. "Seriously? That's great. When?"

"Don't know." He shifted his gaze toward the door. Two other kids wandered into the gym. They froze when they saw us and turned toward the ancient treadmill and Stairmaster. "I don't want to say anything and have Ollie get wind of it."

"Someone will tell him." I gestured toward the camera in the corner. "Guards gossip about everything."

"Yeah. I know."

"I won't say a word."

"I know you won't." He hesitated. "I don't want to get out before you, though."

My throat tightened. "Brother," I choked out the words slowly, "the second you get the green light, fucking *run*. Don't you dare hang back because of me. I'll be fine."

His uncertain stare punched me in the gut.

"I'm serious," I insisted in a controlled voice. "I'll be out soon enough. They can't keep me here past my birthday."

"Yeah, okay." He held out his hand and I clasped it, pulling him in for a loose hug, careful not to crush his bruised ribs.

Hope. There it was again, unfurling in my chest.

What would kill it this time?

FIGHT NIGHT STARTED off normal enough. I won the first round. Eraser won his fight. It should've been time to go upstairs.

"Got a new one for ya," Danny shouted.

The evil laughter in his voice set me on edge.

He dragged a shivering Wiggles to the outside of the ring.

"No." I stared at my former roommate. "Fuck no. He's a kid. He can't fight."

Wiggles crawled to his hands and knees. Danny glared at me.

"What'd you say, Hawkins?" Ollie asked.

I turned toward Ollie. "I said, I'm not fighting him."

"Cash, get in there." Ollie pointed at Eraser, then the ring.

Eraser shook his head and backed away.

Another guard stepped up to the ring. "I'll fight him."

"Fuck yeah," Ollie shouted.

"You're gonna fight him?" I yelled. "What a big badass, beatin' up on a kid."

"No." He stared down at me. "You."

I'd seen the guards challenge some of the other kids. The expectation was that you let them win. So far, they had.

I caught Eraser's eye and he gave me a subtle headshake.

I threw my arms open wide and faced the other guard. "Let's go, big guy."

He snarled at me and whipped off his shirt. His chest was covered in crude tattoos. Prison ink? It wasn't like I had the opportunity to ask. He came at me fast, throwing a punch that glanced off my cheekbone.

He had a bit of a size advantage over me, and he was quick.

But I had rage on my side. I put my head down and charged like a bull, pushing him back a few feet before taking him to the floor.

Fighting from the ground had seemed like a good idea. Until he quickly got me into a headlock. He bent my body in half until

I couldn't draw any air. I threw an elbow, hitting his jaw. The blow loosened his hold for the second I needed to catch a breath and throw another jab. Skin scraped off my knee as I twisted and grappled to turn myself into a less vulnerable position. I ignored the stinging and landed a punch to his chest, then his face.

I staggered to my feet and put some distance between us.

His labored breathing alerted me that he was up.

The wild-eyed kids watching the fight screamed my name.

Two more guards stood off to the side, watching with uncertain expressions.

We outnumbered the guards.

"Watch yourself, Hawkins," Ollie warned. His meaning was clear. I'd put on a good show. It was time for me to lose the fight and make the other guard look like a champion.

My opponent rushed me from behind. He came at me fast. In some kind of crazy super-human move, I crouched, grabbed his arm, and used his own momentum to flip him over my shoulder.

He hit the concrete with a sickening thud.

I stared at his writhing body, stunned at the move I'd just made.

Mayhem exploded around me.

The kids launched themselves at the other two guards.

Breathing hard, I narrowed my gaze on Ollie.

I hated this fucker. Hated the way he bullied kids into fights. Hated his smug face when he won money off our blood and sweat. He deserved to bleed for a change.

"Stand down, Hawkins!" Ollie yelled.

Blood and sweat dripped into my eye. I flicked it away.

I hurled myself at Ollie, tackling him at the knees.

"Roman, no!" Eraser yelled.

I landed several punches before two sets of steel arms pulled me off of Ollie. One slammed a baton into my stomach, knocking the wind out of me.

Another blow exploded at the back of my skull.

Everything went dark.

CHAPTER FORTY-FOUR

Roman

PAIN THROBBED THROUGH MY WRISTS.

My shoulders burned.

I stopped there.

Everything hurt.

I groaned and blinked open my eyes.

"Thank fuck," Eraser breathed out.

My arms were stretched up over my head, leaving me hanging. I put weight on my feet to take the pressure off my wrists and shoulders. I wiggled my fingers, moaning at the pins and needles sensation rushing into my limbs.

Slowly, I turned and found Eraser in a similar position next to me. Blood stained the front of his T-shirt.

"You all right?" he asked.

"No. Are you?"

He shrugged and the chains holding him up clinked together. "Been better."

"Where are we?"

"Solitary."

I glanced around the small cell. "Why are *we* together?"

"Everyone at the fight is in solitary." He let out a sad laugh. "They ran out of cells."

"Shit," I muttered.

How would the guards explain so many of us being thrown in solitary overnight to the day crew? "Surprised they didn't just call the cops and have us carted off to jail."

"I think they have more creative punishments in mind for us."

The metal door creaked and swung open. Ollie hobbled into our cell. Someone obviously went at him after I got knocked out. He held something long and black in his left hand.

I wrapped my hands around the chains tethering me to the ceiling and tugged. Nothing.

He raised the instrument and it made a buzzing sound. "Try anything, and I'll fry your ass," he warned.

I nodded once and relaxed my grip on the chain. He approached slowly. Keys jingled as he pulled them from his pocket.

"We had a good thing going and you ruined it, Roman."

"Good for *who*?" I asked.

A white-hot jab of stinging needles exploded against my side. My entire body twitched.

Ollie laughed. "That was the lowest setting."

There was a click and the pressure on my wrists eased. I fell to the ground still twitching and drooling on my chest.

"You got anything smart to say?" Ollie asked Eraser.

Eraser remained silent.

A few seconds later, he landed in a heap next to me.

Two soft thuds hit the floor in front of us. I cracked open an eye. Two red and green apples rolled our way.

"You two fight over the mattress. Share it. Kill each other for it. I don't give a fuck," Ollie said as he backed out the door and slammed it shut.

I snatched the apples off the ground and rubbed them on the cleanest part of my sweatpants.

"Here." I held out one of the apples toward Eraser.

He smirked at me. "Fucking apples again?"

"I'll eat yours if you don't want it." I crunched into the fruit and immediately winced. My jaw fucking hurt.

"Give me that." He snatched the other apple out of my hand.

Our bodies were battered beyond belief.

But they hadn't broken our spirits—yet.

"How long you think they'll keep us here?" I asked.

He tore another chunk out of his apple and chewed loudly. "I'd keep your expectations low, brother. We ain't gettin' out any time soon."

"My expectations couldn't be lower." Goddammit, I really didn't want to die in this filthy imitation of a horror movie dungeon. "Life's taught me one thing—expectations only lead to suffering."

CHAPTER FORTY-FIVE

Roman

Eighteen.

Happy birthday to me.

Once we were mostly healed, Eraser and I returned to our room.

The guards seemed wary of us now. Everyone seemed to avoid us.

Eraser got his walking papers a few days later. We barely had time to hug each other goodbye and promise to catch up on the outside.

Then it was my turn.

The guards seemed more than happy to see me go.

I was lucky to be leaving on my own two feet and not in a body bag.

Like a prisoner who'd served his full sentence, I walked out of Castle Correctional Center with nothing but the clothes I'd been wearing the night I arrived. The pants no longer fit right, leaving my ankles exposed to the winter air. But I was free and didn't give a shit what I looked like.

Ms. Simpson met me in the circular driveway.

No wonder the guards had gone easy on us after the big

brawl. They didn't want me leaving the place looking too beat up.

"Can I drop you off somewhere?" she asked in a soft voice.

I snorted and shook my head. *Now she's concerned.*

Since Castle was in the middle of nowhere, I didn't have much of a choice. I accepted her offer and folded my aching body into her small sedan.

"Where do you want me to take you?" she asked.

I rattled off the address for Mrs. Shields' house.

Juliet's house now.

I didn't know where else to go. I hadn't written to her in so long, she might not welcome me at all.

But being with Juliet was the closest I'd ever felt to *home*, so I had to start there.

I watched the crumbling building fade away in the side mirror and felt nothing.

Pain sizzled over my bottom lip. I flipped the visor down and stared at myself in the small mirror. My battered face was the least of the injuries I'd come out of that place with.

"Roman—" Ms. Simpson's concerned voice grated my last nerve.

"Don't."

"What happened in there?"

"Why do you care?" I slammed the visor into place and glared at her. "Are you going to do something about it? *Can* you even do anything about it?"

"I can try."

"That's great. I'm sure your efforts will be appreciated." I didn't bother hiding the bitterness in my tone. I was done playing good little foster kid.

I was finally free and in control of my life.

"I'm so sorry."

"You should be." She wasn't the only person who'd fucked up

my life, but she was the most convenient one to take my anger out on at the moment.

"Was it the guards?"

I clenched my jaw and stared out the window.

"I have other kids in there," she said.

"Well, I hope you do a better job for them than you did for me."

She pulled the car into the empty driveway and shifted it into park. "Is anyone home?"

"How should I know?"

She sighed and twisted in her seat, reaching for something in the back. She dragged my old backpack up front. I snorted when I saw it—a relic from my former life.

"What the hell am I supposed to do with that now?"

"I don't know. I kept it for you. In case..."

It was heavy but I didn't bother unzipping it to see what was inside. I didn't care.

She reached behind her for again, then handed me a folder. A small white envelope was clipped to the front. I flicked it open and stared at the cash.

"We usually give something to kids when they..."

"Get thrown into the big, bad world?"

"Yes." She touched the folder. "There are some numbers in there. People you can call to help you adjust..."

"Thanks, but no." I rolled the folder and shoved it in the front pocket of my backpack. "Can I go now?"

I didn't wait for her answer. I grabbed my shit and shoved the door open.

"Good luck, Roman."

The door made a satisfying *clunk* when I slammed it in her face.

CHAPTER FORTY-SIX

Juliet

FAT SNOWFLAKES FLUTTERED FROM THE OVERCAST SKY AND STUCK to my windshield. First snow of the year. Roman's birthday was today. Would they finally let him out? I hadn't heard from him since Mrs. Shields passed away. Mr. Potter promised he had a plan if Roman wasn't released after his birthday.

A terrible thought wouldn't stop nagging me. What if he'd already been released to another facility far away that wouldn't let him contact me? None of my letters had been returned, but that didn't mean anything.

Frustration flowed through my veins and I gripped the steering wheel so tightly my fingers ached. I rolled into the driveway and shut the car off.

Something on the front porch caught my attention.

A man.

My heart leapt into my throat and my hand moved closer to the key in the ignition.

Then he tipped his head up.

"Roman!" I flung my door open and raced over the yard. "Oh my God. You're here!" I shouted, not caring who overheard me.

He stood slowly. His blank expression made my heart stutter, but I kept moving until I had my arms around him.

He winced and I stepped back. My gaze lingered on his black eye and split lip.

"What happened? Did you get mugged on your way here?"

He silently shook his head.

I grabbed his hand, also raw and battered, and dragged him into the house.

"Roman, who hurt you?"

He didn't answer with words. His haunted green eyes captured mine as he kicked the door shut.

I jumped at the noise but the expression on his face didn't change.

"Do you still love me?" he asked.

"How can you ask me that?" I couldn't hide the hurt in my voice. The time away had changed him. Hollowed his cheeks. Sharpened his already hard edges. But it was more than the physical changes. The playful gleam in his eyes had been stolen. His spark dulled.

"Why didn't you tell me you were getting out?" This zombie version of Roman scared me to my soul. I wasn't afraid *of* him. I was terrified of what had happened *to* him. "I'm so happy to see you. You must be starving. Let me get you something to eat. If there isn't enough, we can run to the store." Fear forced an endless stream of chatter out of my mouth. I turned and stepped toward the kitchen.

Roman's hand wrapped around mine, halting my escape. He yanked me toward him.

"Are you still my girl, Juliet?" His blank expression shifted into need.

"Roman," I whispered. My heart raced, warming me all over. He pressed his palms against my cheeks. The chill of his hands jolted me. "How long were you out there? You must be freezing."

"Kiss me."

He covered my mouth with his, swallowing my answer. It didn't matter, my answer would always be *yes*.

He inhaled a sharp breath, then slipped his arms around my waist. His tongue slicked along my bottom lip, and I opened to him. The warmth flowing between us sent shivers of excitement through me.

I'd had this dream so many times. Thank God, he was real. Here in my arms. In my living room.

"You came back for me," I whispered.

"Where else would I go, butterfly?" His hands left me for a moment. He shrugged off his sweatshirt, tossing it on the couch behind him.

"I don't know. You haven't responded to any of my letters lately. I know they were silly but—"

"They weren't silly. Your letters kept me alive, Juliet."

His words were so solemn, I didn't question him or suggest he was exaggerating.

"I'm sorry I stopped answering them," he continued. "I couldn't—"

"It doesn't matter. I'm just so happy you're here now." I was ready to come out of my skin with excitement. I wanted to do everything at once—hug him, kiss him, feed him, shower him with love to make up for all the time we'd missed and to ease whatever had left him with anguish in his eyes.

"How'd you get here?"

"Ms. Simpson gave me a lift."

"Hmm." I had *opinions* about his caseworker but I kept them to myself.

I gently touched his lip. "Did anyone take care of this?"

He snorted.

I didn't know how to reach this hollowed-out version of my boyfriend. It was as if all the sweet parts had been scooped out of him while he was away. I wanted to fill those empty spots with love again but didn't know how.

"Are you hungry?" I asked.

"Starving." He glanced down. "But I really want to take a shower."

"Okay." I loosely grasped his hand.

He picked up his backpack and kicked off his boots, wiggling his toes before following me upstairs.

In the bathroom, he hesitated, leaning against the sink. I hurried to the linen closet in the hallway and gathered a set of fresh towels, a bottle of bodywash, a razor and a toothbrush.

Happy I felt like I was doing something for him, I returned to the bathroom.

With his back to the door, he stripped off his shirt.

Bruises. Welts. Burns.

His broad back and upper arms were covered in ugly marks.

A strangled cry burst past my lips. The towels and supplies landed at my feet as I slapped my hands over my mouth. "Roman," I gasped. "What happened to you?"

Slowly, he turned around and stared at me. The deadness in his eyes chilled my blood.

"Who hurt you?" Anger bubbled inside me. I'd talk to Mr. Porter and see if there was anything we could do. Whoever hurt Roman should pay. I wanted to wrap my hands around a baseball bat and find the person myself.

"Someday." He swallowed hard and turned, glancing at himself in the mirror briefly. "I promise, I'll tell you. But right now—"

"Okay. Of course. I'm sorry." I bent over and picked up the stuff I'd dropped and set everything on the counter. "I didn't know what you might want to use." I picked up the bottle of Cyprus-scented bodywash. "I got this for you a couple of weeks ago. Hoping you'd…well, I figured you wouldn't want to use my roses and vanilla wash…so…" It seemed so stupid now. He was away being tortured and I was worried about what soap scent he might like.

But for the first time, his lips curved into a smile that reached his eyes. He eased the bottle out of my hands, rubbing his finger over my knuckles. "You were thinking of me? Like that?"

"Like what?"

He shrugged. "Thank you."

We stood there staring at each other and I sensed he wouldn't finish until I left. "I, uh, I'll go start dinner." I swirled my hands in front of the medicine cabinet. "Use whatever you want. If there's something you need that's not here, we can go out and grab it." I backed out the door.

"I'll be down in a few minutes."

He closed the door behind me.

The sound of the lock clicking into place rang like a gunshot.

I stood there staring at it for a second before heading downstairs. My mind was a jumble of anxiety, unable to sort through any of my thoughts or emotions. I headed downstairs and into the kitchen.

The house had come with a treasure trove of recipe books from Mrs. Shields. Without Roman around, I'd been afraid to go anywhere besides school, the grocery store, and the house. I didn't even want to invite Vienna over too often, in case her parents started asking questions about why I was living here by myself. All the alone time allowed me to concentrate on schoolwork and plow through the cookbooks. Sometimes, I invited Dex over for dinner. Often, I'd pack the leftovers and bring them to school for Pip. I liked to think Mrs. Shields would be delighted to know how much Pip loved the banana nut muffins I made from one of her handwritten recipes.

I didn't have a lot of food in the house. Tomorrow, we'd have to run to the grocery store. I peered in the refrigerator and pulled out a package of ground beef. Next, I put a large pot of water on the stove to boil. Spaghetti with meat sauce was something I could easily make. It should be filling and leave us with enough for tomorrow's lunch.

I was in the middle of browning the meat when Roman appeared in the archway.

"Hey," he rasped.

I lowered the flame on the meat and covered the pan. "Feel better?" What a dumb question. He was bruised from his neck to his waist. A shower couldn't fix that.

He lifted his shoulders in a half-hearted shrug. "I feel cleaner."

"That's a start." I took a few steps closer. I had to tip my head back a little further to meet his eyes. His damp hair hung over his forehead, covering one eyebrow. I reached up to brush it away.

He caught my hand mid-air.

"Your hair's longer," I said.

His body relaxed. He released my hand and gripped my hips. Instead of pulling me closer, he walked me backward and gently lifted me onto the counter. He wedged his body between my knees and framed my face with his hands.

"Kiss me," he whispered an inch from my lips.

"I don't want to hurt you."

"You could never hurt me, butterfly." The warm weight of his forehead pressed against mine. "I missed you so much."

I took a deep breath, inhaling the fresh, woodsy scent of the bodywash I'd bought him and smiled. "You smell good."

Deep laughter rumbled in his chest. Brief, but it still counted.

He pressed his lips to mine. Hard and demanding. We parted, breathless and staring at each other.

"You don't know how many times I visualized kissing you," he said.

I blinked. "I'm right here."

He caught my lips in a gentler kiss. He trailed kisses along my jaw and to my neck, tugging my shirt to the side to trace his lips over my collarbones.

"Juliet?"

"Hmm?"

"Can we eat dinner later?"

His hands tightened around my waist and he yanked me to the edge of the counter, pressing himself between my legs enough to share exactly what he had in mind.

I looped my arms around his neck. "Whenever you want."

"I need you," he whispered against my lips.

"I need you too."

He lifted me against his body and I wrapped my legs around his waist. In his embrace, I felt complete for the first time in months.

We took a quick detour toward the stove and I leaned over to turn off the burners.

"Hold on." He adjusted me in his arms, then all but sprinted for the stairs. I didn't need to remind him. He knew exactly where to go.

Having Roman's arms around me again was the safest I'd felt in months.

In the bedroom, he set me down. I stripped off my shirt and jeans, eager to be close to him again.

"Roman." I wanted him so much, my voice was nothing but a harsh whisper. I'd help him forget whatever awful memories he came home with. He needed to be reminded how much I loved him and of the future we'd been planning together.

He reached out and cupped my breast, rubbing his thumb over my nipple. My bra was sheer, the fabric so thin, I felt every caress of his calloused hands. His other hand stroked over my ribs, my stomach, and finally pressed between my legs. I went up on tiptoes and dug my nails into his shoulders.

"Ah!" My eyes squeezed shut. I'd missed this so much. "Please, Roman, please," I begged.

"Undress me first."

My eyes popped open. Something was different. More intense.

It hurt so much to imagine what he'd been through.

I slid my hands under his T-shirt and slowly lifted it until he flung it across the room. I gasped. He was leaner, all cut, defined muscle which somehow made all the hideous scrapes and bruises marring his skin stand out even more. He was almost too lean and hard, like food had been scarce.

"Roman—"

He pressed a finger to my lips. "Not now."

A flicker of pain in his eyes caught my breath, but I didn't probe. I'd give him what he needed first and ask my questions later.

Roman

The worry and pity in Juliet's eyes almost undid me. The shame of everything that had happened at the Castle still clogged my soul. There weren't enough showers in my future to wash those memories away. I didn't want Juliet to ever know about the fights. If she looked at me differently, or thought I'd turned into a monster, it would be the death of me.

"Down." I jerked my head toward the mattress. She spread out in the middle with her head on the pillows. I prowled to the foot of the bed.

So much anger still pinged around inside my sore body, I worried I'd be too rough with her. My hands curled into fists at my sides. I needed her so badly I was afraid I'd break her.

"Slide your hand inside your panties and touch yourself."

Her eyebrows lifted. "Roman?"

"Do it." I softened my tone. "For me."

She stared at me, still unsure or shy, I couldn't tell.

"The last few months have been non-stop ugliness," I explained. "Show me something beautiful."

Slowly, she slid one hand down her belly and under her panties.

"Open, so I can see. Please."

She bit down on her fist, which only made her look sexier.

Her panties were sheer but I still couldn't see much. Just the back of her hand pressing against the black material. I moved in closer, sitting on the edge of the bed and resting my hand on her knee.

"Touch yourself." I skimmed my fingers over her soft skin, pressing her legs open wider.

"I'm so wet, Roman," she whispered. "Mmm, you should feel it."

Damn if she didn't know how to make me snap. I stood, shoved my shorts down my legs, and pounced on her. The bed creaked under my weight. She laughed and pulled her hand from her panties.

"See?"

I grabbed her hand, sucking her fingers into my greedy mouth.

"Missed your taste."

Her cheeks turned pink.

"Don't you dare be embarrassed about anything we do together."

"I'm not."

"Good." I snagged her underwear between my fingers and dragged them down her legs, tossing them aside. I shoved her thighs apart and inhaled.

A little pleading sound from her throat made me pause. Calmed me. I moved in and kissed her thighs. Ran my scruff over her soft skin. Her legs quivered and she threaded her fingers into my hair.

One corner of my mouth curled up. "You want me to kiss anywhere in particular?"

"Roman." She sighed and wiggled her hips. "I want you everywhere."

I swooped in and ran my tongue up her slit, stopping to roll it around her clit.

She arched off the bed and let out a short scream. Her legs shook and I grinned. I kept licking and sucking, tasting her until she begged me to stop.

"Please. I need..." She curled her hands over my shoulders.

In my head, when I'd been planning our reunion—if we ever reunited, some days I wasn't sure I'd make it out of the Castle alive—I envisioned this lasting much longer. Spending hours and hours tangled in each other. Worshipping every inch of her body. But now that she was in my arms, I needed her too much. I reached for the nightstand.

"Don't," she whispered.

"What?" My gaze swung to hers. "I need a condom."

"No you don't." She curled her finger at me, inviting me closer to share her secret.

Hard dick in hand, I leaned in.

"I'm on the pill now. I want you bare. Inside me."

I almost came all over the sheets.

In a quick move, I kicked my shorts off the rest of the way and hovered over her body. "You're sure?"

She answered by wrapping her legs around me. I reached behind her, grabbing a pillow and stuffing it under her hips before sinking inside her.

"Oh fuck," I groaned the whole way. Her tight walls of heat gripped my cock sweeter than any fantasy I'd built in my head.

I took her mouth, sucking on her tongue while sliding out and shoving my way back in.

She tore her mouth from mine, gasping for air. "Don't stop, Roman."

I watched, fascinated, as her breasts bounced with each thrust. Deeper. I wanted to be so deep inside her. Crawl inside her warmth and never, ever leave. The numbness in my chest receded.

Crazed with the need to have her every way possible, I pulled out and flipped her over.

"Roman!" she yelped.

"Arch your back," I demanded.

She glanced at me over her shoulder. Even though I must've looked like a maniac, whatever she saw reassured her. She relaxed, resting her weight on her arms, leaving her ass beautifully exposed. I gripped her hips and sank back inside. So good. I squeezed my eyes shut, willing myself to slow down.

"Roman," she whimpered.

I stopped mid-thrust. "What's wrong? Am I hurting you?"

"You're in...*deep*. And you're still very, um, *large*."

A rough chuckle spilled out of me. I leaned over, kissing her shoulder and down her spine, apologizing with my mouth and body. When she was wiggling and moaning for me to take her again, I flopped down on the bed. "Straddle me. Show me how much you can handle."

I didn't have to say it twice. She eagerly swung her leg over my hips and slid all the way down.

"Good?"

"Good," she confirmed. "So, so good."

I closed my eyes and concentrated on not coming. Fuck, she felt incredible.

Her breath grew ragged and her movements jerky. So tight around me. Her body shook and I lost it, pouring everything I had into her.

"Stop. Juliet. Stop."

But she kept going. And going. I wrapped my arms around her and held on tight.

CHAPTER FORTY-SEVEN

Juliet

I UNTANGLED MYSELF FROM ROMAN'S ARMS AND DARTED INTO the bathroom. When I returned, he was sprawled out in the middle of the bed sound asleep. With the sheet tangled around his waist and most of one leg hanging off the bed, he looked more like the boy I remembered.

I wanted to barricade the front door, load a shotgun—do whatever it took to keep evil away and protect him from the world.

"Roman?" I whispered, stepping closer.

His chest rose and fell. I studied the bruising on his pec. A fist most likely. I hoped he'd hit back twice as hard.

Torn between wanting to feed him and wanting him to rest, I watched him for a few more minutes. Finally, I slipped into a pair of loose pants and a long-sleeved T-shirt and headed to the kitchen.

I turned the burners on again and finished making dinner. A few times, I walked over to the stairs to listen for sounds of Roman stirring. I ate dinner by myself at the kitchen table, then packed the leftovers in several containers. I left a note on the counter in case Roman woke up hungry in the middle of the night.

The house was quiet as I made my rounds, checking all the locks. I stood by the sliding glass door at the back of the house and watched the snow still falling. A few inches had already accumulated. Maybe tomorrow school would be cancelled.

Roman

Sunlight. Slow breaths. A warm vanilla scent. Smooth sheets rustled against my skin. Something soft tickled my bare chest.

No screams tearing through the air.

I blinked my eyes open. Dark outlines of tall, bulky furniture. I stretched my legs, grateful they didn't fall off the mattress. Pins and needles prickled my arm and I turned. Juliet. Curled on her side, using my arm for her pillow. Her hair spread out and wild was the source of the sweet scent and ticklish brushes against my skin.

Ignoring the tingling in my arm, I pulled her closer.

"Mmm," she hummed in her sleep.

This wasn't a dream. I'd made it back to her.

At the edge of my mind, vicious memories waited, anxious to replay themselves on a loop.

I brushed Juliet's hair aside and kissed her shoulder. Slowly breathing her in, I pushed back against the darkness and tumbled into sleep.

The next time I woke, I was alone.

Sunlight flooded the bedroom.

I sat up slowly, sharp pains and dull aches reminding me of how close I'd come to death.

Juliet appeared in the open doorway. "Morning."

I reached for her. "Why didn't you wake me up?"

"I wanted you to sleep." Her smile faltered as she came closer.

"I don't like waking up without you." I realized how needy that sounded and my cheeks burned. To cover, I glanced at the clock. "Aren't you going to be late for school?"

Her lips curled. "Which is it, Roman? You don't want to wake without me, or you want me to get to school?"

I ducked my head and laughed. God, I'd missed her.

"It kept snowing. There's a two-hour delay." She held her crossed fingers in front of my face. "I'm hoping it switches to a full snow day."

"Shit." I flipped the covers back. "I better shovel the driveway so you can get the car out."

"Whoa." She pressed her hand against my shoulder. "Easy. I want you to rest. I pushed the snow off the sidewalk with a broom. I'll try to clear a path for the car in a few minutes."

"The hell you will," I growled. "You've lost your damn mind if you think I'm gonna lounge around in bed while you're busting your ass."

I pushed myself to the edge of the bed and winced at the pain in my shoulder.

"Roman," she pleaded. "You're...injured. I want you to rest."

"All I need to do is move. A little manual labor will help." I rolled my shoulders and twisted my neck from side to side. I felt about a hundred and eighty instead of eighteen.

Juliet huffed an annoyed breath and left the bedroom. I snagged my pants off the floor and wrinkled my nose. At some point I needed to go buy some damn clothes.

"Here." Juliet returned with a red and white tube in her hands. "Mrs. Shields must have been in more pain than she let on. She has tons of this stuff all over the place."

I stared at her as the familiar heavy menthol scent filled my nose. "Bengay? Are you serious? My grandmother used that."

"It'll help. I used it when I hurt my knee in gym class."

"Who hurt you?"

"I did." She squirted a generous blob of the white cream in

her hands. "Turn around."

My back probably looked like a horror show. But her warm, slippery little hands felt so good, it was worth the embarrassment.

The menthol burned my sinuses but was oddly comforting. She stopped rubbing around my shoulder blades.

"You done?" I asked in a sleepy voice.

"These look like scrapes and…burns. I don't want to—" Her voice broke on a sob. "Roman."

"Shhh." I turned. "I'm okay."

"What happened to you?"

My gaze dropped to my hands. In the harsh sunlight, the raw scrapes on my wrists stood out. She knelt in front of me, curling her fingers around mine.

"What happened to your wrists?" She traced a line that went all the way around.

"Please, Juliet. I don't want to talk about it right now." *Or ever.* "I can't." I hated shutting her out, but I couldn't even find the words to explain. And I didn't want those images in her head.

Her jaw set in a firm line but then her shoulders dropped and she nodded. My girl was stubborn, yes, but more than that she was compassionate. "Okay."

She stood and leaned in to kiss my cheek. "When you *do* want to talk about it, I'm here."

"Thank you." I glanced at the window. The snow was still coming down slowly in big, fat flakes. Jesus, I didn't even have a winter coat or boots.

"I better go wash this off my hands." She flashed her palms at me.

"Good call." I followed her into the bathroom. Since I'd forgotten the concept of privacy, I relieved myself while she was at the sink. She hurried out and closed the door behind her.

I met her in the hallway. "Is my hoodie still downstairs?" I wanted to burn the thing, not wear it again, but I didn't have anything else.

She frowned and shook her head. "That's not warm enough to shovel snow."

I shrugged. "It's all I got."

"Don't think this is...weird. But Mrs. Shields still had a lot of her husband's clothes." Juliet ran her gaze over me. "He was a big guy. Really tall." She flashed a pained smile. "I think that's why Mrs. Shields liked *you* so much."

I let out a bittersweet laugh. "She was a nice woman." My jaw clenched. "Knowing she was trying to...foster me...it meant a lot. And I feel like shit I never got to thank her."

Her eyes filled with tears but she held them back. "I told her. Many times."

She sniffled once, then cleared her throat. "There are a couple of winter coats of her husband's in the closet downstairs. Boots too. She told me once, she used to leave them on the front porch to scare would-be intruders away. So I'm not sure what condition they're in..."

"Anything will be better than what I've got."

I followed her to the end of the hallway, where she pushed open a door.

"I haven't had the heart to clean out her things yet," Juliet explained, leading me to one of the closets. She slid the door open. "This must have been her husband's closet. It's all men's clothing."

It's not like I wasn't used to hand-me-downs. But I couldn't help feeling like a grave robber rummaging through the clothing of a man I'd never met. My hands brushed against something soft toward the back of the long metal rod. Plaid flannel. Two different patterns. They both appeared to be new with tags still attached. I pulled those forward. They were a size smaller than most of the other shirts and sweaters. The tags had clearance stickers on them from L.L. Bean.

I threw my head back and laughed. "Oh, shit. Eraser would be so jealous. I wish I could tell him this."

"Who?"

"One of my roommates. He was cool." I blew out a breath. Damn, I hoped things were going okay for Eraser with his uncle. "I hope I can find him now that we're both out. I really want you to meet him."

She didn't say anything. I unhooked the two flannels from their hangers and tossed them over my arm. I found two long-sleeved thermal shirts in a dresser and a pair of jeans that would work if I cinched them with a belt. Everything felt clean but had a slight unused scent clinging to them. It didn't matter. I certainly wasn't fussy about my wardrobe.

Juliet followed me back to our bedroom.

"So you made friends while you were there?" she asked.

Friends? I stared at the window, not really seeing anything beyond the frosty glass. "More like brothers. Griff's kinda like that annoying older brother I never knew I wanted. Eraser's more mellow. We looked out for each other. Well, really, they looked out for me."

"Oh."

I turned around to face her.

She stood there twisting her fingers together but a relieved smile lit up her face. "I'm happy you weren't alone there."

"Misery does love company," I said.

What happened to me was an awful lot of heavy shit to lay on the shoulders of a seventeen-year-old girl. So, I forced my mood away and held up the two plaid shirts. "Red or green?"

"Um." She pressed a finger to her lips. "Red. Save the green for when we go out."

"Go out, huh? Where are we going?"

"Grocery shopping." She grinned at me and turned her palms up toward the ceiling. "Apparently, when you're an adult, a 'night out' is a trip to the supermarket."

"Sounds like the kind of normalcy I've been longing for my whole life," I blurted out. Juliet was still in high school. She should have more to look forward to than picking out ripe bananas in the produce section.

"Me too." She backed away. "I'm going to start breakfast."

Suddenly, I was ravenous. I hadn't eaten since...shit, I didn't even know when. "What were you making last night? It smelled really good."

She wrinkled her nose. "Spaghetti and meat sauce? I put it away for lunch—"

"That sounds awesome."

"For breakfast?"

"Yup."

"Okay." Her whole face brightened. "You got it."

The delicious scent of garlic hit my nose when I entered the kitchen a few minutes later. The stove hummed in the background while Juliet set the table.

"Smells good."

She waved her hands toward a shelf in the corner. "I've been entertaining myself going through Mrs. Shield's cookbooks. I usually bring leftovers to school for Pip and—"

"You've been bringing him lunch?"

"Well, yeah." She half-smiled. "Although, he really likes baked goods more."

"He's got a serious sweet tooth." I didn't know what else to say. "I can't believe you've been doing that."

"Well, I'm so worried my aunt and uncle are going to find out where I am or try to make me come back, I pretty much go to school and come right home. Get my homework done. Talk to Vienna. Cook and bake."

"I'm so sorry you've been worrying about them."

She shrugged. "Dex comes by, but he was on the road for a little while."

"Have you heard from your aunt and uncle?"

"No and that freaks me out a little bit."

The oven dinged and she pulled the door down and leaned in to grab a tray.

"I can do that for you," I offered.

"It's okay." She set the tray on top of the stove. Thick, crusty wedges of Italian bread slid to the edge. My mouth watered. "What's that?"

"Garlic bread." She ripped off a paper towel and used a pair of tongs to place one of the slices in the middle, then handed it to me. "Careful, it's hot."

Absolutely ravenous, I tore into the bread, not caring that it singed the roof of my mouth. "Oh, fuck that's good," I mumbled, crumbs dropping everywhere.

She chuckled at me. "Go sit down."

I was only in her way, so I sat at the table and finished my toast while I watched her. She placed the remaining pieces of garlic bread in a basket and set it on the table in front of me. I grabbed another slice and bit into it.

"Do you need me to do anything?" I asked.

"No." She opened the fridge. "Is milk okay?"

"It's perfect." I paid careful attention to where she pulled items from. The glasses came out of the cabinet next to the refrigerator. Looked like plates were to the left of that one. I'd let her wait on me today, but by tomorrow, I wanted to be useful around here.

"Okay." She set a huge bowl of spaghetti coated in rich meat sauce on the table. Fancy serving utensils stuck out of the bowl. "Go ahead."

"Juliet, I'm so hungry, I could gobble that entire bowl."

She hesitated and glanced at the refrigerator. "I can eat a—"

"I'm kidding." I reached for the spaghetti and scooped a generous portion on her plate before taking my own. It was a struggle, but I tried not to shovel the food in like a barn animal. Everything tasted amazing. "Did you make this all yourself?"

"Well, the sauce is from a jar. But I added the meat and vegetables."

"It's so good." I bit into another crunchy piece of garlic toast. "Thank you."

She twirled her spaghetti into a neat ball, before taking dainty bites while I kept scarfing mine down like a homeless dog.

When we finished, I helped her clear the table but she shooed me away from the sink. "I've got this. I have a few more things I want to do out here."

I glanced at the clock. "I better get working on that snow, anyway."

She walked me to the front closet. Mrs. Shields had kept two of her husband's winter coats and a pair of his bib overalls there.

"Uh, the blaze orange is a bold fashion choice."

"Well, I won't lose you in the snow." She grinned at me. "I think Mr. Shields was a hunter."

I ran my fingers over the other one—a newer red plaid wool coat. "Must've been his going out coat?"

She shrugged.

"I'll go with blaze orange for the snow removal."

"Good choice."

"Do you know where there's a shovel?"

"Oh. I used the broom that was on the porch." She bit her lip and turned in a circle before walking down the hall and opening one of the doors. "Maybe there's a shovel in the garage. It scares me, so I don't go out there much."

"You're scared of the garage?"

"Don't judge me, Roman."

I laughed and kissed her cheek. "I'm not. I swear. It's adorable."

She huffed but the way the corners of her mouth quivered, it looked like she was trying not to laugh.

I flicked on the light in the garage. "Oh, shit. No wonder Mrs. Shields didn't park the car in here."

"I know, right?"

The space was full. A workbench took up one whole side of the garage and held more tools than I could identify. Cabinets loaded with even more tools lined the back wall. Lawn equipment was lined up in front of the workbench. I studied the big green riding mower. "Now, that'll be nice in the spring. I won't have to push a mower."

I found a wide walk-behind snowblower under a tarp. "Jackpot. I hope it runs." There were several shovels to choose from in case I couldn't get the snowblower started. So many options. I wasn't sure where to start.

"Oh my goodness." Juliet pointed at my face. "Your eyes are lit up like a kid on Christmas morning."

I glanced around the garage and grinned. While it was a lot of stuff, Mr. Shields had kept everything neat and organized. "It's a lot of machines and tools to play with, for sure."

"Well, I'll leave you to it." She squeezed my hand.

SCHOOL ENDED up being cancelled for Juliet. Good thing. It took forever to get the snowblower running and clear the driveway. But it felt good to be useful and do stuff with my hands. Put something together instead of tearing it apart.

Cold, but happy, I stomped my way into the garage and stripped off my boots, overalls and coat. The warmth of the house blasted my cheeks when I entered the hallway. The oven hummed in the kitchen. Music drifted from the radio. If Juliet was cooking again, I'd be in heaven.

She had her back to me when I entered the kitchen. Leaning over the counter, working on something. "Hey, I'm all done."

"Oh!" She jumped and turned with her hand pressed against

her chest.

I hurried over to her. "I didn't mean to startle you."

"It's okay."

I glanced over her shoulder.

My jaw dropped as I tried to process what she'd been working on. "Is that...are you making me a *cake*?"

"Well, it was your birthday, right?" She curled her fingers in my shirt and pulled me closer. "That's why you finally came home to me."

"Yeah," I rasped, still staring at the cake. Round and covered with thick, white frosting, she'd been spelling *Happy Birthday* across the top with little chocolate chips when I interrupted. "I don't think anyone's made me a cake since I was five."

"It's chocolate, with vanilla frosting." She let out a frustrated huff. "Because that's what I had here. But you can pick out something else when we go to the store—"

"Nope. That sounds perfect." I glanced at the oven. "What's in there?"

She shook her head. "Cookies. Just leave me a couple to take to school tomorrow."

"I'll do my best. But I can't make any promises." I eyed the cake again. "Can we have some?"

"It should go in the fridge for a bit. It's still warm-ish."

I wasn't above a little begging. "Please?"

"As if I could say no to you." She whirled around and opened the utensil drawer.

"Wait." I caught her around the waist and dragged her close again. "Kiss me, first."

"Roman," she pressed her palms against my chest and stared up at me with more love than I deserved, "I'll kiss you first, last, and forever. Just say when."

"Good." My voice cracked. Her words soothed my ragged soul. "Because you're *my* first, last, and forever."

"Mine too." She stroked my cheek. "Always."

CHAPTER FORTY-EIGHT

Roman

AFTER MY RETURN, JULIET AND I CREATED THE DOMESTIC BLISS we'd talked about before I was sent away.

We made a good team. I helped her get ready in the morning. While she was at school, I explored the tools in the garage and taught myself how to fix up the equipment that hadn't been maintained. I made a little cash by helping the neighbors clear their driveways whenever it snowed. Eventually, I needed to find a real job and figure out what I was doing with my life. I couldn't sponge off Juliet forever.

No matter how hard I tried to bury it, the bitterness from my time inside lingered. I finally understood all those stories Ulfric and Dex had shared. Why they rejected society's rules and lived by their own. Not that I was ready to patch in to one of their clubs. Juliet was the only family I needed. She was the person I trusted with my life, and the only one in the world I'd die to protect.

I kept an eye out for Juliet's aunt and uncle. Swore one time I caught her uncle's pickup truck do a slow drive-by of the house. By the time I made it outside, he was gone.

One afternoon, close to winter break, Pip came home with Juliet.

"What're you doing here, kid?" I opened my arms but waited for him to come to me.

He threw his arms around me and hugged me harder than I thought the kid was capable of, considering how much he hated people touching him.

"Why didn't you come back to school?" he mumbled against my shirt.

I patted his back and gently returned the embrace.

Over his shoulder, I caught Juliet's glossy eyes.

"No point. Got my GED while I was at the detention center."

He pulled away. "Squire and Janet got sent away not long after you. They admitted that they set you up. Why didn't you come back?"

"Wasn't given the option." I clasped his shoulder and ducked to meet his troubled eyes. "Who's your roommate now?"

"He's younger than me." He lifted his bony shoulders. "He's all right. Still sucks his thumb. I tell the other kids to mind their business when they give him crap about it."

Pride that was almost painful spread through my chest. "Good job, kid."

"I promised Pip some of those brownies I made last night." Juliet squinted at me, a playful smile teasing at the corners of her mouth. "You didn't eat them all, did you?"

"You hid them on me," I accused.

Her lips twitched. "Maybe."

She tilted her head, inviting Pip to follow her into the kitchen. He stepped lightly, almost tiptoeing, like he was afraid to leave a trace of his visit.

I sat at the kitchen table with them. While he may have been glad to see me, Pip focused most of his attention on Juliet, peppering her with questions. She helped him with an assignment for history class while he snacked on brownies.

It was a nice afternoon.

"Thank you." I curled my arm around Juliet's shoulders once Pip had gone home.

"He asks about you all the time." She angled her head to look up at me. "I hope it was okay—"

"It's your house. You can invite whoever you want over."

Anger lit up her eyes. "It's not *my* house. It's *our* house."

"You know what I mean."

We rarely fought but when we did, it was about me finding a job. Juliet wanted me to enroll in classes at the local community college. I knew whatever Mrs. Shields had left Juliet was for her education, not mine. I'd find a job, eventually.

Turned out, not a lot of places were eager to hire a juvenile delinquent with a GED and limited skills.

We set that aside for the winter break. Too many crappy holidays as children, and the desire to feel like adults, led us to do the minimum. It wasn't until the day before Christmas Eve that we got around to putting up a tree.

She stood back, admiring the undecorated evergreen taking up a quarter of the living room. "Now that it's here, I kind of like it."

"It smells nice." I shrugged and handed her a string of lights. Besides all the tools, I'd unearthed a large collection of holiday decorations in the garage.

Juliet studied the green wiry strand she was holding. "It's weird, I don't remember them decorating a lot during the holidays. I think Mrs. Shields would hang a Santa on the door and some bells and that was it."

"Maybe after their daughter moved out, they didn't bother decorating." I glanced at the boxes we'd dragged into the living room. "It's a lot of work."

"I feel bad. If I'd known they had all this stuff, I would've helped her." She scowled in the direction of the front door. "My aunt and uncle certainly never bothered to do anything."

"Hey." I curled my fingers around hers, loosening her grip on the lights. "We'll make our own traditions now. If you want to light up every inch of the house, we'll do it. If you'd rather string up purple lights instead of red, white, and green, we can do that too."

One corner of her mouth curled up. "Purple? Where are we going to find purple lights?"

"You want purple? I'll find you purple."

"Nah." She stretched the lights between us and started lacing them through the tree branches. "Turquoise. That's my color."

Even though Juliet liked to cook, I was determined to learn a few skills of my own. For Christmas Eve, I made lasagna and didn't burn down the house. We were finishing up when someone knocked on the front door.

We both stared at it like a serial killer was waiting on the other side.

"I'll get it." I pushed away from the table. "Stay here."

I peered through the small window and blew out a relieved breath. "It's Dex," I said over my shoulder.

I opened the door and his eyes widened. He stepped back and leveled a stern stare at me. I crossed my arms over my chest and cocked my head.

"Uncle Dex! You're back." Juliet rushed past me to hug him.

I stepped aside for him to come in the house. He shoulder-checked me as he walked by.

And here I thought we were old pals.

"We were just finishing dinner. Roman made the most amazing lasagna. There's still some left if you're hungry. I made cheesecake too." Juliet chattered at him a mile a minute, either not noticing or ignoring his frosty attitude toward me.

"Sure," Dex answered slowly. "I can't stay long, though. I have to work tonight."

"On Christmas Eve?" Juliet protested.

"One of the busiest nights in the entertainment industry."

I snorted. *Entertainment. Please.*

Other than that slight lapse, I was quiet while he and Juliet caught up. I sipped my coffee and bided my time.

Juliet stood and rested her hand on my shoulder. "I'll be right back."

Dex watched her leave, then zeroed in on me. "Are you living with her now?"

"What's your issue?"

"My issue is you taking advantage of her."

Damn if he didn't know right where to poke. My confident attitude slipped. "I'm not taking advantage."

"No? Let me guess, you got out of jail—"

"Juvenile detention. For something I didn't even do," I corrected.

"Right," he scoffed. "You got out of kiddie prison and aged out of care, right?"

I set my jaw in a firm line and crossed my arms over my chest. He didn't need me to answer since he knew everything.

"It was a stroke of luck, that woman leaving this to Juliet." He raised a hand, indicating the house. "So, you're thinking, what? You'll move in and live off her like a tick?"

"No," I growled. It was a testament to how much I loved Juliet that I didn't clean his fucking clock.

"Uncle Dex." Juliet's harsh voice pierced our glaring contest. "Don't you dare talk to Roman like that." She hurried to my side of the table and stood next to me, her leg brushing against my side. "You have no right."

"I'm worried about you, Julez."

"I haven't seen you in months. You've been off *riding the wind*," she sneered.

Dex winced.

But Juliet wasn't finished. "Then, you show up unannounced and immediately start hassling the one person who actually cares about me?"

"I care about you."

"Yes," she said with a heavy dose of sarcasm. "The post cards you sent from the road were lovely. They didn't do me a lot of good when I was scared here all by myself, worried Uncle Jared would come looking for me."

I tilted my head and stared at her. She always seemed so brave. It hurt knowing she'd been so scared and alone while I was away. I nudged her hand with my knuckle and she curled her fingers around mine.

"He hurt you?" Dex snarled.

"That's not the point."

"The hell it isn't."

She ground her teeth. "I love you, Uncle Dex. And I'm happy to see you. But you don't get to show up whenever it's convenient for *you* and play paternal protector."

Oof. Those last words landed on Dex hard. I almost felt bad for the guy. His shoulders slumped and he leaned forward, resting his elbows on the table. "Juliet, I'm not trying to play anything. I've known guys—"

"What's changed?" Juliet snapped. "You liked Roman well enough before to help him find a job."

It was an odd experience sitting in the middle of their argument—about *me*—and not speaking up. But this seemed to be about more than my presence. Anything I said would've made things worse. Plus, I enjoyed this feisty side of Juliet.

"I felt bad for him being railroaded through the system. But—"

"He still got railroaded!" Juliet exploded. "Not that it's even your business, but did you bother to ask if he even did what they accused him of?"

Dex focused on me and raised an eyebrow.

"Seriously?" I asked. "You're concerned with *my* guilt or innocence?" He remembered that I watched him beat a man half to death once, right?

His mouth twitched, as if he understood the irony, but he continued waiting for my answer.

"No. A guy and girl in my group home set me up." I squeezed Juliet's hand. "I never would've done anything to get taken away from her." My throat burned. "I didn't want to leave. For once, I liked the school I was at. Liked my job. You think I felt like getting my GED in kiddie jail instead of graduating with my class? I didn't. And I sure as fuck didn't enjoy getting the shit beaten out of me as entertainment for the guards."

Juliet gasped. In my fury, I'd gone one too far. Revealed too much.

Dex sat back and sighed. "I'm sorry, kid." Red tinted his cheeks. "I know how the system grinds people up and spits 'em out. I *also* know every inmate claims he's innocent."

"It's really not up to you, either way," Juliet said.

"I suppose you're right." He sat back and drummed his fingers over the table. "You're not even eighteen, Juliet."

"You and Aunt Debbie met in high school," she said gently.

"And look where that got us," he muttered.

Having Juliet in my corner was great and all, but it was time for me to speak up. "Dex, I'm trying. Trust me. I know I don't have shit to offer her. But I'll do anything and everything to keep her safe and make her happy."

"You already do," Juliet said.

"Ah, fuck. I said I'm sorry." Dex pinned me with a sincere stare. "You want me to sing it in a song too?"

"Could ya?" I asked.

"Well." Juliet clapped her hands. "Since I'm not kicking you out, would you like some coffee with the cheesecake?"

Dex chuckled. "Yeah, thank you."

She kept her eye on us while she gathered things in the kitchen.

"Have you been able to find a job?" Dex asked.

"Uncle Dex," Juliet warned.

"I'm just making conversation!"

"Not yet," I answered.

"He's taking care of all the things I can't do around here by myself," Juliet said. "Suddenly caring for a home at seventeen has been a little overwhelming."

"Got your driver's license yet?" Dex asked me.

"We're practicing," Juliet answered for me.

"Jesus Christ, you his fuckin' lawyer now, Julez?" Dex sliced his arm through the air in exasperation. "Let the kid speak."

"She's a good driving instructor." I smirked at him. "And yes, I'm looking for a job too."

"You can get your job with Ulfric back in the spring," Dex said. "He's asked about you. Swears you're the best worker he's ever had."

"Yeah? That's nice to hear." Hadn't done me much good. Not like Ulfric bothered to vouch for me when I got sent to the Castle. Although, that might be unfair. I doubt it would've mattered. "I don't want to wait until spring, though."

"If I hear of something, I'll let you know."

"Thanks."

Juliet set the cheesecake in the middle of the table.

"Now that we're finished grilling Roman about his employment prospects," Juliet side-eyed her uncle, "I need his assistance in the kitchen."

I followed her to the kitchen counter. She set out three mugs, creamer, and sugar. "Will you take that to the table, please."

I leaned down and kissed her cheek, then whispered in her ear, "Thank you."

We brought out the coffee and plates for the cheesecake.

Whatever had crawled up Dex's ass seemed to have gone away. He told us about the trip he'd taken and didn't harp on my lack of employment again, but an uneasiness still hung in the air.

Finally, he glanced at his phone. "I gotta get to work. Thank you, Julez."

She walked him to the door while I cleaned the table.

A few minutes later, she returned with a small green envelope and set it on the table. "Christmas present."

A sadness in her voice stopped me mid-dish-rinse. "You okay?"

"Are *you*? Dex was awfully rude."

"Yeah." My lips curved up and I moved closer to her, slipping my hands around her waist. "You were pretty badass defending your man."

"Damn right. I have your back, Roman." She bit her lip. "I feel bad, though. The dig about him being out on the road... every year he goes on a long road trip around the time Debbie died. I think it helps him forget. I shouldn't have said that. But he ticked me off."

Maybe this time he had a reason to be on the road, but what about all the other times he was in and out of her life?

WE SLEPT under our Christmas tree.

The next morning, as sunlight streamed in through the living room windows, I watched the colorful lights play over Juliet's cheeks.

"Are you watching me sleep?" she whispered.

"Yup." I rolled to my side and propped my head on my hand. "Can't help it. You're pretty."

Her lips curved and she finally opened her eyes. "Merry Christmas, Roman."

"Merry Christmas."

She snuggled closer. "This is already my best Christmas morning ever."

"Mine too, butterfly." I kissed the top of her head.

We slowly got up and replaced all the couch cushions and blankets we'd dragged to the floor to make our bed in the living room. Juliet ran upstairs to the bathroom and I ducked into the one downstairs.

She returned a few minutes later, so damn cute in her black and green flannel pajamas.

"Were you warm enough?" I asked. "On the floor."

She reached up on tiptoes and brushed a minty kiss against my lips. "You kept me warm."

"Come here." I tugged her toward the Christmas tree and pulled a big silver box from behind it.

"Roman, you didn't have to get me anything."

"Of course I did." I hoped she liked it.

She carefully unwrapped the box and tugged the lid off. Layers of tissue paper crinkled as she pawed through it. "Oh!" She pulled out the warm wool coat. "It's so pretty."

"It has a warm, fuzzy hood since I know how much you hate hats."

She nuzzled her face against the hood. "I love it."

Her eyes lit up and she reached for a box under the tree. "This is yours."

"Juliet…" She already did enough for me. Dex had a point last night. I was basically living off of her. "You didn't need to get me anything."

"Open."

The box wasn't heavy, but it was big. Inside, I found neatly folded flannel shirts and jeans. A stack of brand new, *expensive* clothing.

Carefully, I pulled everything out. Juliet knew me so well. My favorite colors. Understated with no flashy logos. Things that would last.

"Juliet, you shouldn't have done this. It's too much."

Her smile faltered. "We're on the same wavelength." She

hugged her coat to her chest. "I needed a coat, you got me one. You need more than Mr. Shields' hand-me-downs."

"I can't keep taking charity from you."

"It's not...*charity.*" A note of indignation colored her voice. Worse, her eyes widened like she was trying not to cry. Why'd I have to get so prickly about this and hurt her feelings?

"I'm sorry." I set the shirt in my hands back in the box. "I just hate feeling like I'm taking advantage—"

"Stop. That's my uncle Dex getting in your head. Forget whatever he said last night. It doesn't matter."

"It's not that."

Her eyes narrowed and her mouth set in a determined line. She shoved the box out of her way and straddled my lap. I shifted my legs to hold her. With our bodies this close, the awkward feelings about the clothes disappeared, leaving room for some *other* feelings to grow.

She teased her fingers over the collar of my shirt. "Maybe," she said in a low, soft voice, "I enjoyed thinking about your body." She dropped her hands to my sleeve, unbuttoning the cuff and folding it a few times. "And how sexy your arms look with your sleeves rolled up." She traced her finger from the crook of my elbow to my wrist, leaving behind a hot, ticklish sensation.

"You got a thing for arms, now?"

"Yours, yes." She cupped my cheek. "I love you. I've never had someone I cared about to buy presents for. It made me so happy. Please don't ruin that for me."

"I'm not trying to ruin anything."

"Hmm." She brushed her lips over my cheek. "Do you like the shirts?"

"I love everything." My lips curved, and I rubbed my hand over one of the soft flannels. "You know me so well."

"Good," she whispered. Her fingers strayed to the hem of my T-shirt, teasing underneath. "Let's try one on."

The warmth of her body so close and the huskiness of her voice sent heat blasting through my blood.

Suddenly, I wished I'd gotten her something a little sexier than a coat for Christmas.

I sat forward, allowing her to pull my shirt over my head and toss it on the couch.

She inhaled a sharp breath. "Merry Christmas to *me*."

I liked the way her gaze flicked to my chest, then lower. And when she traced her fingertips over my abs, my breath caught. My cock instantly hardened.

Her gaze dropped to my lap, and her lips curled. "Looks like I have another present to unwrap."

"I thought you wanted—"

"Are you arguing with me again?" She lifted one eyebrow.

I barely held back my laughter. "No, ma'am."

Juliet

Maybe I was overwhelmed by our first Christmas morning together, which seemed like a miracle. But staring at Roman's bare torso, I was stunned by how much he'd changed since the first time we'd fumbled and fooled around together. "You're so beautiful, Roman."

His lips quirked. "Beautiful?"

I traced my fingers over his broad shoulders and down his well-defined arms. "It's a very masculine beauty," I assured him.

He chuckled, rough and deep. "As long as I turn you on."

"You always have."

His teasing expression softened, and he brushed his knuckles over my cheek. "You have a way of looking at me that makes my heart flutter."

What a sweet thing to admit. "Is that why you call me butterfly?"

"Maybe." He pulled back and studied my face. "The times I've felt dead inside," he tapped his chest. "You're what brought me back to life."

Tears stung my eyes. I couldn't stand that he'd ever felt that way. "I love you so much."

I pressed closer and kissed his parted lips. He groaned into my mouth and wrapped his arms around me, sitting slightly forward. Underneath me, his body shifted. I braced myself against his shoulders and kissed along his jaw. Beard scruff tickled against my lips as I kissed my way to his neck.

I slid one hand lower, right under the loose waistband of his pajama bottoms.

He sucked in a sharp breath. "What are you doing?"

"Unwrapping my present." I pressed a hard kiss to his lips, then scooted off his lap, kissing my way down his chest. "Don't interrupt."

His stomach muscles quivered under my tongue. I curled my fingers in the elastic waistband of his pants and yanked them low enough to free his erection.

"Juliet?" he whispered.

"Shhh." I closed my hand around his cock and brushed my thumb over the tip.

His body trembled. Little panting humming noises left his lips every time I teased his sensitive skin. I stroked and squeezed, enjoying the feel of him. "Is that good?" I asked.

As if his body wanted to answer, he thrust into my hand.

"I love touching you." I stroked faster. "Your skin is so soft. But you're hard as steel."

He let out a shaky laugh. "You're killing me."

I swiped my tongue over my lips, then bent closer to take him into my mouth, sucking soft at first. His hips jerked off the floor.

He groaned and tangled his fingers in my hair.

I pulled away and pursed my lips, lightly blowing on his damp skin. "You like that?"

"Yes."

A powerful feeling slid through me. Roman was usually so strong and controlled. But *I* had the ability to leave him trembling. With a few soft touches, kisses, and licks, he was mine. I savored his desperate noises. When I flicked my gaze up, I found him watching my every move with wide, adoring eyes. His breath came faster. He closed his hand over mine, helping me stroke, showing me how much pressure he liked.

"Yes, show me," I whispered.

He gritted his teeth. "God, Juliet," he rasped. "You have no idea..."

Heat flowed through me, loosening my body but tightening my center at the same time. My heart pounded with excitement.

Two powerful hands gripped my arms and yanked. I released him with a pop and licked my lips. "What are you doing?"

"I gotta tap out now, or I'm gonna lose it."

"But I wanted—"

He cut me off with a kiss. "Later." His hands slipped to my waist and he tugged me into his lap. "I need you wrapped around my cock when I come."

As soon as he said it, I quivered with anticipation.

He stared at me with wild, hungry eyes.

"Take this off." He yanked at my shirt. His fingers worked quickly, unbuttoning my top and flinging it open before I had a chance to react. "Look at you." He traced his fingers down my neck and over my chest. "You're so pretty. All pink." He tilted his head. "You liked that?"

"Yes. You taste good."

He crushed his lips against mine, anchoring me with one hand at the back of my head. His other hand slipped and scrabbled with my pajama bottoms. "Get these *off*," he muttered between hard kisses.

I lifted long enough to work one leg out of my pants.

Bracing myself with my hands on his shoulders, I hovered over his lap. He slowly guided me to him. I gasped with pleasure and shut my eyes shut as he squeezed inside me.

"Ohhh," we moaned together.

I dropped my forehead against his and held on as he slid in another inch.

"That's so good," I whispered.

He squeezed my butt and guided me until he was buried to the hilt. Heart racing, I ground down frantically.

"Juliet," he warned.

I placed a finger against his lips. "I'm close."

He chuckled. "Already?"

"Yes," I panted. Desperation stole my voice. I rocked my hips back and forth, up and down, a frantic, chaotic storm of movement. What I thought had been close seemed to recede.

Frustrated, I reached down and stripped my pants off the rest of the way.

Roman slid my shirt down my arms, leaving me completely naked. "Slow down, butterfly. There's no hurry." He tightened his arms around me. "Relax."

We slid into a slower but harder pace. Our sweaty bodies slipped and strained together. He cupped my breast and leaned down to capture my nipple with his lips, sucking hard. The friction between my legs burned in the best way. I opened my legs wider, trying to take in more.

Roman's fingers tightened in my hair, pulling my head back so he could lick and kiss my exposed throat. A dizzying sensation tingled over my scalp and down my spine.

"Fuck, Juliet," he gasped. "You're so tight."

Wild, wonderful waves crashed over me. My whole being centered on the aching heat where we were connected. Pleasure slammed into me over and over until I lost my rhythm. "Roman!"

"Oh, thank God." He curled his arm around my waist, holding me down while slamming his hips up.

He threw his head back, his breathing as hard and fast as mine. I felt his heart thumping against my palm, where it was pressed against his sweaty chest. He groaned through his release, spilling scalding hot and wet into me. Our lips met, tongues tangling again. He snaked his hand through my hair and kissed me deeply while our bodies slowed.

"Roman." I smiled against his lips while I tried to settle my heart rate.

His lips curved into an impish grin, and he squeezed my hip. "Don't move."

I ran my hands through his damp hair.

After a few seconds, he blinked his eyes open. Together, we pulled the cushions and blankets into a little love nest on the floor and settled onto our sides, staring into each other's eyes.

He traced his finger over my bottom lip. "Thank you for the best Christmas I've ever had."

My heart squeezed. "Mine too."

Was it too much to ask that the rest of our holidays be as perfect as this one?

CHAPTER FORTY-NINE

Roman

THE SNOW HAD BARELY MELTED WHEN ULFRIC OFFERED ME MY JOB at the drive-in again. The drive-in wouldn't be open for weeks, but once again there was a lot of clean-up to be done. At least now I could contribute to the household. Even better, he taught me how to drive bigger trucks and a van around the empty parking lot. I briefly considered long-haul trucking as a career but couldn't stand the thought of being away from Juliet for too long.

When I passed my driver's exam, Dex taught me to ride a motorcycle and helped me get that license. We spent afternoons in the garage sifting through Mr. Shields' old tools. Dex taught me how to fix up a Harley, sold it, then gave me another one to tinker with.

I reveled in my new freedom and couldn't wait to be able to afford a bike of my own.

With a GED and no other job prospects, I picked up more side work for Ulfric and other members of his MC. Dex also threw some assignments my way.

As Juliet's eighteenth birthday approached, we stopped

living in fear that her aunt and uncle might try to force her back into their house. Mr. Porter worked hard to protect Juliet's inheritance and honor Mrs. Shields' wishes. He wasn't going to let anyone interfere, no matter how much her aunt and uncle bitched.

For St. Patrick's day, Juliet and I stuffed ourselves with corned beef and cabbage. Juliet baked an Irish Apple Cake that I was dying to dig into.

"I know it has the sauce, but I think ice cream would be so good with the cake," she said as I helped her clear the table.

It did sound good. "Is that a hint that you want me to run out and grab ice cream?"

She flashed the sweetest smile that I couldn't resist. "Would you? Vanilla."

"Anything for you. Be right back." I kissed her cheek, grabbed my wallet and keys, and headed to Stewarts.

Juliet

Roman was gone for maybe ten minutes when someone banged on the door.

I raced out of the kitchen to answer. "Did you forget your key?"

Without peering through the curtain-covered window, I slid the latch free.

Something hard thumped against the wood, rattling the glass.

The door crashed open.

I let out a short scream and jumped from the intruder.

Uncle Jared.

Instead of relaxing when I recognized my uncle, my body coiled tighter.

"Uncle Jared, what are you doing here?"

Like a snake, he struck. His hand wrapped around my neck. With enough force to shove a car over a cliff, he pushed my back into the wall.

Pressure at my throat choked off my air. I kicked out and clawed at his arm, desperate to breathe.

"Think you're so clever, huh? Got that old bitch to leave you all that money and you're gonna skip out on us? Forgetting all the years we let you live under our roof?"

"Let me go," I rasped. Like a fish on a hook, I kept struggling to free myself.

"Letting that criminal live here. Acting like a whore. Your aunt's sick to her stomach. What would your mother think?"

I couldn't answer any of those questions. His hand was too tight.

My vision darkened at the edges.

No.

I kicked out again, too feeble to do damage. My foot missed his crotch by inches and he laughed.

"Trying to hurt me, little girl?" He slapped my cheek. "Try again."

He released me. I crumpled to the floor.

Air. Breathe!

I wheezed and gasped.

My gaze strayed to the broken front door.

There was nowhere to run *to*. He'd follow me into the street and drag me back by my hair. No one would hear me scream.

"I liked you better when you were little," he spat. "When you listened to me."

"I was *scared* of you." I coughed. "You hurt me."

He tore a vicious hand through my hair and jerked me into the living room, throwing me on the couch.

"We're not blood-related. My wife is gone for the weekend." He wrapped his calloused hand around my jaw and squeezed. "I never hurt you that bad. What happens stays between us. No one else needs to know."

Once again, he was trying to make it sound like I wanted or invited this madness into my life.

I hadn't.

I never had.

CHAPTER FIFTY

Roman

I WALKED IN ON A NIGHTMARE.

Juliet.

My girl red-faced. Clothes torn. Hair tangled.

And that motherfucking uncle of hers standing over her, undoing his belt.

"What the fuck!" I shouted.

I'm not even sure what happened after that. Red vapor clouded my mind, narrowing my body down to one purpose.

Kill.

Everything I learned at the Castle returned with lightning speed.

I struck hard and fast.

Two shots to his kidneys.

Jared went down on both knees.

I kicked him in the face. Blood spurted everywhere from his broken nose.

My next kick landed in his gut. He rolled to his back and I straddled his chest. My fists crashed into his face, punch after punch.

Juliet's cries and her little hands tugging on my arm finally snapped me out of the red fog.

On my knees, I crawled away from Jared's battered body and wrapped myself around her. "Are you okay, baby?"

"I'm okay," she rasped.

I pulled away and studied her face. Red cheeks. Red rings around her neck.

Shaking with rage and fear, I held onto her as hard as I could without hurting her.

"Is he alive?" she whispered.

"Who gives a fuck?"

Ignoring me, she crouched over Jared and searched for a pulse.

"Well?" I asked. "Are we calling Dex to help us bury the body? Or the cops to take Jared to jail?"

She blinked and stared at me. Was that too much info about Dex? Oh, well. I couldn't be bothered to worry about his secrets right now.

"He's alive," she said.

I yanked out my cell phone and dialed 911.

HOURS AND HOURS OF QUESTIONS.

"Your aunt and uncle are your guardians, but you live here?" one officer asked.

Juliet nodded. "My attorney's been handling my affairs."

The vague answer seemed to satisfy the cop. I had Mr. Porter on speed dial, ready to call if they tried to take Juliet anywhere.

The cops were finishing when Dex burst through the busted front door.

His accusing eyes found me immediately. "What the hell happened?"

I blamed myself too, so he wasn't alone.

"And you are?" the officer asked.

"Her uncle. What happened?"

"As long as there's finally an adult present," the officer said, "we'll get going. They can tell you what happened. Mr. Samson will be taken into custody." He threw a glance at me. "If he recovers."

"Jared did this?" Dex seethed.

"Stay away from him." The cop eyed Dex's leather cut, zeroing in on the Lost Kings MC patch. "Let the system handle him."

"Absolutely, officer. No problem. I feel safer already knowing you're on the case," Dex sneered.

Damn, it was hard not to like him.

"Since it's clear he broke in and attacked the girl, we won't be pressing charges, Mr. Hawkins." The cop nodded at me. "But don't go anywhere."

"Not planning to."

The officer shook my hand and motioned for his crew to follow him outside.

Juliet told her story one final time before I took her upstairs to bed.

She winced and I almost lost my mind when she stripped off her shirt and I saw the bruises forming on her back.

"I should've killed that son of a bitch," I said through my teeth.

"Don't say that," she whispered.

"He hurt you. He didn't give a damn about the damage he was inflicting. I should kill him for scaring you alone."

"I don't want that on your conscience, Roman," she said as I tucked the covers around her.

Her weary expression kept my mouth shut. This wasn't about me or my need for revenge.

It was about protecting Juliet and making her feel safe again.

Murder could come later.

I stayed by her side until she fell asleep, then returned downstairs.

Dex and one of his club brothers were quietly cleaning up the debris and fixing the front door.

"Thank you for staying and doing that," I said.

Dex turned and nodded at his red-headed buddy. He had a dense beard that made it impossible to tell if he was closer to my age or Dex's. I supposed it didn't matter, I was just happy to have someone help me clean up the mess. When Juliet woke tomorrow, I wanted no trace of the wreckage to remind her of what happened.

"Murphy, this is Roman, Juliet's boyfriend," Dex introduced.

The emphasis he added to *boyfriend* made me think Dex wasn't all that thrilled with me at the moment.

Murphy and I nodded at each other. "Thank you for coming over." I'm sure he had better things to do on a holiday than clean up this mess.

"No problem. If Dex calls, I answer."

Dex rolled his eyes. "You're not a prospect anymore. You're the RC for fuck's sake."

Murphy smirked and punched Dex in the arm.

"RC? That's road captain, right?" I asked.

Murphy slowly tapped the patch on his cut that plainly spelled out *Road Captain* as if I was an idiot.

Funny fucker.

Since the night Dex had taken me on my first adventure into the world of vigilante justice, I'd read up on motorcycle clubs. And I certainly learned more about the secretive side from Eraser and Griff. "You plan the trips, right? Maintain the bikes for the club?"

Dex nodded with approval. Like he was proud I'd done my homework.

"Yeah." Murphy seemed to warm up to the conversation. "Dex says you're turning into a good mechanic."

I was more interested in Murphy's trip-planning skills than an assessment of my mechanical skills. "I do all right."

Eventually, I wanted to take Juliet away. Go on the road for a while and leave all this crap behind.

Murphy and Dex shared a look I couldn't decipher. "You should come hang out at the clubhouse one night," Dex suggested. "We have a nice spread out in the woods."

I'd *also* heard about the way a lot of motorcycle clubs partied at their clubhouses. None of it sounded like an environment I'd take Juliet into.

I narrowed my eyes at Dex. "Is Juliet invited? I don't go where she can't go."

His mouth twitched. "Maybe on family day."

Murphy snorted, as if family days were a rare occurrence.

Dex nodded at the door. "Help me screw this plate in."

When we finished, the three of us sat down at the kitchen table. I hated digging into Juliet's apple cake without asking her, but I wanted to offer them something for their trouble. Knowing her, she'd do the same thing.

"Juliet made Irish Apple Cake for St. Patrick's. You want a slice?" Juliet must have been in the middle of slicing the cake when Jared knocked. One piece was on a small plate and a knife with cake residue was on the counter. I sliced two more pieces and started a pot of coffee.

"So domesticated," Dex quipped as I set the plates on the table.

A sharp retort burned on my tongue but I wanted to be respectful, so I held back.

When the coffee finished, I set everything on the kitchen table and sat with them.

Dex took a quick sip of his coffee, then set the mug down

with a harsh clunk. "So tell me, Henry Homemaker, what are we doing about this situation?"

I rolled my eyes at the homemaker joke. Last time he accused me of leeching off Juliet. I couldn't win with this dude.

"*We* aren't doing anything," I answered. "I'm going to kill that motherfucker if he gets out on bail."

"You go at it stupid, cops will cart you off to jail next." He glanced at the stairs. "Then who's gonna look after Juliet?"

He had a point.

"Cops seemed to be worried *you'd* do something about it too," I reminded him. "Seems like your club's got a less than sterling reputation."

Murphy chuckled and glanced away, like he couldn't believe my audacity.

"We'll come up with a plan," Dex said, ignoring the jab at his club. "One that doesn't land either of us behind bars."

"They'll probably hold him at the county jail." Murphy glanced at Dex and lifted an eyebrow. "We know people—"

"No," I cut him off. "He's *mine* to deal with."

If anyone was going to snuff the light out of that prick's eyes, it would be me.

CHAPTER FIFTY-ONE

Juliet

I SPENT A FEW DAYS AT HOME RECOVERING WITH ROMAN BY MY side. If we needed something, he called Dex and it was delivered to the house.

"What do you think about a road trip?" he asked me the night before I went back to school.

"Where?"

He shrugged. "Anywhere. Everywhere." He cast a sideways look my way. "After graduation, of course."

"How would you feel about selling the house?" I asked. "We can go on the road. Live like nomads for a while. Then pick a place to settle down."

"What about college?"

"I can go to college anywhere."

"It's *your* house. I can't tell you what to do with it."

I glanced around. None of it felt like *mine*. I was forever grateful to Mrs. Shields, but after Jared's attack, it felt tainted. Even though it had been fixed right away, I couldn't look at the front door without bile burning the back of my throat.

My aunt still lived down the street. A constant reminder that one day soon Uncle Jared might be in the same house while he waited to go to trial or if he accepted a plea deal.

"It's *our* house," I insisted. What was mine would always be his.

"I'm okay with it if you are."

"I'll talk to Mr. Porter."

SCHOOL SEEMED to move at a snail's pace. I so desperately wanted to graduate and move on with my life. At least the ice cream shop opened and Ulfric hired me for the season again. It gave Roman and me more time to spend together. Every night after he finished at the front gate, he'd help me close the stand.

"You want to stay for the second movie or go home?" he asked one Saturday night.

I glanced toward the big white screen. Through one of the back windows, I caught a glimpse of the horror movie playing. "We already saw it last night. *And* last weekend."

Someone knocked at the front window. Cursing, I hurried to answer. I hoped they wanted something simple.

I raised the window with a whoosh and click. The guy standing on the other side was so tall, I had to bend over and stick my head halfway out to see his face. Thick hair, strong jawline, tentative smile.

"You wouldn't happen to be Juliet by any chance, would you?"

I studied his wide shoulders and thick biceps. No ink that I could see, but it wasn't like I wanted to ask him to take off his shirt. I couldn't tell if he was a biker friend of Dex's or someone else.

"Who's asking?"

He smiled wider. "I'm a friend of Roman's."

"Eraser!" Roman shouted. He hurried through the small

space and cracked open the side door that led to the parking lot. "Holy shit, brother. What are you doing here?"

Curious, I followed Roman outside. The two of them tackle-hugged each other.

Eraser thumped Roman on the back. "Good to see you on this side, brother."

"You too."

They moved to where I was standing at the side of the shack. Roman slipped his arm around my shoulders. "Juliet, this is Easton Cash. He saved my ass on many occasions while we were at the Castle."

"Family can call me Eraser," he said, extending his hand to me.

"Oh! Roman's mentioned you." I quickly shook his hand.

"I was in the area." He gestured toward Roman. "Remembered you said you worked here. Took a chance thinking maybe you got your old job back."

"I'm glad you did." Roman tilted his head. "Griff's not with you by any chance, is he?"

"Nope. But he's doing all right. We're all gettin' together tomorrow afternoon at my uncle's racetrack if you want to come. Place isn't open yet. But we're having a cookout. I'd love to have you both there."

"You sure it's not a family thing?" Roman asked.

Eraser tilted his head and gave me a can-you-believe-this-guy eyeroll. "I just said you're family, did I not?"

Roman glanced at me and raised an eyebrow. Was he looking for my *yes*, or for me to give him a reason to say *no*. I couldn't think of any reason not to go. Besides, I wanted to learn more about the friends Roman had made at the Castle. He still wouldn't open up about what happened there.

"We don't have to work until six. I'd love to go," I said.

Roman's smile seemed genuine, maybe even relieved, and I felt good about my decision.

"We'll be there," Roman promised.

"Do you want ice cream?" I asked Eraser. "I'm about to close up but I can make you a milkshake or something."

He ducked his head and gave me a sheepish grin, like he really wanted one but didn't want to ask me to make it. "Do you have strawberry?"

"I sure do." I squeezed Roman's arm. "You two catch up, I'll go make it."

Ulfric gave me permission to give free ice cream to my friends when he hired me. Vienna didn't eat ice cream and I really didn't have any other friends who came to visit besides Roman, so I didn't get to take advantage of that perk often.

When the shake finished, I capped it, grabbed a straw and slid it onto the counter.

"Thanks, Juliet." Eraser said.

I made two more and set them aside, then broke down the machine and cleaned everything.

Roman walked in the side door as I was finishing up. "Sorry, you should've waited for me to do that."

"It's my job." I waved my hand at the windows. "I wanted you to catch up with your friend."

His expression slid into an animated smile. "I'm so happy he's doing okay. He'd been trying to get placed with his uncle for a while. And it sounds like it's working out."

"Was he in foster care too?" I asked.

"Yeah. In and out."

That vague answer was all Roman would say. But I guess Eraser's story wasn't his to share.

CHAPTER FIFTY-TWO

Roman

JULIET HANDED ME THE CAR KEYS THE NEXT AFTERNOON.

"What's this?"

"You should drive us out to your friend's place." She opened the passenger side door. "You've got your license now."

We were running late, so I didn't argue. I slid behind the wheel and moved the seat back. "You worried I don't want my friends to think I'm whipped or something?"

She chuckled and rolled her window down. "No."

"Because I'm not one of those guys who has a problem with his girl driving him around."

More of her sweet laughter. "I know you're not."

"You get to play co-pilot, then."

"No problem." She studied the directions Eraser had scribbled on a napkin last night. "Take a left when we reach Main Street. Looks like we follow that for a while."

Uncomfortable sensations crawled over my skin. That was in the direction of the Castle. I didn't want to be anywhere near that place. But I swallowed the brutal memories and put the car into gear.

Juliet guided me there easily. Only the last few steps gave us trouble. The sign for Zips was sun-faded and covered by years of overgrowth.

"I think that was the right back there," Juliet said.

No one was coming from the other direction, so I whipped the car around and sped back to the turnoff. I took it slow over the gravel and dirt path until we encountered an eight-foot chain-link fence. The gate was open but the whole place looked abandoned.

"You sure this is it?" I asked.

I caught Juliet's shrug from the corner of my eye. "*Zips.*" She pointed to a sign above us. "Must be the place."

"All right." I continued on the dirt path, finally entering what looked like a parking area. In the distance, I spied what looked like stands to sit in, a racetrack and some other scattered buildings.

I parked next to a shiny black late'60s Mustang Fastback.

"Cool car," Juliet said.

"Eraser's uncle is supposedly into all kinds of classics."

"Well, he owns a racetrack. So that makes sense."

"Smart-ass." I leaned over and kissed her. "Thanks for coming out here with me today."

"Why wouldn't I?" She studied my face for a moment, then hesitantly opened her mouth. "I, uh, was happy to meet one of your friends. You don't talk much about what happened when you were…away."

My jaw tightened. I didn't ever want to talk about that. "*You're* my best friend, Juliet. Always."

Her eyes softened. "You're my best friend too. That's why I want you to know you can always tell me anything."

Wrong. The things I'd been through were too ugly to put inside her head. "Thank you." I left it at that.

We stepped out and I glanced around. Music thumped from the direction of the racetrack.

"Snazzy Buick!" someone called out.

I turned my head and my eyes landed on a happier-than-the-last-time-I'd-seen-him Griff loping across the pavement. He'd let his hair grow since he'd been out. It kept flopping into his eyes and he impatiently pushed it back.

"Fuck!" He slammed into me, hugging me so tight, my ribs creaked. "It's so good to see you outside in the sunshine, brother!"

I squeezed him back. "You look good."

He pulled away, keeping his hands on my shoulders. "Same. Freedom agrees with you."

Wide-eyed and tentative, Juliet came up beside me. I pulled her closer. "Juliet, this is Griff. He was one of my roommates at the Castle."

"Oh damn!" Griff whistled. "You *are* pretty. I always figured Roman was exaggerating." He held out his hand and, laughing, she took it for a quick shake.

"Roman always says you saved his butt." Her gaze skipped my way and back to Griff. "I always *hoped* he was exaggerating."

"Eh, I showed him a thing or two," he answered with easy evasiveness.

"Where's Eraser at?" I wanted to move away from this topic.

Griff waved toward the track. "Trash-talkin' himself into a race, probably."

We followed him through an unmanned entrance gate right up to a high white, wooden wall that kept the stands separate from the track. Griff stopped and waved for Eraser to join us.

"Wow, it's so much bigger than I expected it to be." Juliet turned and took in the racetrack with wide-eyed appreciation.

"That's what all the ladies say." Griff tipped his head and gave his version of a humble shrug.

I glared at him.

"Oh, you meant the racetrack." Griff let loose with a devilish grin. "Yeah, that's big too."

"Hilarious," Juliet deadpanned.

"Ooo." Griff pointed at Juliet. "I like her."

A dark-haired guy slightly taller and maybe a little older came up behind Griff and bear-hugged him, lifting him off the ground.

"Motherfucker!" Griff shouted. "Get off me, Remy."

Remy bounced his buddy in the air a few times before setting him down.

"Psycho," Griff groused, brushing off his shirt. He jerked his thumb over his shoulder. "This is that asshole I told you about, my brother from another mother, Remy."

"You've gotta be Roman." Remy stuck out his hand. The dimples in his cheeks disappeared. "Thanks for lookin' out for my boy."

"He's the one who looked out for me," I corrected, shaking his hand.

"Griff said you're a natural fighter."

I shrugged off the compliment. My time in the ring wasn't something I was proud of. Nor was it something I wanted to discuss in front of Juliet.

Eraser joined us with two other guys at his side. "So glad you two could make it." He leaned in and gave me a quick hug, then embraced Juliet.

She smiled widely. "Thanks for inviting us. This place is amazing."

Eraser nodded and slowly looked around. "Needs a lot of work. But we'll get it back to what it used to be." He turned and slapped the guy on his right. "This is my cousin Torch," Eraser introduced.

I leaned in and shook his hand. Did he get that nickname for the shock of bright orange-ish hair growing straight up on his head, or some other reason? "Hey."

"And my buddy Spoons." Eraser pointed to a guy sporting an Elvis-worthy jet-black pompadour and an arm covered in a full sleeve of tattoos.

I wanted to ask if Ella was here too, but if she wasn't, it was probably a sore topic and I didn't want to bum Eraser out today.

After all the introductions, Eraser walked us over to a glossy-white Chevy Camaro with black rims. I wasn't as well-versed in cars as he was, but he explained what we were looking at without making us feel dumb.

"It's a '68. Custom paint. My uncle dropped a small-block V8 in it last summer. Runs like a dream."

"It's incredible," Juliet said, peering inside at the black leather interior. "But it doesn't look that old."

Eraser's mouth twitched. "He updated it with all modern equipment. Not another vehicle like it out there."

I might not know as much about cars as these guys did but that must've cost a fortune.

He walked us toward a row of vehicles, explaining different things about each one. I squeezed Juliet closer. "Sorry if this is boring."

"Not at all." She beamed. "I never knew you could do so much with old cars. They're really beautiful."

"See one you like?" Eraser asked.

"Honestly, that Mustang we parked next to was really neat," she answered quickly.

Spoons patted his hand against his chest. "Girl after my own heart. That's my ride."

"Careful, Roman," Griff teased. "She's going to get the bug and you'll spend your weekends combing junkyards searching for parts and panels with the rest of us."

"Roman can fix anything," Juliet said. "So, I bet he'd be good at it."

"Easy, butterfly." I loved that she had so much faith in me but I knew I wasn't near this level of competence. "Tinkering with lawn mower engines isn't the same as restoring a car."

"You racing lawn mowers?" Torch asked.

"What? No."

"People do that?" Juliet asked.

"Hell, yeah. People will race anything with an engine."

"Purely residential use," I explained. "I fixed up some old mowers and a snowblower we had. Been slowly getting some side-work fixing up other people's mowers out of our garage."

"Nice." Remy nodded. "Budding entrepreneur here."

"Roman can't sit still," Juliet said. "He's always busy. Working on something."

I shrugged.

Torch and Spoons wandered over to an open garage, leaving the five of us next to a white Chevy pickup. "You're not racing this, are you?" I asked.

"Nah."

"What else can you fix?" Remy asked.

"Motorcycles," Juliet answered quickly. "And he takes care of my car."

"Her uncle's been showing me a few things," I explained, not wanting to make more out of it than it was.

The smoky scent of grilling meat wafted through the air.

Like hounds, the guys sniffed the air and Eraser pointed us toward a pavilion next to the garage. A mountain of a man was behind a grill the size of a truck. He flipped burgers onto a platter. "East! Come set this out!" he called.

"Come on." Eraser jerked his head toward the grill. "Let me introduce you to my uncle."

Griff skirted past us and grabbed the hamburgers, delivering them to one of the picnic tables.

"Uncle Pax," Eraser said. "This is Roman."

"Roman!" Pax boomed. He set his tongs aside and maneuvered his big body around the grill. He gripped my hand in a hearty shake. "Heard a lot about you from my nephew. Real happy to finally meet you."

Even with my natural inclination to be wary of people, I liked Pax. Eraser had always spoken about him with respect and affection. "Good to finally meet you too, sir. Eraser mentioned you often." I pulled Juliet forward. "This is my girlfriend, Juliet."

"Welcome to Zips, sweetheart."

"Thank you. Is there anything I can do to help out?"

"Nope. You're a guest. First visit's free." He winked. "After that, we put you to work."

Eraser led us to a table. We stuffed ourselves with hot dogs, hamburgers, chips, and heaping portions of potato salad.

"Better than the dog food we ate at the Castle, right?" Eraser said.

"Bro, that shit doesn't even qualify as food," Remy added.

I flicked my gaze across the table and met Remy's ice blue stare. "You did time there too?"

"Unfortunately." He glanced at Griff. "I *was* trying to keep this fuckhead *out* of there but—"

"Shit happens." Griff rolled his eyes.

Eraser raised his can of Sprite. "No going back."

"Yeah, bro. Now it's *actual* jail," Remy added.

"You little shits stay out of trouble," Pax shouted.

"Yes, sir!" The guys all saluted him. I ducked my head and laughed.

Juliet hadn't said a word. I glanced at her staring at her cheeseburger like she was about to cry. "What's wrong?" I whispered in her ear.

"Nothing." She shook it off and bit into her burger.

Juliet

Overwhelmed. Charmed. Amused. That's how I felt around the guys.

"We're getting our own fighting ring together." Remy clasped his hands on the table, leaning toward Roman. The impishness dissolved from his face, transforming him into someone wiser than his age. "Eraser says you're fearless and skilled. It won't be like the Castle. We'll have rules and you'll actually get your cut at the end—"

"No thanks," Roman said quickly.

"At least check it out one night," Remy insisted. "We send a text with the location—"

"No," Roman answered with more force.

Eraser reached around Griff and shoved Remy.

A chill of fear washed over me. Fighting ring? If someone started a fight, Roman would end it. And he always protected me. But willingly go into a ring like some boxer just for sport, no. I couldn't picture him doing that willingly.

My mind flashed back to Roman's battered body and broken spirit the night he was finally released from the Castle. He refused to talk about it. Not knowing what to think, I assumed the guards used severe punishment. Or did the kids fight each other? Remy said there would be rules, implying there were none at the Castle. My mind created all sorts of horrifying scenarios.

As we finished eating, more cars rolled into the parking area. They backed into spaces at a diagonal, creating a neat row.

"Show-off night," Eraser explained to me. "We'll peep under each other's hoods, talk some trash, challenge each other, and then do a little racing."

"Sounds dangerous."

He cocked his head. "It can be, yeah."

A few vehicles that didn't look like they were here to race cruised by the row of muscle cars. A fuchsia Volkswagen Beetle, a black Mini Cooper, and an orange Jeep parked in a cluster away from the show-off cars.

"Fan club's here," Pax grumbled and shot an accusatory glare at Torch.

"What?" Torch shrugged. "Lorraine races that Mini."

"The hell she does." Spoons craned his neck to stare at the

girls. "Bet Sandy could race that Beetle with a few mods, though."

"*Yeahhh,*" Pax drawled, slow and mocking, "Those girls ain't here to race and y'all know it."

It was more than the two girls Torch and Spoons named. Like a backwoods racetrack version of clown cars, at least four half-dressed young women extracted themselves from each vehicle.

"Jealousy's an ugly color on you, old man." Torch slapped Pax's shoulder and dashed off to meet the new arrivals.

"Living dangerously, that one." Pax shook his head.

Spoons smirked and took off to join his friend.

The girls who didn't stop to talk to Torch and Spoons studied our table with an almost predatory interest. I curled myself around Roman's arm and pretended not to notice.

Remy leaned over the table. "Racing brings *all* the girls."

"No different from the ring bunnies showing up to the fights," Griff added in a bored tone.

Roman curled his arm around my shoulders. "Sounds like fun." His tone made it clear he thought it was anything but.

"Duh." Remy smacked the side of his head, his lips tilted in apology. "Forgive me, Juliet."

I shrugged.

"Eraser, Keely keeps asking about you." Remy wriggled his eyebrows.

Eraser answered with a glare and a clipped, "I've got a girl."

Remy opened his mouth—to shove his foot all the way down his own throat, maybe—but Griff elbowed him in the side.

"Don't go there," Griff warned just loud enough for me to make out the words. The two of them ended up wandering over to join Torch, Spoons, and the fan club.

Pax grunted and stood, clearing the empty plates from our table.

Eraser turned to watch everyone for a second. "Once the soap opera dies down, we'll get to racing."

"We have to get going soon," Roman said.

"Shoot. Forgot you're both working tonight."

"I definitely want to watch you race one day," I said.

Eraser grinned. "You're welcome back here anytime. And if you ever want to give it a go, I'll find a car for you."

"Oh no." I shook my head vigorously. "I don't think I could do that."

"You can do anything you put your mind to." He tapped the side of his head. "Just have to visualize it."

Roman groaned. "Not this."

"Mock me all you want. But those nights when we were bruised and hurting, I was picturing exactly this." Eraser spread his arms wide. "And now here we are."

I reached across the table and squeezed Eraser's hand. "Thank you for including Roman in that picture."

He nodded and stood.

I burrowed closer to Roman and he tightened his arm around me. "Sorry."

"For?" I lifted my head and raised an eyebrow.

"Them. I don't know."

"I like the guys." Despite the teasing, the undercurrent of brotherly affection they had for one another was evident. "The few family dinners I can remember before my mother and aunt died were always full of gossip and fights. It was always ugly and my mother would be upset the whole way home."

"I'm sorry."

I laughed. "At least these guys insult each other to their faces and it seems to be done with love."

"Yeah, I guess." His expression brightened. "I'm glad you're here with me."

"Me too."

He leaned in and captured my lips. His hand cupped my cheek and I angled my body closer.

"Woo! Go, Roman!"

He groaned and pulled away. "Wrong place."

I swooped in and planted a kiss on his cheek. "I don't care who sees how much I love you."

"I don't either. I just don't want you to be uncomfortable."

"I'm fine."

This time, he leaned in and planted a softer kiss on my forehead. "Let's get going. I know Ulfric doesn't care if we're late, but I don't want to abuse his good will."

"Never know when we'll need the extra time," I agreed.

We stood and said goodbye to Pax. Roman took my hand and led us over to the row of cars where Eraser was checking out a red Camaro.

"You two headed out?"

Roman nodded. "Gotta get to work."

Eraser pulled him in for a hug and slapped his back. "Glad you could make it." He released Roman and gave me a quick embrace too. "You too, Juliet."

"Thanks for having us. This was fun. We'll have to invite you guys over to our place soon."

"Roman's got my info now."

Griff jogged over and hugged Roman tight. "Don't be a stranger."

We said our goodbyes and made the long trek back to the parking lot to our car.

Roman dangled the keys in front of my face. "Still want me to drive?"

"Sure."

This time we took the Thruway—the fastest route to get us to work on time. I waited until we'd cleared the toll booth to ask my questions.

"What did Remy mean about there being no rules at the

Castle? And how does he know you're a skilled fighter? What does that even mean? I know you did martial arts when you were a kid, is that what he was talking about?"

Silence, so thick I couldn't take a breath, filled the car.

"Griff taught me to fight. Bare-knuckle, dirty fighting. Eraser too."

I punched my fist in front of me. "Like boxing?"

"Like staying alive."

I tried to stay calm and keep my emotions out of the conversation. "Fighting the other kids? Or..."

I let my voice trail off, hoping he'd pick up the thread.

"I don't want you to see me that way." His white knuckles and quiet voice said so much more than his words.

"What way?"

"The way I had to be in that place."

I reached over and set my hand on his leg. A light touch. Enough to say I was here and listening.

"Inside, a monster inside of me was set free." His hands clutched the steering wheel even harder. "It's back in its cage now but—"

"You're not a monster. It sounds like you were fighting *off* the monsters."

"Maybe." The hollowness in his voice chilled me to the bone. "But even when you're fighting monsters, you have to be careful you don't turn into one."

CHAPTER FIFTY-THREE

Juliet

THE DRIVE-IN WAS NOW OPEN A FEW NIGHTS A WEEK IN ADDITION to the weekends. We weren't busy yet, though. Some of the weeknights only one or two cars would show up for the movies.

The ice cream shop was a different story. Since it served the public *and* the drive-in customers, the second the weather warmed, we had a line of customers at our window.

During the first movie, I finally had a lull in customers and walked outside, hoping to catch Roman's eye.

I found him talking to Ulfric and stopped. They were so deep in conversation, it didn't seem like a good idea to intrude. Roman frowned, then finally nodded. A second later the two of them headed my way.

"How's it going tonight, sweetheart?" Ulfric called out as they crossed the wide, gravel parking lot.

"Pretty good." I gestured toward the building at my back. "Finally had a bit of a breather." I didn't want him to think I was goofing off so I could drool at my boyfriend, although that's kind of what I was doing.

Roman met my eyes but I couldn't decipher whatever he was

trying to tell me. Ulfric clapped him on the back. "Spend a minute with your girl. I'll meet you by my truck."

"Okay," Roman nodded.

We both waited until Ulfric entered his small office building next to the ice cream shack.

"What's going on?" I asked.

Roman's gaze skipped to the side. "Ulfric asked me to help him with something. If I'm not back by closing—"

"Wait a minute. Where are you going?"

He shrugged. "I didn't get a lot of details."

"Who's going to watch the gate?" Not that many cars would come this late into the movie.

"His sister's taking over my shift."

"Why can't *she* help him out?"

He cocked his head but didn't answer.

"Is this a job for his club?" I asked in a low voice.

"Juliet..." he dragged my name out as if it pained him. "You know if it's something for his club, I can't tell you."

I stepped closer. "Is Dex okay with this?"

He lifted an eyebrow. "Your uncle doesn't own me."

"I didn't say he did. It's just—"

"I think Dex is aware of everything that goes on, whether it's in his territory or not."

Somehow, that wasn't reassuring. I'd never given Dex's motorcycle club or their *territory* a lot of thought. He'd worn a Lost Kings MC cut and ridden a Harley for as long as I could remember.

But now, working for Ulfric, who was the head of a *different* motorcycle club, I had a lot more exposure to bikers. And it became clearer and clearer that they didn't always operate on the right side of the law. After the way Roman was railroaded into juvie jail, the broken way he'd returned, and the awful things he'd finally confided in me, I viewed the clubs' outlaw ways in a different light.

Roman sneaking off with Ulfric worried me. No one needed to tell me these "jobs" were risky.

I didn't want to lose him again.

"Roman, we don't need the money. I have enough from the trust Mrs. Shields—"

"I'm not gonna sponge off you. You know me better than that." His gaze landed on something over my shoulder and he lifted his chin. "I gotta go." He leaned in and kissed my cheek.

I watched him go and prayed he'd return in one piece.

CHAPTER FIFTY-FOUR

Roman

"Remember, if the job goes sideways, you don't know anything," Ulfric reminded me for the thousandth time. "Above all else, keep my club's name out of your mouth," he said casually while he screwed a silencer onto the business end of his pistol.

I didn't need the gun pointed at my head to understand the threat.

"Wolf Knights, *who?*" When he didn't respond to the joke, I added, "I'm not a snitch."

He grunted in acknowledgement.

His biker brothers, Merlin, Whisper, and Hudson, crowded around us and my nostrils filled with the scents of sweat and gasoline.

Why had I agreed to this again?

Money. Right. The job would put a lot of dollar bills in my pocket. More than I saw after a month of working at the drive-in.

Here's where I should probably ask some questions. Stuff like, what's with the gun? Should I have a gun too? How sideways could this possibly go?

I kept my mouth shut.

"Vipers got no idea who you are." Merlin patted my cheek with a grease-stained hand. "They'll still be suspicious. Won't like a stranger knocking on their door."

"You look too young to be a cop," Hudson added. "So they shouldn't get too worked up about it."

Whisper side-eyed the younger brother and Hudson shrugged. "What? It's true."

None of this boosted my confidence.

Ignoring his brothers, Ulfric continued explaining the plan. "Knock. Whoever answers, ask if you can use their phone to call a tow truck."

"What if they offer to help?" I gestured toward Ulfric's white pedo-van we'd driven to Ironworks in.

He snorted. "They ain't gonna offer to change your tire."

I was eager to end the conversation, do the job, and get back to Juliet. "They'll probably say no, right? So, then what?"

"Get me a head count. How many bikers in the building? Let me know if they got women in there."

Merlin snorted. "Who gives a fuck?"

"I do," Ulfric growled, shooting a sharp look at his biker brother.

"Okay." *Head count. Make sure it's just patch holders inside.* I could handle that.

"Look for crates of coffee beans while you're at it," Merlin added.

Ulfric sneered. "That ain't his concern."

"Make our job easier," Merlin grumbled.

"Once we get inside, we could use his help carrying the shit out. If we know exactly where to go, we can get gone quicker," Whisper added.

"Guys, the whole conversation's gonna last about fifteen seconds," I said. "I won't have time to get a count on bikers *and* do your grocery shopping."

"Just let us know how many we gotta deal with." Ulfric thumped his hand between my shoulder blades a few times. "And once we go inside, keep the van running. Ready?"

"As I'm gonna be." I clenched my fists a few times and jumped up and down, much like I had before a fight at the Castle. The two situations felt oddly similar.

I left the four bikers leaning against the van and walked with purpose down the cracked, uneven sidewalk. A light spring breeze kicked up, swirling bits of trash along the curb. My gaze landed on a two-story garish red snake insignia painted on the side of the painted-white brick building. The clubhouse of the Vipers MC.

What a dump.

While it looked unappealing from the outside, they must've had something to hide. An eight-foot-high chain-link fence surrounded the parking lot attached to the building. Barbed wire and security cameras lined the top. Motorcycles and a few cars were tucked safely behind the barrier. Out of the corner of my eye, I studied the parking lot and estimated there were at least twelve bikes.

Fuck.

Jamming my hands farther into my pockets, I hunched my shoulders and continued to the front door. Painted the same shade of red as the aggressive snake on the side of the building, it was wide and covered with iron hardware. I gripped the rough metal bar of the door knocker and rapped a few times.

When that didn't yield any results, I threw my fists against the hardwood planks.

Locks clicked on the other side and the door swung open.

A beefy biker a few inches taller and a lot of inches wider than me filled the space. His black leather cut was adorned with too many colorful patches for me to decipher. But I caught the Sergeant-at-Arms one and groaned.

He crossed his inked-up arms over his chest and glared without uttering a word.

Better make this story as convincing as possible or there's a good chance this guy snaps me like a matchstick.

My heart thudded but I stuck to the script. "I'm so sorry to bother you, sir." I gestured wildly toward the sidewalk. "My van broke down. Do you mind if I give my dad a call? No one else would answer their door." I prayed like fuck he hadn't used any of the cameras lining the fence recently or he'd catch me in my lie.

"We ain't gotta phone. Get lost."

Jesus, did this dude gargle with rocks instead of mouthwash in the morning?

"You sure?" I tried to peer inside. My gaze snagged on at least four other people in the room. "I swear I'll be quick. I don't need to come in. If you got a cell or—"

Slam.

I stumbled backward to avoid the door smashing into my nose. Well, at least they didn't shoot me.

Crack! Splinters of wood flew past my face.

Fuck, they shot at me. *They actually fucking shot at me!*

Frozen in fear, I stood there for a second, my brain frantically flipping through my options. Which way to run? What path would lower the odds of getting a bullet in my ass to zero?

In a burst of speed, I darted across the street in a diagonal line from the Vipers' clubhouse. By the time they'd be able to see me from one of the small, high windows, hopefully I'd be out of range. I didn't hear any other shots, but I kept hauling ass.

Ulfric was waiting by the van and approached as soon as he saw me. "What happened?"

Heart hammering, I took a moment to catch my breath. "They fucking shot at me."

"Shit. You all right?" he asked, looking me over for fresh blood, I guessed.

"I'm fine." I shook off the fear and sucked down a lungful of air, willing myself to calm down and act cool. No need to prove I couldn't handle myself in front of these guys.

"Motherfuckers," Merlin grumbled. "Let's go. Right now."

"Calm the fuck down," Ulfric urged. He lifted his chin at me. "How many?"

"Big dude, their SAA, answered the door. Saw about four other bikers in the main room. But they didn't let me in and I don't know who was upstairs or anything." I squeezed my eyes shut, replaying the last few minutes of my life. "Twelve bikes in their parking lot."

Whisper and Ulfric shared a look. Ulfric nodded and Whisper pulled out his cell phone.

"They've got cameras all over the place," I added.

"Hudson's got that covered." Ulfric jerked his thumb toward the van. "He'll jam the signal or whatever the fuck he does to shut 'em down. Park your ass inside the van. You did good, kid."

I hoisted myself into the driver's seat and stared out the windshield. We were maybe fifteen miles away from the drive-in, but I might as well have been on another planet.

Not even ten minutes later a horde of Wolf Knights MC brothers rumbled down the street.

Nothing like announcing your presence in another club's territory.

"Let's go get our shit." Merlin jammed a pistol in the back of his pants and zipped a plain, black sweatshirt up over his cut.

No one bothered to introduce me to the new arrivals but I didn't take offense. I was too busy rethinking a lot of my life choices. Making new friends was low on my list of priorities.

The entire neighborhood remained eerily silent. I studied the dark, shadowy buildings around us. The curtains in one of the windows rippled. "Guys, even if you cut the cameras, people are watching. Someone's gonna let them know we're here," I said.

Ulfric grunted at my warning but everyone else ignored me as they slipped on sweatshirts and tight-to-their-skulls knit caps.

"You got this?" Merlin slapped me on the arm.

My gaze strayed to Ulfric. "I'm ready."

"Just back the van down the alleyway like I taught you," he encouraged in a paternal sort of way. Well, paternal for an MC president.

I should've known all those driving lessons would serve a purpose one day.

"Put that on." He flung a heavy vest against my chest. "Keep the van running and pay attention to your surroundings. You see cops or more Vipers coming, hit the horn."

"Got it." I shrugged into what I assumed was a Kevlar vest and zipped it to my chin. *Would've been nice to have this earlier.*

Ulfric and half his crew jumped in the back of the van. The rest of the brothers thundered over the sidewalk, running toward the front of the clubhouse.

I climbed into the driver's seat and adjusted my mirrors. Last thing I needed to do was announce our arrival by backing into the damn clubhouse.

"We ain't got time for ya to fix your makeup," Merlin shouted.

"Fuck off," I grumbled.

Ulfric told him to shut it, then leaned over the seat and clasped my shoulder. "You got this, Roman. Ease it in nice and slow."

Beads of sweat popped on my forehead as I turned the steering wheel and guided the van into the narrow, trash-filled alley.

"Keep going," Hudson murmured.

With painful slowness, I continued until the chain-link fence of the Vipers' parking lot appeared on my left.

"Little closer," Ulfric said. "Closer. Okay, stop." He reached over and patted my shoulder again. "Stay here. Keep it running."

For a big guy, Ulfric moved with extreme stealth, silently hopping out of the back of the van and landing on the pavement without a thud. The rest of the guys filed out behind him. They left the wide doors open, but it was too dark to see much. I slid my window down so I could hear what was going on and kept my eyeballs glued to the wide side mirror. Hudson and Whisper wielded what looked like a large black log, slamming it into the back door with a thundering crash.

Well, they're gonna know we're here now.

A similar crash came from the front of the building.

Ulfric used two fingers to motion his guys through the door. He followed right behind them.

Gunfire exploded through the air.

Are Kevlar hats a thing? I should probably invest in one if they exist.

I slid down in my seat but kept watching the mirror.

A shadowy figure darted out of the back door and ran in a crouch toward the van. Something scraped over the metal cargo area and the van rocked. More guys scurried out of the back of the clubhouse, each one sliding heavy barrels into the back.

Gunfire and shouting continued.

The urge to ask if everything was okay burned my tongue. But I kept my mouth shut. They were having a shoot-out. Things were obviously *not* okay.

Sirens pierced the air.

Cops. Shit.

My hand strayed toward the horn. But I didn't actually see any cops. Yet.

Screams and more shouts.

"Wrap it up!" Merlin yelled. "Let's go! Let's go!"

"Ulfric's down!" Whisper yelled from behind the van.

I jerked the door open and slid out, running toward the danger before I knew what I was doing. He might have brought me into this nightmare of a job tonight, but Ulfric had been good to me. If he'd been shot, I needed to help him, no matter what.

I stumbled over him just inside the door. He had one arm wrapped around a cannister. His other hand was pressed to his leg. Blood seeped out from under his fingers.

"Shit!" I knelt next to him and grabbed his arm. "Come on. Cops are coming."

He blinked at me. "You're s'posed to be in the van."

"Whisper said you were down."

He groaned as I helped lift him off the floor. Noise and shouting from the rest of the clubhouse increased. Gunfire sounded closer. We needed to get the fuck out.

I half carried, half dragged Ulfric to the back of the van. Merlin and Whisper helped me bundle him inside.

"Go grab his stash," Merlin said.

"Cops are coming. We gotta get out of here."

"Hurry up." Merlin shoved me toward the open door.

I crept inside again. The cannister was right where we'd left it. I snatched it off the floor.

As I stood, there was a click behind me.

Something hard pressed into the back of my skull. "Set it down. Slow."

Fuck.

It couldn't be a Viper. They would've just blown my brains out.

"Lace your fingers behind your head."

Nope, it was worse.

"You're under arrest."

CHAPTER FIFTY-FIVE

Juliet

ULFRIC AND ROMAN NEVER RETURNED TO THE DRIVE-IN.

Worried, I finished closing down the ice cream shop. Usually Roman waited right outside the back door and we'd catch the rest of the second movie together.

"Where's your *boyfriend*?" my co-worker, Chris, sneered at me. "He's gonna get fired for taking off in the middle of his shift."

I rolled my eyes. "He went to help the *owner* with something, so I think his job is fine." I shooed him out of the way with the dishcloth in my hand. "Are you working or yapping?" If I didn't stay on top of him, he'd let me do all the closing work myself.

"Working," he grumbled.

We finished our tasks in silence and Chris left without slinging any more attitude. I checked the windows and locked the door on my way out. Outside, in the cool night air, I hesitated. Should I go home? Or wait for Roman? My gaze landed on a few other employees scattered over the grounds. There seemed to be more employees than customers.

Another horror movie was playing on the big screen to my left. I stood in the darkness watching the poor hapless babysitter hide from a knife-wielding madman for a few minutes. A chill ran down my spine. I'd been alone at the house before. But for some reason, tonight the idea of going home alone left me jittery.

I pulled out my cell phone and sent Roman a text.

Do you want me to wait or go home?

I stared at the screen for several minutes.

No answer.

He probably couldn't check his phone. What had Ulfric roped him into?

I sat in the car, drumming my fingers against the steering wheel. Finally, I took out my phone and dialed Dex. He answered and by the background noise, I assumed he was at a party.

"Dex?"

"Give me a second, Julez."

Eventually the noises faded and he came back on the line. "You okay, sweetheart?"

"I'm fine. I'm still at work. Roman took off with Ulfric tonight and they haven't come back yet." I swallowed hard. Directly asking about "club business" wasn't allowed. It was an unspoken rule, and I'd always followed it. Until now. "Do you know where they are?"

A long silence stretched over the line. He didn't like the question. Well, too bad. I wasn't a little girl anymore. If Roman was involved, I was involved and Dex would just have to suck it up.

"I don't know what Ulfric had him working on," he finally answered. "But I'll make some calls. See what I can find out. Do you need me to come over to the house?"

"No, I'll be fine."

That was a lie. I'd be up all night worrying about Roman.

Dex must have heard the anxiety in my voice because when I pulled into my driveway forty-five minutes later, he was waiting for me. Casually leaning against his bike, the bright light of his phone's screen lit up his face in an ominous way. Thank God it also helped me recognize him.

I slid the car in next to him and turned off the ignition.

He opened my door.

"What are you doing here?" I asked, grabbing my bag and stepping out. Fear trembled down my legs. "Is Roman okay? Did you find out something?"

Employer or not, I'll kill Ulfric if he got Roman hurt. The savage thought stopped me cold. Roman was mine and I'd protect him as fiercely as he protected me.

"I can't get ahold of Ulfric," Dex explained, walking me to the front door. "And no matter how friendly our two clubs are, none of his brothers are gonna give me details about what they're up to without Ulfric's approval."

That was a lot for Dex to share with me. It didn't ease my concerns, but I appreciated him talking to me like an adult. "Roman's never been out this late without me."

The corners of Dex's mouth twisted in a wry smile. "He's an adult, Juliet."

Heat blasted my cheeks. "I'm just worried about him."

"Roman's smart. He'll be fine."

That Dex seemed so laid back about the situation helped calm me as well. *Maybe I was overreacting.* Dex probably did whatever he wanted whenever he wanted and found my fussing strange. "Do you want something to drink?"

"Nah. I didn't come here so you could wait on me." He reached out and roughed his hand over the top of my head. "You want me to stick around until he gets home?" He lifted his chin toward the couch.

"You don't have to do that." I wanted him to stay but I'd never ask. "I'm sure you have other things you'd rather do tonight?"

I'd never asked Dex many questions about his personal life

since Debbie died. Part of me didn't want to know if he'd started dating. The other part of me wanted him to find someone and be happy.

He was slow to answer. "I'm going to stick around. Maybe lecture him when he walks in."

I snort-laughed. "As long as it's not with your fists."

"Nah." A slow smile spread over his face and an evil gleam that I wasn't used to seeing shone in Dex's eyes. "That's only if he ever hurts or disrespects *you*."

"You don't have to worry about that." No one had ever been as gentle or kind to me as Roman.

"Go on." Dex waved his hand toward the stairs. "Get some rest. I'll be here. You don't have to worry about anything."

My heart melted and I rushed over to hug him. "Thank you," I whispered against his chest.

He held me tight for a few seconds. "You don't have to thank me, Juliet. I shoulda been looking out for you better all these years," he rasped.

"You did when you could. I've always been happy to see you."

"I know, peanut." He patted my back.

I pulled away and glanced at the couch. "You don't have to sleep there. There's an extra bedroom upstairs."

"I'll be fine here." He stepped back and his lips quirked. "I wasn't kidding about wanting to have a word with your man when he gets in."

A short burst of laughter escaped me. "Okay. Okay. Have your manly chat."

Feeling reassured by Dex's presence and his confidence that everything was fine, I hurried upstairs and got ready for bed.

BEFORE THE SUN kissed the sky, my phone buzzed. I groaned and reached for my nightstand, accidentally knocking the phone on the floor.

"Damn." Fully awake, I opened my eyes and leaned over the side of the bed and scooped it up, hurrying to answer before the call went to voicemail.

"Hello?"

A robotic voice answered. "You have a collect call from Ironworks County Jail. Will you accept the charges?"

My stomach chilled. "Yes, I'll accept," I said.

"Juliet?" Roman's hoarse voice squeezed my heart.

"Roman." My body jerked upright. "Thank God. What happened? Why are you in jail?" I couldn't help the rising hysteria in my voice. This had to be a mistake.

Angry, rage-filled tears blurred my vision as he gave me vague details.

Fearing our time was running out, I cut him off. "I'll gather money and post bail. Do you know how much—"

"Don't."

"What?"

"This is bad, Juliet. I don't want you involved." He paused and I strained for sounds he was still on the phone with me. "Finish school and...stay away, Juliet."

His words eviscerated me. "Stay away? Roman—"

"I love you. But obviously, I'm no good for you."

"No good for me? Roman, stop."

"I don't want to drag you down with me."

"We take care of each—"

The line went dead.

My bleeding heart leaked out on the floor along with my will to exist.

CHAPTER FIFTY-SIX

Roman

COCAINE. A LOT OF IT. THAT'S WHAT THE WOLF KNIGHTS WERE so desperate to retrieve from the Vipers' clubhouse.

They got out of Ironworks with most of it. While I got left holding the one cannister.

It still contained enough to put *me* away for a long time.

I'd gone and fulfilled the prophecies of everyone I'd ever known. Except Juliet. For some reason she saw something good in me. She was wrong. And that's why I told her to stay away. I wouldn't have her put her life on hold. Visiting me in prison once a month. Hoping one day I might be free. No way. She didn't deserve that kind of life.

No matter how hard the cops tried to break me, I wouldn't give up Ulfric and the others. Cops asked me about other crimes I might have witnessed—even the guy Dex had beaten the shit out of last year. That one got an eyebrow raise out of me. But still, I stayed silent.

So many different cops asked so many different questions, I started to wonder if the Wolf Knights had set it up as some sort of fucked-up loyalty test.

Finally, I was tossed in a cell.

Exhausted, I thanked whatever higher power had placed me by myself. I climbed into the bottom bunk and stretched out on the blanket, feeling the metal coils beneath the mattress poke into my ribs.

County jail was considerably nicer than the Castle, so that was a bonus.

I'd need to keep to myself and watch my back harder than ever in here, though.

DAYS DRAGGED ON FOREVER. At least at the Castle, they'd pretended to have some activities that would keep us entertained. Chores to do. This was relentless boredom. On the plus side, so far, I hadn't been thrown into any gladiator rings and told to fight for my life.

"Hawkins," someone shouted.

I blinked awake.

"Hawkins!" the CO shouted over the din of the Ironworks County Jail. He banged a metal rod against the bars. "Let's go! Your lawyer's here to see you."

I yawned and stretched. My overly eager, recently graduated public defender never had any good news. I wasn't even sure he'd passed the bar yet.

I was royally fucked.

I shuffled into the interview room and stared at a man I didn't recognize. Now *he* looked like a criminal defense attorney. Sharp and a shade slimy. Turning to the guard, I shook my head. "He's not my lawyer. There's been a mistake."

"Barry Hansen." The man stepped forward and offered his hand. "I was hired by a friend of yours to represent you, Mr. Hawkins."

"Juliet?" Damn her, I told her to forget about me. No matter how you looked at it, I was facing a long prison sentence. There was no point in her wasting money hiring an expensive lawyer for my hopeless case.

"No." He flashed a warm smile. "A family friend who prefers to be anonymous."

Had to be Dex or Ulfric. They probably wanted to make sure I'd keep my mouth shut. And if the lawyer sensed I was about to snitch, I bet he'd report back to whoever was paying his bills. One day I'd be headed to the dining area, and someone would shove a makeshift knife made from a toothbrush and razor blade between my ribs.

"Okay." I studied him while I slowly took a seat. The guard left us to talk in private, closing the door behind him.

"I have a meeting with the district attorney on Monday," Mr. Hansen said. "From what I've been hearing, they're willing to offer a plea deal."

"What do I have to do in exchange?" I asked warily.

"They might want you to tell them who else you—"

"No."

His mouth twitched and he scribbled down a few notes. "Let me talk to him first before we make any decisions. You're a young man, Roman. You've got options."

"Snitching isn't one of those options."

I might as well hang myself with my bedsheets now if I planned to snitch.

CHAPTER FIFTY-SEVEN

Roman

A WEEK LATER I WAS CUFFED AND SHACKLED, TOSSED INTO AN Ironworks County Correctional van, and driven to the County Courthouse for a meeting with my attorney.

The guards brought me in through a back entrance. I kept my gaze glued to my feet. Not out of shame. The shackles hurt like fuck, messed with my balance, and dug into my ankle bones with every shuffle.

Mr. Hansen was waiting in a small room and stood when I entered. The guards uncuffed my wrists, unshackled my feet, and shoved me into a chair.

"What's going on, Mr. Hansen?" I asked after he shook my hand.

A brief smile flitted over his face. "You can call me Barry. I'm not sure how or why, but the DA is dropping the charges." He frowned and studied the folder in front of him.

Cops had a solid case. Caught me red-handed. I understood Barry's confusion.

I clenched a mental fist around any hope threatening to materialize in my chest. No point getting excited. I wouldn't believe it until I was a free man. "Are you sure?"

"That's what I was told." Another wrinkle formed between his brows. "It's unusual for the district attorney himself to handle a case like this."

I didn't know anything about how that worked, but I'd take his word for it.

"There has been minimal media attention and Tony's already got the next election locked down," he muttered to himself.

None of that mattered to me. I just needed my freedom. I had to see Juliet. Never expecting to be released, I'd cut her off. Refused her visits. Ignored her letters.

What if she'd moved on?

She was stubborn, but I hadn't answered any of her letters.

Stupid. At the time, pushing her away seemed like the right thing to do.

"All right." Barry stood and motioned for me to do the same with a quick flick of his hand. "Let's get you out of here."

I latched onto those words like a starving dog who'd been thrown a bone. The rest of Barry's instructions were drowned out by impatience. If I was really getting out, I wanted out *now*.

The guard returned to escort me into the courtroom. Apparently, Barry couldn't be trusted to walk me ten feet.

"Good morning, Tony," Barry brushed by me and offered his hand to the other attorney. They made small talk while I dropped into my seat and stared straight ahead. I didn't have any faith this was going to work out the way Barry said it would. Freedom would be dangled in front of my face and then yanked away. That was my curse.

The judge took the bench and slammed his gavel down. "District Attorney Cain, I see you've decided to grace us with your presence this morning," the judge said with a wry twist of his mouth. He was either amused or annoyed with the DA, I couldn't tell.

As long as it didn't delay my release, I didn't care.

The DA stood and buttoned the top button of his suit jacket.

His whole demeanor dripped with arrogance, but my inner foster kid recognized the hard exterior it probably took him years to cultivate. He wasn't some soft trust-fund kid kind of lawyer, who'd lucked into his position using his family's connections. No, he had the rough edges of someone who'd clawed his way to the top from the very bottom and had no intention of returning to his hellish roots. I could certainly relate to and respect that.

"Your Honor, we've agreed to drop all charges against the defendant," Mr. Cain said.

"That's it?" the judge prodded.

My entire body tensed. Was it possible the judge wouldn't allow my case to be dismissed? Could he do that? I leaned over to ask my lawyer, but he shook his head. The guy seemed almost as on edge as I was.

"We've obtained new information that leads us to believe Mr. Hawkins was incorrectly identified as the suspect."

Incorrectly identified? Bet the cop who'd arrested me enjoyed having to change his story.

All the reasons I should leave town as soon as I was set free started to stack up around me.

"We'd like the case dismissed with prejudice," my lawyer added.

Tony cast a don't-get-carried-away look at our table.

"Request granted." The judge scribbled down some notes, then glared at the DA. "Next time maybe be more thorough in your investigation before turning a young man's life upside down."

If the judge only knew this was one of many tornadoes that had upended my life over the years. Sure, it was more serious. My actual freedom was at stake, but it wasn't really a surprise. The counselors, hell even teachers had joked my whole life about how foster care was just a stop on the way to prison.

I didn't want that to be my life, but somehow I wasn't doing a stellar job at staying out of trouble.

A few more things were said. I signed a stack of papers.

"Ms. Kendall, come on up," the judge barked. We must've been taking too long to vacate the table. I wanted to shout at the judge, "Trust me, I'm trying!" but managed to stay cool.

A tall, pretty redhead pushed through the wooden gate. Her heels clicked softly over the wood floor as she approached the table and placed her briefcase on the chair the DA just vacated. There wasn't much room between our two tables. Barry scooted over to her side with an eager expression stretched across his face.

"Good to see you, Hope. Are you finally dabbling in criminal work?"

"Gosh, no." She laughed. "Although you make it look pretty easy." She caught my eye and gave me a warm smile. "Congrats," she whispered.

I blinked and stared. She didn't look at me like I was a criminal who'd gotten lucky. Maybe she hadn't been a lawyer for long.

"Come on." The officer yanked me to my feet by my elbow.

"I'll be downstairs to talk to you in a minute," Barry said over his shoulder.

"Okay."

The woman peered around Barry and caught my eye again. "Good luck."

I nodded a thanks. *Lady, you have no idea.*

As I shuffled my way downstairs, I felt like the luckiest bastard in the world to skip away from the charges. It seemed like a once-in-a-lifetime get-out-of-jail-free—*literally*—card had fallen in my lap.

It wouldn't happen twice. So, I needed to get my shit together and stay out of trouble for good.

After more "processing," I was finally free.

How would I get home?

An even better question—*where* was my home now?

After telling Juliet to forget about me, I couldn't show up on her doorstep, arms open wide and announce, "Honey, I'm home!"

The answer to my problems waited outside in the parking lot, smoking a cigarette with three of his similarly leather-clad brothers.

Motherfuckin' Dex.

Was his presence a good sign? Or did he and his MC brothers show up to silence me for good? To make sure I never told anyone what actually went down. Or were they here to protect me from Ulfric and the Wolf Knights MC? Or worse, the Vipers MC? I had, after all, been part of the shoot-out at their clubhouse. Jesus Christ, in one stupid night I managed to paint a target on my back for every motorcycle club in the area to shoot at.

Nah, Dex didn't like me enough to shield me from a rival club. Hell, maybe the Lost Kings were pissed I made them look bad or something.

The possibilities made my head throb.

CHAPTER FIFTY-EIGHT

Roman

DEX PULLED ME IN FOR A HEARTY HUG AND SLAPPED ME ON THE back a few times.

"Come on." He lifted his chin. "Truck's over there."

I said hello to the only other Lost King I recognized, Murphy. Dex introduced the other two as Bricks and Teller.

Teller and Murphy took off on their bikes ahead of us, while Bricks got into the back seat of Dex's truck. They insisted I take the front seat.

An uneasy sensation rolled through my gut.

Christ, they were probably taking me somewhere to blow my brains out and dump me in a shallow grave.

I sat sideways to keep an eye on Bricks.

Dex noticed my tense demeanor immediately. "Relax, kid. You did good. Fuckin' proud of you for not breaking once."

"I still got picked up."

"Happens to the best of us," Bricks assured me.

"Point is," Dex added, "you're not a snitch. Ulfric sends his regards. He was impressed with how you handled yourself. Risked gettin' shot to go back for him."

I couldn't believe he was praising me for getting arrested. "The cops seized what I was carrying."

"Cost of doin' business," Bricks said. "Don't sweat it."

"Speaking of." Dex reached across and unlatched the glove box. He pulled out a thick yellow envelope and handed it to me. "Ulfric wanted me to give this to you. Your cut of the job."

As much as I wanted to play it cool and stuff the envelope in my pocket without taking a peek inside, I flicked the flap open and glanced at the thick stack of cash. A knot of tension inside my chest unraveled. At least if I couldn't go back to Juliet's, I'd have enough money to find a new place.

"Seems like a lot," I said.

"They got most of their stash back thanks to your help. Wolf Knights honor their debts."

"And if he didn't," Bricks slapped Dex's shoulder, "Dex woulda set him straight."

Uncomfortable talking about my arrest, I wanted to move on to more important topics. "You seen Juliet lately? She okay?" *Does she hate me? Has she found someone else?*

He smirked and briefly slid his gaze my way. "You have one hell of a one-track mind, kid."

"Have you seen her or not?" I asked in a sharper tone.

"Of course, I've been looking out for her. She's madder than a wet kitten that you wouldn't let her visit."

"I—"

He held up a hand. "I get why you did it."

"Did you tell her I was getting out today?"

"Wasn't sure you'd actually *be* getting out today, so no." He shrugged. "It's up to you to fix things with her now."

"You think I can?"

He tipped his head back and closed his eyes for a second, like I was unraveling his last nerve. "You looking for my permission, Roman?"

"Not exactly."

Dex glanced over. "Her graduation's tomorrow."

Thank fuck. I got out in time. I was so damn proud of her. I may not have had the chance to walk the stage and have a diploma handed to me, but I wanted to see her do it more than anything.

"Where are we going?" I asked, still not convinced he wasn't planning to execute me.

"You'll see."

It's not like I had any other pressing matters to attend to—like a job or school. So, I played along.

He pulled in behind Crystal Ball, the strip club he worked at or managed or whatever.

"If this is my surprise release party, you can drop me off somewhere else," I said, jerking my chin toward the club. "I told you I'm not interested in this scene."

"Calm down, Saint Roman." Dex chuckled. "I promise not to taint your virgin eyes."

"Ain't nothing virgin about these eyes," I muttered.

He smacked me on the back of the head. "Don't you talk about my niece like that."

Bricks reached over and punched Dex's shoulder. "He didn't say anything about *her*, dipshit."

Apparently their version of brotherhood meant you enjoyed both verbally and physically harassing each other constantly. Not much different than hanging out with Eraser and Griff. Except I never worried one of them was planning to kill me.

Dex parked in front of a small white garage and motioned for me to get out.

"Is this where you interrogate rival club members?" I asked.

"Shut up." He laughed and shook his head.

Bricks keyed open a padlock and unwrapped a length of chain from around the metal garage door's handles.

An all-black Harley Electra Glide sat in the middle of the concrete floor.

"What's this?" I asked, staring at the two bikers.

Dex shrugged but couldn't stop grinning. "Graduation present."

"I earned my GED a while ago. Try again."

Dex scratched his head. "Are you always so difficult, Vapor?"

"What? Is it a 'thanks for not snitching' gift?"

Bricks chuckled. "That's exactly what it is."

I ran my gaze over the bike again. It was a couple years old. In good shape. Still out of my price range.

Dex ran his hand over the seat. "Juliet mentioned you two wanted to take a cross-country trip."

"We talked about it." Before I got arrested and thrown in jail. *Was she still willing to go with me?*

"Probably be good for her to get out of town for a little bit. See some new scenery. Be good for both of you."

"I can't afford this, Dex."

His smile slipped. "What part of *gift* confuses you?"

Bricks slapped his hand on the handlebars. "This one's the carbureted model. Got almost the same power delivery and throttle response as the fuel-injection ones. Plenty of horsepower and torque to haul you, your girl, and some shit wherever you want to go."

"Yeah, thanks for the specs, Bricks. But I can't—"

"Shut up, Vapor," Dex said.

This time I frowned at the strange nickname. "Why do you keep calling me that?"

"It's about time you had a road name."

Bricks spread his hands wide. "Ulfric said you moved all silent and deadly sneaking into the house to help rescue him."

"*Rescue* is a bit of a stretch."

The smile slid off Dex's face. "You've given me the

impression you're not interested in patching in to any one particular club."

I shook my head. Thanks to Dex, I'd gotten a taste of how a couple of different clubs worked. I liked and disliked things about each of them. Pledging my life and loyalty to one club? Nope. There was only one person in this entire world who I wanted to devote all my time and energy.

If she still wanted me.

"Nothing personal, Dex. I'll help you out whenever you need me," I promised, because holy fuck did I owe him one hell of a debt now. "But I'm not interested right now."

He nodded. "Long as you take care of my girl, you're a friend to *my* club. I'll always have your back. You've earned Ulfric's loyalty as well."

I swallowed hard, fighting off showing any emotion.

"Vapor can exist in two states simultaneously." He poked me in the chest. "That's you. Civilian and outlaw."

"Plus, the silent and deadly thing," Bricks added.

Vapor. I kinda liked the name, even if I wasn't ready to admit it yet. I squinted at Dex. "A little pretentious, isn't it?"

"Yeah," Dex answered with a hint of a smirk. "But so are you."

"Me?" I burst out laughing. "The foster kid?"

"Be thankful. We got a brother down in Virginia with the road name *Pants*," Bricks said. "So, it coulda been worse."

As much as I enjoyed yanking Dex's chain, the thought he'd put into choosing a nickname for me left an unfamiliar warm sensation sliding through my chest. For the first time in my life, I felt like I belonged. Maybe in a few years, I'd rethink prospecting for his club.

Dex slipped a leather cut off of a hook on the wall. "This goes with the bike." He turned it around, showing me the blank back and the rocker on the bottom that simply said "Nomad."

Nomad. That word resonated. No home. Always moving from place to place.

"You can't wear our colors if you haven't been voted into the club." Dex tapped a small, rectangular patch on the front. "But you've earned one of these."

It was the same patch I'd noticed on Dex's cut the day I met him.

Respect Few, Fear None.

"For doing time without snitching," he explained. "Any Lost King you run into will understand what it means."

My throat tightened. I could only take so much of this emotional torture before I'd break. If I teared up in front of Dex, I'd never live it down.

He pulled me in and hugged me, slapping my back a few times.

"Thanks, Dex," I rasped, returning the hug.

"You got it." He glanced at the bike. "Come over Sunday. I'll help you map out a route. Murphy has some numbers and names for clubs that you can safely stop at wherever you go."

"Thank you. Appreciate that. I gotta save up more money first."

"You wanna paint this up nice, you come see me," Bricks said. He glanced at Dex and stroked his hand over his chin. "Rock—our president—needs an extra set of hands in his shop if you're planning to stick around over the summer and need some cash."

Wary, since I just got out of jail, I stared at the two of them before answering. "Legit mechanical work?"

"He'll probably pay you under the table." Dex shrugged. "But fixing up bikes. That's it."

"He gets real busy at the start of summer," Bricks explained. "He's a demanding boss. But fair."

Just what I needed. More terrifying bikers employing me. "Yeah, I'd like that."

"Go on. Go see Juliet." Dex shoved me toward the bike. "She should be at the house soon."

Bricks held out his hand and we shook one last time.

Then I threw my leg over the bike, twisted the throttle a few times and roared away from the parking lot.

I was going to go get my girl.

CHAPTER FIFTY-NINE

Juliet

DULL WASN'T A STRONG ENOUGH WORD TO DESCRIBE LIFE without Roman. The days were all the same. Lifeless. Joyless.

He'd gone silent. Not responding to my letters. They never got returned, so I assumed he read them. Somehow that hurt even worse.

Dex told me Roman was okay, and that he was working on it, but that was the only information I could pry out of him about the case.

Without Roman around, Dex insisted on either staying at the house with me or making me sleep over at his place. He seemed to have taken our Christmas Eve argument to heart and wanted to be there for me. I gave him grief over his endless fussing but secretly I was happy not to be alone.

Somehow, I buckled down, blocked out everything, and managed to study for finals. No matter how I felt about Roman, I needed to finish school strong and figure out a future for myself.

"You did it!" Vienna bounced up and down next to my locker, tugging on my arm. "Number three in our class!"

"Phew." I blew out a breath and rested my forehead against

the cool metal locker door. High enough to earn the scholarship I'd applied for and low enough not to give any speeches at graduation.

She shoved a piece of paper in my face with the list. Her name was only a few spots below mine. "Way to go, V." I wrapped my arms around her and squeezed.

"Not bad, right?" She pulled away and casually rubbed her knuckles against her shirt as if she possessed an ounce of modesty. "Top ten."

"I knew you could do it."

"My parents said I can have a party Sunday. Will you come?"

The last thing I felt like doing was celebrating. "You bet."

"What are you going to wear for graduation?" Vienna asked.

We'd been fitted for our gowns weeks ago and that was the last time I'd thought about it. I'd been too consumed with studying.

"Ugh, now I don't even want to go," I grumbled.

"You *have* to go. You've had a shit year and you've worked too hard not to be there. Besides," she added in a lower voice, "wouldn't Roman want you to go?"

How would I know? I couldn't ask him. He'd cut off all communication.

"Purple. You should wear purple," she declared with a nod that sent her hair tumbling into her face. She blew the strands out of her eyes with a quick huff of breath.

Her serious tone about what I considered a frivolous topic finally pulled a smile from me.

"Come on, let's go try on dresses." Vienna clamped her hand around my arm and dragged me toward the parking lot, tugging her keys out of her pocket with her free hand.

"Slow down." I tried to dig my heels into the pavement, but it was no use. Vienna was a force of nature that would not be denied.

"Let's take my car," she pleaded. "I'll drive you to school tomorrow."

"It's out of your way."

She tipped her head back. "I don't care," she shouted at the sky. "We're free!"

Laughing, I opened the passenger side door of her shiny hunter green sports car and lowered myself into the smooth buttery seat. An early graduation present from her parents, it had replaced her last car that wasn't even a year old.

I sighed and stared out the window. I had a knack for turning a fun occasion into a pity party.

"Are you okay?" Vienna's hand grazed my leg. Her usually bubbly voice had turned somber. *Could I be more of a buzzkill?*

I forced a bright smile. "Just thinking about which shop we should try first."

"How about Macy's?" She turned the key in the ignition and the powerful engine roared to life. It reminded me of being at the track with Roman and hanging out with his friends. Then I was sad all over again.

"They have a huge junior's dress department," Vienna said.

"Okay." Thanks to Mrs. Shields, I wouldn't have to rely on Vienna's charity to obtain a dress. I'd be able to afford it on my own. My chest ached at the thought of Mrs. Shields and I briefly closed my eyes. She probably would've baked a cake to mark my graduation. I hoped if she was watching over me, she was proud and that she understood how much her generosity meant to me.

I tried to force myself out of my funk and follow Vienna's happy chatter. By the time she slid the car into a parking spot at Macy's, I was mentally drained.

"Come on!" Vienna flung open her door and hopped out.

"Snap out of it, Juliet," I whispered to myself. I tugged the visor down and stole a glance at my wild hair. After a quick attempt to tame it with my fingers, I gave up, grabbed my purse, and stepped out of the car.

Vienna was a seasoned shopper. She started at one end of the large dress department, ruthlessly flipping through racks of dresses. "Nope. Nope. Prom dress from hell. No, no, no," she muttered to the tune of screeching metal hangers.

I wandered away toward a display of lacy dresses in shades of pink and peach. "Vienna," I called.

"Oh!" she squealed and hurried over, grabbing a dress in a bright shade of peach and pressing it against her chest. "It's perfect, don't you think?"

"Honestly, yes." I nodded toward the dressing room. "Go try it on."

"No, let's find something for you, first." She draped the dress over her arm and pushed me toward a wall display of flowered dresses.

Bright orange and purple caught my eye and I reached out to touch the fabric.

"Oooo," Vienna sighed. "I like that."

"You do?" I plucked the hanger off the rack and held up the dress for inspection. Abstract flowers in vibrant shades of purple, lilac, and magenta were splashed against a sherbet-orange background.

"Let's go." She snatched the dress out of my hand and hurried us toward the dressing rooms.

We closed ourselves in adjacent dressing rooms. Carefully, I slid into the dress. I couldn't quite reach the zipper, though.

"I need to find a plunge bra." Vienna knocked on my door and pushed it open without waiting for my answer.

"Can you zip it?" I asked.

I turned and held up my hair while she tugged the zipper into place. Together we stared at ourselves in the three-way mirror.

She placed her hands at my waist. "This is perfect on you."

Gauzy sleeves fluttered at my shoulders, and a deep, wide V showed off more of my shoulders and cleavage than I was normally comfortable with. The flowing skirt ended right above my knees. "You don't think it's too...I don't know, bold? It's a little mature for me, no?"

Vienna's pretty face screwed into a scowl. "You're eighteen. It's your *graduation* dress. It should be 'mature.'" Her expression softened and she tugged on the ends of my hair. "It looks really pretty on you. Enhances your coloring."

"Thanks." I glanced down again and twisted my hips, smiling at the way the fabric danced around my legs.

"But," Vienna added, "we need to find you a strapless bra." She skimmed her fingers over my shoulders, skipping over my bra straps.

My cheeks heated. I'd never had a mother to teach me the fundamentals of dressing up. Anything I'd learned was from Vienna.

"And I need something else." She pointed to her chest. The lacy dress was rather demure for Vienna, but the front panels dipped low enough that her bra peeked out.

We dressed in our regular clothes and Vienna marched us to the lingerie department. I tried on several bras with the dress before finding the right one.

Last we hit the shoe department.

"These," Vienna declared, thrusting a pair of deep purple suede heels in my face.

"I'll break my neck." I reached for the shoes and ran my fingers over the velvety leather. "They're pretty, though."

"They're really not that high," she insisted.

Once again, she thrust me out of my comfort zone and into something I thought I'd never wear. The three-inch heels were easier to walk in than I expected. While Vienna tried on and discarded several pairs of shoes, I practiced walking across a stage.

"Hopefully, I won't face-plant when I accept my diploma." I dropped the shoes in the box and closed the lid.

"Yay!" Vienna punched her fists in the air. "I'm so happy you're getting them."

Laughing, I adjusted the bags in my arms. "When you're right, you're right, V."

She grinned. "Let's go to the food court and grab pizza."

I groaned. "Can what they serve even be considered pizza?"

"Come on." She tugged me into the mall.

I wasn't looking forward to going home, anyway.

The food court was jam-packed, but Vienna and I managed to find a table. I tucked my bags between my feet and nibbled on my too-hot-to-eat-yet pizza, while Vienna cut her slice into neat triangles.

"Hey, polka dots."

I groaned when I recognized the voice.

"Douchebag Dougie," Vienna sneered. "Shouldn't you be on the curb with the rest of the trash?"

The two guys with Doug guffawed and punched his shoulder. I recognized one who'd graduated a year earlier and the other was Jameson.

"Juliet, right?" the older guy said.

Surprised, I grabbed a napkin and dabbed my lips. "That's me."

"You know my boy Frankie, right?" Doug slapped his friend's chest. "Took our team to the State Championships last year."

"Frank," he corrected, sliding into the seat next to me. "I didn't spend much time on the field this year."

"Uh…" I shot a confused look across the table at Vienna, but she was too busy talking to Doug and Jameson

"So, you're graduating tomorrow, right?" Frank asked. "I heard you're number three. Congrats. You excited?"

How'd he know that? I shrugged and half-smiled at Frank. "I guess."

"Cool." He grinned and nodded like a happy Golden Retriever puppy.

The guys started talking football and baseball. I tuned them out, focusing on my pizza. Vienna ignored every one of my scowls.

Frank nudged my elbow and leaned in closer. The warmth of his body felt so wrong, I inched away.

"Not into sports?" he said against my ear.

"Not really." I shrugged and swiped my napkin over my mouth again.

"Got plans for graduation weekend?"

I flicked my gaze across the table. "Vienna's supposed to have a party."

"I'm throwing the party." Doug thumped his chest as if it was some great achievement. "You two can come."

Ignoring him, I nudged Vienna under the table with my foot. "I need to get home."

"I can give you a ride," Frank offered, sliding out of his chair.

"No thanks." I nudged Vienna with my toe again. I loved her but good God, it was like her brains slid out of her ears any time a boy paid attention to her.

Finally, we made our escape.

"I thought you hated Dougie," I hissed at her as we walked back to Macy's.

"I do." She clasped her hands in front of her, letting her shopping bags slide down her arm. "But I was thinking, wouldn't it be total revenge if I hooked up with him at his party and then ghosted him after?"

That was the dumbest thing I'd ever heard. "Revenge for who? I think he'd be getting exactly what he wants. The only one you'd be screwing over is yourself."

"So wise, little grasshopper." She patted my head. "Well, Jameson's off-limits. He and Chloe just broke up. I don't want to be *that* girl."

"Good."

"What'd you think of Frankie?" She nudged me with her shoulder again. "He's really cute."

I couldn't even remember a single detail about his appearance.

"He seemed really into you," she persisted.

"I'm not...I can't." I swallowed hard. Date someone else? I couldn't picture it. Even though the situation seemed bleak, I wasn't over Roman.

I'd never be over him.

Roman

Now that I was a free man with a job lined up, I needed to get serious about my future.

Our future.

Maybe it was an excuse to delay things, but I fired up my new ride and took the long way to the mall.

Showing up at Juliet's house empty-handed wasn't an option.

When I got there, I circled the parking lot twice before going inside. What the fuck do you get your girlfriend when you're not even sure she's still your girlfriend? Hallmark probably didn't sell hey-honey-I'm-not-going-to-prison-still-wanna-be-my-girl cards.

A dazzling display caught my eye. I wandered into one of the mall's jewelry stores and went straight to the case with the engagement rings.

Under the store's bright lights, I felt as conspicuous as a flea on white velvet. I shifted and hooked my thumbs in the back pockets of my grubby jeans.

If I wanted to propose, I was gonna need to know how much money I needed to save.

"Looking for a gift for someone special?" the clerk asked me.

"Yeah." This dude was probably two seconds from calling security on my grungy ass. "I'm, uh, not sure how much…"

He launched into a long speech, explaining more than I'd ever need to know about diamonds—cut, color, clarity. Blah, blah, blah. My gaze wandered over the glittering rows, landing on a small one in the corner. I leaned in closer.

It had a small center diamond with what looked like shimmering leaves fanning out around it. A solid, glittering daisy. "How much is that one?"

"Oh, excellent choice." He pulled the ring out of the case and held it up in front of me. "The center gem blooms like a spring flower with its glittering leaves." He wiggled his fingers over the ring like a magician. "Very understated and elegant."

Understated must've been code for "not expensive."

"She likes daisies and that kind of reminds me of one."

His face broke into a wide grin. "It's called the Daisy Duchess."

"The ring has a name?"

"Oh yes."

"Well, how much to take her highness home with me?"

He chuckled and named a price.

My eyes bugged.

He leaned in closer. "I can probably get my manager to let me take a little off the price for you."

"Can I put it on hold?"

"Absolutely."

I pulled the envelope of money out of my pocket and plucked a crisp hundred-dollar bill out of the stack.

He wrote up a receipt and some paperwork. I stared at the number at the bottom. It could take me most of the summer to earn enough money to pay off the balance.

While I waited, my gaze wandered to another case. It landed on a gleaming little gold butterfly suspended on a thin gold chain. I was afraid to ask, but still needed a present for Juliet. "Can I see this?" I asked.

The clerk keyed open the case and handed me the small velvet box holding the necklace. It had two tiny diamond chips on its wings.

"It's solid gold, so it will last her a lifetime," the clerk said. He named a price that seemed downright reasonable after the ring.

"I'll take this today."

"Excellent." He snapped the box closed with a quick *thwack*. "Do you want it wrapped?"

"That'd be great."

For the first time in months, hope flickered in my chest as I walked out of the store and into the mall. I had a job that wouldn't get me tossed back in jail and a plan to propose to my girl.

Now, I just needed to win her heart again. I'd done it before when I had nothing to offer her. I could do it again.

Should I show up at the house? Call her? Pick her up from school? Visit her at the drive-in? I couldn't do any of it because I didn't know her schedule.

I flipped through all my options as I approached the food court. The place was jam-packed. My stomach growled. I hadn't exactly eaten a lot in jail. I drifted toward the pizza counter when someone caught my eye.

Juliet.

Was it really her? Or was I seeing things because she was so heavily on my mind? Damn, she was even prettier than I remembered.

I was so busy staring at her, it took a few seconds for the other details of the scene to register. Vienna had her back toward me, but I recognized her easily. She kept turning and looking up at the two guys standing next to the table. Doug, that jackass from school. I thought Vienna hated him. Why was she so obviously flirting with him? Jameson also seemed to be angling for Vienna's affection. Where was Chloe? Those two had always been attached at the hip.

But all those thoughts were to distract me from the worst part.

A guy sitting all cozy with Juliet. They were pressed up tight, touching from shoulder to elbow as he leaned in to say something in her ear.

Fuck. I couldn't watch another second.

I was too late. She'd done what I asked.

She'd moved on and found someone else.

CHAPTER SIXTY

Juliet

THE UNCOMFORTABLE FEELING FROM THE MALL FOLLOWED ME ALL the way home. I tried to convince myself it was the crappy food court pizza landing wrong in my stomach, but it was more than that.

"Are you sure you don't want to sleep over at my house tonight?" Vienna asked, while flipping on the blinker for my driveway.

"I have a bunch of stuff to do to get ready for tomorrow." I needed time to decompress. Maybe take a long, hot bath.

She gasped and hit the brakes so hard, my hand flew forward to brace myself against the dashboard.

"Juliet." The awe in her voice made my head snap up.

"Wha—?

Roman. In my driveway.

Waiting for me?

Somehow, he seemed taller and broader than ever. More menacing too, as if he'd kill any man who stood in our way.

He leaned on a black motorcycle I didn't recognize. A stab of hurt poked me in the chest. How long had he been out? Why didn't he contact me? Obviously, he'd been free long enough to buy a motorcycle. That stung.

Where was he living?

Who was he living *with*?

His arms were crossed over his chest and the short sleeves of his T-shirt showcased powerful forearms. Beard scruff darkened his jaw, adding an extra dose of menace to his sexy scowl.

No longer the boy I'd fallen in love with.

He was now a man I didn't know.

"Why are you sitting here drooling?" Vienna's voice yanked me out of my trance. "Go climb that man like a tree."

Without answering Vienna, I flung the door open and jumped out of the car.

Roman turned and the frightening expression on his face melted into pure affection.

Even though I wanted to be furious with him, I couldn't fly over the blacktop fast enough. My hands were dying to run through his thick, messy hair. My legs couldn't wait to wrap around his waist.

My heart thumped against my ribcage as if urging me to pump my legs faster. Get to him quicker.

Our bodies collided and he caught me, burying his face in my hair while I squeezed the ever-loving daylights out of him.

"Juliet," he rasped. "I missed you."

"Me too. Me too," I whispered.

He squeezed me tighter, then he pulled away to stare at me for a few agonizing seconds before fusing our lips together.

We kissed for what seemed like the first time in our lives. Except, the burning sweetness felt like home. His lips were as demanding as I remembered. In his arms, I was safe. I inhaled his crisp scent—now mixed with oil and leather.

Leather.

Only when we parted, and my heart stopped racing, did I

tear my gaze away from him long enough to take in the leather vest he was wearing. Similar to Uncle Dex's but without the same patches.

"Where'd you get this? And the bike?" Anger and hurt crept into my tone. "How'd you get out? When? Why didn't you call me?"

"Easy." He kissed my cheek. "One thing at a time."

"I missed you."

His eyes softened. "Missed you too, butterfly."

I slugged him in the stomach, which probably hurt my hand more than his gut. "I'm *mad* at you. Furious."

His steady gaze drilled into me. "You have every reason to be."

We stood there staring at each other. Anger and love warred inside me. I was so happy he was here but still mad he hadn't let me be there for him when he needed me.

He lifted his chin toward Vienna's car. "You two have plans?"

"We went to the mall to try on graduation dresses."

His jaw tightened for a brief second. "You find one?"

"I did. My stuff's still in V's trunk." Nervous and flustered, I rushed over to the car and she smiled at me.

"Lucky wench." She popped the latch of the trunk and stepped out. "Welcome home, Roman."

"Hey, Vienna." Roman's quiet greeting seemed off. But he accepted a quick hug from her before pulling away.

"Got everything?" Vienna asked me.

I held up my bags and nodded.

"All right." She climbed into her car again. "If you still need a ride, let me know." Her gaze flicked toward Roman. "But I think you'll have it covered."

"Thanks, V." I waved as she backed out of the driveway.

Then Roman and I were alone.

Strong arms slipped around my waist and he pulled my back

against his chest. His warm breath slipped over my cheek. "I want to see the dress you bought."

"I don't think I'm going to the ceremony now."

"Yes, you are."

I turned and lifted my gaze. "I want to spend time with you."

He leaned down, staring into my eyes. "And *I* want to watch you graduate."

Roman

I wasn't letting my girl go without a fight.

Seeing her with some other guy shook me for a minute. But I hadn't survived all the bad in life by giving up whenever a situation seemed bleak. Juliet and I were embedded in each other's souls. A little jail time couldn't alter our destiny.

I would've sat in her driveway waiting all damn night if I had to.

And if that guy came home with her, I would've slugged him in his smug, preppy face a few times just for thinking he was good enough for my girl.

"Why didn't you go inside?" Juliet asked as she keyed open the front door. "Did you lose your key? You still haven't told me when you got out."

Anger turned her questions into accusatory word bullets.

Fuck. The realization of what showing up with a new bike must suggest to her slammed into me. She thought I'd been out for days—maybe longer—and hadn't bothered to see her.

"I got out this morning. The bike was a thanks-for-not-snitching gift from Dex's club. Or Ulfric's. Dex was fuzzy on the details." I had to tell her at least that much. She deserved to know. And if Dex didn't like it, too bad.

"Dex knew you were getting out?"

Now she just sounded hurt.

"Why didn't he tell me?" she persisted.

"I don't think he knew for sure they'd let me go today." I rested my hand on her shoulder. "Maybe he didn't want to get your hopes up in case I wasn't released."

"Hmm."

Her hum neither agreed nor disagreed with my statement. She tossed her bags on the end of the couch and kicked off her shoes. "Are you hungry? I ate at the mall." She clutched her stomach. "The pizza didn't agree with me, though."

I'd certainly lost *my* appetite at the mall. "No? You looked satisfied to me."

Oh, fuck. Why had *that* come out of my mouth?

"What?" She stared up at me with wide eyes. "What are you talking about?"

"Nothing." I ran my hand over the back of my head. Damn, I needed a haircut. Maybe some super glue for my mouth too. "I stopped there to get something. Saw you and Vienna in the food court with some preppy guys and that jockstrap-for-brains Doug."

She blinked and frowned.

I'd said all that in English, right?

"You seemed, uh, kinda cozy with the one guy," I added.

Might as well dig my grave nice and deep.

"Frankie?" Her frown intensified. "I just met him today."

I closed my eyes and blew out a long, relieved breath.

She popped her little fist against my abs, like she'd done out in the driveway. It tickled. I caught her hand in mine.

"What'd you think? I was on a date?" she snapped.

"Kinda, yeah." I shrugged and leaned over to brush my lips against her knuckles, silently asking her to forgive my big mouth and all the dumb stuff shooting out of it.

"Well, he *did* ask for my number," she said.

I froze.

Note to self, locate Frankie and kill him.

"I didn't *want* to give him my number," she added. "I mean, I didn't."

I met her eyes. "I told you to forget about me."

"As if I'd ever forget you, Roman." She jerked her hand out of my grasp. "I love you. I wanted to be there for you."

Her voice rose with each word.

"I know you did." I held my arms out at my sides. "I was trying to do the right thing. It wouldn't have been fair to stress you out right before graduation. I've already fucked up my life. I didn't want to be responsible for fucking up yours too."

"You haven't fucked up your life." She tilted her head. "Besides, it's *my* uncle who dragged you into whatever it is you're involved in." She waved her hands in frustration.

"He didn't drag me into anything, Juliet. My options are limited."

She let out an annoyed huff of air and turned toward the kitchen. "Are you hungry or not?"

I glanced down at my clothes, feeling grimy and uncertain. "You mind if I take a shower first?"

"Of course not." She jerked her head toward the stairs. "All your things are right where you left them."

Something unfamiliar like relief, or maybe disbelief, unlocked the tension in my chest. This was the first time I'd ever returned anywhere and had my belongings in the same place. The first time I didn't lose everything. She had no idea how monumental this was for me.

Or maybe she did. "Thank you."

She nodded and turned away. My stomach let out a ferocious growl as she pulled cold cuts out of the refrigerator. I hurried toward the stairs and into the bedroom. Everything looked the same. Bed neatly made, closet door slightly ajar, books stacked on the nightstand. In the bathroom, I shed my clothes and cranked up the hot water. Lord knew there hadn't been long, hot showers in jail. Eager to return to Juliet, I didn't stand under the spray for long.

I emerged feeling renewed and hopeful about the future.

When I returned to the bedroom, Juliet was sitting on the bench at the end of the bed staring at the door. Our eyes met and she shifted, tucking her hands under her legs.

"What's wrong?" I approached her slowly, my feet silent over the carpet.

"Nothing. I wanted to continue our talk." She flicked her gaze at my bare torso, then down to the towel at my hips. "It can wait, though. I know you're hungry."

A different sort of hunger was building inside me, but things still didn't feel right between us yet.

The bags she'd returned home with sat on the edge of the bed. "Will you show me what you bought?"

She cocked her head. "What do you want me to do? Put on a fashion show for you?"

Laughter rumbled in my chest. "No."

She stood and I took her place on the bench, whipping the towel around my neck off and rubbing it over my damp hair. When I opened my eyes, Juliet was standing in front of me, holding an orange and purple dress against her chest with one hand and a pair of dark purple shoes in the other.

"Wow, that's eye-catching."

The corners of her mouth turned down and she lowered the dress. "You don't like it?"

"No, I like it a lot. It's pretty. Just different from what you normally wear." I shrugged, feeling stupid. It's not like I knew a damn thing about women's fashion.

"Well, duh. I don't graduate every day." She flashed a quick smile and stalked over to the closet, sliding the door open and hanging the dress inside.

I peered past her. Like she promised, my clothes were where I'd left them. I stood and walked over to the dresser I'd taken over when I moved in and slid the top drawer open. All my clothes were still neatly folded inside. I swallowed hard over the lump in my throat. She hadn't tossed my stuff in a bonfire in the backyard. She had faith I'd return to her. More faith than I'd had in myself.

"Did you think I was lying about your stuff not being here?" she asked.

I wrapped my fingers around a pair of black sweatpants. I couldn't turn to face her yet. "No, although I wouldn't have blamed you if you threw it all in the trash."

"Don't be ridiculous."

I finally turned but she was scooping up my clothes, not looking my way. "You're supposed to hang up your cut." She shook my leather vest. The box with her butterfly necklace tumbled out of the inner pocket, landing on the carpet with a quiet thump.

Her wide eyes blinked and stared up at me. "What's that?"

I hurried over and scooped it off the floor. "The reason I went to the mall." I slipped my hand around hers and tugged her toward the bench. This wasn't quite how I envisioned doing this, but it's not like I'd come up with a better plan.

We sat side by side on the bench. I turned her hand up and placed the box in her palm. "I wanted to give you this for graduation. I'm so proud of you."

She unwrapped it and gasped, "Roman." The box was small and flat. Nothing like the kind of box an engagement ring should come in. But the name of the jewelry store was embossed in shiny silver script on the top of the box.

"Open it," I encouraged.

She popped off the lid and let out a sigh. "It's so pretty."

"Butterflies have a lot of meanings but one of them is growth and transformation." I gently pried the necklace out of the box and held it up. "You've grown and changed a lot since the day I tried to break into your locker."

She laughed softly, then turned and held up her hair. "Some say they symbolize eternal love, too."

I leaned forward and kissed right below her ear. "You already have mine."

"You have mine too," she whispered.

I slid the chain around her neck, worked the tiny clasp open and secured it. "There."

"Thank you." She let her hair down and turned to face me. "You got out of jail and the first thing you did was swing by the mall to pick up a present for me?"

"I didn't want to show up empty-handed."

"This is your home too." She laid her hand over mine and squeezed. "Get dressed. You need a decent meal. And I want to talk to you some more."

"Yes, dear."

Laughing, she leaned in and gave me a quick kiss, then hurried out the door, closing it behind her.

I returned to the dresser and pulled out a T-shirt and a pair of sweatpants. Sighing as I slipped into the clean-scented clothes, I felt better than I had in weeks. I grabbed my damp towels and hung them in the bathroom before heading downstairs.

In the kitchen, Juliet was seated at the table, munching on a bag of chips. I took the seat next to her and stared at the huge roast beef sandwich she'd prepared. Oozing with mayo, it was stacked with tomatoes, lettuce, and a thick layer of roast beef. Just the way I liked it. She slid a small bowl full of something white that looked like chunky mayonnaise in my direction.

"Horseradish mayo. Dex has a thing for it. I thought you might like it too. Careful, it'll set your sinuses on fire, though."

"This looks perfect as it is, but I'll give it a try," I promised before biting into the closest half. "Ohmygod," I mumbled while chewing, not caring about manners. "Best damn thing."

She chuckled and bit into another chip.

Feeling wrong about eating in front of her, I nudged my plate toward her, offering her the other half.

She held up her hand. "I stuffed plenty of roast beef in my mouth while I was putting yours together."

So overwhelmed by the behemoth of a sandwich, I'd overlooked the macaroni salad she'd neatly scooped into a bowl for me. I shoved a forkful in my mouth. "You're the best damn cook."

"It's hardly cooking."

"Don't care." I slathered the horseradish mayo on one corner of my sandwich. "You're the best."

She watched me in silence as I destroyed the meal she'd lovingly put together. But it was a comfortable, easy silence.

Finally, I sat back. "Thank you."

"There's more if you're still hungry."

"I'm good for now." I shifted, unsure of where to go next.

"What happened?" she asked.

"Today?"

"All of it." Her steady gaze drilled into me. Fearless. Juliet wanted the truth, no matter what.

So, I told her all of it. From the Wolf Knights' plan to the container full of cocaine the cops caught me with. My time in jail, all the way to the surprise change in lawyers, my swift unexpected release, Dex meeting me and giving me the bike. All of it.

Juliet absorbed the story in silence until I purged every last piece.

"Thank you for trusting me."

All of Dex and Ulfric's warnings to "keep women out of club business" returned but I didn't care. This woman had my back unlike any other person I'd ever known. Her loyalty deserved truth from me. "I trust you more than I've ever been able to trust anyone, Juliet."

She chewed on her bottom lip. "Is Dex...is that what his club is involved with, too? Drugs?"

"I don't think so, but I've never directly asked. The job he hooked me up with is going to be strictly fixing up bikes."

"Or so he said," she muttered.

I huffed a quick laugh. She had a point.

"Who hired the lawyer for you?" she asked.

"Dex's club or maybe both clubs did once they knew I wouldn't snitch? I didn't get to ask. Everything happened so fast. Barry said it was a family friend. I assumed it was you at first."

"Why didn't you tell the cops the truth? You weren't involved."

"What truth? That I didn't know there was coke in the cannister I picked up?" I shrugged. "They wouldn't believe that unless I came up with some details about the Wolf Knights MC. Overall, Ulfric's been good to me. I didn't want to burn him or his club. What good would that have done? Cops asked me about Dex too, but he's your family. I wouldn't snitch on him either."

Her eyes widened at the mention of Dex's name. "Ulfric kept telling me not to worry, that they'd take care of you, but he wouldn't give me any specifics."

"I'm not surprised. He's got...opinions about women being involved in club stuff."

"But *you* told me."

"Like I said, I trust you, Juliet." I sighed and glanced away. "I think in Ulfric's head, not sharing is a means of keeping the people he cares about safe."

For anyone else, the next logical question would've been was *she* in danger now that I'd told her the truth. But we'd both lived through enough events that taught us to be loyal to the people who've been loyal to us regardless of whatever might be the "right thing."

Technically, Ulfric might be a criminal. Dex too, but they'd both protected and provided for us when the rest of the world let us down.

"Enough about me. What's been going on with you? Tell me everything I've missed, Juliet."

A sad smile flickered over her lips and she sat back. "Well, I tried inviting Aunt Susan to my graduation but that didn't go over well."

"Why'd you do that?"

She shrugged. "I thought, maybe with Uncle Jared no longer clouding her judgment, she'd...I don't know, remember that I'm family? She's the last connection to my mom, you know?"

Hurt shadowed her words. I reached over and slid my hand over hers. "I'm sorry." At least the last member of my bio family —my grandmother—had done everything in her power to protect me.

"She's pretty bitter about all this." Juliet waved her hands in the air, indicating the house Mrs. Shields had left her.

"Yeah, she thought she'd have you toiling away as her slave a little longer."

Her lips set into a grim line and she nodded. "That's what I got from our brief conversation."

"What else?"

"I'm taking summer classes at the community college." She hesitated, biting her lip. "They have an Automotive Technical Services program you might be interested in."

I opened my mouth to shoot down her suggestion. *No money, sick of school*, and a dozen other reasons jumped to mind. But how the hell was I supposed to take care of Juliet with few legit ways of earning money? "I'd like to check that out."

The lines of tension around her eyes softened with relief. "I'm going to work part-time in a doctor's office too. Mr. Porter helped me find the job with one of his friends. And at the ice cream shop nights."

"Busy, busy," I teased.

Her expression remained somber. "I wanted to make sure I filled my time, so I didn't miss you so much."

Guilt slugged me in the stomach. "Come here." I held out my arms, inviting her closer.

She pushed her chair back with a squeak and closed the short distance.

I pulled her into my lap, hugging her tight. The weight of her felt so good against me. "I missed you, Juliet. Every night you were in my dreams and I was so angry to wake up and find you weren't there."

She carefully traced a line down my cheek, along my jaw, and to my shoulder. "Maybe our spirits met up in our dreams because you were in mine every night, too. And I wanted to cry in the mornings when I woke and you weren't beside me."

"Never again," I swore. I swooped in to seal my promise with a kiss. "I love you."

"I love you too." She lifted and adjusted until she was straddling my lap, feet dangling on either side of the chair.

I pressed my lips against hers harder and she looped her arms around my neck.

"Let me show you," I whispered.

She drew back, one eyebrow lifted in a teasing expression.

I slid my hands along her thighs to her butt, squeezing gently. "Hang on."

She squealed as I gripped her and stood. "What are you doing?"

"Words are cheap. I want to show you how much I love you."

"How?" She touched her forehead to mine.

"By worshipping your body for the rest of the night."

CHAPTER SIXTY-ONE

Juliet

I WOKE UP WITH A SMILE STRETCHED ACROSS MY FACE. THE weight and warmth of Roman's body sprawled next to me made me sigh with happiness. He was home, safe, and free. Graduation Day was already perfect.

Quietly, I tossed the covers aside and slipped out of bed. I had so much to do to get ready for the ceremony, but I didn't want to wake Roman until I absolutely had to.

I slipped downstairs and went about my morning routine, using my favorite shampoo scented with roses and sandalwood. Excitement and nerves jounced through me while I slicked conditioner through my long, thick hair.

Would I trip as I walked up the stairs to collect my diploma? I'd never worn heels so high before. It was probably a dumb idea. What if the small points stuck in the grass as I walked to my seat and I face-planted in front of an entire stadium of people?

Eh, except for Vienna, I never planned to see any of those people again. So, who cared? Not like most of them knew me anyway.

I had my head flipped over and was working a wide-bristle

brush through my hair while aiming the blow dryer at it when I sensed movement. Roman's bare feet came into my field of vision.

I flicked the dryer off and flipped my hair back, standing straight. "You're up."

"Why didn't you wake me?" He lazily stretched his arms over his head and braced his hands on the doorframe, allowing me to study his naked torso. My gaze dipped to the sweat shorts hanging loosely at his hips. It was such a casually sexy pose, my brain fizzled.

"Juliet? You all right? Are you nervous about today?" Concern crept into his voice with each question. He stepped forward and tugged the blow dryer from my hands. "Let me help you."

I reached out and traced my fingers over his abs. "Sorry, I was momentarily distracted. Morning looks *good* on you."

He chuckled and ducked his head. A slight pink spread over his cheeks.

How could he be embarrassed? "This can't be news to you, Mr. Hawkins." I hooked my fingers in the waistband of his shorts and yanked him closer. "I thought I showed you last night how sexy I think you are."

"You sure did." He cupped my hips and leaned in to drop a kiss on my forehead. "But if you keep giving me those bedroom eyes, you're going to miss your graduation." He waved his hand in the air in a hurry-up motion. "Flip your hair over again."

I grabbed my brush and bent at the waist, shaking my hair out before brushing it smooth. The hot air from the dryer followed my hands and after a few minutes, I stood straight, grabbed my round brush, and styled my wild hair into place.

"That's good!" I shouted over the noise of the dryer and flashed a thumbs-up at Roman.

He flicked it off. "You look fantastic."

"Thanks." I picked up a small barrette and clicked it open

and closed a few times. "I feel like I should pull it up or back or something, but it'll be easier to get the cap on if I leave it down."

"Probably." He wiggled his fingers toward my barrette. "Bring your clip thingie. In case you change your mind."

I smiled at "clip thingie." Such a guy phrase. "I'm going to pack some stuff in case I need it. Will you mind holding onto it for me?"

"Whatever you need." He popped another quick kiss on my forehead. "Come on, though. You're going to be late. You need me to make breakfast?"

"I ate when I got up. Sorry—"

"Juliet, I can feed myself. Go get ready."

I scurried into the living room. A glance at the clock lit a fire under my butt and I raced up the stairs to the bedroom. My phone was buzzy dancing across the nightstand and I scooped it up.

"Hey, V."

"You need me to pick you up?" she asked.

As much as I was dying to take a ride on Roman's new motorcycle, I didn't want to risk ruining my pretty dress. "Actually, yes. We never picked up my car last night. Are you sure you don't mind?"

"Nope. Gives me an excuse to get away from my parents. They're driving me nuts."

Her parents were hell-bent on her going to dental school and joining the family practice one day. I could picture them lecturing her about *only* making it into the top ten in our class. "I bet."

"Ugh. I'll be there in fifteen minutes."

Sheesh. I shouldn't have spent so much time on my hair.

We hung up and I hurried to strap myself into the new bra and panties, found a slip, and finally tugged the dress off its hanger.

"Need help?" Roman asked.

I jumped and turned. "To zip it, yeah."

He approached slowly. "I'm afraid of dirtying it with my grubby hands."

"You're not grubby."

Warm, rough hands skated down my spine. Heat from his body simmered against my back. His soft lips brushed against my shoulder. "It pains me to cover you up," he said in a rough voice.

A happy shiver danced down my spine. "I promise you can take it off as soon as we get home."

He kissed my shoulder again before sliding the zipper into place.

I turned and tugged the fabric away from my hips as if I was about to dip into a curtsy. "What do you think?"

"It's different."

My eyes widened. "You don't like it on me?"

"I didn't say that. It's...colorful. Bolder than what you normally wear." He shrugged. "It's pretty on you."

"Hmm." I turned and stared at myself in the mirror. "Well, I like it."

I caught him rolling his eyes in the mirror. "My idea of dressing up is a freshly laundered T-shirt, clean jeans and shitkickers. So, I'm not sure why you care what I think."

"Of course I care what you think."

"Juliet." He leaned closer and rested his chin on my bare shoulder. Light scruff tickled against my skin. "I think you're stunning." He dropped his gaze. "I think if I catch staring at your cleavage today, I'm going to gouge out their eyeballs."

"So violent," I muttered.

"You have no idea."

I wiggled my shoulders, testing the strength of the dress and new bra to keep everything in place. "I'm going to stuff a wrap in my bag. Just in case."

"What do you want *me* to wear?" he asked.

"It's going to be hot and the ceremony is outdoors." I glanced out the window. The sun was already beating down something fierce. "So jeans and *shitkickers* might not feel great." I walked over to the dresser and pulled out one of the bottom drawers. "I wasn't sure if you'd be getting out...or when you might...but I was hopeful. I ordered some summer clothes for you." My voice caught and I paused to clear my throat. "I hope everything fits." I reached out and tickled my fingers over his ribs. "You, um, bulked up a bit, while you were...away."

He grabbed my hand and pulled it up, dragging his lips over my knuckles. "You did that for me? Even though I...even though I might not be coming back?"

"I wanted you home with me. So...I tried to plan for things as if you *were* coming home."

"Juliet." He wrapped his arms around me, crushing me to his chest. "Thank you."

"Don't thank me, yet. It's just some shorts and—"

"It doesn't matter. You always believe in me. Even when I don't believe in myself."

I wrapped my arms around him and hugged him tight. "And I always will."

Roman

A few hours later, I found myself cooking in the bleachers of my former high school's football field while waiting for Juliet to walk the stage and collect her diploma. As hot as it was, the sun felt good on my vitamin-D-deficient skin.

"Jesus," Dex groaned and wiped sweat from his brow. "They couldn't have offered the families some seats in the shade?"

I searched through the bag of "supplies" Juliet packed before we left the house. My fingers grazed a slippery tube and I pulled it out, handing it to Dex. "SPF 50 should help, Casper."

One corner of his mouth lifted in an amused smirk and he snatched the tube out of my hand. "What else you got in your purse, Vapor?" He tapped Juliet's quilted tote bag with the toe of his boot.

I yanked the handles apart and peered inside. "Besides the sunscreen? Juliet packed water bottles, granola bars, an umbrella, bug spray, wet wipes, deodorant, lip balm, toothbrush, Tylenol, uh, some hair ties and a brush—"

He rubbed his hand over the top of my head. "Can't let your pretty locks get ruffled, huh?"

"Har, har. That stuff's for *her*, obviously." I lifted my chin. "She was worried about the cap messing up her hair."

"You two are already like an old married couple."

I shrugged but inside I was pleased with his observation. "There's an extra pair of shoes in here too." I pulled out one glittering purple sandal. "If you wanna change out of those stinky boots later."

He barked out a laugh and elbowed me in the ribs. "Gimmie one of those granola bars, smart-ass."

While he tore into the snack, I scanned the field. Way toward the back, a row of graduates emerged and lined up, then marched toward the lawn. I craned my neck, searching for Juliet in the sea of black gowns.

"There she is." I nudged Dex.

Juliet scanned the bleachers and I waved to capture her attention. Her gaze finally landed on us and she beamed the brightest smile. Dex was busy taking photos. Thank fuck one of us remembered. At one of the middle rows, Juliet stopped and let a few of her classmates go ahead of her, waiting for Vienna. They giggled and hugged before taking seats next to each other.

"They swap spots?" Dex asked me.

"So they could sit together, yeah."

He chuckled and snapped a few more pics.

"Roman?"

I turned and grinned at Pip who stood in the aisle, nervously shifting from foot to foot and biting his lip. "What're you doing here?"

"They let us come to the ceremony to see the older kids." He flailed his arms toward the field. "But I snuck away to look for you."

Guilt washed over me. I should've asked Juliet about Pip.

I stood to make room for him to pass but he flung himself against me, hugging tight. Damn, the kid practically cleared my chin now.

"Look at you! What'd you do, grow about a foot taller?" I returned the hug, not caring that people were giving us weird looks. "You doing okay?"

"Yeah. It's not too bad."

"Good." I patted his back and pulled away, motioning for him to sit next to me.

I introduced him to Dex and they shook hands. Dex didn't ask why the kid was sitting with us, just accepted his presence.

The ceremony dragged and the speakers droned on and on but I managed to tune most of it out. A pang of regret struck me halfway through the speeches. If things hadn't gone to shit, I would've been sitting right next to Juliet waiting to accept my own diploma.

I shook off the useless regret. What was done was done. I had my GED. That's all that mattered. It's not like I had parents or a family who gave a damn about watching me march across some stage.

"Juliet Hayworth," the principal announced.

The three of us stood up and cheered.

From the stage, Juliet turned and waved in our direction. She smiled wide and said something to the principal before hurrying down the stairs and back to her seat.

There were a lot of kids to get to between Hayworth and

Zimmerman. I squirmed and sweated in my seat, wishing I could scoop Juliet up and run away.

Finally, it ended. The graduates threw their caps in the air. The noise of people shouting for their kids and students yelling for their friends rose to a thundering cloud around us.

"Thank fuck," Dex groaned. "I thought it would never end."

"Amen," I muttered.

"I better get back before they notice I'm gone." Pip stood. "I want to congratulate Juliet, so I'll find you guys in the crowd, okay?"

"All right, buddy."

He gave me another hug before hurrying away.

"Nice kid," Dex said.

"I feel bad I haven't been around to look out for him."

"Well, you're home now." He slapped my shoulder and stood. "Come on, grab your purse. Let's go find our graduate."

I rolled my eyes and slung Juliet's tote bag over my shoulder. Dex easily pushed his way through the crowd, clearly not giving a crap about the people who side-eyed his leather cut and biker patches.

A short blonde jumped in front of him at the bottom of the bleachers, blocking our path. She hugged him in a way that looked more like a jungle cat marking her territory—rubbing her breasts up against his chest and arms. It was not family-appropriate and awkward as hell to witness.

"Is this your son?" she asked with wide eyes, pointing at me with one long, red fingernail.

"No. Good to see you, Courtney. We gotta find someone." He wrapped an arm around my shoulders and tugged me away without an introduction.

"Girlfriend?" I asked.

"No." He raised an arm and waved. "Juliet!"

His voice easily carried over the rest of the noise. Juliet turned and ran, dodging her classmates until she reached us.

She launched herself into my arms and I caught her, swinging her around wildly. "So proud of you, baby."

"I thought I was going to trip when I went down the stairs." She turned and motioned toward the stage.

"Couldn't tell," I assured her, setting her down. "You want your other shoes?"

"Not yet." She beamed at Dex. "Thank you for being here. I'm sure it was boring as heck for you."

"Wouldn't miss this for anything, Julez." He picked her up and kissed her cheek. "Real proud of you, peanut."

"Thank you."

Vienna dragged her snooty-looking parents over to greet us. The mom was an older, bonier version of Vienna. Her dad twitched and stared at his daughter—he looked more like a confused grandpa, than a proud father.

Mr. Broom worked his way through the sea of students and families to greet us. He smiled broadly when his gaze landed on me and held out his hand.

"Good to see you, Roman."

Surprised he even remembered me, I took a moment to shake his hand. "Thanks. Uh, you too."

He moved closer and added in a lower voice, "I know things have been unstable and I'm sorry I couldn't do more...I don't know what your plans are, but I hope you'll still find creative outlets. You have a lot of talent, Roman. Don't forget that."

Shock froze my tongue. So many people had let me down in life, I'd lost count. Mr. Broom wasn't one of them. "Thanks, Mr. Broom. I learned a lot from you. Your classes were my favorite during my short time here." I hesitated, not sure this would make him feel any better. "Got a motorcycle I'm planning to customize with a little artwork, if that counts." I mimed painting with a tiny brush in the air and he laughed.

"That absolutely counts. Feel free to send me pictures."

"Thanks, I will."

He turned toward Juliet. "I know you've got your heart set on nursing but you're also a fantastic photographer. I hope you'll find time to keep developing that skill." His lips quirked at the pun.

"Thank you, Mr. B." Juliet blushed and glanced my way. "Sounds like I'll be taking photos of Roman's bike."

"Excellent." Mr. Broom let out a hearty laugh. Juliet introduced him to Dex and they shared a few words before he moved on to other students.

"I don't think the school knows how lucky they are to have him," Juliet said as she watched him stop to talk to his students.

"Probably not," Dex said. "The good ones usually get shafted in favor of the ass-kissers. I'm sure it's no different in education."

Well, if that didn't sum up my life experiences so far, I didn't know what would.

CHAPTER SIXTY-TWO
Juliet

HIGH SCHOOL GRADUATE.

Somehow it all felt so anti-climactic. The weight of my future and what it might hold pressed down on me as soon as I accepted my diploma. One thing I knew for certain, I wanted Roman in my life.

"Do you mind if I stop by my locker?" I asked him. "I think I left a few notebooks in it and don't want them thrown out."

Dex glanced at his watch. "I have a reservation for us for dinner—"

"You do?" I cringed at my shrill tone. But all week long, I'd listened to other students bragging about where their parents were taking them to dinner after graduation.

"Yes, peanut." He turned and glanced at Vienna and her family busy talking to the principal. "Do you want to invite your friend and her parents?"

"No, that's okay." I grabbed Roman's hand. "Just the three of us together would be nice." I loved that the two most important men in my life got along so well.

I held Roman's hand as we made our way through the

school's poorly lit hallways. It seemed so empty and foreign. Yesterday, I belonged. Today, I felt like an intruder.

When we reached my locker, Roman traced his finger over the scarred black metal. His lips curved. "This is where we met."

A warm, happy sensation fluttered in my chest. "How could I forget? You were trying to break into my locker."

He let out a rich, rumbling laugh. "Wish I knew who messed up my locker assignment so I could thank them."

"We would've met anyway." I squeezed his arm.

Dex sighed and shifted.

"Sorry, Uncle Dex. Didn't mean to get all mushy in front of you." I laughed and opened my locker. My stack of notebooks was on the top shelf. I grabbed them and stuffed the pile into my tote bag. Even though I had a perfectly clear view of my empty locker, I peered inside, checking the top shelf to make sure I wasn't missing any stray items.

"You sad to be leaving high school?" Dex asked.

I closed my locker door and considered the question. "I don't know if *sad* is the right word. It felt like it took forever but also like I was a freshman yesterday."

Dex pinched his lips together, like he was trying not to laugh. "Hate to burst your bubble, but that's a pretty accurate description of life in general."

"I guess so."

We left the building and headed to the back parking lot. Many of my classmates were celebrating by screaming and running around like animals. Dex's bike was a few spaces away from my car.

"We'll follow you, okay Uncle Dex?"

"Yup." He gave Roman the address in case we were separated.

Roman was quiet as we settled into the car. "Was it weird for you to be here today?" I asked. How had that not occurred to me sooner?

He blew out a long breath before answering. "A little bit. I've been to so many different schools. But at this one, I was actually happy for a while."

I reached over and slid my hand over his. "I want to make you as happy as you make me."

He squeezed my fingers. "You already do."

Roman

For someone who looked so rough around the edges, Dex sure had expensive taste. The restaurant he'd picked featured a giant fountain out front. The prices on the menu made my eyes bug out.

We were finishing dessert when Juliet excused herself. "I'll be right back." She brushed a quick, sweet kiss against my cheek.

Dex watched her with an amused smile stretched across his face.

I waited until she disappeared around the corner, then leaned forward to pull out my wallet. "Let me—"

"Put that away." He drilled me with a stern stare and I jammed the wallet back into my pocket.

"I just—"

"I appreciate it. But I invited *both* of you."

"Thanks," I mumbled, feeling stupid. I shifted my gaze to the large window next to our table. The fountain out front was now lit up in a rainbow of colors.

A couple, maybe a few years older than Juliet and me, stood in front of the fountain. The guy suddenly dropped to one knee and held out his hand to the woman.

Damn, this would be a nice place to propose. Since finding the ring, I'd been thinking of different ways to ask the question. Once I had the money to actually bring the ring home, anyway.

Dex must've noticed my wistful expression.

He chuckled. "Don't tell me you were planning to propose to Juliet tonight, princess."

"Nope. Today's all about her." I flashed an evil grin. "I picked out a ring and put a deposit on it yesterday, though."

"That's what you did the day you got released from jail?" Even in his hushed voice, his amused disbelief was easy to detect.

"Damn right." A slower smile tilted my lips up. "Don't worry. We celebrated in other ways, too."

He scowled. "Don't make me toss you in that fountain, kid."

"I'm hoping to have it paid off by the end of the summer."

He nodded but sadness seemed to settle over him, replacing the teasing atmosphere. Desperate to return to our light banter, I asked, "Do I need to get your permission or something, first?"

One corner of his mouth lifted but the sorrow etched into his face didn't disappear completely. "Nah. Already told you, I'm not her dad." He glanced the way Juliet had gone. "Besides, she's fully capable of making her own decisions."

"Yes, she is."

Juliet reappeared, hurrying to our table. "Did you see the couple outside getting engaged?" she gushed as she dropped into her chair. "They're *so* sweet." She clasped her hands under her chin, her lips tilting into a dreamy smile.

Dex caught my eye and smirked.

Damn, I really wish I had that ring *now*.

CHAPTER SIXTY-THREE

Roman

BEADS OF SWEAT CRAWLED DOWN MY FOREHEAD BUT I KEPT working. It was early August and I almost had the ring paid off. Rock's garage was slammed with people bringing their bikes in for last-minute upgrades before some big rally up north at the end of the month. I didn't care about the details, I just wanted to keep those sweet dollar bills stacking up.

Rock worked me hard but treated me fairly. He paid damn well, too.

"Jesus," Bricks groaned as he squatted on the cement floor next to me. "What's this RUB got you doing to his weekend ride now?" He patted the pristine leather seat of the custom orange Street Glide.

"Cold air intake."

He nodded. "Should bring an extra five per cent bump in power or so."

"That's what Rock said." I tapped the gas tank. "Adding an External Breather System too."

"As you should." He patted my shoulder. "So wise now, little grasshopper."

I smirked but kept working. "Thanks, old knowledgeable one."

"Gettin' to be a cocky lil' shit now too, huh?" He let out a hearty belly laugh. "I like it."

"You harassing my guy, Bricks?" Rock called out as he crossed the path that led from the side of his house to the garage we worked out of.

From what I'd seen, he ran his motorcycle club in a stricter, more hands-on way than Ulfric seemed to run his. The brothers who stopped by Rock's house on a daily basis seemed more like family than just bikers he shared a patch with.

Not that it mattered. I still wasn't ready to patch in myself.

"Now, how is he gonna learn if I don't harass him on the regular, boss?" Bricks said.

Rock circled the bike, studying the work I'd performed. My body tensed, waiting for his verdict.

His heavy boots stopped beside me. "Looks good."

I breathed a sigh of relief. "Thanks."

"Bye, Rock," a high, feminine voice trilled. Heels clacked over the pavement. I glanced up and caught a skinny blonde wiggling her fingers at us. "Hey, Bricks."

"Later, Jan," Rock called without moving an inch.

"See you tonight?"

"Maybe, darlin'."

A car door slammed and an engine rumbled to life.

"Such a heartbreaker, Prez," Bricks said, slapping Rock's shoulder.

"Don't you have to be a pain in the ass somewhere else?" Rock growled.

"Yeah, I gotta run," Bricks said. "See you at Crystal Ball later?"

"Yeah," Rock answered in a weary tone. For a guy who managed a strip club, he never sounded too thrilled about it. "I'll be in soon."

I finished tightening the last bolt and stood. "Think your customer will be pleased?"

"Definitely," he said, still staring at the bike. "You do good work, Vapor. Glad you were able to help me out this summer."

Uh-oh, that sounded like I was about to get my pink slip.

Maybe my expression showed my fear of losing my job. Rock slapped my shoulder. "Relax. I still have plenty of work to keep you occupied."

"Thanks."

"In fact," he reached into the inner pocket of his cut and pulled out a white envelope, "here's what I owe you for this week."

Unless he was paying me in singles and fives, it looked like a lot more money than I was actually owed. I didn't want to pull it out and count it in front of him, though. Lord knew, the ruthless MC president might see that as an insult and slit my throat. I studied the bills quickly, estimating there was enough to pay off Juliet's ring and add to our nomad travel fund.

"Figure most of that'll end up right back here." Rock's eyes crinkled at the corners as his lips pulled into a smirk. He nodded toward my bike. "You've got a few mods left from what I can tell."

"Some upgrades I still want to make," I agreed. "Custom paint too." I didn't want to get crazy like the guys who came to Rock and dropped their entire paychecks on fancy gadgets. I had bigger goals in mind.

"Whatever you need." Rock spread his arms, indicating his shop. "You're welcome to use the space."

"Thanks. Appreciate it." I slapped the envelope against my open palm, feeling the weight of the bills inside. "Right now, I'm going to go pay off my girlfriend's engagement ring."

The easy smile slid off his face. "Dex's niece, right?" He wobbled his hand from side to side, in what I interpreted as meaning he knew Juliet and Dex weren't actually blood-related, but *niece* was the best way to describe their relationship.

"Yes, sir. Juliet." I braced myself for the "you're too young to settle down" speech every other biker seemed to give me whenever I expressed my lack of interest in strippers and random hook-ups.

"Dex know?" he asked.

"I mentioned it to him a while back." I lifted my chin and squared my shoulders, prepared to tell him to mind his own business if he tried to talk me out of proposing to Juliet.

"You two have been through a lot." Rock's solemn voice shook my defiance.

Some days it still amazed me she didn't tell me to fuck off when I got out of jail. "Even when I screw up, she has my back."

"That's good. It's not a crime to be wrong." He chuckled. "Fuck knows, we go through life being wrong about lots of things. It's part of being human. Not admitting your mistakes and learning from them is the crime. If she can help you through that, never let her go."

I turned that over in my head. Juliet forgave me easily. I hadn't forgiven myself. I could see the mistakes I've made in my past. I wasn't sure if I'd learned from them yet. "Yeah. She always has faith in me. Even when I don't have any in myself."

"You're lucky to find that in someone at your age." He blew out a long, heavy breath. "Always make her your priority. Protect her with your life."

Wait, what was happening here? My jaw dropped. Considering that I'd rarely ever seen the same woman leaving his place twice, I expected him to give me the biker version of "variety is the spice of life" or something equally gross.

"I do," I answered lamely. "I will."

"All this stuff is nice." He gestured toward the row of bikes lined up against the opposite wall. "But it's just *stuff*. It won't listen to you when you have a rough day or kick your ass when you need it."

My mouth curled up. "Juliet definitely kicks my butt when I need it."

"I bet she does." He chuckled and patted my shoulder. "Congratulations."

"She hasn't said yes, *yet*."

"She'd be crazy not to." He nodded to the tools scattered around the bike I was working on. "Clean up and knock off early. He's not coming to pick this up until next week."

"You sure?"

"Yeah, go on." He jerked his thumb over his shoulder, "I need to lock up and head down to Crystal Ball anyway. Fuck knows it's one emergency after another down there."

An eerie sense of calm settled over me as I finished work and headed to the mall. The future I wanted to share with Juliet sprawled before me. I couldn't wait to take this next step with her.

CHAPTER SIXTY-FOUR

Juliet

"Why am I up before the sun?" I asked with a deep yawn.

Roman answered by squeezing my hand and hurrying me outside.

Cool, dewy air brushed my cheeks and tickled my nose. "Roman, where are we going?" I blinked up at the inky sky. *Darkest before the dawn,* isn't that the saying? I yawned again.

We stopped next to his bike and he pushed my helmet into my hands. "It's a surprise."

I yawned loudly, this time stretching my arms up over my head. "The sun isn't even up yet."

Rough fingers tickled over the sliver of my stomach that peeked out between my jacket and jeans. I quickly jerked my arms down but couldn't stop my laughter. "Knock it off. That tickles." I pushed his hand away and righted my jacket.

"Come here." He gripped my waist and yanked me closer. "I love you." He leaned in and brushed his nose against mine, then dipped lower, pressing a soft kiss against my lips.

My knees turned to jelly. Good thing he was holding onto me. "I love you too."

"Let me take you for a ride."

"I'll go anywhere with you, Roman." I tucked my hair up under my helmet and secured it into place.

A few minutes later, I was in my spot on the bike, gripping him tight. While I loved riding with him, the rush of the pavement beneath our feet and the movements of the bike still felt unnatural.

The deafening rumble of the Harley's engine shook the ground. Our neighbors were probably cursing us out.

"Hang on," Roman shouted. He always warned me right before taking off.

"Eee!" I yelled as he slowly rolled the bike forward, then shifted and took off. The roar drowned out anything else. I squeezed my eyes shut and held on tight, remembering to move my body with the bike.

The angle of the bike shifted as if we were climbing a mountain. The air cooled. I opened my eyes. Bits of magenta and orange touched the sky, pushing the velvet darkness away.

We were headed to Fletcher Park.

Absolute delight tickled me. I squeezed Roman tighter. He pushed the bike faster.

The park wasn't quite open this early but Roman rolled the bike to a stop outside the gate blocking off the main overlook.

I dismounted first. "What are we doing?" I asked in a loud whisper.

"Shhh." He grinned as he took off his helmet and set it on the seat. He took mine, then grabbed my hand, pulling me toward the stone wall overlooking Empire valley below.

We weren't alone. A few other people were walking along the sidewalk. Some had tripods and cameras set up to catch the sunrise. "Oh, Roman, we should've brought a camera."

"Next time. Promise." He stopped at a spot roughly in the middle of the stone wall, where we had a perfect view of the rising sun. Roman shrugged off his jacket and laid it on the chilly stone wall.

Arguing that he'd ruin his jacket would be pointless, so I carefully arranged myself on it, making sure not to smudge my damp boots against the leather. He sat next to me and I curled my hand around his. My breath caught in my throat as the sun made its appearance. It seemed to happen slowly but also all at once. I squinted but couldn't look away from the colorful sky.

Next to me, Roman shifted off the wall, kneeling in the grass in front of me.

"What're you doing?" I whispered. "You'll get in trouble for being on the other side of the wall. Or fall off the cliff."

He glanced behind him. "There's plenty of room here. I'll be fine."

"That's probably what everyone says right before they fall off the edge."

"Juliet." He squeezed my hand.

At the catch in his voice, I stopped breathing and took him in. Down on one knee, both hands wrapped around mine. He swallowed hard and bit his lip.

"Juliet," he rasped.

My eyes widened. "Roman?"

"I fell in love with you the day you caught me breaking into your locker," he said in a rush. "Once we struck a bargain to share the space, I knew I was going to marry you one day." As he continued, he seemed to relax and ease into the words.

My heart pounded.

"We've lived and experienced more than most people our age. You make the hard things seem easy. Your courage inspires me. Your smile motivates me to work hard. Whenever we're apart, I can't wait to be home with you again." He paused and squeezed his eyes shut for a second. "I love you so much. I want to build our life together. To take care of each other forever. Will you please be my wife?"

Tears spilled down my cheeks. "Yes! Roman, of course I want

to marry you. I can't wait to be your wife." I ran my fingers through his hair. "You want to be my husband? Really?"

"Yes." His voice shook and I realized he was as emotional as I was but trying to hold it together. "So much."

I wrapped my arms around his neck, clinging to him. He scooped me up and awkwardly lifted and carried us over the low stone wall to the safety of the sidewalk. He sat again, holding me in his lap.

"Oh my God," he groaned and released me for a second, shoving his hand in his pocket and producing a pretty velvet box. "I'm supposed to give you this. Sorry."

"You got me a ring?" I whispered.

"Of course I did. I couldn't propose without one."

"Yes, you could have."

"*Pssh*. Open it, please."

I carefully popped the lid. The sunlight dazzled off the ring inside, blinding me for a moment. A ring set with a small round diamond, surrounded by petals of yellow gold and smaller sparkling diamonds, rested inside.

"Roman," I gasped. "It's beautiful. It looks like a daisy."

"I know." He grinned and gently tugged the ring from its holder. He took my left hand in his. "Will you marry me, Juliet?"

"Yes."

He slid the ring on my finger and it fit perfectly.

"Wow." I wiggled my fingers, unable to look away from the glittering stones. "It's so perfect."

"One day, I'd like to get you a bigger diamond—"

"Don't you dare. I love this." I held my hand to my chest, covering the ring with my other hand to shield it from his threat to replace it.

"Kiss me," he demanded.

"Always." I cupped his cheeks and mashed my lips to his, sealing our promise.

CHAPTER SIXTY-FIVE

Juliet

BUTTERFLIES WOULDN'T STOP CHASING EACH OTHER IN MY stomach. I lifted my gaze to the mirror but instead of looking at my own reflection, I watched Vienna moving behind me.

"Are you nervous?" she asked, adjusting my veil.

"A little, I guess."

"Who would've thought you'd be marrying your locker buddy," she joked.

"I did," I whispered. "There was something about him. I think I knew the day we met." I couldn't imagine a life without Roman in it.

"Yeah, I could see it, too." Instead of the teasing I expected, Vienna leaned in and hugged me tight. "I'm so happy for you two."

My eyes prickled. "Don't you dare make me cry," I scolded, pulling away.

"Trust me, I won't." She circled her finger in front of my eyes. "I did such a damn good job, I should be a makeup artist instead of studying biology." She picked up the tube of liquid eyeliner she'd used on me and waved it in my face. "This stuff's like paint, though. A few tears won't wash it off."

"Great." I peered in the mirror and admired her work. I barely recognized myself. Whatever she'd done with the liner made my eyes look bigger and bluer. "It looks great. Thank you."

"No problem."

Someone knocked on the door. "It's me," Dex shouted.

"I'm all dressed, come in!"

He appeared in the doorway. "Can you give us a minute, Vienna?"

"Sure. I'll go check on the golf cart."

"Thanks, V," I called after her.

I held my arms out and twirled in a circle. "What do you think?"

No answer.

I stopped spinning and took in Dex's serious expression.

"Stop looking at me like that, Uncle Dex," I warned.

"How am I looking at you?"

"Like you're going to cry. If you cry, I'll cry. Vienna will kill us both if she has to re-do my makeup." He didn't need to know my liner was allegedly bulletproof.

He scoffed but at least the melancholy lines around his eyes softened.

"Don't tell me we're too young, either," I added. Enough people had expressed that opinion while we were planning our wedding. I was tired of people judging us.

He rolled his eyes. "That's not what I was thinking at all. Although now that you mention it..." He tapped his finger against his cheek in a playful way.

"Dex!"

The smile slid off his face. "I was thinking how much I wish Debbie was here to see you." He smoothed his hands in the air in front of me. "You look beautiful."

I swallowed hard over the lump in my throat and tugged at

the light, airy fabric at my hips. "You think I look wedding-ish enough?"

"You're a beautiful bride." He reached out to flick a stray piece of netting from my veil away from my eyes.

I'd chosen an elegant white sundress embroidered with dozens of tiny sunflowers and daisies that gave it little pops of color in yellow, orange, and light green. Thick, ribbon-like straps in orange and yellow tied at my shoulders. The flared skirt fell to my knees. Sunny yellow leather ballet flats seemed more appropriate for the terrain than heels, so that's what I'd chosen. They'd been expensive but I'd be able to wear them again after today.

Around my neck, I wore Roman's butterfly pendant.

"You need one more thing." Dex reached inside his cut and pulled out a small teal velvet box.

I blinked and stared as he handed it over. The slightly rusted hinges creaked as I flipped the lid open. I gasped and pressed my hand to my chest, my jaw dropping. "They're beautiful." I studied the simple but elegant earrings. Yellow gold metal caps carved to resemble flower petals extended into twisted stems holding a diamond and freshwater pearl at the bottom. The metal looped into a small oval with a clasp at the back. I wasn't an expert, but they had to be expensive. Something about them tickled a memory at the back of my mind.

"Debbie wore them when we got married," Dex explained in a slow, raspy voice. "She wanted to pass them to our daughter…" He glanced away. "She'd want you to have them."

Now I knew where I'd seen the earrings. In their wedding pictures. Tear pricked my eyes. I threw my arms around Dex's neck and kissed his cheek. "Thank you, Uncle Dex. They're so beautiful. I promise I'll take good care of them."

He patted my back gently. "I know you will. Come on, let's not mess up your dress and everything."

I pulled away and carefully pinched the fabric of my dress

into place. "Did you tell Vienna about these?" I asked as I set the box in his hand and plucked one of the earrings out to work into my ear. "She was adamant that I didn't need to wear earrings today because they'd get caught in my veil."

One corner of his mouth tipped up. "Yeah, I asked her to leave the earrings out of your wardrobe planning."

"Well, she did a good job." A nervous laugh slipped out of me as I secured the second earring. I turned my head from side to side. Dex nodded and I ran over to the mirror to see how they looked. "They're perfect," I whispered. "Thank you."

"Let's go!" The door swung open and Vienna peered inside. "Your golf cart awaits."

The park had generously allowed me to use one of the ranger's cabins to get ready. We'd paid extra to rent a small, motorized cart. Dex would drive Vienna and me down the wooded path and across the road to the spot where Roman and I would say our vows.

"I'm ready," I declared, turning and beaming at Vienna. I angled my head to show her the earrings.

"Oh, they're beautiful!" She clapped her hands together and tossed a smile Dex's way. "So much prettier than what I was going to pick out."

He returned the smile. "Thanks, V."

I picked up my bouquet of daisies and sunflowers wrapped with a sunny yellow satin ribbon. "Ready."

Vienna stepped closer. "You're not nervous at all?"

I held my hand in the air parallel to the ground. "Steady as stone."

She opened her arms and gingerly pulled me closer, careful not to muss my dress or hair. "I'm so happy for you, babe. You two deserve all the good things."

I choked over the lump in my throat that hadn't gone away since Dex's gift. "Thank you. For everything."

"You got it." She released me and pulled away, quickly dabbing at the corners of her eyes. "Let's go."

At least my dress was short. I didn't have to worry about it dragging on the ground and collecting dirt or pine needles. Vienna carefully laid a blanket on the front seat of the cart, then wrapped me up like a burrito once I was inside.

"What are you doing?" I poked my chin out of my individualized blanket fort.

"It's all dirt down to the road." She gestured toward the path in front of us. "I don't want your dress all covered in dust before you get to the wedding."

Why hadn't I thought of that? "Thanks."

"That's what I'm here for." She tapped the side of her head. "My anxious brain is always in overdrive worrying about every possible scenario."

I grabbed her hand and squeezed. "Well, I appreciate it."

"Glad someone does." She forced a smile.

Dex's boots scraped over the gravel and stopped in front of the cart. "All set?" The corners of his mouth tipped up when he took in the blanket.

"Getting a little sweaty under here," I admitted.

Vienna chuckled and hurried to the back of the cart. I turned and watched her tuck a blanket around her short, strapless yellow chiffon dress. "Ready!" she called.

The golf cart tipped and swayed as Dex folded his bulky frame behind the steering wheel. His knees smushed into the dash. He grunted as he searched for a lever to move the seat but came up with nothing.

"Sorry."

"It's a short trip." He flashed a quick smile. "I'll be fine."

Even though Dex kept the speed low, my hair and veil rippled in the wind. Laughing, I held onto the veil until the cart jerked to a halt. I peered past Dex, searching for Roman.

Bright sunlight sparkled off the autumn leaves. Although I'd said I wanted to marry on the edge of a cliff, it wasn't practical —or allowed by the park. Roman had done his best, though. A temporary arch had been set up in front of the fence overlooking the prettiest view of the mountains.

"It's perfect."

"Eee!" Vienna squealed and jumped off the cart. "I'll go tell Roman you're here." She clutched her bouquet and hurried down the narrow gravel path leading to the archway.

Dex rounded the cart and stood by my side, offering his arm.

This was really happening.

I held onto his arm harder than necessary as he walked me down the aisle.

The few people we'd invited stopped chattering as we approached. I was too nervous to look directly at anyone. My gaze locked on Roman. *Oh my.* He'd rolled up the sleeves of his fitted black dress shirt and it was a very good look on him. He turned and our gazes collided. His eyes widened and a slow smile spread over his face.

He reached for me and I took his hand as I joined him in front of the judge.

"Do you give this bride away?" The judge asked Dex.

"I do." Dex nodded, his voice calm and confident. I'd marry Roman no matter what, but to have Uncle Dex's approval meant the world to me. He stepped over to Roman's side and nodded.

Roman

Weddings might make some guys nervous. Not me. I couldn't wait to marry Juliet. I knew I'd made a good call adding Griff, Eraser, and Remy to our short guest list when none of them busted my balls or made "it's not too late to escape" jokes. No one had offered to take me to a strip club for "one last night of freedom" or any of that bullshit, either. We'd spent last night at the racetrack and had a blast.

It wasn't fear that had me strung tight. Nope. It was the need to see my bride. To publicly promise to love each other for the rest of our lives.

The moment she stepped on the gravel path that would lead her to our altar, a sense of peace settled over me. Much like the first day we'd met. Every wish I'd made since that day was about to come true. She was the most beautiful bride I could've imagined.

Long, wide curls bounced around her shoulders. A filmy white veil billowed behind her as she took slow steps. The ribbons at her shoulders fluttered in the soft autumn breeze. My heart thundered so hard I was afraid it would burst out of my chest.

Dex's grim face was hard to read as he acknowledged giving Juliet away. He was either trying not to cry or planning to toss me over the cliff. I hoped if it was the latter, he'd wait until *after* we said the "I dos." I didn't want to leave this world without being Juliet's husband, even if only for a few seconds.

The judge settled his stern gaze on us. He flashed a warm, fatherly smile, then began the ceremony.

"Welcome family and friends. Thank you for your presence today. We are gathered here, surrounded by the beauty of nature, to celebrate the wedding of Juliet and Roman."

"Woo!" Someone behind us whistled. I turned slightly and caught Griff mid-clap. The grin on his face faltered as no one else joined in.

"Too soon?" he asked.

Everyone laughed, even the judge.

Juliet grinned up at me.

I couldn't help but go off script. I leaned down and whispered in her ear, "You look beautiful."

She peered at me from under her lashes. "You're quite dashing yourself."

Dashing. I liked that. It was worth all the discomfort the fitted dress shirt and tie around my neck had caused me this morning.

The judge cleared his throat.

I stood straight and faced him again.

"We're here to celebrate the love this young couple has discovered in one another and to support their decision to commit themselves to a life of happiness together."

The judge closed the book in his hands and dropped it to his side. "Love is not a fairy tale. But it is *your* story, Roman and Juliet. The deep, enduring affection two people find is both magical and irresistible."

Magical. Yes, that's how I felt when I was with Juliet. *Irresistible.* A grin tugged my cheeks up. It's like the judge could tell how much trouble I had keeping my eyes and hands off my fiancée.

Wife.

Holy shit! Juliet's about to be my wife!

I tuned into the judge's words again. "The world is a tough place."

Understatement of the century. I peered down at Juliet. We both knew better than most how cruel the world could be.

"Life can be rough. Show each other tenderness. Make your marriage a refuge from life's harshness."

That's exactly what Juliet and I had managed to create together—a safe haven.

"Put down roots together wherever you create your home."

Juliet and I had never had roots. We grounded and centered each other. Home to me was wherever she was.

I wanted to love and protect this woman for the rest of my life. Together we had everything.

"Finally, I hope you will have many long years together to delight in each other's company."

"Thank you," Juliet whispered. She stole a quick glance at me as if she feared she wasn't supposed to say anything.

The judge bestowed a fatherly smile on both of us. "Now, Roman Hawkins and Juliet Hayworth, do you both present yourselves of your own free will to be joined in marriage?"

We turned to face each other and smiled. "We do," we answered together.

"Do you promise to care for each other through every twist and turn of the sometimes-rocky paths you might face?"

"We do."

"Roman, do you take Juliet to be your wife and promise to love, comfort, and honor her, in sickness and health, as long as you both live?"

"I do."

"Juliet, do you take Roman to be your husband, promising to love, comfort, and honor him, in sickness and health, as long as you both live?"

"I do."

"Wonderful." The judge glanced at each of us. "For thousands of years, couples have exchanged rings as a token of their vows."

Dex nudged me with his elbow. I glanced down and accepted the slim wedding band he passed to me. Juliet tucked her flowers under her arm and took my ring from Vienna.

"Your rings are a symbol of the past, present, and future of the love you share."

I took Juliet's hand and slid the ring on her finger. "This ring is my promise to be your husband, partner, and best friend to the end of my days." My voice cracked on the last word, but I smiled through the emotions crashing over me.

Juliet paused and cleared her throat. "Roman, this ring is my promise to be your wife, partner, and best friend to the end of my days." She slid the gold band into place, pushing so hard it was as if she wanted to mark me for eternity.

"Easy," I laughed.

She wrinkled her nose. "Sorry."

"Now that you've exchanged rings and said your vows, the

love shared between you has been strengthened. In accordance with the laws of the state of New York, it is my honor to declare you husband and wife. You may now seal your vows with a kiss."

I wrapped my arms around Juliet, lifting her in the air so fast, she squealed and squeezed me tight. Our mouths met and fused together.

Our friends clapped and whistled. Dex thumped me on the back, either to congratulate me or to warn me to cool it. I didn't know or care.

Juliet pressed our foreheads together. "You're all mine now, Roman."

"I've been yours from the day we met. But I'm so happy to be your husband now."

She curled her fingers in my hair at the back of my neck and reached up to kiss me again.

The hurricane of life had stolen my family when I was too young and powerless to do anything about it. I'd been tossed around in an ocean of brutality for years. My whole life, more than anything, I wanted to belong to someone.

And now, Juliet and I had created our own family.

CHAPTER SIXTY-SIX

Juliet

"That's everything." Roman plopped a milk crate of tools on top of our already precarious stack of cardboard boxes.

The only things that mattered to us fit into fewer boxes than I'd expected. I couldn't stand to sell Mrs. Shields' car yet. So we'd rented a garage to store everything while Roman and I hit the highway. The larger tools and equipment had been either sold off or given to our friends.

"Excellent." I checked off one more entry on our "to do" list.

"I talked to Pip earlier," Roman said.

"Is his new house okay?"

"Yeah. He seems happier. Said the kids are closer to his age. Eraser promised to pop by the school and check on him once in a while." He pulled a slip of paper out of his pocket. "I have the address and said we'd send postcards."

I plucked the paper from his hand and pulled out my phone to snap a picture. "There. That way we won't lose it."

He curled his arms around my waist. "So clever."

"Mr. Porter has the keys. He said he'd contact us if we need to do anything else for the closing."

"We won't be far at first. Dex hooked me up with their charter near Virginia Beach. We can hang there for a bit."

I couldn't stop my nose from wrinkling. Roman's time in jail still haunted me. But as much as I wanted him to stay away from Uncle Dex's motorcycle club, they always seemed to help us when we needed it. "No side work, I hope."

One corner of his mouth curled. "Nothing dangerous."

"Roman," I sighed.

"Everything's going to be fine. I'm never leaving your side again."

"I'll hold you to that." I poked him in the chest and he winced. "Oh, no! I'm sorry."

I peeled his T-shirt up and checked the bandage covering his freshly inked skin.

"I'm fine. I should change that before we go, anyway."

I grabbed my purse and followed him into the bathroom. I bit my lip while he carefully eased his T-shirt over his head.

"Stop looking at me like that, butterfly. There's no furniture left in the house."

I fluttered my lashes at him. "Who needs furniture?"

"Juliet." He growled my name like a warning.

"Okay, okay." I carefully eased the tape away from his skin and uncovered the grinning skull tattoo. Roman had created the design himself and I loved it. A butterfly in shades of red, orange, and yellow perched on a skull resting in a bed of daisies and roses. He said it represented us. The way he didn't truly feel alive until we met. It still made me choke up every time I thought about it.

I studied the tattoo carefully. The skin under the lines was still slightly red and irritated but otherwise everything looked like it was healing. "Does it hurt?"

"Just itches a little." He raised his curled fingers as if he wanted to scratch, then dropped his arm to his side.

He stood still, quietly watching me in the mirror as I cleaned and dried the area.

I took out the plastic bag of supplies and instructions from the tattoo artist, then carefully applied the thin sheet of tattoo film over the area. "Looks good."

"Thank you." He leaned in and kissed my forehead. "Still think you're going to sit for yours?"

"Yup." I tapped my left shoulder where I planned to have a matching skull-head butterfly inked.

He brought me to life the day we met too.

Roman

"Are we ready to go, now?" I asked.

I was sure ready to leave. Juliet's Uncle Jared had gotten out of prison not that long ago. Dex and I had thrown him a special "welcome home" party. So now was a perfect time to get lost on the highway.

Payback was a motherfucker.

"Let me check." Juliet jogged upstairs. Overhead, I heard her soft footsteps walking through each room. A few minutes later, she bounded down the stairs.

"I think we're good to go!" She grabbed her helmet from my hands.

We only had a vague idea of where we were going and what we wanted to see. For now, that suited us fine.

For weeks, maybe months, we planned to live like nomads. Ride from town to town. Move on when we'd seen enough. See things we'd only read about. Let our hearts lead the way.

And that's exactly what we did.

EPILOGUE

Vapor

A few years and many roads later...

"ARE YOU ALL PACKED?" I SHOUT DOWN THE HALLWAY. JULIET'S been dawdling which isn't like her.

I want to get on the road before sunrise.

"Just a minute!"

"Babe." I tap on the bathroom door. "Can I bring your bag downstairs?"

She hesitates before answering. "Sure."

We have a long ride ahead of us to get to Florida. We're meeting up with Dex at a bike rally.

Sometimes Juliet gets annoyed with Dex for hooking me up with side jobs for Lost Kings all over the country. He's vouched for me with other clubs he's friendly with too. Through those connections, I've managed to carve out my own niche. Patched by no particular club but respected by everyone I do business with. *Vapor*—silent and deadly—is how I'm known now. Silent, because I'll never snitch. Not to cops or to other clubs. Deadly, because betrayal ends in bloodshed.

The riskier jobs get under Juliet's skin the most. But me not working a regular nine-to-five means we get to spend a lot of time together. And we take impromptu road trips whenever the mood strikes.

Either way, last I knew, she was looking forward to seeing Dex. So I don't understand the sudden hold up.

"Roman," she calls out. "Come here. I want to show you something."

My mouth quirks. "Already saw all of you this morning, butterfly."

I push the bathroom door open and stare at my beautiful wife dressed in nothing but a pair of white lace panties. Like the greedy bastard I am, I stand there and drink all of her naked beauty in.

"You're killing me," I groan. "I wanted to be on the road early. But now I want to take you back to bed."

"Roman." She draws out my name in a low, singsong voice and waves something in my face.

"Is that a tampon? You want to push the trip back a few days?"

She doubles over laughing. "No, you goof."

I look closer. *Rapid Pregnancy Detection.*

"What is that?" I ask slowly.

"Really, Roman?" She's the only person in our lives who uses my real name anymore. Love hearing it from her lips.

Holy fuck!

"Are we having a baby?"

"Ding! Finally." She sets the test stick down and throws her arms around me. "What do you think? Can an outlaw-nomad like yourself take some paternity leave?"

"Butterfly, I can do whatever I want. What about you? You love your job."

She rubs her hand over her still-flat stomach. "I want this more. I want to give our baby all the love, attention, and chances you and I never had."

Her earnest words punch right through my chest. I'll never leave my child at the mercy of the system like I was. "Think it's time for us to move back to New York?"

"Maybe."

"Eraser asks about ten times a week when we're moving back."

Her mouth curves. He's still one of her favorite people. "I'd like to live closer to him and Ella." Her smile widens. "And the other guys too, of course."

My phone buzzes and I pull it out of my pocket. "It's Prophet. Give me a second."

She rolls her eyes. "What does he want now?"

I tap out a quick text telling him I'm headed out of town, before returning to Juliet.

"You gonna tell Dex when we see him?"

"No, maybe we shouldn't tell anyone yet. Just in case. It's too early."

Fuck, now that she's told me, I don't want to take any risks. "Maybe we should cancel the trip."

"No way. We've been planning this for months. Besides, it might be the last road trip I take for a while."

Riding without Juliet at my back? Just the idea seems wrong.

"If we have a girl," Juliet says in a soft voice, rubbing her hand over her stomach, "I'd like to name her Emma."

"For Mrs. Shields?"

"Yes." Juliet glances around our swanky one-bedroom condo. "Without her, we would've struggled an awful lot our first few years."

"Damn right," I agree. "I wish she was here to see that we've turned out okay."

One corner of Juliet's mouth kicks up. "I like to think she's watching over us and she knows."

"Might be time for me to trade in the Green Flame for a

cage." I'd put a lot of hours into fixing my Harley but suddenly it didn't seem as important.

"I'd never ask you to get rid of your bike." Her voice drops. "I love you, Roman. I always want you to be happy."

"Love you too. *You're* what makes me happy." I brush the hair out of her eyes. My gaze drops to her naked chest. "You look good." I yank her up and against me and carry her out of the bathroom. "Let's go back to bed and celebrate."

I fuse my mouth to hers. Soft minty breath washes over me and I stroke my tongue against her bottom lip.

She pulls back, blinking at me. "What about Florida?"

"It's not going anywhere. I want to celebrate the addition to our family."

Family. I loved our life the way it was. But for the first time, I could visualize another person in the picture. A little one to guide and help grow. Someone to shower with the love and attention Juliet and I had been cheated out of.

We started out as two battered souls.

By seventeen we had suffered more heartache than anyone should have to experience in a lifetime.

Then, we found each other.

Two lonely, damaged spirits became one.

The open road healed both our souls.

Our love mended them together for eternity.

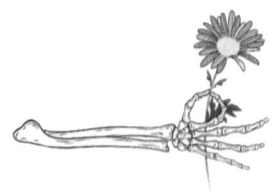

THE LOST KINGS MC® WORLD

by USA Today bestselling author Autumn Jones Lake

Renegade Path can be read as a standalone. But if you're curious about how it fits into the

Lost Kings MC Series, this is my suggested chronological reading order.

1.Kickstart My Heart (Hollywood Demons #1)

2.Blow My Fuse (Hollywood Demons #2)

3.Wheels of Fire (Hollywood Demons #3)

4.Renegade Path (A Lost Kings MC World Novel)

5.Slow Burn (Lost Kings MC #1)

6.Corrupting Cinderella (Lost Kings MC #2)

7.Three Kings, One Night (Lost Kings MC #2.5)

8.Strength From Loyalty (Lost Kings MC #3)

9.Tattered on My Sleeve (Lost Kings MC #4)

10.White Heat (Lost Kings MC #5)

11.Between Embers (Lost Kings MC #5.5)

12.Bullets & Bonfires (A Lost Kings MC World Novel)

13.More Than Miles (Lost Kings MC #6)

14.Warnings & Wildfires (A Lost Kings MC World Novel)

15.White Knuckles (Lost Kings MC #7)

16.Beyond Reckless (Lost Kings MC #8)

17.Beyond Reason (Lost Kings MC #9)

18.One Empire Night (Lost Kings MC #9.5)

19.After Burn (Lost Kings MC #10)

20.After Glow (Lost Kings MC #11)

21. Zero Hour (Lost Kings MC #11.5)

22. Zero Tolerance (Lost Kings MC #12)

23. Zero Regret (Lost Kings MC #13)

24. Zero Apologies (Lost Kings MC #14)

25. Swagger and Sass (Lost Kings MC #14.5)

26. White Lies (Lost Kings MC #15)

27. Rhythm of the Road (Lost Kings MC #16)

28. Lyrics on the Wind (Lost Kings MC #17)

29. Diamond in the Dust (Lost Kings MC #18)

30. Crown of Ghosts (Lost Kings MC #19)

31. Throne of Scars (Lost Kings MC #20)

32. Reckless Truths (Lost Kings MC #21)

33. Rust or Ride (Lost Kings MC #22)

...and many more to come!

ABOUT THE AUTHOR

Autumn Jones Lake is the *USA Today* and *Wall Street Journal* bestselling author of over twenty novels, including the popular Lost Kings MC series. She believes true love stories never end. Her past lives include baking cookies, bagging groceries, selling cheap shoes, and practicing law. Playing with her imaginary friends all day is by far her favorite job yet!

Autumn lives in upstate New York with her own alpha hero.

www.autumnjoneslake.com

[f] facebook.com/autumnjoneslake

[g] goodreads.com/autumnjoneslake

[p] pinterest.com/autumnjoneslake

[o] instagram.com/autumnjlake

[BB] bookbub.com/authors/autumn-jones-lake

www.ingramcontent.com/pod-product-compliance
Lightning Source LLC
Chambersburg PA
CBHW030850030726
47495CB00005B/1458